THIS LAND
OF
MONSTERS

By
Tim Gabrielle

Ink Smith Publishing

www.ink-smith.co

This book is dedicated to my loving, patient, adorable wife, Heather...and also the New England Patriots.

Chapter 1

Nash couldn't remember the last time he'd slept in an actual bed. The rain pelted against the bedroom window, and all he thought about was how many times they'd slept in the trunks of abandoned cars and on top of cargo trucks in order to stay safe from the madness that surrounded them. Houses were a luxury of the past and offered little protection in this new world. Still, as he lay in the dusty bed, he couldn't help but appreciate the small comfort of the past.

Moonlight broke through the storm clouds and illuminated the decorations on the dimly lit walls. The name "*Melissa*" was scrawled in neat, colorful cursive above the door, with pastel butterflies that floated among the hand-painted letters. Posters of bands he hadn't thought of in years hung on the walls and their forgotten songs crept through his head.

He propped himself up on his elbows and surveyed the destruction around him. A bookcase lay smashed on the floor, magazines and CDs strewn about the room. A wooden chair, broken in two, covered a large dark blotch on the carpet in the middle of the room. With each flash of lightning, the large spot would come into focus, with smaller stains that led away toward the open hallway door. He hadn't known Melissa, but he was overwhelmed with sadness. He knew what had happened to her in this room.

Dried blood had ruined the thick blanket that was on her bed, which was fine, as the single sheet he'd found in a linen closet was more than enough for the hot July night. A small backpack sat beside his bed, filled with items he'd collected on their travels. He'd lost his favorite knife months ago and instead had found a sturdy axe, which leaned against the wall beside the bed. He felt odd sleeping in Melissa's bed with his muddy shoes still on, but he knew this would probably be the last time that he or anyone else rested there. Muddy sheets were a small price to pay when a quick escape might be needed.

As he watched the rain continue to crash against the window, a small circle of orange glowed brightly, and then softened in the reflection of the glass. The smell of cigar smoke wafted into the room, a smell he had grown accustomed to but still hated. His stepfather, Duncan, had a way of not making his presence known unless he wanted it to be. This was one of those times, as Nash had been awake for hours and hadn't heard or seen him at all.

He laid quietly and watched the dark silhouette as the glow of the cigar continued to brighten and fade. Not a single flash of lightning came as he watched Duncan's reflection in the window, which made his presence all the more unnerving. Nash heard the familiar sound of ash being tapped off and the thud of a half-smoked cigar as it tumbled onto the messy floor. Duncan had a habit of never finishing cigars, usually finishing them only halfway before he tossed them away. It never made sense to Nash, but he knew better than to ask; it was Duncan's world and Nash was simply along for the ride.

Duncan's footsteps echoed through the hallway as he left to go back to his bedroom. Nash was alone again, something he was rarely granted and greatly appreciated. They'd spent the greater part of the last two years together as they ran, hid and survived. Survival meant close quarters, which made privacy a luxury rarely attained. As the storm crashed violently against the house, the two men silently enjoyed their time away from each other.

Somewhere far away in the dark landscape, Nash heard an unnatural scream as it escaped from the belly of a monster.

Lightning crashed across the dark sky as he tried to force himself to sleep.

Chapter 2

The storm clouds from the night before dissolved, allowing the morning sun to warm the room as Nash slung his backpack over his shoulders. It was light, as it only contained a couple paperback books and some survival items he'd collected from abandoned homes they'd searched. He hardly had time to read, but he liked having a couple books with him for the rare times they found themselves somewhere safe.

The sounds of the morning echoed through the house and reminded Nash of the time before the monsters had come. Back then, his mother had still been with him, and Duncan had been nothing but a side note. He remembered pancakes and bacon, coupled with the slow melodic music she had listened to every weekend as she stood in front of the stove. The sounds and smells had crept slowly up the stairs to wake him every Sunday, his favorite day of the week. Duncan had always been gone on Sundays, which left Nash and his mother alone.

It was a Sunday that she had died, trapped in an overturned car as they waited for an ambulance to arrive. Nash had been in the car with her and had been fortunate enough to be there as she died, holding her hand while she was pinned in the crumpled sedan. The fact that Nash had shared her last moment was something Duncan resented, causing an even greater rift in their already tattered relationship.

The memories of his mother dissolved as another scream echoed through the halls of the home. It wasn't the sound of someone calling for help, but the sound of madness that echoed far off in the distance. It was a sound that Nash had learned to aggressively avoid, no matter the cost.

The world had undergone a drastic, violent change since his mother died. The first reports had been of sickness that spread quickly across the world. Those infected became either incredibly violent or docile. It had advanced rapidly and changed those who were infected within minutes, and the world had settled into a madness it had been completely unprepared for. Watching the world decay around him, a large part of him was thankful his mother had passed before it had all started. She had been too kind for this new world.

Nash adjusted the straps of his bag as he stepped forward and looked out the window, spotting a figure in the yard below. It was partially hidden from his view by an overgrown tree, and moved slowly from side to side in an almost hypnotized movement. He could tell it was what he'd come to call a slowpoke. Some people became violent, driven by rage and bloodlust after becoming infected, but others became lethargic, living the remainder of their days standing about and waiting to die as they faded into nothing. Slowpokes had no will to eat; other than their infected blood, they posed no true threat to the living. He couldn't help but feel sad as he watched from his window, the figure moving listlessly in the overgrown grass.

He left the slowpoke standing below and rummaged through the remains of Melissa's room, searching for supplies they could use in their travels. Most of the room had been torn apart in the carnage that had occurred, but he wasn't going to leave until he searched the remains of the room. He turned over a dresser drawer, which had toppled to the ground, and found a pile of underwear and socks underneath. A wave of embarrassment washed over him as he looked at the girl's undergarments displayed on the carpet in front of him. He started to lower the drawer back over her things when a yellow envelope fell from it and scattered pictures onto the bloodied carpet.

He crouched and collected the pictures, remembering his own friends and family as he thumbed through the prints. The set was from a family vacation at a cottage and showed people in canoes, lakefront scenery, and family dinners at sunset. He thought about the time before Duncan, when he and his father's family had vacationed together. He'd never met his real father, who had died of cancer before Nash could remember, but Nash and his mother had always been closer to his father's side of the family than his mother's.

The last picture he picked up was of a girl he recognized from the framed pictures on the main floor. Her long, blonde hair was pulled back in a loose ponytail as she smiled at the camera. She stood on an old dock with a bottle of Dr. Pepper in her hand as the sun reflected off the still lake. A smile crept across his face as he looked at the picture while he tried to remember the taste of Dr. Pepper.

With the exception of the last photo, he slid the prints back into the envelope and placed them on the foot of the bed. Something about having the dock picture with him made him feel at ease, as if she'd been a long-forgotten friend. He slid the photo into his back pocket and took another quick look out the window. The slowpoke still stood there, swaying softly in the morning sunlight.

The hallway outside Melissa's room was covered in debris. Pictures had fallen off of the wall and sprayed glass across the floor, which was cluttered with the belongings of the previous inhabitants. The dried mud on his boots left crusty footprints and the glass splintered into smaller fragments as he did his best to move quietly through the hallway. The room that Duncan had slept in the night before was now open and empty. Another half-finished cigar lay on the floor next to an overturned bottle of bourbon, something Duncan had likely found before turning in.

Nash crept carefully down the cluttered staircase, filled with chairs and end-tables that he'd placed there the night before in order to give them warning if anyone, or anything, tried to reach them while they slept. He had put himself in charge of securing the areas where they took refuge, as Duncan was usually more concerned with finding booze and cigars. He ducked around a bookcase toward the bottom of the steps and stepped onto the main floor, which was in considerably worse shape than the upstairs.

Almost every piece of furniture or décor had been torn apart and tossed to the floor, destroyed at some point before their arrival. As he stood among the wrecked furnishings of the previous residents, he heard the faint sound of liquor sloshing back to the bottom of a bottle as Duncan drank alone in the kitchen. A loud belch echoed through the home, followed by a soft chuckle and another slosh of liquid.

Before he went into the kitchen, Nash crept to the back of the house and looked through a window at the slowpoke that stood in the backyard. It was a woman in her mid-thirties, with long, straggly brown hair that hung loosely around her slender shoulders. She wore no clothing, only a single thong sandal that barely clung to her left foot as she stood awkwardly in the wet grass.

He backed away from the window, feeling ashamed that he had even looked at her naked chest. She was beautiful, there was no denying that, and he knew without looking that Duncan had watched her from the kitchen all morning. Nash looked at slowpokes with a sense of pity, while Duncan took his anger out on most of the ones they came across. His weapon of choice had always been a large Bowie knife that he kept with him at all times, using it to hack and slash at them through a storm of laughter and curses before he finally killed them with a blow to the head. The more alcohol in his system, the more sadistic he was with his attacks, which Nash routinely tried to avoid seeing.

He found Duncan with his feet up on the kitchen table, leaning back in a chair that looked as if it would break apart at any moment. He held an almost empty bottle of wine loosely at his side while he fiddled with an unopened condom in his other hand. The large window across the table from him had been shattered long ago, its glass and wood sprayed out across the lawn. The naked slowpoke stood just outside, her feet bloodied from the broken shards of glass.

"You see this shit?" said Duncan, pointing at the woman outside with the bottle in his hand. He looked at Nash with a delighted grin. "Now do you see why I keep a pack of rubbers on me at all times? We picked the right house, didn't we, *Buddy Boy*!"

Nash hated when Duncan called him Buddy Boy. It was never in an endearing manner, usually only used when he was drunk and feeling belligerent. Nash turned away from him and continued into the kitchen, opening up the cabinets and drawers as he rummaged for anything of value.

"Take a good look, it's probably the closest you'll ever get," Duncan said as he leaned forward and slammed the bottle down on the table, snickering at his joke.

The woman outside noticed the noise from the kitchen and leaned forward to see inside. Her long, dark hair fell forward and covered most of her exposed chest.

"What are you doing out there all alone, *sweetie-pie*?" Duncan said as he motioned with both hands for the slowpoke woman to join him in the kitchen. "Come on in and we'll have a good time! You, me, and my Buddy Boy over here!"

"You're disgusting," said Nash, as Duncan broke into a fit of laughter.

"Think what you want. I wasn't planning on sharing her with you anyway."

Nash left out of the front door as Duncan erupted into another drunken giggle. The street was lined with cars and trucks as he came to a stop at the edge of the yard and listened to a crow caw from a dead power-line. Except for a few slowpokes in the middle of the road, staring lazily into the sky, the road was empty. The houses that lined the street were left in ruin, having been torn apart or completely burned to the ground.

They needed to collect supplies and judging by Duncan's mood, he knew he'd be doing it alone, but Nash knew that Duncan couldn't be left alone with the defenseless creature in the state he was in, especially after the comments he'd made in the kitchen. He had seen that look in Duncan's eye before and knew what he had planned for her as soon as Nash left. Nash's body involuntarily convulsed in disgust. His decision made, Nash made his way to the back of the house, his boots squishing in the wet grass.

He picked up an old musty blanket, soaked from the night's rain and dragged it behind him with one hand, his axe rested securely in the other. The naked slowpoke noticed him immediately as he came around the house. He made his way toward her in the hot morning sun, the wet blanket still grasped in his hand as it dragged behind him.

Nash had seen the fear in the faces of some of the slowpokes Duncan had cut into and had watched as a few of them even tried to slowly escape from him in vain. He'd witnessed groups of them as they walked together, as if part of an old clique before their deaths, and even the occasional couple that held hands and made their way aimlessly through the world. Nash had witnessed Duncan kill dozens of slowpokes, in all manner of ways, in the time they had traveled together. Nash, however, took no joy in the few times he had killed one, but as Duncan sat and watched her, Nash swung his axe and planted it into the back of the slowpoke's skull. The feeling of the axe as it came to a stop in her head sickened him. The woman's personality had left long ago but she was still a life, and that belief was responsible for his hesitation when it came to killing any of the vacant, docile slowpokes. Blood sprayed up and sideways as she fell to the ground.

"*What the hell, Nash?*" Duncan yelled angrily from the kitchen.

Nash draped the musty blanket over the now deceased woman and took one last look at her sad face before he fully covered her from head to toe. He walked away from her, knowing she wasn't a slowpoke any longer, just a victim of the crumbled society in which they lived.

Nash wiped the blade of his axe with the blanket and grabbed his bag before he walked back to the abandoned street. He heard the backdoor open and close as Duncan came outside to inspect his previously intended prey. She was at peace; whether or not Duncan moved forward with his plan, Nash didn't want to know.

Chapter 3

Nash walked down the street and observed the devastation that had once been a nice neighborhood. White picket fences now lay on the ground, trampled and broken by passing monsters. A flagpole laid in the ruins of a crushed fence, the American flag flapping in tatters on the street, its white stars streaked with blood. Most of the houses were ransacked to the point where he deemed them pointless to search, with the exception of one. The windows remained unbroken and the exterior of the house was still intact as the door hung partially open. It looked mostly untouched, and if any house would have something of value, this would be the one.

Nash was always weary about walking into houses alone but knew he was better off than if he had brought Duncan with him this morning. Given the way he'd left him, anything done with him would have ended up being more of a liability than an asset. His nerves slowly tightened as he approached the house. He looked from the walking path into the home through the open door as he clutched his axe tighter. For as long as he remembered, he'd always been a little on the nervous side, but nervousness was a sensation that could no longer be afforded.

A wooden porch wrapped around both sides of the home, painted white, with dead potted flowers sitting at the opening of the stairs. The steps creaked softly under his feet as he made his way onto the porch and listened for any signs of movement through the partially open door. The interior was in worse shape than the outside and Nash wasn't sure if his initial observation about the house would pan out.

He used his axe and slowly pushed the door open further. He was relieved to hear no squeaking as it swung inward. He was always extra cautious not to make any noise that would attract unwanted attention. Within the first month of being on the road, Duncan had kicked open the door of a house he thought was good for looting. The door had exploded into shards of wood that sent shockwaves through the house as three howlers spilled into the foyer and chased them into the streets, separating them for hours. Nash still remembered Duncan's laughter as two of the howlers wildly pursued him into the distance.

Howlers were the opposite of slowpokes. They were the reason most of the world was in ruin and Nash had learned long ago to avoid them at all costs. They were fast, angry, and full of rage as they burst into homes and buildings, moving freely across the country. Something left over in their decayed psyche alerted them to the fact that people had once lived in homes, which drove them to crash through windows and doors in search of their next victim.

There was no rhyme or reason as to what dictated if someone turned into a howler or a slowpoke. Nash had spent countless hours trying to make sense of it. He carried a notebook he'd used to detail hundreds of the dead he'd seen, cataloguing everything from gender, size, approximate age, original bite location, and even eye color when possible. Pages and pages of detailed notes had left him with no answers at all. He couldn't find any features that connected the two groups, which left him just as confused as anyone else still alive in this dead wasteland.

Nash stood in the open doorway and saw a set of steps just inside the foyer. They were completely broken apart with gaping holes that lead to the upper floor. A gust of hot, rotten breeze flowed around him as he stepped inside, a telltale sign something inside was decaying. The source of the smell was identified as he stepped further into the foyer; an outstretched arm hung out of an open hallway door.

Nash stared at the rotted skin and slender fingers of the decaying arm, pinned underneath the hallway door, which had been torn from its hinges. He gripped the handle of his axe tighter as the monster's index finger twitched. The rest of its fingers closed into a loose fist before opening again.

Careful that he made no sound, he crept forward and peaked around the broken door. A rapidly decaying slowpoke lay face up in a pool of dried blood. It looked up at him with eyes a mile away as its dying mouth formed into a sad frown. Its gray skin looked tight against its skeleton as it looked up at Nash with mindless, confused eyes. He knelt down beside the dying slowpoke while he fished an old screwdriver out of his bag.

Nash locked eyes with the monster before him as the shaft of the screwdriver slid easily into its temple with a soft squishy sound. The life drained quickly from its eyes. Nash continued to kneel and stare at the dead man in front of him, struggling to embrace the sadness he always felt when he killed a slowpoke. He'd gone months without having to and today he'd killed two before lunch.

Nash made his way through the main floor of the home and found nothing worth taking among the debris. He stepped gingerly over the dead slowpoke as a pool of black blood slowly inched its way across the hallway floor, saturating the hardwood as it grew. Nash came to a stop at the foot of the broken staircase, more destroyed than he'd originally noticed. Most of the middle of the stairs had caved in, which left a trap of splintered wood and nails in its wake. Slowly, he made his way up the side of the staircase; he carefully placed each footstep as if he expected the stairs to give way at any moment. He looked down into the large, dark holes as he moved and while he knew that there was nothing more than the area under the stairs, he imagined an endless cavern of darkness readied to swallow him whole.

He exhaled fiercely after he reached the top of the steps; he hadn't even realized he'd held his breath. The room at the top of the steps remained untouched, which gave him hope that the climb up the dangerous stairs had been worth it. He stood still in the doorway and listened for any sign of danger before he began his search. Howlers were often loud when they could smell a meal, but there were some howlers that were more predatory than creatures of opportunity. Sometimes they stood still and waited for someone to cross their path.

He walked quietly into the bedroom and went straight for the dresser drawers to scan their contents for supplies. The first contained mostly socks and underwear, exactly what he had expected to find. Opening the other drawers proved to not be as exciting as he had hoped it could have been, as they were filled with nothing but clothing.

The bottom drawer turned out to be a junk-drawer, filled mostly with items he had no use for. Nash pushed the items back and forth and found a box of wooden matches and an unopened pack of gum. He knew the matches would be kept under Duncan's guard, just another instrument in his growing cigar addiction, but the packs of gum went straight into his pocket to be enjoyed later. There was a small part of him that was excited to give the matches to Duncan, as he knew it could possibly smooth over the backlash from earlier in the morning. He slid them into his bag and hoped they insured him a smooth afternoon.

He placed his bag on the bed and ran his hand along a line of hanging shirts in the open closet. It looked like the previous inhabitant had been about his size, so he took a few of them off the rack and stuffed them in his bag before he removed his own shirt and slid on a new one. The fabric felt crisp and clean as it fell onto his torso, a feeling he hadn't enjoyed in months. He slung his bag around his back and left the room, his bloodstained shirt on the floor behind him as he made his way back to the hallway.

The next door in the hallway was closed and it would remain that way. He wasn't about to get bit by a howler as he searched for supplies while Duncan sat outside and drank in the sun. At the end of the hall was a linen closet that sat open between two open doors. The room on the left was a study, complete with a computer desk, bookcase and a few filing cabinets. The room across from it was a bathroom, where he found another collection of useful items.

He walked away with his bag filled with Tylenol, peroxide, gauze, and mouthwash. There were days when he would have traded half his belongings for a container of mouthwash if given the chance. Nash grabbed a few clean towels from the linen closet before he made his way into the study. He ran his fingers across the top of the desk, which left dark, wooden streaks overtop the dusty surface. The drawers were locked, and remained that way as Nash looked in vain for the key. Sitting on top of the desk, though, was a sturdy letter opener, covered in so much dust he almost missed it. He picked it up and brushed it off as he felt the weight of it in his palm. He could tell it had been expensive and could easily be used as a weapon should the need arise.

A thunderous crash from the hallway rattled the walls of the house and his fingers instantly tightened around the letter opener. He crept slowly toward the doorway, hoping the sound had been Duncan—knowing it wasn't. Even Duncan wouldn't be stupid enough to make a commotion like that. Another crash echoed through the hallway and Nash flinched. He continued to creep forward until he heard the deep, wheezing breath beyond the wall.

Nash steeled himself and darted to the corner of the office beside the large, wooden bookcase, fighting the urge to cry out. He fixated his eyes on the reflection of the open door in the window across from him. He held the knife-shaped letter opener in front of him; his fingers were turning white as they wrapped tightly around the handle. The howler continued breathing heavily, a wheezing sound that he could hardly bear.

The sound of footsteps filled the upstairs as the howler moved into the hallway. Nash listened to its heavy, labored breath as it spewed foamy saliva and blood with each exhale. In between bouts of heavy breathing, it sobbed softly, as all howlers did while they stood alone and unattended. The sound of their cries always brought on a feeling of hopelessness in him. They had all once been alive, trying to survive just like he was, but they now stood trapped in a prison to which there was no escape.

He waited in the study for another half hour and listened as the howler alternated between angry breathing and sobbing. He knew it was only a matter of time before the howler decided to wander into the room. There was no way to signal to Duncan, which meant he was on his own to get down the stairs and back onto the street. The window on the opposite side of the room was too high to jump from and the sound it would make would send the howler screaming into the study, its jaws gnashing open and shut. The floor hadn't creaked at all when he'd made it to the top, which he knew would be his only saving grace as he tried to escape the howler down the hall.

Nash moved slowly to the doorway and hesitated for a moment before he poked his head into the hallway. It was empty, just as before, but now there were dirty footprints that led into the room where he had found the matches. He made his way into the hall, taking care to make as little noise as possible with each step. He would need to pass the room in order to get back to the stairs.

The howler's shadow painted the floor of the doorway like a black hole and filled him with dread as he made his way toward it. He stopped short of the open door and peered in as relief washed over him when he saw that the monster stood with its back toward him. It panted and spewed moisture onto the bed in front of it and sent ribbons of bloody saliva onto its tattered shirt. It had begun to sob again as Nash moved slowly against the wall opposite the bedroom, the sound echoed harshly in his ears as he inched his way toward the steps. He knew the sounds would revisit him in his dreams that night, as they always did. Nash kept his eyes locked on the bloodied, battered howler that stood before him.

It wasn't tall, maybe five foot seven, with a bald head that revealed jagged strips of skin, which hung loosely from its infected scalp. The howler's black t-shirt was torn open down the back, revealing a long gash from its shoulder to its waistline. Its light colored jeans were stained black from dried blood that led down to his heels, which were stained crimson with blood and dust.

Nash continued toward the stairs, his eyes locked on the howler with every silent step. It paused its sobbing and released a gurgling howl into the air before returning to short, heavy breaths. Its hands moved up to its head and pulled the flaps of skin from its bloodied scalp, which added a painful tearing sound to the symphony of its horrid breathing. Nash stopped, situated just near the top of the stairs, barely out of the howler's line of sight. He watched for a moment as it pulled more strips of skin off its head, caught in a trance of revulsion. He held back his disgust until the howler began sobbing with its head down again, which gave him the opportunity to proceed carefully down the stairs. He placed each foot softly on the broken staircase and began the slow descent to the main floor.

Footfalls filled the foyer as Nash neared the halfway point on the stairs. The howler remained sobbing, somehow unaware of the sound that came from the lower level as it stood in its own sadness. Duncan stood in the foyer below and looked at

Nash with a smile as he held a baseball bat at his side. He opened his mouth to shout something but somehow, through all the morning booze he had consumed, he noticed the panicked look on Nash's face as he stood silent on the stairwell.

Duncan looked up into the upper level, and from where he stood he could just see the howler in the open door. Nash lifted his index finger to his lips as he signaled Duncan to keep quiet, who, somehow in his inebriated state, complied. Duncan motioned him to come down the stairs slowly. Nash made one small step forward and that's when all hell broke loose.

"Ding, ding, ding, ding, ding!" yelled Duncan at the top of his lungs. "Who's the next contestant on the Price is Right?"

Nash jumped from the middle of the stairway and came crashing down onto the foyer floor as a bloodcurdling scream echoed through the empty house. The howler stepped to the top of the staircase, fresh strips of skin hanging loosely over its face as it surged toward them in a frenzy. It leapt from the top of the stairs and made it to the bottom, landing awkwardly on the floor as its ankles snapped loudly.

"We can't have you chewing on Buddy Boy here, now can we?" said Duncan as he raised his baseball bat over his head. "Close your mouth, *Buddy Boy*!"

With one swing of the bat, Duncan obliterated the howler's skull and sent a spattering of blood across the foyer floor. Nash struggled to his feet and wiped the gore from his shirt. Duncan placed two more punishing blows to the howler's head, a smile plastered on his face.

"Practice makes perfect, *am I right*?"

Nash leaned against the wall and exhaled, his eyes closed as nervous energy flowed angrily through his body. He easily would have gotten out quietly if Duncan hadn't shown up, but it was over now, and he did feel somewhat relieved.

"Move," said Duncan as he tapped the bat against Nash's elbow and motioned toward the door.

Nash stepped out onto the porch and looked up and down the street to make sure Duncan's attack hadn't brought any unwelcome attention. He locked eyes with a slowpoke that stood in the middle of the street when his face was jolted backward with a foul smelling cloth. Duncan breathed heavily into his ear, the stale liquor on his breath hot on Nash's skin.

"What you did at the house this morning; don't you ever pull that shit again! You hear me? Don't you interrupt my plans—or I'll interrupt that life of yours!"

Duncan let go of him roughly, sending Nash crashing onto the wooden porch. He pulled the cloth from his face and the smell lingered as he realized it wasn't a cloth at all. Nash looked in horror at the face of the woman he had killed earlier this morning, staring back at him from the porch floor.

"What is wrong with you!" yelled Nash. "What if I got her blood in my mouth?"

"Oh, settle down," said Duncan as he chuckled. "I cleaned it beforehand."

Nash reached into his bag and splashed a bottle of water over his face and used one of the towels he'd collected to make sure he was clean. Duncan laughed from the street and watched Nash hunch over as vomit spilled out onto the porch. Tears welled in his Nash's eyes as he sat on his knees and stared at the empty eyes of the slowpoke's face.

"Let's go," Duncan said from the street as he dragged his bat across the white picket fence at the edge of the front yard.

Nash stood up, composed himself as best he could, and tried his hardest not to look at the woman's face. He opened his bag and took out the box of matches before closing it again. He held the box in his hand, squeezing it slightly so that the corners bent inwards. He took one more steadying breath and tossed the box onto the lawn. The wooden matches spilled out onto the wet grass as Nash slid his bag over his shoulder and followed Duncan.

Chapter 4

Three days after the run in with the howler, Nash woke up in the back of a black Mercedes. He remained hidden and protected throughout the night, as the tinted windows had remained intact throughout the apocalypse. Duncan had disappeared up the congested interstate to find his own place to sleep, as he always did. It was just another moment of privacy that Nash looked forward to daily. He rubbed his eyes and silently yawned while he took out the picture of Melissa.

He held the photo in front of him and analyzed every inch of it. He almost felt the warm breeze that had caught her hair and the bubbles of the Dr. Pepper on his tongue. He imagined doing a cannonball off the dock, landing with a splash in the cool lake as everyone laughed from the bank. He smiled again while he looked at the photo, as if it was his own memory and not Melissa's. A loud thumping outside of the car startled him as he fumbled to put the picture away.

"Time to get a move on, dumbass," yelled Duncan, his voice muffled as he strained to see inside.

Nash stepped out of the car into the muggy air as the dark clouds from the last few days slowly disappeared into the distance. Duncan had already moved a long way up the interstate and looked back every so often to make sure Nash checked cars for supplies. Duncan only stopped to loot cars when there was something in plain sight that piqued his interest, while Nash took his time and inspected most vehicles that didn't look like they'd already been picked through. Other than a few books of matches and some packaged granola bars, he'd found only decaying bodies and pools of dried blood. Nash stopped and watched Duncan furiously rummage through a car far up ahead of him.

"Damn perverts!" he yelled back to Nash as he held up a Playboy magazine above his head for. "Good thing I came along first. Don't want any kids seeing this filth, eh Buddy Boy?"

He laughed loudly as he rolled up the magazine and slid it into the back pocket of his dirty jeans. Nash was surprised that an old tattered Playboy was even worth the effort for him, considering the amount of slowpokes he'd known Duncan to have his way with. It's why he always carried a box of condoms with him. Duncan was reckless, but not enough to be suicidal—a thoughtful rapist. He held his axe tightly in hand and scanned the area for any activity. Duncan's voice had carried loudly along the congested road and could have easily attracted nearby howlers. Other than a few slowpokes that had taken notice in the large open field beside the road, everything looked safe as Duncan made his way further up the road ahead.

The two of them spent almost the entire day walking along the dead interstate, looking through abandoned cars and listening for any nearby howlers. It was common for Duncan to disappear far ahead while they scavenged, leaving Nash alone to fend for himself. Every so often, Nash heard a hoot from up the road as Duncan found some trinket he found funny or entertaining. Normally, Nash found the separation between them slightly unnerving, but on a clear day like today where he could see all around that they were not in danger, he appreciated the distance. He hated the safety that traveling with Duncan provided, but knew that having Duncan with him meant an extra layer of protection, even if Duncan was a danger in his own right.

Duncan erupted into a fit of laughter as he leaned through the window of a rusted-out pickup truck about 100 yards away. Nash watched him in disapproval, hating that his stepfather couldn't keep his voice down anywhere. A little Toyota Corolla shook slightly as Nash approached. When he was about ten feet away from the car, the door creaked open slowly.

Nash dove quickly behind a car and sat with his back against the bumper while he listened with a nervous ear. A car that had flipped during an accident had its side mirror pointed directly at the car door, which allowed him a good vantage point to watch.

He stared at the mirror as a bloodied foot fell from the driver's side door and hit the pavement with a thick, squishing smash. The monster in the car wore gray sweatpants, dark and crusty from a gash on its abdomen. Its left hand was wedged awkwardly in the inside door handle while its right hand sat wedged in the steering wheel.

Nash stayed hidden behind the mangled car while he listened for any sign that it was a howler. He peered around the edge of the crashed vehicle as the hand on the door handle released and fell limply against its crusty leg. Nash stood calmly, knowing it was nothing more than a slowpoke, but kept his axe in hand just the same.

He looked up the road to try and find Duncan but only found another slowpoke that stood alone in the middle of a pile of cars. The slowpoke in the car in front of him tried to slide itself out of the driver's seat, only to fall to the ground awkwardly like a newborn deer. It grunted as it reached up and used the car door to help itself up. A loud creaking sound echoed loudly from the abandoned car as the slowpoke pulled itself up from the pavement. It looked Nash in the eye, its nose viciously broken from the fall, as dark blood flowed from its nostrils into its clueless, open-mouthed smile. It was apparent to Nash that there was a small part of all slowpokes left inside their confused exterior, memories trapped deep inside their new existence. The one that stood in front of him was no exception.

It continued staring at Nash as the blood flowed freely from its nose and down over its lips and chin. It had started to show signs of malnutrition; its skin was dry and flaking away as a bite on its left arm oozed with infection, sending dark blue veins all the way to its fingertips. Its face was shallow, which made its eyes start to sink into the darkened circles that surrounded them. During his time spent with the smiling slowpoke, Nash hadn't even realized that Duncan had doubled back in the trees along the road and crept up behind them.

"Look at this fucking guy! You tell him a funny joke or something?" He leaned on the trunk of the car the slowpoke had sat in and smiled back at the grinning monster. It looked at Duncan curiously as its smile widened to the point where Nash thought the corners of its mouth would split apart.

"Goodness he's a smiley fucker, isn't he?" said Duncan as he tapped the slowpoke in the gut with his bat. The monster slowly moved its eyes between the two of them, still pleased with the emergence of its new friends and oblivious to the danger that Duncan represented to it. Duncan slid his knife out of the sheath on his belt and let the sun gleam off the shining blade.

"Put your knife away," said Nash. "Leave it be."

Duncan looked at Nash with a furrowed brow. Then he turned back to the slowpoke as it slightly choked and splashed blood out of its open mouth.

"I've had something stuck in here all day. Don't you hate that?" said Duncan as he raised the blade to his mouth and used the reflection to look at his teeth.

"Just leave him alone, Duncan."

"Can you believe this guy?" Duncan said to the slowpoke while he pointed at Nash with his knife. He threw his head toward the sky and laughed, the echo pinging off the abandoned cars. The slowpoke looked to Nash as if awaiting a reaction, not breaking its smile for a single moment as it stood confused in front of them. Duncan abruptly stopped laughing and planted his muddy boot into the stomach of the slowpoke, sending it backward into the open car door. The metal hinges creaked loudly and gave way as the door folded backward with the weight of the tall, dead thing.

"Get your shit together," said Duncan as he walked over to the slowpoke and kicked it in the side of its head. "I'm gutting the next one!" Duncan stormed off down the highway like a petulant child.

The slowpoke struggled to stand up, stumbling back to the ground a couple times before Nash covered his hands with his sleeves and approached it. Making sure to keep clear of its blood, Nash helped the slowpoke to its feet. It didn't even look to where Duncan went, but stared at Nash with a saddened look on its bloodied face. Duncan's boot had torn a fresh flap of skin away from its cheek and sent blood flowing onto its tattered t-shirt. The smile it had previously had on its face had completely faded away and was replaced with a look of sheer confusion and abandonment as it searched Nash's face for an answer.

Nash reached into his bag and fetched out a bottle of water and threw the cap to the ground.. He placed the bottle in the right hand of the slowpoke and it immediately started to hold onto it with both hands like a toddler. It squeezed the bottle a little and sent water bubbling out of the top like a geyser. A strip of red cloth was tied around its left wrist, with no lettering or logos at all; just a simple strip of ragged, dirty cloth, hung somewhat loosely from its wrist.

"I'm sorry this happened to you."

It raised the bottle to its bloody mouth as Nash made his way around it and joined Duncan. Slowpokes didn't eat, but they drank water. You could find them congregating at water sources, which was why bottled water was so special. You couldn't be certain that their blood hadn't contaminated a water source. He could see Duncan not far up ahead as he rifled through an open trunk and muttered to himself as usual. Duncan pulled his head out of the truck with a lit cigar between his teeth and smiled while he gave Nash a thumbs up, his right foot up onto the tire of a car beside him. Nash thought he looked ridiculous, like some sort of cheesy sea captain, and if it had been anyone else he may have even laughed.

A crow cawed loudly in the distance as a soft whizzing sound registered in Nash's ear, seconds before a loud crunching came from behind him. He spun around to find the slowpoke with a confused look on its face, the bottle of water obliterated in a pool of water and blood on the pavement. The slowpoke's hand was bloodied and mangled as it looked down at the busted water bottle.

"Get down!" yelled Duncan from far up the road.

Nash stood in shock and locked eyes with the slowpoke as its head cocked sideways and sprayed blood on the idle vehicles next to it. The slowpoke fell sideways, landing in a crumpled heap as its eyes somehow remained locked onto Nash's. Nash gazed at the dead slowpoke as hands wrapped around his ankles and pulled him abruptly to the ground. He fell hard, landing on the hot pavement with a loud thud as the air vacated his lungs.

"When I tell you to do something I mean it!" whispered Duncan, angrily. "There's a sniper somewhere across that field."

Nash rolled onto his side and tried in vain to refill his lungs with air. His arms were bleeding, having taken most of the impact from his fall. He winced, his head radiating from connecting with the car as he fell.

"Quit your bitching and help me search the tree line."

Hot air rushed into Nash's chest as his airway finally re-opened. He rolled onto his chest and looked under the car with Duncan as they both tried to find the source of the gunshot. An overgrown field stretched out in front of them, spanning a few hundred yards from the road and ending at a small forest. He looked briefly at Duncan and saw no form of remorse on his stern face for pulling him so harshly to the ground.

"I thought you'd done that," said Nash.

"I was giving you a thumbs up when it happened, dumbass. Did you see me holding a rifle in my other hand?"

"Can you blame me for thinking that after you kicked him like that?"

"*Him*?" said Duncan as he briefly broke his gaze on the trees to give Nash a look of disgust. "*It* was nothing but a dumb hillbilly. That sniper should have taken a shot at you for wasting a bottle of water on it. Don't come crying to me when you're thirsty."

As if Nash would go to him for anything other than tips on killing or smoking.

There was a long stretch of silence as the two scanned the horizon together. The midday sun was intense, which made the pavement feel like hot, smoldering embers, as sweat dripped from their skin onto the scorching road.

"Do you think he's still there? We can't lie here in the open all day," asked Nash.

"Why don't you stand up and give it a test. Go check on your friend over there."

The two remained still on the pavement, hesitant to even so much as breathe too loudly. The sun had started its final descent towards the horizon, but the asphalt still continued to bake them as they sat motionless against the broken car. Duncan lowered himself to the pavement again, looking out across the field from below the car to try and see any kind of movement.

"Do you see anything?" whispered Nash, seeing the rolled up Playboy still secured in Duncan's back pocket.

Duncan remained silent, ignoring Nash as he often did. Nash sat with his back pressed against the car and scanned the trees behind them for any howlers that might pass. Duncan turned and looked back at the trees, assessing them as a possible escape route before he returned his gaze back to where the shot had come from as an angry scream echoed loudly across the pavement.

Four howlers screamed and smashed into each other as they made their way through the dead cars. The fastest of the group, two males, tore at their skin and left chunks of flesh and gore hanging from their chests. An older woman in a tattered housecoat, as well as a woman in her twenties, followed close behind. The older woman was covered in dark blue veins as her bloodied housecoat hung loosely from her frail body, while the younger woman looked as if she'd been turned within the last day or two.

"Keep your head down!" yelled Duncan as he lunged to his feet and ran toward the woods behind them. Nash hesitated a moment, watching Duncan disappear into the woods as the howlers continued their sprint. He'd grown used to running and hiding from howlers, but snipers were a whole different story, and he was frozen in fear. Another whizzing sound filled the air as another bullet connect with the skull of one of the male howlers, sending it crashing to the ground about twenty feet from him. Nash finally sprinted towards the woods, his head down as he imagined bullets flying past him in all directions. He felt slightly relieved as he made it into the woods until his foot caught on a twisted root.

"Duncan, wait!" he screamed, trading glances between the trees Duncan had disappeared into and the tangled root around his foot. He was grateful to have made it into the woods without being shot, but a more dangerous threat was now on its way, ready to bear down on him any minute.

A vicious cracking sound echoed from the road as the remaining male howler slipped in a pool of blood formed from the dead slowpoke, breaking its leg and sending jagged bone through its skin as the two others flew past. The female howlers briefly became wedged between two cars as they made their way toward him, bottlenecking with each other as they each tried to force their way through. The old woman made her way through first, gnashing her teeth and growling as she stepped forward. Her housecoat caught on the bumper of a car, sending a tearing sound into the air as she wiggled herself away from it. Her naked body was wrinkled and covered in dark veins from head to toe, showing that the infection had completely invaded her entire being. Nash freed himself but hesitated for a moment when he noticed the red strip of cloth tied around the younger woman's wrist.

"What the hell is wrong with you?" yelled Duncan as he lifted Nash to his feet by his arms. "Let's go!"

The two maneuvered the forest quickly as the younger female howler kept pace behind them. Her angry yelps filled their ears as they weaved in and out of the trees, hoping to lose her along the way. Younger howlers were better nourished than ones that had been dead for a while, making them much harder to escape or hide from.

Duncan unbuttoned the leather snap that kept his knife sheathed in his belt and pulled out the shiny blade. Nash could see a nervous determination on Duncan's face as he carefully adjusted his fingers around the handle of the knife, his knuckles turning bone-white. Duncan stopped and turned to face the screaming woman, the knife held out in front of him as she locked her furious gaze on him. Her black hair flew behind her in wispy strands, the left strap of her dirty white tank top fallen aside to expose her breast as she ran at them with outstretched arms. With better timing than either of them could have hoped for, Duncan sank the blade into her forehead as she crashed into him at full speed. The two of them went crashing onto the damp ground, the dead woman on top of Duncan with her chest pressed against his face.

"Whoa! No thanks, honey!" scoffed Duncan as he pushed the dead woman off himself with a strained chuckle.

He stood up and wiped her blood from his hands as he looked down at the bleeding mass on the ground. As he stared down at her, Nash found it hard to ignore how pretty she had been as part of her humanity returned while she lay peacefully in the wet leaves. With the exception of the dark infected bite on her right forearm, her body was void of any of the typical dark winding veins found on older howlers.

"She's the second I've seen today with that red bracelet," said Nash.

"Who gives a fuck." Duncan knelt down beside her and pulled the knife out of the top of her head. It created a squishy popping sound as blood flowed out of the slender wound. Duncan smiled up at Nash while he used his knife to jiggle her breast as it sat awkwardly outside her tank top.

"Not too shabby, eh, Buddy Boy? Want a turn with her? I doubt she'd give you much trouble."

Nash responded with silent disgust and looked up to scan the trees for the old woman. They could hear her far back in the woods as she panted and howled in the distance, but to their benefit she'd gotten lost along the way.

"You're too serious, Buddy Boy. What happened to the males that were with these two broads?"

"One got hit by the sniper. The other fell back at the road. He must have broken his leg because he didn't get back up."

"You gonna go back and make a splint for him? Maybe clean up those wounds on his chest? He probably saw you give smiley that bottle of water too. We don't want him getting jealous, now do we?"

Duncan sheathed his knife and began to walk deeper into the forest, but not before he took one last look at the half-topless dead woman. Nash knelt down and closed her cloudy eyes.

"Really?" asked Duncan as he watched Nash kneel beside her

Branches cracked behind them, followed by a sound they hadn't heard in months; the gruff voice of someone other than themselves.

Chapter 5

"Don't move," boomed the voice from behind Duncan.

Nash looked up from the dead woman and saw a large tank of a man who stood about five feet away. He held an automatic rifle, pointed directly at them. He wore dark camouflaged army fatigues with heavy black combat boots that weighed deep into the muddy ground. His thick, brown beard hung straggly from his face, his eyes hidden behind dark sunglasses.

"Your weapons and bags; place them on the ground and step away slowly," he said with an unflinching face.

Duncan unclasped his knife from his belt and tossed in in front of him, followed shortly after by his bag. Nash took his time, unbuckling the axe from his own belt. He imagined it slipping out of his hands as he threw it forward—crashing into the man's legs, and the man responding by opening fire on them. He took a steadying breath and awkwardly tossed the axe on the ground in front of them. Nash and Duncan both backed away from their belongings slowly, hands in the air.

"Kneel on the ground with the boy," the soldier ordered.

Nash immediately kneeled. Duncan turned around slowly with his hands out to his sides and stared up at the man as he joined Nash on the ground. Nash could see a large hunting knife sheathed to the man's boot, as well as smaller knives around his beltline.

"Let's just calm down, sailor," said Duncan as he looked at the man with a determined gaze.

The soldier ignored him. "I'm going to look through your stuff. Either of you so much as sneeze and your throat will be open before you blink."

He pulled his knife out of the sheath on his boot and plunged it into the ground in front of him. Nash's eyes locked onto the long blade as it glistened in the afternoon light. If it hadn't been for the threat of killing them, he would have seemed polite in the way he handled their belongings. Nash had expected him to gruffly dump everything onto the ground, but instead he gently rustled through their open bags as if they were his own.

"What's your name, big guy?" asked Duncan as he watched the man finish rummaging through his pack and move on to Nash's. The man ignored him and continued his search. It looked as if he were almost done until he froze, his eyes fixed on something inside.

"How do you know this girl?" he said as he held up the picture of Melissa. Duncan let out a sigh as he looked down at the ground in frustration. The soldier hadn't broken his gaze with Nash and waited in silence for him to reply.

The image of the glistening blade filled his mind as Nash tried in vain to think of something to say. If he said he knew her, it could end badly; if he said he didn't know her, it could end even worse. His eyes fixed on the knife again as he struggled to decide what to say. The man picked it up by its handle and placed it back into its sheath.

"It's okay, kid," he said, speaking softer than he had before.

"I don't know her. We stayed in a house a few nights ago to get out of the rain and I slept in her bedroom."

Duncan gazed at Nash with a disgruntled face as he explained how he'd acquired the picture. The only thing that cut the silence was the distant sound of the housecoat howler as she sobbed loudly and wandered naked through the dense trees.

"I thought she was pretty. She just looks so happy and it reminded me of better days."

The soldier remained crouched in front of them, listening as Nash explained himself. Duncan looked at the photo, recognizing her from the house they'd stayed at during the storm. Another loud, high-pitched squeal echoed through the forest as the dead thing far behind them cried in frustration.

"How far back is she?" asked the man.

"Who knows? She wasn't nearly as fast as this hussy," said Duncan as he motioned toward the dead woman on the ground. Nash glared at him as Duncan's eyes once again lingered on the dead woman's exposed chest.

"Stay here," he said. "I think it's clear at this point what will happen if you make a break for it."

The soldier stood up and walked into the woods in the direction of the weeping dead thing. The two remained on their knees and kept quiet until he had completely disappeared into the woods.

"So you've been carrying that hot little number around in your bag this whole time and you didn't think to share with me?" asked Duncan as he stood up and brushed off his knees.

"Where are you going?"

"Stand up, you twit," he spat. "I'm not going anywhere and neither are you. I'm just through with being on my knees for Mr. Macho."

Duncan gathered his bag and reattached his knife to his belt while Nash stood and watched.

"Aren't you gonna get your shit together? You should put your girlfriend back into your bag before he decides he wants it for himself," said Duncan with a grin. "As a matter of fact..."

"Don't touch it," said Nash. He reached down and grabbed it a second before Duncan could.

"Oh relax, drama-queen," said Duncan as he reached into his back pocket for the now-muddied Playboy. "Fine by me!"

Duncan bopped Nash on the head with the magazine as the crying in the distance crested into a vicious squeal, followed by the abrupt return of eerie silence. Nash and Duncan stood together in the late afternoon air and listened to the soft sounds of the forest. Nash always valued these moments, when the sounds of the old world crept through the madness. It comforted him to know that no matter what happened in the lives of men, the natural world moved onward, unscathed. The birds still sang and the fish still swam, unaware the world around them had gone through a fundamental change.

The soldier returned shortly after, his knife at his side and a red strip of cloth in his other hand. He bent down and cut the strip off the dead woman, then placed them both into his pocket.

"Get your gear on kid," he said as he stood to his feet and sheathed his knife.

Before he grabbed any of his things, Nash knelt down and readjusted the dead woman's tank top. Duncan rolled his eyes as he watched and looked to the man for a reaction but got nothing from him. Nash slid his backpack onto his shoulders, picked up his axe, and stood at the ready in front of the two men.

"I'm going to take the two of you to my camp. There are people there, and it's safe. I will not hesitate to remove you quickly should there be any disruption of the peace. Are we going to have any problems?" he asked as he turned his gaze to Duncan.

"No problems here chief," he said as he put his palms slightly in the air in a submissive posture. "You think we can manage that, Buddy Boy?"

Nash didn't respond and left Duncan standing with his hands in the air.

"We weren't just running from her," said Nash as he looked down at the dead woman. "There was someone out on the road with a scoped rifle. Was that one of your people?"

"No," he said flatly after a short pause. "We should get to camp. Let's get moving."

Duncan walked in front of Nash, with the man behind them as he scanned the forest. The screaming dead woman had scared most of the birds away, but they slowly returned to fill the air with their melodies.

"How far is this little love-shack of yours?" said Duncan as he kicked leaves into the air as they walked. "I don't think we've even done proper introductions!" Duncan turned around with his hand extended toward the man, a big, smile on his face.

The man grabbed Duncan by the hand and placed a pair of handcuffs on him, so fast that Nash barely saw it happen.

"What the hell?" yelled Duncan as he looked at the cuffs now strung between his wrists.

"Consider that your first hint as to how interested I am right now in pleasantries. Keep talking and I'll tape your mouth shut."

Duncan scowled at the man as he turned and continued walking, quieter than Nash had ever expected him to.

"That red strip, the one you took off that girl back there. I saw a slowpoke that had one on its wrist earlier today, too."

"Slowpoke?" said the soldier, motioning for Duncan to keep walking as he turned around to see why they weren't moving. His face was sour as he watched as the man and Nash talked to each other.

"Oh, sorry. That's what we call the slow ones that don't attack," said Nash, forgetting that he'd coined the term himself.

"I knew what you meant. We can talk about this more once we've gotten you settled at camp. Let's keep moving, it's getting dark."

The two resumed walking as the late afternoon gave way to early evening.

"My name's Sullivan," said the man, quietly so only Nash heard.

"I'm Nash, and that's Duncan."

"What's your business with him?" asked Sullivan.

"He's my stepfather. *Was* my stepfather? I'm not so sure anymore."

Nash was fully aware it could be naïve to put his trust in the man they'd just met, considering minutes ago he'd had his gun focused on them, but something told him that Sullivan was trustworthy. It seemed that Sullivan was not at all blinded by the repulsive charm Duncan emanated. In Nash's eyes, and in the eyes of his mother, Sullivan was "good people."

He hadn't thought of his mother and good people in a long time, and Nash smiled slightly as they walked.

Chapter 6

The sun had begun its fast descent over the horizon by the time they reached Sullivan's camp. It was impossible to tell how much daylight they had left, as the farther they moved into the woods, the denser the canopy of trees above them became.

"Stop here," said Sullivan from the back of their walking formation. He made his way past them, patting Nash on the shoulder as he moved. He disappeared into the thick woods ahead of them, once again leaving the two of them alone.

"Well you two seem chummy," said Duncan as he looked at his agitated wrists. "You bunking with him tonight? He seems like your type, *Buddy Boy*."

Nash ignored him and tried to see where Sullivan had disappeared. He strained his eyes against the increasing darkness, finding it impossible to see anything in the dense woods. He gasped as strong hands dug into his shoulders before he was thrust backward against a large tree. His teeth smashed down hard on his tongue, which sent the familiar, metallic taste of blood into his mouth. Duncan was in front of him quickly, his handcuffs pressed against his neck.

"When I ask you a question, you answer me," sneered Duncan. Their faces almost touched as he glared at Nash. The burning stench of alcohol crashed out of Duncan's mouth as he spoke. "You've been ignoring me a lot lately and I'm not liking it at all. I don't care if you don't like me, as a matter of fact I prefer it that way, but when I ask you a damn question, *I expect a damn answer*."

His voice was filled with a desperate need for control. He spoke softly, a manic grin on his face as he continued to spew his stinking, boozy breath at Nash.

"Tell me…do you plan on shacking up with Mr. Macho over there." His smile transformed into a sneer. "A boy like you needs protecting and I'm damn near ready to retire from that job."

Nash struggled for breath as a bead of blood trickled out of his mouth from when he'd bit his tongue. With each second, Duncan pressed more of his weight against him and dug the cuffs against his throat, shortening his air supply. His head radiated with waves of pain and his eyes blurred from the intense pressure. Nash heard a slight rustling before the butt of Sullivan's gun connected with the side of Duncan's head, sending him sideways into the musty dirt. Nash fell to the ground in pain, the indents of the metal cuffs still outlined on his neck as he gasped for breath. Sullivan crouched down over Duncan and placed one of his giant hands around his throat. He squeezed tight, Duncan's eyes filling with panic.

"This is your last warning. Anything like that once we're inside my camp and I'll escort you to hell myself."

Nash was shocked at how calmly Sullivan spoke as he loomed above Duncan. Duncan looked up, his eyes a furious red. Sullivan kept his grip long after he was done speaking.

Duncan inhaled deeply as Sullivan suddenly released his grip. He gasped for breath, the sound echoing through the trees as fresh air filled his choking lungs. Sullivan stood up, grabbed Duncan by the handcuffs, and pulled him behind like a set of rollaway luggage. Nash walked behind them and watched as Duncan pulled back and forth attempting to find some weakness in the cuffs; instead the cuffs dug deeper into his increasingly agitated wrists. He stared into Nash's eyes with a deep, seething anger, letting him know that he'd be punished at some point in the future. The punishment he would inflict on him later was the last thing on Nash's mind though. Duncan was receiving what he had deserved for months, and Nash was happy to watch.

After struggling in vain against Sullivan's strength, Duncan finally relented and allowed himself to be dragged through the dirt in silence. Duncan's wrists fell and smashed against the ground as the three of them stopped in front of a long, thickly camouflaged chain-link fence. It rose about six feet into the air and was coated in mesh and forest debris, which made it nearly impossible to see through it. A small rectangle opened up in front of them and revealed a set of eyes peering back at them.

"Welcome back, Sully!" said a cheerful female voice from the other side of the fence. Duncan rolled onto his stomach and onto his knees, quickly back on his feet as the eyes watched from behind the wall.

"*Sullivan* and two guests," said Sullivan to the woman inside, clearly annoyed by his name being shortened.

"Yeah, yeah, yeah. Come on in, Mr. Fancy."

The rectangle closed, followed by the sound of multiple locks being undone. It hadn't occurred to Nash until then, but he faintly heard the sound of people on the other side of the fence. It had been a long time since he'd been in the company of anyone other than Duncan, and the curiosity of what lay beyond the fence bubbled inside him.

A portion of the disguised fence creaked inward. The sweet voice that they'd heard did not at all match the woman standing in front of them. She was almost the same height as Sullivan, with broad features from head to toe. Her long, matted hair was tucked behind a red bandana and looked just as scraggly as Sullivan's beard. The new, dirty world had taken its toll on her, but her smiling eyes could brighten any room. She looked disapprovingly at Duncan and took note of his handcuffs. She didn't allow his manufactured smile to sway her, either.

"Are you sure this is a good idea?" she asked with a concerned glare. She folded her arms under her large bosom as she looked at him.

"Seemed like it at the time," Sullivan said as he shrugged his shoulders, slightly smiling at her. "Nash, this is Dianna. She's our gatekeeper."

"It's nice to meet you, young man." Nash's hand disappeared into her much larger one as they shook hands between the gate entrance.

"I'm gonna get Duncan here put away someplace safe," said Sullivan as he walked with Duncan in front of him.

"Hold on now, I thought this was *America*! Nash, call my lawyer!"

"I'm just going to say sorry right now for anything he does, or says," said Nash as he watched Sullivan forcefully move Duncan through the camp.

"No need to worry, sweetie; we've dealt with his type before. I assume he's your father?"

"He's my stepfather, technically speaking. He's always been awful but it's gotten much worse. I'm sure you've seen how this world changes people."

"I don't agree with you about that," said Dianna as she locked the gate behind her. "This world just amplifies what you already are; it brings out the truth in people. Don't fool yourself, kiddo. He was always like that."

"Never thought about it like that. I guess you're right," said Nash.

"I'm always right," she said as she placed her large hand on his shoulder. "Welcome to the Treefort, Nash."

A feeling of safety settled over him as he looked at the space inside the fence. People walked about the space, smiling and talking as if the world outside the fence was nothing but a distant memory. The camouflaged fence stretched far into the woods in four sections and formed a square around the people living inside. The back part of the fence was lined with two rows of RVs, each neatly placed behind the other. Nash watched as Sullivan unlocked a small pop-up trailer and forced Duncan inside, making sure it was locked again before he walked away.

"This place is amazing," said Nash.

"You're right about that, sweetie," she said. "It used to be an old camp retreat. Sullivan found it and retrofitted it into what it is today. We should get you settled in before the sun goes down."

Dianna led him through the Treefort toward the area where the RVs were parked. There was a large fire crackling in the middle of the square that sent flecks of light into the sky as people stood talking together as twilight settled upon them. They smiled and waved as Dianna and Nash walked by; Nash awkwardly returned their friendliness as they moved through the camp. Nash heard Duncan banging on the walls inside the small holding trailer as they came to a stop in front of the RVs.

"They all look brand new," said Nash as he looked up and down the line.

"You don't miss a thing, do you Nashy-Boy?" she said with a chuckle as she squeezed his shoulder. "There was a dealership nearby and Sullivan was able to bring twelve of them here. Parked them all and built the fence around them. We can get you settled in this one."

Dianna stepped forward and opened the door of the RV in front of them. She held up a battery-powered lantern as they stepped inside together. With the exception of the king-size bed at the end of the RV, everything else had been stripped away.

"I know, it looks weird with everything torn out. Sullivan did it to all of them to make room for as many people as possible. Most everyone sleeps with sleeping bags and blankets on the floor and take turns in the bed. That's what works for the majority here, but you and your stepdad can decide what works best for the two of you."

"How many people are there here?"

"I'm thinking there are roughly six out of the twelve RVs with eight people in each. With you and your stepdad, it makes about fifty people."

"If half the RVs are empty, why doesn't everyone spread out?"

"I think it makes people feel safe," she said. "I tried myself one night. I moved into an empty RV to be alone and I simply couldn't take the silence. The snoring, the smells, the shared heat of the summer nights; it was more comforting than being alone."

The two stood silent for a moment and listened to the voices of the people outside. The flickering light of the campfire filled the RV as it danced on the walls like a prehistoric television program.

"We have a food truck!" she exclaimed to break the silence. "Why don't I walk you over there?"

"That would be great; I'm starving."

He placed his bags on the floor and leaned his axe on the wall near the door. He already felt safe at the Treefort, but if he had to leave in a hurry, he wanted his axe accessible.

The two of them stepped out of the RV into the warm summer evening. Smaller fires had popped up all throughout the camp, which gave the entire Treefort a campfire glow. Laughter and chatter rose from the Fort as an unseen man played an acoustic guitar and sang lyrics Nash had never heard. He watched as a young couple sat together on two swings, holding hands as they gently swayed back and forth.

"How do you keep this place safe? I know there's a fence but it seems like any noise could easily attract someone...or something."

"It's never been much of a problem out here, and trust me, it's been tested. You'd be surprised how well the fence around this place and the trees outside nullify any noise in here." Dianna gave a hearty high five to a teenage boy who walked past them. The sound rippled across the Treefort as the boy giggled at his now tingling hand. "Sullivan, myself, and a group of six others have an RV to ourselves and take turns surveying the border nightly. There's never a time when the fence isn't being watched."

The two of them continued their walk toward the food truck through a sea of smiles and curious glances.

"The food truck closes down around 6:00 every night. It's not that we don't trust everyone to police themselves with their food intake, but it's easy to forget how important it is to keep our food supplies rationed. It gets pretty jovial in here sometimes, can't have too much merriment!"

"I didn't expect it to be an actual food truck," said Nash, smiling as they walked up to the large food service truck. It was almost as big as the RVs, but much older. The side of the truck had a large sliding window, as well as a metal shelf below the glass. The glow from the fires illuminated a cartoonish painting of a Latino man who wore a large sombrero and held a taco in each hand. Harsh, artificial light reflected off the glass as a figure moved about inside the truck.

"Let's get you some grub," she said while she knocked gently on the sliding-glass door.

"One sec!" said a younger female voice from inside, followed by the sound of ruffling papers as she moved toward the window. "Is that you Dianna?"

"Yeah, honey, it's me. I've got a newcomer here who needs some of your fine cooking." After some more rustling from inside, the window slid open as the girl leaned outside.

"Who's the new guy?" she said as she looked directly at Nash and smiled.

Her long blond hair was wrapped in a messy bun with strands that hung down over a pair of large framed glasses, the lenses missing.

Melissa.

Chapter 7

Melissa handed a bundle of food and water to Dianna, who stood amused at the dumbfounded look on Nash's face. When he had taken the picture from her bedroom, he had assumed she'd been killed. Her room had been destroyed and streaks of blood and mayhem spanned the entirety of the house. The thought had never occurred to him that she may have survived, let alone that she'd be giving him food and water out of an old taco truck.

"Nash, this is Melissa! Our food truck extraordinaire!" said Dianna, who easily picked up on the awkwardness that washed off him in waves. Melissa looked to Dianna with a confused smile as Nash continued to stare at her.

"Hey, wake up sailor!" Dianna put a large hand on Nash's shoulder to shake him. "She's not that pretty!"

"Hey!" said Melissa, who reached through the window and smacked Dianna in the shoulder with a giggle.

"Sorry," said Nash as he looked at Dianna with a bashful smile. "I'm pretty exhausted and hungry. Guess I zoned out for a moment. I'm Nash."

"I know," she said with a smile as they shook hands through the window.

"We'll let you get back to what you were doing, Mel. Just wanted to grab Nash some food before he settles in for the night."

Nash was back to staring at Melissa as she smiled back at him.

"Come on, Casanova," said Dianna. She pulled Nash by his arm and winked at Melissa as she led him away. "You two will have plenty of time to get acquainted."

The two walked back to the RV as Nash continued to make sense of his introduction to Melissa. It now made sense why Sullivan had taken issue with the picture he'd found in his backpack. He looked backward at the truck, hoping to get another glance at Melissa, as if she was a figment of his imagination. The window was still open but she had returned to the inside of the truck to continue her work.

"She's cute isn't she," said Dianna with a smile as they came to a stop at his RV.

"I feel like I need to tell you something," he said with worried eyes. "I don't want Sullivan to tell you before I have a chance to explain myself. I don't want any problems here."

"What is it, sweetie?"

"When Sullivan found us, he went through our bags before leading us here. I had a picture of Melissa in my bag." Dianna listened as he spoke, her face still jovial but showing small signs of worry. "Duncan and I had stayed in a house a few nights ago…her house. I stayed in her room and it was a complete disaster. There was blood everywhere, things were turned over and torn apart. I'd just assumed she was dead. I saw this photo of her and for whatever reason I took it with me."

They stood silent together as the worry melted away from Dianna's face.

"I don't think you have anything to worry about," she said as she pulled him in for a hug, which he hadn't expected but appreciated. "I saw the way Sully interacted with you. He trusts you already. You're going to fit in here just fine."

Dianna released him from her embrace as Nash locked his eyes on the trailer he'd seen Sullivan deposit Duncan in earlier. He was surprised at how quiet Duncan had been during his time in captivity.

"We'll keep an eye on him. It's not your job to take responsibility for him," Dianna said, noticing the worried look on

Nash's face. "This place is peaceful and happy, but it's that way for a reason. We have safeguards in place; anyone who we think poses a threat to what we have here, we watch very closely."

"It's not going to be easy with him, I can tell you that."

"I'm sure Sullivan made it clear to him what's expected when it comes to living here. I'm not worried, and you have nothing to worry about either. Regardless of his behavior, you can stay here as long as you'd like."

Nash saw the light turn off in the food truck as Melissa left and walked toward the fire. She joined an elderly couple and handed them both a snack before she sat between them.

"All that blood in her house..." said Nash as he watched her smile and talk with the couple.

"It was her mother's. Her family had survived in their home for a while, but her dad eventually got bit. Melissa and her mom barricaded themselves in her bedroom but it was just a matter of time before he found his way to them. Her mom tackled him and he tore her apart, giving Melissa enough time to escape."

"That's horrible..."

"We found her living inside the food truck at the RV dealership. Sullivan found her on the last run to bring the RVs here. She didn't come out sooner because she was scared, so she's lucky that Sullivan took an interest in Juan and his big sombrero. I don't think she would have lasted much longer on her own. She cried for days after we brought her back here."

They watched her in silence for a moment. Every time he'd seen Melissa, she'd had a smile on her face. Nash was astonished at her demeanor, given everything that had happened to her.

"When did Sullivan build this place?"

"It's been around for just over a year. I was the first person he found to bring back here. For a while it was just the two of us, the fence, and one of the army tents."

"Are you two...?"

"Well *that's* a damn good question, isn't it," said Dianna with a smile as she watched Sullivan walk along the fence. "When he first set up shop here, yeah, we were something. As we started finding more and more people to bring here, our relationship took a backseat as we focused on keeping people safe. He has a strong sense of responsibility to keep everyone here safe."

Nash watched as she followed Sullivan's continued inspection of the fence. He could tell that she had more to say but she didn't.

"Look at me; I just met you and I'm blathering on about my love life! I'm gonna let you turn in. That's my subtle way of saying I desperately need to turn in myself."

"I'm more than okay with that," said Nash as Dianna let out a booming yawn.

"Goodnight sweetie, sleep as long as you'd like. We'll do grand introductions tomorrow."

"Thank you. Goodnight to you, too," he said.

"Goodnight, *sweetie*," said Duncan from the holding trailer. His voice was muffled but Nash easily picked up on his mocking tone.

He stepped inside his RV and shut the door behind him. The inside was comfortably warm and the walls were still filled with the flickering lights of the fires outside. He thought about going back outside, saying hello and meeting some of the people around the fire, but the rumbling in his stomach was more insistent.

He opened the bundle of food and found a bag of barbeque flavored chips and quickly devoured them. The can of processed ravioli didn't last long either as he used his fingers to scoop out the contents into his mouth. He found himself thankful he was in the privacy of his RV as he licked the ravioli sauce from his messy fingers. He downed a bottle of water quickly, a trickle of water running down his chin as he gulped. Bottled water was something that he and Duncan had always had trouble finding so it always felt like a treat. He'd sipped from enough puddles, creeks, and lakes that he knew the value of a small plastic bottle of water.

He stuffed the empty can and bottle into the chip bag and placed it on the floor. The bed at the end of the RV looked inviting and he made his way to it as fast as his weary legs would allow. He stumbled slightly as he peeled of his shoes and shirt, chuckling a little as he regained his balance.

"Come on, Buddy Boy, almost there," he said to himself as he lurched toward the bed.

The fact that he had talked to himself in a manner that he was used to hearing from Duncan had not eluded him, but he was too exhausted to examine the reasons for it. He climbed into bed, let his head crash heavily against the soft pillow and fell asleep instantly.

Chapter 8

Nash stood in the empty RV with his face buried in his hands. He wept softly as tears rolled warmly down his wrists. His mind was lost in a sea of anger as he squished his toes in a large pool of blood that had formed around his feet. His chest was bare, covered with deep lacerations which he had dug himself in the midst of his madness.

The inner walls of the RV were alive with intense firelight from outside, contrasted by deep shadows that danced along the walls like a sadistic ballet. Through bloodshot eyes, he could see that the Treefort was completely ablaze with faceless shadows that ran from side to side as they tried to escape the licking flames of the wildfire. The sounds of their screams did nothing but fuel his anger as he released a nightmarish screech into the emptiness of the RV.

The door of the RV flew off and sputtered across the flaming ground as Duncan leapt inside. His chest rapidly pulsed as he filled the space with his rotten, boozy breath. He stood with his legs spread wide and wore no clothes except for a single shoe on his left foot. His stomach had been cut open and his entrails hung loosely in front of him, a trail of gore behind him. He smiled with a face full of demonic anger, his features twisted like a reflection in a funhouse mirror.

The two stood facing each other as they screamed and tore at their flesh. Nash dug his fingers deep into his skin and pulled apart muscle fibers underneath as blood continued to flow wildly from his self-inflicted wounds. Duncan put his fingers into his mouth and pulled hard at the corners. His demented smile widened as the skin split across both cheeks with a wet, tearing sound. It seemed like a competition between the two to see who mutilated themselves to the fullest.

From across the Treefort, a scream echoed loudly above all the rest like a piercing alarm. The two men looked at each other and released a collective squeal before they lunged for the door. Duncan reached it first and kicked Nash backward with a splash of blood before he bounded gracefully into the night air. Nash tripped awkwardly in his attempt to leave the RV and fell hard onto the ground with a thud. Dirt coated his open wounds as he lay on the ground, spitting saliva and blood into the dirt as he pushed himself to his feet.

Shadowy forms ran panicked throughout the Fort as Nash and Duncan searched for the source of the scream. At the other end of the burning Fort, Melissa stood trapped inside the food truck as she feverishly tried to escape. Her hands were bloody as she smashed her fists against the glass, tears running down her face.

Nash and Duncan took off in unison toward her, running at full speed, not breaking stride. Duncan's innards still hung from his abdomen, which sent splashes of thick blood onto them both. Nash tore flesh from his chest and gnashed his teeth wildly as they closed the gap between themselves and the food truck. The look of fear on her face filled Nash with a burning hunger.

Duncan pulled ahead just as they reached the truck and catapulted his body against the window. Melissa ducked as the window shattered inwards, showering the inside of the truck with pieces of jagged glass. The impact had caused monumental damage to what was left of Duncan's abdomen. Fresh blood gushed onto the truck and cascaded down to the ground like a crimson waterfall. His legs kicked wildly as he stretched his body and laced his fingers in Melissa's hair as she wailed in fear.

Nash echoed her scream as he grabbed onto Duncan's knees and pulled with all his strength. Duncan let out a gurgling, bloody whine as Nash pulled him from the window, pulling Melissa partially out with him. Duncan and Nash fell backward onto the ground and left a string of Duncan's guts still wedged underneath Melissa as she tried to force her way back into the truck. Nash pulled her out of the window and threw her to the ground in a heap and leapt on top of her before she had a chance to escape. He saw the veins in her neck pulse, but there was something else that had drawn his attention away; a small strip of red cloth, tied around his left wrist.

He leaned forward to bite her as a pair of hands wrapped around his ankles and pulled him away. Melissa shot to her feet and stumbled into the forest, leaving Nash behind in the dying Treefort. Duncan stood behind him like a ghoulish mirage, his chest and abdomen torn completely open. Nash could see Duncan's exposed heart beating wildly while the fire continued to flicker around them. Nash clawed at his eyes, blood and tears merging on his face. Duncan's outstretched hands locked onto his forearms and dragged both of them into the fire, screaming as the flames licked up their tattered bodies.

****

Nash jerked awake with enough time to brace himself for impact as his head smashed against the floor of the RV. Tears immediately filled his eyes as he returned to consciousness.

"Stay out of my bed, asshole," said Duncan, climbing into the bed.

Nash ignored him, taking slow, deliberate breaths. He listened to Duncan snore as images from his nightmare replayed in his head like a macabre slideshow. He curled up for a moment on the ground and cried quietly while Duncan's snoring continued to fill the RV. The hatred and anger that had coursed through him as he sprinted toward Melissa made his skin crawl and left him wondering if that's what it actually felt like to be one of the dead. He shook the phantom memories from his head and focused on the flames from the fires outside still flickering on the walls. He wiped tears from his eyes as new ones materialized. He couldn't understand why he had dreamed so vividly about killing Melissa. He'd barely even had a proper introduction to her, but he decided, in that moment, that he would never let anything happen to her. He would protect her as long as he was able.

After a long, vain attempt to fall asleep, he stood and stretched with his arms above his head, letting his muscles stretch and pop. He could see Sullivan through the window, standing alone at the fire. Nash knew he'd be unable to go back to sleep with the nervous energy that flowed through him, so he decided to go outside. It was better than listing to Duncan snore.

He slid his pants and shirt back on and took time to verify the gouges in his chest were just memories. The door clicked softly behind him, but loud enough in the quiet night that it made him pause to make sure Duncan didn't stir. The sound of loud, uninterrupted snoring affirmed that he was in the clear.

"He woke you up didn't he?" asked Sullivan as Nash made his way to the fire.

Nash dug his hands into his pockets and looked back at the RV. He half expected Duncan to come crashing out with his innards hanging loosely in front of him. "A little bit, yeah. I wasn't having the best night's sleep anyway."

"Most people don't start the nightmares until they are here for a while."

"How'd you know I was having a nightmare?"

"For starters, you look white as a ghost. It happens to most of us here, myself included. Something about safety in this world brings out the worst in our subconscious. When you're out there surviving, it's hell every day. My guess is that our nightmares are a reminder of what is outside the fence, and what can happen if we aren't vigilant."

The two of them stood in silence for a moment as they watched the fire crackle and burn. Nash turned his eyes from the fire and looked at the food truck. A sheet of relief fell over him to see it was not smashed and covered in blood.

"Earlier you had mentioned the red cloth around the dead woman's wrist," said Sullivan as he pulled one out of his pocket. Nash watched as he worked the fabric between his fingers.

"Before we started running from the sniper, we found a slowpoke with one tied on his wrist too. What do they mean?"

Sullivan continued working the fabric in his hand, staring into the fire as he did. "I have no idea. We've been seeing them for a while. Outside of you and I, only my security team knows about them. I'd like to keep it that way until I have a better idea of what they mean."

Nash nodded in agreement as a man approached them from the fence. He was short, with balding hair and a thick Fu Manchu mustache. He wore an old pair of blue jeans, both knees cut open, as well as a tattered AC/DC shirt that clung tightly to his large potbelly.

"We have a few spots on the north wall that need to be fixed, but everything seems mostly in order," said the man as he handed a clipboard to Sullivan and joined them at the fire.

"Thanks Stu. This is Nash; he and his…"

"Stepdad is fine," said Nash.

"Stepdad it is. He and his stepdad Duncan joined us today."

"Ah, yes!" said Stu as he reached across Sullivan and shook Nash's hand. "I saw the three of you come in earlier. He seems like he could be a handful."

"That's putting it lightly. He's all about appearances though. He'll be a regular Mr. Rogers while here."

Stu laughed loudly, his hands on his belly as it jiggled under his black shirt. "We shall see, won't we? Should be pretty quiet for you, Sullivan. I'm gonna turn in."

"Thanks Stu. Get some rest."

"Nice to meet you Nash! Looking forward to learning lots from Mr. Rogers!"

"You should have seen him when he first got here," said Sullivan as Stu disappeared into the darkness. "He's a big guy now, but six months ago, he was easily a hundred pounds heavier. He's lucky we found him when we did because the area outside was thick with dead ones, and I don't mean the slow ones. What did you call them earlier?"

"Slowpokes. I've been calling the aggressive ones howlers."

"Howlers? That seems appropriate." He stood up and slid his gun-strap over his shoulders. "I have to start my nightly rounds."

"Do you go outside the fence?" Nash stood with him.

"Not at night, unless a situation calls for it. Typically, I'll just patrol the fence, making sure it's in good order and listening for any activity in the woods. Care to join me?"

As much as he wanted to join Sullivan, the nervous energy from the nightmare had finally begun to dissipate and he was starting to feel somewhat tired.

"I should probably get some sleep."

"Tomorrow then. Find me after you're up, I'll show you around."

"Thanks, I will. Have a good night." Nash turned and walked away, his hands in his pockets as he released a wide, open-mouthed yawn.

"Don't worry about Duncan," said Sullivan from behind. "My security team does more than just patrol the border. We'll have our eyes on him, but if there's anything going on behind the scenes that we aren't seeing, please let me know."

"I will," said Nash.

He gave Sullivan a small wave as he turned and walked toward his RV. The amount of kindness he'd felt from the people of the Treefort in the short time he'd been there was overwhelming. The knowledge that he'd no longer have to rely on Duncan settled over him and he was ready to embrace what the Treefort community had to offer.

He opened the RV door and stepped in, relieved to find Duncan's face still buried in the pillow, fast asleep. He found three cushions, left over from a couch that used to be fixed to the wall of the RV, and laid them on the ground as a makeshift bed. A silent, wide-mouthed yawn escaped him as he stretched out onto the set of warm pillows. The last of the firelight danced on the wall as closed his eyes and drifted quickly into a long, dreamless sleep.

Chapter 9

The early afternoon light had begun to raise the temperature inside the RV as Nash slowly opened his eyes. He had started to sweat underneath the blanket he'd used in the night, which laid crumpled on the floor next to him. He listened to the sounds of people outside as their voices intertwined with the rhythmic melodies of the birds overhead.

His back popped while he worked out the kinks. The floor hadn't been as bad as he'd thought it would be but he was still sore. The relief of having a safe place to sleep dissolved into anxiety as he realized he was alone in the RV. The bed was empty, which meant Duncan had ventured into the Treefort alone while Nash was asleep. He hurriedly knelt beside his bag and pulled out an old watch with a crack across the face. He rubbed some dirt off the glass as he held it by the last leather strap that remained.

11:13 am.

He'd never intended to sleep so long and he quickly readied himself to do damage control for anything Duncan might have done. Looking outside, he saw many more people than he had seen last night. He slid his shoes on, excited to get outside and explore the Treefort, after he located Duncan.

"Morning, princess," said Duncan, as Nash stepped out of the RV.

The words stopped Nash in his tracks as he shut the door. Duncan sat in a sturdy plastic chair and leaned backward so it rested on the back two legs. "Don't get too comfortable. I still call the shots. When I wanna leave, we're leaving."

The anxiety of not knowing what Duncan had done while he slept gave way to the fear of being dragged back into the savage world outside the fence. "I'm not leaving."

"Excuse me?" The front two legs of the chair hit the ground. Nash walked casually toward the fire to join Sullivan and his group as he tried to hide the rush of excitement he felt from questioning Duncan's authority.

"Hey, Nash! Come back for a minute! I had something I wanted to ask you!" A cheesy smile crept onto his face. "Just for a minute, I had an idea for something."

His heart sank into his stomach as he turned toward Duncan, who stood in a relaxed position with a fatherly grin. Duncan was doing exactly what Nash thought he would, only he was doing it much better than expected. The show was on.

The people from the fire watched as the he walked toward his smiling step-father. They could see Duncan place a hand lovingly on Nash's shoulder, but none of them felt the pain as his fingers angrily dug in and stopped just short of Nash reacting to the pain. Nash looked into the smiling face of a man he didn't know. Even his eyes sparkled with a friendliness he had never encountered.

"Listen here, you little shit," said Duncan, the sour words flowed from his glowing face. "I don't want you getting close with these people. Keep your distance, because when I say it's time to go, you'd better-fucking-believe it's time to go."

Nash's eyes filled with tears as he tried in vain to keep his emotions hidden. As much anger as he felt for the man now in front of him, there was a time where all he wanted was the smiling façade that gazed at him now.

"One more thing," said Duncan as he released his shoulder and used his hand to playfully tussle Nash's hair. "I know who's here. I met that little twat this morning when I went to get my breakfast. Have your fun with her while we're here because she's not coming with us. Hell, I might even take her for a spin before we leave!"

Nash turned sharply and walked off. He wiped his eyes dry and tried his best not to show the anger that bubbled inside.

"Maybe we can do that together later! Sound like a plan, Buddy Boy?" Duncan sat back down in his chair with one leg crossed over the other, pleased with himself.

"Don't worry about it," said Sullivan as Nash joined him at the fire. He stared at Duncan through his dark sunglasses. Duncan's smile hadn't faded in the least. "He's not fooling anyone."

"Not fooling me one bit," said Stu, staring at the fire as it crackled softly. "Stick with us, kid. You'll be fine."

Dianna stood up and inserted herself next to Nash, which pushed Sullivan aside in the process. "How was your first sleep, sweetie?"

"It was good. It's a little warm in there but it's better than being out on the road."

"We need to have a briefing," interjected Sullivan. Dianna and Nash watched as he walked away toward a smaller army tent across the Treefort.

"No problem boss," called Stu as they watched Sullivan walk away.

"I'll gather the team and head to the war room," said Dianna.

"War room?" asked Nash while he watched Sullivan disappear into the army tent.

"It's just what we call the place we have our security briefings," said Dianna. "Kind of an odd name, given that there's no one around here to go to war with."

"He's worried about something," said Stu, his arms crossed over top his belly. "In all our time here, I've never seen him worried like that."

Nash pulled the red strip from the night before out of his pocket. "I assume you know about these."

"Oh I know *all* about those things. Sullivan must be starting to connect the dots."

Nash glanced at the food truck. Lunch approached and people had started to gather, waiting for Melissa to hand out their food.

"I have a pretty good feeling food is not the reason you want to go over there," said Dianna as she squeezed his shoulder and pushed him toward the truck.

He smiled as he lurched forward. He made his way toward Melissa as the people who stood at the truck walked away with their packs of food. She leaned out of the window, deep in thought as she monitored the day's food rations. Her hair was still in a messy bun, the glasses with the lenses popped out rested squarely on her nose and she poured over an old clipboard.

Apprehension washed across her face as she looked up to meet Nash's gaze, a much different greeting than she'd given him on their first meeting. Nash stopped and looked backward toward Duncan, who smiled mockingly and waved at him from his chair.

"Damn you," he said under his breath, putting his hands in his pockets as he continued toward Melissa. He readied himself to do damage control, realizing what Duncan had done that morning.

Melissa pulled herself back into the window as he came closer. "Hungry?"

"Yeah, a little," said Nash. He stood back from the truck to ease her nervousness. He had no idea what Duncan had told her and no idea how to act around her. She disappeared for a moment and came back with a handful of items. She placed some prepackaged food on the metal shelf, as well as a few pieces of fresh produce.

"You grow food here?"

"Yep, over behind the RVs," she said as she pointed toward the back of the Treefort.

Duncan sat on his chair and smiled as he watched the trouble he caused pay off.

"Whatever he told you about me…"

"He said you have been carrying a picture of me around with you." She was stern with her words, but also nervous. "He made you sound like a bit of a pervert, to be honest."

Nash felt the embarrassment rush through him and his face turned a deep shade of red. He looked down and exhaled deeply as she glanced at Duncan, her features twisting into disgust, he smiled back.

"I should have known better," she said, leaning out of the truck toward him. "He has CREEP written all over him."

"I do have a picture of you, he wasn't lying about that. I'm not a pervert though. He's the one who had a rolled up Playboy in his pocket when Sullivan found us."

She gave a soft laugh and looked back at Duncan's now hardened face. "How'd you find a picture of me?"

"A few nights back, a storm came through and we had no choice but to find somewhere to ride it out. It was your house."

"Oh?" said Melissa as a small flash of sadness fell across her face before she shook it away.

"I always check houses for supplies and that's when I found your picture. It was you on a camping trip."

"So you were in my underwear drawer then," she said with a smile. "You're not helping your 'I'm not a pervert' stance."

"I imagine I'm not," he said, chuckling a little while he fidgeted with his hands. "I'd been traveling with Duncan, and *only* Duncan, for so long. It was nice to see someone else, even if it was just a picture. It's a nice picture of you and it just reminded me of the times before everything happened."

She laughed slightly while she tossed her hair comically. "I just figured you thought I was pretty or something!"

"I do." The words were out of his mouth before he could stop himself. She stood with a red-faced smile, trying her hardest not to look away from him.

The tension released a bit when Stu came trotting up behind them. He pretended to be riding a horse like a Civil War general. He galloped beside them and trotted back and forth, acting as if he was fighting for control of the imaginary steed. "Sir, you've been summoned to the war room."

Confusion settled over Nash as he watched Stu trot back and forth in front of them. "Me?"

"That's right, big guy! Sully's orders!"

Melissa giggled as Stu continued to guide the pretend horse. Sullivan stepped out of the war room and watched them, noticeably irritated by Stu wasting time.

"No, seriously we should go," said Stu, releasing the imaginary horse as he shrank from Sullivan's gaze.

"Thanks for the food," said Nash as he grabbed the package she'd made him. She slid a chocolate bar across the shelf and smiled with a finger over her lips.

"Come by later, I'll show you around." She slid the window shut and disappeared inside. Nash stood outside for a moment and smiled back at the empty window.

"Sullivan's gonna wring my neck if I don't get you to the war room," said Stu as he stepped up beside him. "You can smile at the food truck later, Casanova!"

The front of the war room was open and the security team was inside. The hot, sticky air assaulted Nash's senses as Dianna zipped the flaps of the tent shut.

Stu took his seat with a smile and watched Nash's reaction to the stifling heat. "Should have warned you that it can get a little stuffy in here."

The members of the team flicked on battery-powered lamps, which lit a long table that spanned most of the length of the tent. Sullivan stood at the end of it, his head almost touching the top of the ceiling. The room glowed with the artificial light of the lanterns, illuminating a bag that sat on the table in front of him.

"I know it's hot in here, but it's best to keep these matters private for now."

The long table formed the shape of a T. Stu and Dianna sat on each side of Sullivan. Nash took the last empty seat near two women and two men he hadn't met. Sullivan opened the bag in front of him and dumped the contents across the tabletop. Red strips of cloth cascaded onto the wooden table, intertwined with each other like exposed intestines.

"We've all seen these. You've been collecting them for a while now and we know nothing more about where they came from than we did when we started seeing them. I think it's time we get to the bottom of it before it's too late."

"What do you mean 'before it's too late'?" asked one of the men that sat at the table in a thick southern accent. He wasn't very tall, but what he lacked in height he made up for in muscle. Everyone in the room came dressed for the day, but the man that questioned Sullivan sat shirtless, with black flame tattoos stretching down both arms. He had his boots on the table, chair tipped back slightly, tattered jeans frayed at the bottoms and a cowboy hat.

"Before being brought into the Treefort, Nash and Duncan had been traveling the interstate out past the tree line. They had encountered one of the dead ones with a strip on its wrist. Nash says it was killed by a sniper."

Silence hung over the group as sounds of laughter and camp life crept in from outside.

"Whoever fired the gun took three shots." said Nash. "He missed the first time and then hit the slowpoke… right in the head on the second shot. Duncan and I took cover until we got chased into the woods by a pack of howlers…the fast ones, I mean. The shooter killed one of them too."

"I like your terms for the dead," said one of the women sitting at the table.

"I can't help but think the sniper and the red strips are connected," said Sullivan as he collected a handful of cloth in his hand.

"What do you supposed we do?" asked the shirtless man as he placed his feet back on the ground.

"I think we need to send out a party to gather information. We've spent most of our resources on keeping the Fort safe and I'm wondering if there is another camp somewhere nearby. If we can find who fired those shots, we might be able to shed some light on the red strips."

The shirtless man stood up immediately and almost knocked the chair over behind him.

"I was already going to ask you, Cole," Sullivan sighed. "Nash, this is Cole Philips. I'd also like you to meet Eliza Barnes, who I'm also asking to join Cole and I on our expedition."

The woman who sat next to Nash reached over to shake his hand. She was slender, with thick red hair that popped out from underneath a thin beanie.

"Hi," she said in a squeaky, feminine voice. "Nice to meet you."

Nash could tell she wasn't wearing a bra, which wasn't much of a concern, as she was almost as flat chested as him. The plunging neckline of her thicker white tank top revealed the tattoos covering most of her arms and chest.

"Welcome to the Fort," Cole nodded from across the table.

"Nice to meet you. I wish I had more information for you about the shooter but we didn't see a thing."

"It's okay," said Sullivan. "We know someone's out there, that's a start. Hopefully, they're friendly. If not, we need to be prepared. I plan on having a meeting with the Fort before leaving. I'm still not going to tell them anything about the red strips, but I think people around here need to be aware that we may not be alone."

"When are we leaving," asked Eliza.

"I'm hoping to talk to everyone within the hour and leave shortly after that. While I'm gone, Dianna and Stu are in the lead. I want to have more people involved in securing the Fort and the woods around us, so Scott and Meghan, I'd like you to spearhead that effort."

Scott and Meghan sat across from each other and nodded in understanding. It was clear to Nash that they were siblings. Meghan had short black hair and abnormally large blue eyes that sparkled like distant stars in the harsh lantern light. Scott had shoulder length black hair and a short beard, with the same striking eyes as his sister. They were both short and slender, with small features from head to toe.

"Find a few people who you think would be good for security detail," Sullivan continued. Until we have more people on our team, I want the two of you out there every day, monitoring the grounds."

"Understood," said Scott, with an unusually husky voice.

Meghan put her hand on Nash's shoulder and smiled as Scott gave a small wave from across the table.

"I don't want either of you approaching any howlers, unless they pose an immediate threat to the Fort. If they have one of the red strips, just log it in your field journals. I want this to go as smoothly as possible while I'm gone."

"You've never encountered any other groups?" asked Nash.

"No, actually," said Eliza. "I've always found it strange, but we've never run into any groups larger than maybe five or six survivors."

"Nothing large scale, like us," added Cole.

Large scale, Nash thought to himself. He let the idea sink in. Fifty was large scale in today's world – fifty used to be a child's birthday party, not an entire community.

"There's another group out there, I feel it. The red strips are connected and we're going to figure out how," said Sullivan.

The implications of the task at hand hung over the group while they sat in silence and pondered the pile of red strips on the table in front of them. Sullivan walked around to the front of the war room and unzipped the door, which let fresh air and sunlight bathe the inside of the enormous tent. "Scott and Meghan, can you please gather everyone at the meeting place. I'm going to bring the Fort up to speed before we leave. Cole, Eliza; meet me at the gate as soon as the meeting is done."

Everyone left the war room together, with the exception of Nash, Dianna and Stu. Through the opening in the tent, they saw the rest of the inhabitants of the Fort, going about their business as they enjoyed their day, unaware of the possible threat that loomed in the distance. Nash understood their level of comfort, as he himself had become accustomed to it quicker than he ever thought he would.

"He's really taking this seriously. I can tell he's nervous," said Stu, watching as Sullivan walked across the Fort to prepare.

"He's nervous; has been for a while," said Dianna. "This was his world before everything happened. Conflict, strategy, war; he can smell it in the air. Something's coming."

"Was he a soldier before everything happened?" asked Nash.

"In some capacity, yes," said Stu.

"He's a mystery to all of us and I think he likes it that way," said Dianna.

The news about Sullivan's meeting spread quickly, as members of the Fort began to gather in the center of the grounds. Melissa walked past the war room and noticed that the three of them still sat inside.

"Is everything okay?" she asked nervously, standing just outside the open flaps.

"Just some things that have come up that need to be addressed," said Dianna. "Don't worry sweetie. Sullivan will go over all of it."

"I'll walk with you." Nash stood up and exited the tent with Melissa. Dianna and Stu looked at each other and smiled as they watched the two of them walk away together.

"Something's going to happen between those two; mark my words," said Dianna.

"Sooner than later, I hope," said Stu with a worried look on his face as he collected the red strips from the table and stuffed them back into the bag.

"Don't be so morbid." Dianna slapped Stu on his back as she stood. "Sully may be worried, but he can handle whatever is out there. We're lucky to have him. Let's just take it day by day. He'll get us through it."

Dianna and Stu joined the group and settled near the back next to Nash and Melissa. The four of them looked over the group as Sullivan stood on a small, elevated platform, preparing to address the crowd. Scott and Meghan joined them with a couple other people, the group now mostly gathered together. Scott nudged Nash to look toward the line of RVs as Duncan sat alone, leaning back in his chair with his feet propped up on an old propane tank, fast asleep.

Nash shook his head at Scott. "Even if he was awake he wouldn't care." Scott put his hand up in the air and gave Sullivan a thumbs up.

"Hello, everyone. Thanks for gathering. I'm sure by now; a few of you have met Nash and his step-father Duncan. They'll be staying with us for as long as they'd like." The group members near Nash patted him on the back or shook hands, while a few others in the back let out a few whistles and claps. "I found them out on the road yesterday, running from a few of the fast ones. Finding the fast ones around here isn't out of the norm, but Nash tells me there was a sniper taking shots at them."

The crowd grew silent. Duncan was awake again, sitting in his chair and listening from afar.

"Maybe the gunman thought the two of them were dead ones, we don't know, but I intend to find out. Myself, Cole, and Eliza, will be heading out shortly to gather supplies and find out anything we can about the shooter. While we're gone, just stay calm and remain vigilant."

The group gave a round of nervous applause as Sullivan exited to the side of the platform.

"I don't know what any of us would have done without him," said Melissa as she watched him disappear into his RV. The crowd slowly evaporated while they stood together, the afternoon sun beating down on them.

"Dianna told me about what happened before Sullivan found you," said Nash, taking the quiet moment after the meeting to give his condolences. "I'm sorry about your parents. It looked like you had a nice life."

She stood quiet for a moment as she fiddled with her fingers and looked down at the ground. He hadn't been sure if he should have said anything at all, or if this was the time to bring it up, but he'd wanted it said since Dianna had told him what had happened.

"Thank you," she whispered. "Can I ask what happened to your mom?"

"She died in a car accident before all this happened. Right before, actually."

"And Duncan is your stepdad, right?"

"Unfortunately; he wasn't always like this. I mean, we weren't ever close but he made my mom happy at first so I was happy. He just always had an edge to him. Nothing like what he is today, but there was always something that seemed *off*. I have no idea what my mother saw in him but that's not my question to answer, I guess."

"What about your real dad?"

"He died when I was really young, in a car accident, just like my mother."

"Nash, I'm so sorry," she said as she took his hand softly in hers. His heart raced from the feeling of her soft skin against his as she moved close to him and leaned her head on his shoulder. He felt his shirt dampen as fresh tears flowed from her eyes.

As if by some long dormant instinct, Nash took her by the shoulders and wrapped his arms around her. Her head came to rest on his chest as her tears continued to wet his shirt. Duncan watched them, his eyes narrowed. There was a threat lingering there, but Nash wasn't sure what it was.

"Don't leave," she said softly.

"Why would you think I'm leaving?" he asked, his eyes still firmly locked with Duncan's.

"I see the way he looks at this place. I can tell he's not gonna be staying long."

"What he does is his business." Duncan broke his gaze and quietly entered the RV. "I'm staying."

She pulled away from him with a soft smile as she wiped her eyes with the back of her wrist. "I'm sorry, your shirts wet now."

"It's ok," said Nash with a smile. He thought back to her house and the framed pictures that were smashed onto the floors from the carnage her parents had created. He'd never thought she was still alive, let alone that he would ever meet her.

"Let's say goodbye to our fearless leader," said Dianna as she appeared nearby. The two backed away from each other awkwardly as she chuckled. "Am I interrupting something?"

"You're always interrupting something, Dianna!" Melissa laughed. They all looked toward the front of the Fort where Sullivan, Eliza, and Cole stood with a growing group of people. "I'll go get their food ready."

Nash watched as she skipped back to the food truck, the loose bun of hair on the back of her head bounced as she moved.

"Moving a little quick there, aren't you, big guy?" said Dianna as she slung her thick arm around Nash's shoulder. He looked at her nervously, afraid that she had confirmed what he had already feared. She flung her head back and let out a loud chuckle. "Don't worry honey; she likes you. It is moving fast, but there's no time to waste nowadays!"

Nash watched as she disappeared into the food truck. "I've never actually dated a girl."

"I think she's in the same boat as you, honey. I don't know what you two were talking about, but I've never seen her open up to anyone like she did to you."

The mass of people around the front of the Fort had grown as everyone joined them, crowding around to wish them good luck. Melissa wedged her way through the group with a duffle bag filled with supplies for their trip. Sullivan took it from her and tossed it over his shoulder, winking at her with a smile as she joined the crowd.

"We'll be back as soon as possible, but we won't be longer than two days. Our plan is to load up on as many supplies as we can carry and hopefully gather more information on the shooter. Well see you all soon."

Sullivan stepped aside and let Cole and Eliza go through the gate first, handing his rifle to Cole as he passed by. He stepped toward Dianna and wrapped his arms around her as she nuzzled into his embrace. The crowd dissipated as the two stood in each other's arms. Dianna cried softly into his broad shoulder. Nash and Melissa watched from afar as Sullivan whispered into her ear and her sobs slightly subsided as he held her by her shoulders and kissed her. It was a long kiss, both of them frozen in each other's embrace as Cole and Eliza watched from the other side of the gate.

Sullivan hugged her one more time before he walked through the gate and pulled it closed behind him. She applied the locks and stood listening to their footsteps as they disappeared into the woods.

"You okay, honey?" asked Stu, joining her and placing his hand on her back. She turned around, her face red with fresh tears.

"He said he loved me. He's never said that before. I had no idea."

She buried her face in her hands and tried to stifle any sounds she made.

"Please come back Sully, please come home safe to me," she whispered into her hands as they stood together in the warm afternoon light.

Chapter 10

During the two days after Sullivan, Cole and Eliza's departure, the camp took on an almost mechanical precision as the inhabitants went about their days. They tended to their responsibilities and tried to ignore the possible threat outside the woods. The sound of camp simply became the sound of surviving.

The respect the group had for Sullivan was evidenced by their quiet reserve as everyone waited in reverence for his arrival, but as the third day came and went with no triumphant return, the silent calm began to crumble, with Duncan at its core. The morning of the fourth day, Stu and Dianna called a meeting in order to ease the growing tension in camp. The group wearily crowed around the same area that Sullivan had given his speech the day he left, the same nervousness nagging at each of them.

Stu started off as the fear flowed from the crowd toward him in waves. "We all know he's not back, but it's going to be okay. It's far too early to panic. We don't know what's happened. For all we know…"

"He said two days, Stu," interjected a man with curly, orange hair from the middle of the group. "He's not the type to say something unless he means it." The man stared intently at Stu as the crowd started to become restless in agreement.

"The ginger's right!" yelled Duncan from the back of the group. Some of them turned to look at him, giving him disapproving glances before they turned back to Stu.

"As I was saying, we don't know all the facts. He's a survivor, more so than any of us here. For all we know, they could have found more people in hiding or found a store with supplies still intact. The fact of the matter is, we just don't know."

"They could also be dead," interjected Duncan with a flat tone. This time, the entire group turned and stared with a mixture of anger and agitation. "Why are you looking at me like that? You all know it's true. Tubby, up here, is filling your head with all these possibilities of new friends and wonderful cash prizes, but the reality is the three of them could be running through the streets right now, biting and tearing at their chests."

The initial shock of Duncan's statement dulled as the harsh reality he had presented settled in. He was right, and they all knew it. There was a very real chance that they had been killed.

"He's saying it like an ass, but he isn't wrong," said Dianna as she stepped up beside Stu. "I think sometimes we forget how harsh the world is outside of these woods of ours. Let's just give it time. If he's not back by tomorrow morning, we'll send Scott and Meghan out to look for them. For now, let's keep our heads down until it's time to act."

Stu and Dianna gave a slight nod as they started to move off the platform together. Duncan began clapping loudly, smacking his hands hard from the back of the group as everyone nervously moved away from him. Dianna continued off the platform and grimaced at Duncan's unsmiling face as she moved. Stu remained in place, his gaze fixed on Duncan. Duncan stood unfazed, continuing to loudly clap his hands together in a mocking roar of applause.

"You're a real asshole Duncan. Feel free to leave anytime."

"I'll keep that in mind, you fat redneck." Stu's face reddened as he geared up to snap back at Duncan.

"Don't bother," said Nash. "It's not worth it. Trust me, he's gonna get himself kicked out for something sooner than later."

"Listen to the boy, Tubby. He's right, and trust me, when I do leave this shithole, you'll have a front row seat." His tight grin stretched into a wide, toothy smile. Seeing his lips peel away from his teeth reminded Nash of a rabid dog, and for the first time in his life, he was genuinely afraid of what he was capable of.

Duncan didn't move an inch. His twisted, angry smile stayed in place as Stu and Nash walked off toward the food truck. The clapping started back up again as they walked away, leaving Duncan alone at the meeting place.

"I'm treating his actions today as a threat. As soon as Sullivan's back, I'm going to have a long conversation about what to do about him."

"I honestly don't know what to tell you," said Nash as he nervously smiled at Melissa inside the food truck as they approached. "He's always been aggressive and hard to deal with, but this is different. It's almost like this place is making him worse."

Stu stopped in his tracks and grabbed Nash's arm. "He's your stepdad. Are you going to be okay with…"

"Do what you need to do. We survived together out of convenience, that's all. He's nothing to me now." Stu let go of his arm and nodded in understanding. "I actually wanted to ask you something."

"What's that?"

"If Sullivan isn't back tomorrow and you have to send Scott and Meghan to search for him, I want to be one of the people helping outside the fence while they're gone." Stu looked at Nash, cracking his knuckles while he pondered the idea. "I know how to handle myself out there and I want to help. Even after Sullivan gets back, I want to be part of the security team."

"Ok," said Stu while he rubbed his balding head reluctantly. "I'm not making the final call on this, you'll have to talk to Sullivan when he gets back, but for now I'm fine with it. Meghan and Scott come back around noon to get lunch. I'll let them know you're gonna tail them today to get the lay of the land."

"Thank you," said Nash as he reached out and shook Stu's hand.

"Just be safe. Listen to Meghan and Scott. They know what they're doing out there." He put his hand on Nash's shoulder and squeezed slightly. "I've got faith in you. You're here for a reason, kid."

Stu disappeared into the middle of the Fort, leaving Nash with a greater feeling of acceptance than he'd felt since he'd first arrived.

"What was that all about?" asked Melissa from the open food truck window.

"I was just asking him if I can help patrol the woods if Meghan and Scott have to go looking for Sullivan."

"Oh," she said, pausing for a moment before she turned to grab his food.

"Everything okay?" he asked as he sensed her sudden apprehensiveness.

She put his food on the ledge and locked eyes with him for a silent moment. She placed one of her slender hands on top of his. "Just please be safe." She squeezed his hand gently and sent his heart racing over the feeling of her hand on his. "I like you, you know."

"I like you too." The two chuckled at their awkwardness. The words hung uneasily between the two of them as they stood in silence, hands together while they smiled. It was as if nothing else existed in that moment. The image of her being pulled from the truck by her hair flashed across the back of his eyes and his face flinched with horror.

"What's wrong?" she asked as he shook the panic out of his eyes.

"Doesn't look like anything's wrong from my point of view!" said Dianna as she appeared near the front of the food truck and walked toward them.

"How long have you been over there?" asked Melissa who took her hands back, her face again filling with color.

"Long enough to hear the two of you blathering on about how you like each other! Don't stop on my account. Keep on!"

Stu opened the front gate as Meghan and Scott walked in together. They talked briefly while they looked over at Nash with a smile. Even from the distance, Scott and Meghan's eyes glistened like nothing Nash had ever seen.

"I should go. Thanks for the food, Mel."

"No food for you today!" quipped Melissa to Dianna as the two of them chuckled loudly behind him. He smiled as he made his way to the front of the Fort, ready to explore.

"Just going to grab some lunch, then we'll be on our way!" said Scott as they walked past him.

"They won't be long, they usually eat quickly," said Stu as Nash joined him at the gate. "Let's head over to the armory to get you strapped with a sidearm. Have you ever fired a gun before?"

"Never," said Nash, nervously. He and Duncan had always used quiet weapons like bats and knives. He knew that guns were loud and brought attention. He'd never felt at ease with guns, even before the dead had taken over.

"Nothing to worry about, it's for a worst case scenario. Nobody's ever had to discharge a weapon while on patrol."

The armory was an old Winnebago, covered with burn marks and dirt on the outside. An old man with long, stringy gray hair sat in a shredded lawn chair, half asleep as they approached. He wore a pair of tattered denim overalls that hung loosely over his aging frame. The name "Mark" was stitched onto a stained auto garage button-up shirt.

"Wake up, soldier!" yelled Stu as they came to a stop in front of him. The loudness of Stu's words shook the man from his sleep and made him almost fall out of the raggedy old lawn chair in the process.

"Good lord, Stuart!" yelled the man as he stumbled to his feet in a frenzy, proceeding to knock the chair over. He waved a homemade cane in Stu's face with a smile. "I've got half a mind to pop you one, you know that!"

"Wouldn't be the first time, old timer! Have you had a chance to meet Nash?"

"Nope, I haven't had the pleasure!" said Mark, as he extended his hand out to Nash. As they shook, a wave of sour body odor permeated the space around him. He tried his hardest not to make it known he'd noticed the smell, but his face grimaced slightly as the inside of his nostrils began to burn. Mark flung his head back and revealed a mouth void of teeth as he let out a bellowing laugh.

"It's okay, Nash," said Stu as he shielded himself from the foul odor. "Mark doesn't really worry about hygiene."

"And proud of it! Why bother? Look around boys! It's a dirty world we live in!"

Mark unlocked the padlock and opened the door, taking his seat again as Nash and Stu stepped inside. One of the walls of the Winnebago was completely covered with racks of guns and ammunition, while the opposite wall was covered with close combat weapons like axes, knives and baseball bats. Stu took a small holster from a rack at the end of the Winnebago and helped Nash secure it to his side.

"Like I said, worst case scenario." He held up a handgun and a clip of ammo. "Pick out a combat weapon to bring with you, whichever you're most comfortable with. I'll be outside when you're done to go over the gun with you."

Stu stepped out of the trailer and left Nash alone in front of the large assortment of close combat weapons. He viewed each one closely, vetting their usefulness in his head as he looked from piece to piece. He reached for a knife with a long blade, sheathed in a black leather case with a compass situated in the leather. He took it off the wall and slid the blade out, admiring the shape and shine of the clean metal. It reminded him of one he'd lost long ago as he hid with Duncan in an abandoned gas station. He'd had it since the first week of their time on the road and he'd always regretted losing it. A bead of sweat formed and ran down his forehead as he realized for the first time how incredibly hot it was inside the Winnebago. He clipped the knife to the waist of his pants and stepped outside to join Stu.

The temperature noticeably changed as he stepped outside into the open. He coughed from Mark's foul stench and moved aside as Mark closed the door behind him. Scott had joined Stu outside and smiled as Nash moved away from Mark's putrid odor. Meghan joined them with a look of disgust on her normally bright face, which made Mark laugh even louder.

"Have you ever fired a gun before?" asked Scott. Nash nervously shook his head no. He looked down at the holstered weapon with a curiosity he never thought he'd have toward a firearm.

"Here, lemme show you," said Scott as he took the gun from its holster and removed the ammunition clip. Meghan and Stu walked back to the gate together as Scott gave Nash a quick lesson.

Duncan sat near the RV in the same chair he always sat, leaning back as he watched them. Nash choked back excitement as he listened to Scott's instructions; he knew that Duncan was dying to know what was going on and that filled him with satisfaction. He holstered his gun and clutched the handle of his knife firmly as he and Scott made their way toward the gate.

"Be safe, kid," Stu said as they joined Meghan and Scott at the gate. "Just listen to them and you'll do fine."

"Nothing to worry about," said Nash as he moved through the open gate to join Meghan and Scott.

"I'm not worried," said Stu, smiling as he locked the gate behind them.

But Nash felt a twinge of guilt. He was leaving the rest of them with Duncan, Melissa included.

Chapter 11

It didn't take long for Meghan and Scott to realize that Nash knew what he was doing outside the Fort. Nash was the newest resident in the Treefort, which meant he'd spent the most time surviving on the road, and it showed in the way he carried himself. He moved silently across the leaves and broken branches that covered the forest floor as Meghan and Scott branched out in other directions to search for anything that could be considered a threat to the Fort.

Security outside the fence was very much based on the rules he already followed while out on the road. Slowpokes were to be left alone, as they posed no immediate threat. Howlers were to only be handled if they were in the direct vicinity of the fence, which from what he'd heard from everyone, didn't happen very often. Everyone on the team was given a watch upon leaving and each hour they met at the front gate in order to report anything of concern and to regroup. A few hours had gone by and he already checked in three times; the forth check-in was rapidly approaching.

With the exception of the songbirds and the soft wind that wound its way through the trees, the forest was completely silent. Anything posing a danger would be heard long before it became a threat to anyone outside the fence. He walked slowly through the woods, enjoying the scenery as he scanned the area for anything out of the ordinary. After months of hiding out in broken cities and destroyed towns, the peaceful nature of the breeze reminded him of the times before the fall of the living. Standing in the warm afternoon sun, he had almost forgotten the world that lurked just beyond the woods.

The surprisingly heavy weight of the gun secured in its holster felt as if it were pulling him toward the ground, a feeling he wasn't particularly fond of. He stopped, unclicked the holster, and slid the gun out into his hand. The air around him remained warm as the sun made its slow descent into early evening, but the metal of the gun against his palm felt unnaturally cold. Compared to the natural feeling and grip of the knife, the gun felt completely foreign to him.

He re-holstered it and snapped the leather strap into place. He shook himself and looked back toward the Fort, shocked at how far he'd wandered.

"Way to go," he whispered to himself, frustrated by his lapse in judgment. The last thing he needed was to get lost on his first day. He wanted to feel useful and the security team felt like a good fit. He turned to make his way back to the Fort when the echo of running water in the distance registered in his ears.

He walked a few yards deeper into the woods and reached the edge of a shallow, high-banked creek. It wasn't large, roughly six feet wide and six inches deep, but the banks rose five feet into the air. It wasn't the creek itself that demanded his attention, but rather the multitude of slowpokes bent over as they slowly shoveled water into their mouths.

He knelt down fast and scanned the distance around the creek, knowing that oftentimes howlers were attracted to groups of slowpokes. He listened closely for the telltale sounds of a nearby howler but only the symphony of thirsty slowpokes echoed around him.

He counted twenty-one slowpokes loitering, each with a red cloth tied around its left wrist. A male in a tattered business suit crouched next to a teenager in bloody basketball shorts, both staring into the sky without purpose. Farther down, a younger woman sat with her legs spread out in front of her in the middle of the creek, slowly running her fingers through the cool water. Her toes popped out of the creek like little towers as she gazed at them with a look of wild amusement. Crouched beside her on the shore was an older man that laboriously tried to get water into his mouth as it repeatedly ran through his fingers and down his arm. His long, bony hand reached down for more, only to end up in the same predicament.

Down the creek in the direction he wasn't looking, one of the slowpokes fell face first into the water, sending ripples in every direction. The rest of them up and down the watering line hardly paid notice as she slowly struggled to get back to her feet. Standing beside her, looking directly up at him from the edge of the water, was a slowpoke that immediately demanded every bit of his attention. It was a male, wearing tattered pants with a button up shirt, both covered in old dirt and grime. The buttons of its shirt were unbuttoned halfway, which revealed its dirt-covered chest underneath, and a well-worn denim jacket that hung loosely from its torso.

The slowpoke's eyes bored into Nash from behind a collection of thick, brown, dreadlocks. It smiled at Nash with a set of well-cared for, gleaning white teeth. Its grin widened into a deep, dumb chagrin as it stiffened its gaze on Nash.

"How's it going, rookie?' asked Scott as he joined Nash at the creek. Some of the slowpokes stopped to look at them as Nash told Scott to be quiet by placing his index finger over his lips. The look on Scott's face turned to concern as he slowly crouched down beside Nash.

"Oh my," whispered Scott, looking down at the mass of slowpokes drinking, many of them now staring at them from the creek bed. The slowpoke with the dreadlocks hadn't looked away.

"Have they always been here?" asked Nash as he tried not to make too much eye contact with the smiling slowpoke.

"We usually find a few huddled around the water but not this many." Scott continued to look up and down the creek in awe of the group. "I was down here three days ago and there was only three or four of them. They're either just following the waterline or they've been herded here."

"I assume you see what I see," asked Nash, knowing Scott would have already noticed the red strips.

"First thing I noticed," he said as he stood from his crouched position and locked eyes on the slowpoke with the dreadlocks. "He's kind of creeping me out. I've seen them smile before but seriously, his eyes are on fire!"

Nash thought back to the slowpoke on the road that had been killed by the sniper. Its happy, clueless face was something he would never forget, nor the sound of its body hitting the ground after the bullet tore through its skull.

"It's getting close to final check in," said Scott, his eyes still fixed on the raggedy slowpoke. "We should head back."

The two turned and walked back toward the Fort in silence. Meghan was already waiting for them when they reached the gate. She looked disapprovingly at her watch as they approached.

"Honestly, let me explain before you start in on us," said Scott as he held up his hands in surrender. Dianna and Stu opened the gate and joined them as Nash and Scott explained what they'd found at the creek.

"If it wasn't for the red strips, I wouldn't be worried in the least," said Dianna. She had deep, black bags under her eyes that showed the level of exhaustion she'd felt since Sullivan's departure. The smallest noise had her twitching, her hand immediately finding the handle of her knife at her hip. She was scared.

"Finding one or two every so often wearing those damn things is stressful enough, let alone a whole group of them meandering around together," said Stu, his arms folded across his chest. "It's starting to feel like some sort of message. How many were there exactly?"

"Twenty-one, by my count," said Nash. He could see across the Fort that Melissa was sitting alone waiting for him to join her.

"That's concerning. That's too many at once," said Stu as he twirled his fingers through his mustache nervously. "Assuming that tomorrow we still haven't heard from Sullivan, Meghan and I will continue the security detail around the Fort. Nash and Scott, I'd like the two of you to follow the creek in the direction that they came from. Try and see what you can find."

"Let's just keep this between us for now," said Dianna. "Get some dinner, have a relaxing night and then start back up early tomorrow." The group nodded in agreement and broke off into the Fort to recharge. Dianna grabbed Nash by the forearm as he tried to walk away. "Good find today. That amount of them all in one place, moving together, that could be a big break in figuring this out."

"Thank you," he said with a smile.

They both looked over to where Melissa sat as she tried to pretend she wasn't watching them. "She's been nervous all afternoon."

Nash's face flooded with color, and as flattered as he was to hear she worried for him, he was more concerned with Duncan.

"How was Duncan while I was gone?"

"Noticeably agitated," said Dianna with a grin. "You didn't tell him what you were doing today, did you?"

"Should I have?" he asked as he second-guessed his decision to not tell Duncan about his training. He felt no obligation to fill Duncan in on anything he did around camp, but he hadn't thought about the drama he could have created by keeping him in the dark.

"To hell with 'em," chirped Dianna as she broke into a loud chuckle. "He can leave whenever he is good and ready." She gave him one last smile before she nodded in Melissa's direction before wandering away.

He locked eyes with Melissa as she walked toward him, soaked in her smile and sent one back in return. Her face turned to concern as she looked over his left shoulder.

"Where were you today, *Buddy Boy*?" sneered Duncan as he came to a stop in front of him. Nash tried to move to the side to go around him, but Duncan grabbed him hard by the forearm and spat his putrid breath into Nash's face.

"Get off me!" yelled Nash, pushing back hard enough that it almost made Duncan lose his footing. The look of shock on Duncan's face after Nash's retort was quickly replaced by determined anger.

"You're not in charge here, *asshole*!" The words were spewing from Duncan's mouth with a quiet hatred, only loud enough for the two of them to have heard. "You don't leave these walls without me. All these people here might be making you feel like Mr. Bigshot, but you and I know you'd have been dead long ago if it weren't for my fucking generosity."

"Get away from me," said Nash sternly, using his other hand to push hard against Duncan's chest. The sadistic smile Duncan had shown Stu that morning crept on his face, his lips peeling away from his teeth as he tightened his grip on Nash's forearm.

"I've got a promise for you," he whispered into Nash's ear. "I'm gonna *fuck* that little girlfriend of yours."

The demented smile left Duncan's face the moment Nash's fist connected with his bottom jaw. Duncan's fingers peeled away from Nash's forearm as he rubbed his mouth, opening it wide as if to verify it still worked. Stu and a few men from the group came sprinting over to defuse the situation, as Duncan pulled Nash close by his shirt collar.

"*Right in front of you, dickhead. Front. Row. Seat.*"

Duncan released him and stormed off toward the RV as Stu and another man followed after him. Melissa was at his side in a flash and knelt beside him as she threw her arms around him.

"It's fine," said Nash, watching as Stu stopped Duncan before he could get into the RV. They exchanged some choice words before Duncan stepped into the RV, leveling more insults about Stu's weight and hairline before he slammed the door shut behind him.

"He's awful," she whispered to him, her voice full of nervous tension as they watched.

"I know. Stay away from him, okay? If he even so much as talks to you, let me know right away." Duncan's threat rang in his ears as he held her in his arms.

"If Sullivan isn't back soon, we're gonna have to make a decision on what to do with him," said Stu as he furiously marched up to them. Melissa released Nash from her embrace as he approached.

"What have you done in the past with people like him?" asked Nash.

"That's the thing, we've never had anyone like him here. If Sullivan isn't back tomorrow, I think the safest thing is to exile him before he causes any real damage."

"Fine by me. I want to be part of it though," said Nash as he looked at Stu with determination. If they were to be rid of Duncan, he wanted to be there to see it through. He *needed* to see it through.

"Of course," said Stu. "Melissa, take the night off. We can handle feeding the masses tonight."

"Thank you!" she said as he walked toward the food truck. "Looks like my night's free! Got any plans?"

"Well, I'm definitely moving into one of the other RVs, but other than that, I think I'm wide open." They put their arms around each other's waists and walked to the middle of the Fort to the main fire.

The temperature dropped as sunset came quickly, which basked the Fort in the familiar firelight glow.

"So how was your first day out in the woods?" Melissa asked as she leaned into Nash.

"It was good, actually. It feels like a good fit for me."

"You were safe, I assume?" She looked up at him with false, comedic concern.

"I made it back in one piece, didn't I?"

"Don't be a jerk!" Melissa chuckled. "I haven't seen anyone even close to our age since I got here. I like having you around."

"What? You don't like all the old-timers?"

"Who you calling *old-timer*, sonny?" said Dianna from across the fire.

"Well you're no spring chicken, Dianna," Stu said, putting his hands up expecting her to land a punch on him...which she did with a smile.

They all chuckled together as Nash reached into his pocket and pulled out the picture he'd taken from Melissa's room and handed it to her. "Never did I imagine I'd end up sitting here with you."

She held the picture as they both looked at it in the pale light of the roaring fire. Tears welled in her eyes.

"It was so much easier then. I miss them terribly." Nash raised his arm and placed it around her, his hand resting on the top of her right shoulder. Before long, she was asleep and breathed nervously onto his chest as she made her way through some mysterious dream.

Dianna and Stu stood up together as Dianna expelled a booming yawn. She stretched her arms high above her head as her back popped loudly. "I'm so glad Sullivan found you, but you should get her to bed."

Stu and Dianna walked off together and disappeared into the night. Nash spoke softly to Melissa and gently squeezed her shoulder. She opened her eyes slowly and smiled up at him, the glow of the fire beautifully illuminated her eyes. He wanted nothing more than to kiss her in that moment, but thought better of it. He knew things were moving quickly and he didn't want to scare her off. "We should get you to your bed."

She nodded in agreement and removed herself from his shoulder as he helped her to her feet. She slipped her hand into his, interlocking their fingers. They walked with her head still rested on his shoulder, moving carefully through the darkened Treefort. He could see movement inside his RV and realized he wasn't prepared to deal with Duncan's wrath. After the altercation earlier that day, he knew his move to one of the empty RVs would not be an easy thing for Duncan to accept.

They reached Melissa's RV, the sounds of snoring flowed freely from inside. She looked at him with a sour face and knew that because she had stayed up later than everyone, she'd now have to tip toe through the sleeping campers to get to her spot. He smiled and wrapped his arms around her and pulled her in for a hug before they parted for the night.

"Goodnight," she whispered to him.

She kissed him softly on his cheek before pulling away. The small, sweet kiss sent his mind into a tailspin and made him instantly regret not kissing her first at the fire. Everything about that moment had been perfect. So perfect, he didn't want to chance ruining it.

"Goodnight," he said and closed the RV door behind her. The rest of the Treefort was mostly deserted as the fires began to die down on their own. Most nights, there were a least a few people that remained around the fire and stayed up late talking and sharing stories. With Sullivan still away, there really wasn't anyone who was interested in socializing.

He walked to his RV and stood outside, looking at the closed door. He knew Duncan's time at the Fort was limited, so he took a deep breath and opened the door. The second he stepped inside, a heavy object slammed against him and knocked him onto the floor. He hit the ground hard, hardly having any time to brace his fall. The object that had slammed into him was his backpack, repacked by Duncan while he'd been sitting at the fire with Melissa.

"We're leaving tonight," said Duncan, who stood above him with all his belongings secured on his back and side. "Keep your damn mouth shut and get up. I hope you had your fun with that little bitch you've been hanging around with."

Nash scooped up his backpack and scrambled to his feet. "Leave if you want; I'm not going anywhere."

"Oh, *you're going*, make no mistake about it. You've got no say in the matter. I told you when we got here that *I* say when we leave, not you. You've got ten minutes. Go bang one out with blondie before I do it myself."

Nash stood in disbelief of the man in front of him. The cruelty and hatred that radiated from him was overwhelming. He said the only thing he could think of in the moment. "My mother would be so disappointed in what you've become."

The words left his mouth and seemed to grow and fill the entire expanse of the RV. Duncan stared back at Nash, stern-faced and stoic as he pondered the abrasive truth of the statement. He moved forward slowly as his muddy boots clopped loudly on the floor. He stopped in front of him and stared intently into his face.

"You're right," said Duncan, just before he plunged his fist deep into Nash's stomach, forcing the air out of his lungs as Nash fell to the ground.

"Your mother was an idiot!" He reached down and pulled Nash up by his shirt with both hands. Nash gasped for breath and used his hands to grab onto each of Duncan's wrists. "*And a whore!*"

Duncan tossed Nash against the door of the RV, which sent it crashing backward as Nash tumbled hard onto the ground. His backpack came flying out of the open door and landed next to him as he lay on his side and tried in vain to regain his breath. Duncan jumped from the RV door and slammed his feet directly in front of Nash's head, spraying dry dust and dirt into his face.

"Come along now, little faggot. We've got places to be!"

Duncan picked up Nash by the foot and pulled him behind. The noise had attracted attention from people in the camp as lanterns illuminated the RVs. The door to Melissa's RV flung open in a fury as she leaped outside.

"Stu! Dianna! Someone help, *please!*" she yelled as she made her way to Nash.

"*No!*" yelled Nash as he lifted his hand toward her to tell her to stop. She stopped where she was, holding a battery-powered lantern that revealed a look of horror on her face as Duncan pulled Nash behind him. As he finally regained his breath, Nash spun around onto his back and used his other leg and tried to kick Duncan's knee, but missed and connected with his calf. Duncan screamed in fury and released his foot, which gave Nash time to back away on the ground a few feet.

"Where do you think you're going, *cocksucker*?" bellowed Duncan as he grabbed onto Nash's foot with more strength than before. Nash was almost completely depleted of energy, but with one final triumph of will, he slammed his free foot against Duncan's mouth, splitting his lip and sending bloody saliva into the dirt.

Duncan fell backward and laid on the ground a moment before he lifted himself back up to his feet. A long string of blood, saliva, and dirt hung from his busted mouth as he smiled the demented smile Nash hated. He could see through the blood and mangled lips that all of his teeth were somehow still intact and glowed back at him in the night. Nash readied himself to take another blow as Stu sprang forward and tackled Duncan to the ground.

Melissa was there in a flash, helping Nash get away from them as Duncan and Stu wrestled for control on the ground. Dianna came running but flew past all of them toward the front of the Fort, which left Nash and Melissa with a second of confusion before they refocused on the fight in front of them. Duncan quickly gained the upper hand and was on top of Stu with his knees planted in the dirt.

"*DING, DING, DING*!" yelled Duncan as he pinned Stu to the ground and began pummeling him with both hands. A few people from the group ran forward to help, but were swiftly pushed aside by Duncan. It was if he was expelling the strength of ten men as people were flung away while he continued his assault. Stu's face was bloodied in no time as Duncan continued to land blow after blow, letting blood and saliva flow freely from his busted lips. Duncan let his bloodied fists rest and leaned forward in front of Stu's face. "I told you, *fatso*; the day I leave, you'd have the best seat in the house."

He raised his fist for one last vicious blow when a pair of strong, tattooed arms wrapped under his armpits. He tried his best to turn and see his captor but was unable to. Pain erupted inside his head as a gigantic hand grabbed a tuft of his hair and pulled him up slightly. He let out a piercing yelp when Sullivan's massive fist connected with the side of his head with the force of a sledgehammer.

Chapter 12

Cole released Duncan from his grip and slammed him face first into the dirt. The realization that Sullivan had returned spread quickly through the camp as he stood over Duncan's motionless body. Dianna swallowed the excitement of his return as she tended to Stu, his face a bloody mess from the attack.

"I'm so sorry Stu," said Nash as he crouched down beside him. "I should have just left with him. I'm so sorry."

"You didn't do anything wrong, kid," said Stu as he pushed himself up on his elbows. Melissa flicked on a battery-powered lantern to reveal that while Duncan had landed a significant amount of blows, he hadn't done as much damage as they'd originally feared.

"There isn't a person in here that would have let him take you away," said Dianna while she helped Stu to his feet. Stu's bottom lip had been split open, sending thick blood down his chin and onto his shirt. Dianna and Stu slowly walked together, heading toward the trailer they used as their medical area.

"Well let's get the fire going again!" someone yelled. The crowd clapped in agreement, excited by Sullivan's return.

"I appreciate it, but not tonight," said Sullivan. He turned to the crowd. What was left of the firelight illuminated the dark circles underneath his eyes. Eliza and Cole had already moved off into the dark, heading to their beds for the night. "I don't want to leave you all wondering so I'll just tell you right now that we didn't find anything about the shooter. There's nothing out there. It's quiet." The crowd stood silent in the dying firelight, not knowing what to think. "The good news is, we did make it back with a lot of supplies, so I need some volunteers to help bring it all into camp."

People moved forward to help, and Sullivan directed them to the outside of the fence. The five volunteers walked together with a lantern as Sullivan picked up Duncan and slung him over his shoulder in one swift motion. He reached across his broad chest and patted Duncan on the butt as his legs dangled in front of him. "It's good to be home." The crowd chuckled as he made his way through them and motioned to Nash with his free hand to follow behind him.

They made their way through the quickly dispersing crowd, Nash following behind while watching Duncan's head bob up and down. Nash felt an overwhelming guilt over what Duncan had done to Stu and followed quietly behind Sullivan as they walked, not knowing what to say. They came to a stop at the trailer Duncan had been kept in their first day. He opened the door and tossed Duncan in without caution, letting his body crash limply to the floor. Sullivan closed the door and secured the lock.

"He's being exiled tomorrow," said Sullivan as he double-checked that the lock was secure before he turned to address Nash fully. The prospect of no longer having to live with Duncan merged into reality with those four simple words. Nash stood quietly before the hulking leader of the Treefort before a dark fear pulsed through him.

"I can still stay, right?" he whispered softly. He couldn't believe that the words had left his mouth, but the fear of leaving the Treefort and being shackled to an even more vicious version of Duncan had taken hold of him.

"I wouldn't have it any other way. I assume you want to be there when he's taken out to exile?"

"Yes," he said. It was a simple but powerful response. He needed to be sure he was rid of Duncan for good.

"We'll go as soon as you're up tomorrow," said Sullivan as he re-checked the lock a third time. "I don't know what happened to start all this, but it's not your fault. This was going to happen eventually and I'm glad it happened sooner than later."

Without saying another word he disappeared into the darkness to find the rest he visibly needed. The trailer where Dianna had brought Stu was illuminated by harsh lantern light as three silhouettes moved about inside. He made his way through the empty Fort to join them. The door swung open on his approach as Melissa stepped out with a worried look on her face.

"Everything okay? I saw you leave with Sullivan before I came in here." She frantically inspected his face to see if Duncan had done any damage to him during the fight.

"I'm fine," he said, smiling as she scanned his body for injuries. "He wanted to let me know that we're exiling Duncan tomorrow."

"Good," said Dianna from inside, her voice muffled by the trailer. "That prick should be put down like the animal he is."

"How bad is it?" asked Nash as he stepped into the trailer. Dianna had put stitches into Stu's bottom lip, as well as both cheeks and chin. Bandages covered his cheeks and Dianna was gingerly applying the last bandage to his chin. In the pale lantern light, Nash could see that his left eye was almost completely swollen shut.

"I've been better," said Stu in his usual comical tone with a noticeable twinge of pain. Just hearing him speak sent waves or relief through Nash. "You'll have to take my place tomorrow during the exile. I have a feeling I won't be up to it." He shook a bottle of painkillers in the air.

"Ok, settle down there, pill-popper. Let's get you to bed." Dianna closed her first aid kit and helped him to his feet. "You can use one of the empty RVs until you're all healed up."

Nash opened the door and helped Dianna and Stu out, Melissa following close behind. Dianna started to make her way toward the line of RVs as Stu leaned on her, but stopped and turned back toward Nash. "How is he?"

"He's tired. Look over there and you'll see why." Nash pointed toward the front of the Fort. Situated on the ground were ten duffle bags, each almost bursting with supplies.

"Holy cow," she whispered. "Just get those things into an empty RV for the night boys! We'll go through it tomorrow morning," she yelled to the volunteers.

"Yes ma'am," said a gruff, southern sounding voice from the front of the Fort.

"Goodnight you two," Dianna said as she continued into the darkness with Stu.

The fire still glowed lightly as they stood holding hands. Most everyone had retired back to their sleeping quarters, ready to sleep easy knowing that Sullivan's group was back safe.

"You sure you're okay?" she asked, putting her arms around him as she nuzzled into his neck. "It looked awful. I thought he was going to kill you."

"I'll be sore tomorrow, but I'm okay." He stood holding her as the exhaustion of the evening took over.

The two of them walked hand in hand to toward the RVs, barely able to keep their eyes open as they moved. He started to turn toward her RV to escort her like he had before, but she nudged him toward his own RV.

"It's okay, you don't have to. Just get some rest." She walked away, holding hands a little while longer so that her arm was outstretched before softly letting go. He stood watching her as she disappeared in the moonlight.

The door of his RV still remained open from when Duncan had thrown him through it. He closed it, having to now pull up slightly for it to latch, as one of the hinges had come loose. An eerie calm filled the empty RV as he released a silent yawn, ready to crawl into his bed. He knew that in time, there would be other survivors brought into camp and the RV would have to be shared, but he fully intended on enjoying his alone time while it lasted.

Duncan's belongings were packed in bags on the floor from when he'd chased Nash from the RV. Nash collected them all, opened the door, and flung them into the darkness outside. With the door open, he could see Sullivan and Dianna at the holding trailer, struggling to stich Duncan's lip the best they could. It sounded to Nash that Duncan was still out of it, trying to curse at them as they worked but his words came out as incomprehensible gibberish.

Nash realized how surreal it was that the RV was now his alone. Duncan no longer had any claim to anything that belonged to him. He shut the door for the night with the knowledge that his life would be completely different tomorrow. He'd never contemplated life without Duncan and now that it was becoming a reality, he couldn't be happier. He undressed and crawled into bed as flashes of his nightmare appeared in his head. He rubbed his eyes, shaking the images out of his head the best he could as he tried to fall asleep.

His mind was racing as he continued to try and force himself to sleep. The ceiling of the RV began to look as if it were moving as he stared at it. As he gazed up at the speckled design, the image of his mother appeared, which was something that hadn't happened in sometime.

As much as he missed her, he was happy that she had passed before everything had happened to the world. He was even happier that she had never been around to see the monster that Duncan had become. Duncan was a mean-spirited, spiteful man, but he'd always retained some form of a sense of humor during their travels. It wasn't until they entered the Fort that he had descended into the madness that now seemed to have overcome any goodness that had remained inside him. Remembering his mother's smiling face, Nash finally drifted to sleep.

****

He was back in Melissa's room, the dreadlocked slowpoke staring up at him from the yard outside. The slowpoke wildly pointed with both hands at the house, his wicked smile gleaming in the darkness.

A hungry shriek pierced the air, and Nash clapped his hands over his ears. Dozens of decomposing howlers flooded past the dreadlock-slowpoke and swarmed the house; their impact was enough to rattle the walls. Nash fled to the stairwell, and was greeted by the swarm. Clawing at one another, the howlers pushed forward towards their intended victim. Terrified, Nash rushed back to Melissa's room and barricaded himself inside. He wrapped his hands around his stomach trying to calm his frantic breathing. He slowly backed toward the window, his eyes firmly set on the door – the hinges screaming against the weight of the howlers.

Strong, knife-like fingers dug into his shoulders and slammed him against the wall. It was Duncan, but not Duncan — his features twisted with rage, his eyes sunken back in his skull. He shoved Nash out the window, letting him dangle above the masses.

"You'll never be done with me, Buddy Boy," Duncan hissed, his bottom jaw unhinging and flapping against his chest. Nash clung to Duncan's hands, fear clogging rational thought as he looked below him.

Staring up at him were familiar faces — the residents of the TreeFort looked up at him with hungry rage. Stu stood below him, tearing at his throat, blood gushing down his chest. Scott leered over Meghan's limp body, covered in her entrails. Dianna kneeled in the grass, Sullivan behind her; ripping out her hair in sticky clumps. But the most horrific, was Melissa.

She wasn't one of the dead. Instead, she was being tossed around, the dead ripping pieces of flesh from her body as she screamed. Duncan's broken mouth pressed against his ear.

"Never," he hissed, the words slurred. And then Duncan let go, and Nash plummeted toward eager hands.

****

Far off in the distance of his thoughts, the sound of the RV door being unlatched echoed in his mind, followed by the soft sound of someone creeping inside. The footsteps of an unknown intruder pattered across the floor and moved silently toward him to thrust him into the throws of another nightmarish reality. In a moment of vibrant realization, his eyes opened to the silhouette of someone standing at the foot of his bed. Sleep induced terror grasped his mind: Duncan. He raised himself up onto his elbows, ready to fight, when a familiar voice eased his mind.

"It's me," whispered Melissa. "You sounded like you were having a nightmare." He rubbed his eyes and squinted in the darkness, confirming that it indeed was her

"Is everything okay?" he asked as he sat up more. "What's wrong?"

She crawled into his bed in silence, pulled the blankets down beside him, and slid inside next to him. With his senses still on high alert from the nightmare, he assumed Duncan had escaped and she had come to hide from him, but that thought washed away as her lips met his.

They rolled onto their sides, facing each other as they continued to kiss in the darkness. They kissed long into the night, holding each other close under the blanket until they fell asleep in each other's arms. It was a long, dreamless sleep for both of them.

The best night sleep Nash had experienced in months ended to the sound of yelling outside. The bed beside him was empty. The bright morning sun had already begun to heat the inside of the RV, and sweat beaded on his skin. He flung the blanket off and scooted to the end of the bed. From outside one of the windows he could see Duncan pointlessly trying to struggle against Sullivan's might as he kicked and yelled incoherently. Nash smiled, knowing the day had come. Duncan would be out of his life for good.

He thought back to the night before, the feeling of Melissa lying next to him as he ran his fingers through her hair. The smile on his face widened until the thought that he'd imagined the entire evening crept its way into his head. A wave of disappointment settled over him until he noticed a small bundle of food on the corner of his bed.

Wrapped together with a bow was a small box of cereal, a pack of Pop Tarts, a chocolate granola bar, and a large bottle of water. There was some assorted fruit as well, all swathed together with a heart drawn on the silver package of the Pop Tarts. His hunger eclipsed the sentiment of the gift as he opened the package of Pop Tarts and devoured them quickly, followed by the fruit and granola bar. He placed the cereal aside, deciding to eat it later before he took a few sips from the bottle of water, leaving the rest for throughout the day.

He took the empty package of Pop Tarts and placed it in one of the zipper compartments of his backpack. The small heart drawn on the side was her first gift to him and he wasn't about to toss it aside. He dressed quickly and stepped out into the bright morning light. From across the Fort, he could see Melissa at the food truck as she dispensed food packages to a long line of people. They shared a quick smile before he was brought quickly back into Duncan's lunacy.

"You hear the news, *Buddy Boy*? I'm shipping out!" Sullivan applied a pair of handcuffs as Duncan wiggled to make it as difficult as possible. "Things are getting kinky over here, pal!

Why don't you go get that little girly of yours and meet me in the RV!"

"You shut your damn mouth before I pull those stitches from your lip," Sullivan said calmly, pulling upwards on the handcuffs, which sent blasts of pain into Duncan's arms.

Duncan's face was puffy from his scuffle with Sullivan and his shirt was covered in blood. He'd woken up before everyone and torn all his clothes to bits, yelling like a madman and mocking Sullivan and Stu throughout the night.

Dianna joined Nash as Sullivan moved Duncan toward the front gate, gripping his forearm tightly as they walked.

"It's a fresh start for you today, sweetie," she said, standing next to him. She exhaled deeply, a sound full of stress and relief. "This is a first for us."

"I'm so sorry for everything he's done," said Nash, watching as Duncan said something to a passerby. Sullivan shoved him forward, almost tripping him in response.

"Enough of that honey. He's not your responsibility. We all knew it from the start. He's his own kind of monster, and he's not our problem after today."

The two of them walked to the front of the Treefort where Sullivan was waiting for them. Eliza had joined him and held a large duffel bag as well as Sullivan's enormous rifle, which hung loosely around her back. He considered going to say a quick goodbye to Melissa, but with the line for food having stayed the same since he last looked, the two of them exchanged a bashful smile as he moved toward his soon to be exiled stepfather.

"Oh *he's* coming?" exclaimed Duncan loudly at Nash's approach. "What about Tubby? How's his face feeling after last night?"

Duncan fell to the ground in a fit of laughter as Sullivan pushed hard against his back. He laid on the ground and squealed like a pig, blood starting to seep from the stiches on his lip as he rolled on the ground.

"Just get him out of here," said Dianna as Sullivan pulled Duncan up from the ground by his handcuffs. Duncan erupted into a loud screech of pain as he was yanked upwards.

Duncan fixed his eyes on Eliza with a smile. "You coming with me, sweetheart? I bet we could have all kinds of fun out in the wild." Sullivan wrapped a blindfold hard across his eyes as another screech of discomfort roared out of Duncan's mangled mouth.

"Let's go," said Sullivan, letting Eliza and Nash lead the way as he trailed behind.

Eliza wound them through the woods on a predetermined path, each of them with a bag of Duncan's belongings on their backs. Eliza purposefully moved through the woods in directions they never intended to follow, simply to disorient Duncan. They reached a small bridge at the creek that rose only a few feet above the water. It was far away from where Nash had encountered the slowpokes the day before, but it reminded him that he still needed to talk to Sullivan about what he'd found. Their boots echoed loudly on the wooden bridge.

"Close your legs, sweetie," said Duncan from behind as the smell of the shallow, murky water below hit their nostrils. "Or don't, actually. I think I like it."

Sullivan pushed Duncan hard off the bridge and sent him splashing into the dark water below. He went in face first and quickly rolled himself over, gasping into the air as fresh lacerations appeared on his face from the shallow creek. Sullivan jumped off the bridge, his boots landing in the water on each side of Duncan's torso. He knelt down over him, their eyes inches apart as the two of them angrily glared at each other. The sounds of birds chirping and the steady flow of creek water filled the air as he stood over Duncan in the water and waited for him to make a move.

"This is your final warning. Anything else from you and I will gag your mouth with dirt until we're ready to be done with you for good."

He pulled Duncan from the water and back onto the bridge before motioning to Eliza to continue farther into the woods. Nash had expected Duncan to press his luck for the remainder of the walk, but he was pleasantly surprised when he stayed quiet for the rest of the trip.

The temperature rose quickly as they left the shade of the tree canopy. A black SUV sat dormant along a winding dirt road that stretched endlessly in both directions. Eliza opened the hatch and each of them threw Duncan's belongings in without a care, letting them fall on top of themselves like dirty laundry. Sullivan placed a bag of provisions in the back to leave with Duncan at the exile point. Dianna had spent a good portion of the morning trying to convince him not to pack the bag, but in the end Sullivan had insisted this was an exile and not a death sentence.

Eliza and Nash got into the middle row, shut the doors, and sat behind the dark tinted windows. The SUV looked and smelled brand new, with black leather seats that matched the exterior paint. The inside of the vehicle felt like a hot box as they waited for Sullivan and Duncan to join them inside. Sullivan opened the passenger side door and gruffly pushed Duncan inside, attaching his seatbelt across his chest.

"Safety first," said Duncan without a smile, looking straight forward with the blindfold still tightly wrapped around his eyes.

Sullivan sat in the driver's seat and turned the ignition. The dirt road erupted like a dusty tornado as they peeled away. Other than the occasional broken down car, the road remained mostly unobstructed. Sullivan turned on the air-conditioner, a luxury that Nash had all but forgotten about.

"I could get used to this," said Eliza quietly as she smiled with her eyes closed and her head back against the seat.

"You can say that again," said Duncan who still looked forward with his blindfold on. Sullivan reached over and closed his vents, which sent a wide smile onto Eliza's face.

They exited the forest and continued on the dirt road, driving alongside the dead interstate, cluttered with slowpokes and the occasional frantic howler. Sullivan took many twists and turns, taking the time to drive into fields just to end up back on the same road, headed in the same direction. The goal was to have Duncan completely disoriented before they dropped him off, making it nearly impossible for him to find his way back to the Treefort.

They'd been driving for close to an hour when they entered a deserted town named Hillsborough. It was remarkably small, small enough that it reminded Nash of a movie-set. A handful of homes, a post office, and a convenience store were all that remained of the once populated town. A lot of the buildings had been burned to the ground, leaving only charred skeletons and scorched rubble in their place. As Sullivan slowed the car to a stop, a howler came screaming out of the broken glass of the post office door toward their vehicle. It snapped its teeth frantically as it moved, its arms out stretched toward them with its fingers clenching open and shut. Sullivan rolled down his window and planted the blade of his knife in the howler's skull as it reached his door. It fell silently backward from his knife with a sickly liquid sound when the knife slid out of its forehead.

"Ohh, I know that sound!" cooed Duncan from the passenger seat as he clapped his shackled hands together.

Keeping the engine running, Sullivan blasted the horn three times. "We'll sit here for a moment, wait to see if we have any other local howlers," he said.

A few slowpokes stepped out from the shadows, and stood aimlessly in the street. Sullivan rolled up with windows and nodded to them. "Clear."

Sullivan cut the engine and they filed out of the SUV.

"Weapons ready while we're on the move," said Sullivan as he opened the hatch of the SUV and grabbed the bag he'd packed for Duncan. Each of them collected one of Duncan's bags before Sullivan closed the door again. He set off down the street, passing a few burned buildings before he stopped in front of a yellow ranch. The small house was set back a bit from the main road, tucked back against a few untamed hedges.

"Is this our new home? *Can I pick my room*?" said Duncan. "I hope there are other kids my age in the neighborhood!"

"Stay here," said Sullivan and left Eliza and Nash with Duncan as he disappeared inside. Nash looked up and down the street, more slowpokes were funneling into the road from the abandoned buildings. Nash felt a pang of sadness for them because he knew what Duncan would do to them once left alone. But Duncan couldn't stay at the Treefort.

"You're making the mistake of a lifetime, Buddy Boy," said Duncan as he looked straight ahead into the street while he addressed Nash. "These people, that place…it's a shit show. You'll see, and once you do, it'll be too late."

"Shut up," said Eliza.

"I'm talking to you too, *whore*," he said as he turned his head toward Eliza's voice. "You all feel safe right now, but give it time. You'll be standing on the roadside with a dumbass smile on your face, or maybe you'll be chasing your friends around trying to take a bite out of them."

"Quiet," said Sullivan as he came to the open door and pulled Duncan backward into the empty house.

Nash and Eliza followed them into the hollowed shell of the home. Sullivan was already pushing Duncan up a flight of stairs as they followed behind, keeping their ears trained for any danger around them. Sullivan had closed all the doors in the hallway at the top of the stairs with the exception of one, which hung open to reveal a tidy bedroom. He led Duncan into the open room and motioned for them to place Duncan's belongings down beside the bed.

"Here's how this works, Duncan," said Sullivan while he had Duncan face away at the foot of the bed. "We're gonna leave you here, and you'll be on your own. Your bags are all here, as well as a survival bag we've packed for you. If you find your way back to the Treefort, you will be killed on the spot. Do you understand?"

"Trust me, *when* I make my way back to your campsite, it'll be you with your throat torn open, not mine." His voice seemed to echo from the pit of his stomach, not quite a growl. Chills shivered down Nash and Eliza's spines as his threat sank in. He turned his head and somehow found Nash's eyes through his thick blindfold. "And for you, *Buddy Boy*, my promise still stands. I'm gonna *fuck* that little girlfriend of yours!"

The butt of Sullivan's gun connected with the back of Duncan's skull, knocking him unconscious as he fell forward onto the dusty bed. Sullivan positioned him fully onto the bed and positioned his head to make sure his airway was not obstructed. The image of Duncan's final, blindfolded threat burned in Nash's mind, echoing back and forth as he tried to force it from his mind.

"It's part of the exile plan to knock the person out, that way they don't know which way we came from and can't track us easily. I should've done it sooner to avoid all that. I'm sorry," said Sullivan.

"Let's just get out of here," said Nash as he looked at Duncan's limp body on the bed.

Nash and Eliza left first as Sullivan followed behind after doing another quick check to make sure Duncan was breathing. He contemplated leaving the door hanging open, which would allow a howler to come along and rip his body apart while he slept. Instead, he closed the door and set the lock.

Chapter 13

Nash spent the time on the drive back to the Treefort telling Sullivan about the slowpokes he'd found by the creek, specifically how they had all worn the red strips. Sullivan remained quiet, as usual, but listened intently as he absorbed the information.

"Show me when we get back to the woods," he said. "We haven't had much time to talk since you got to camp. Are you settling in okay?"

"Everything is great, especially now that Duncan's gone. Everyone around camp has been so welcoming."

"Are you okay though, after dumping him off like that?" asked Eliza from the backseat. He hadn't thought much about how he felt about the situation, but the overwhelming feeling he had was relief.

"Yeah. We only traveled together because it was safer. He's not safe to be around any longer."

They drove for a few moments of silence. The countryside was rich and overgrown, covered in a sea of green and gold that scrolled past them in a flash as they watched from behind the tinted glass.

"Melissa slept in his RV last night," Eliza blurted with a mischievous smile. Nash smiled in return as he continued looking out his window.

"Not surprised," said Sullivan as he sat firmly behind the wheel with a smirk. "Treat her good, kid, or you'll be exiled next."

"Stop!" cried Eliza from the backseat, her voice like a siren. Sullivan slammed on the brakes, making them all lurch forward as the SUV screeched to a halt.

"*What's wrong?*" yelled Nash as he scanned the area around them before he saw the reason for her alarm. Far in the distance, down a large over grown hill, was a man who ran toward them with his arms flailing wildly. The three of them sat in the middle of the road as the SUV idled and watched the man sprint toward them in a frenzy.

"He's alive, right?" asked Nash, watching the man as he approached them.

"Stay inside," said Sullivan. He stepped out of the SUV, leaving the door open behind him. Nash watched the man as Sullivan retrieved his gun from the back of the SUV before he walked to the edge of the field. The man slowed and came to a stop at the sight of Sullivan and his rifle.

"Please," said the stranger, panting with exhaustion as he crashed to his knees in front them.

Sullivan stood firm with the gun held in front of him, sizing up the man as he stared frantically back at him.

"I just need help, *please!*" he said while tears rolled down his cheeks as he spoke. "I can't be out here alone any longer!" The man's face was covered in fresh scrapes and bruises and his clothing was dirty and worn. "Please, I mean you no harm. I'm unarmed, you can see for yourself."

The frail whisper of a man shook with fear while he silently pleaded for their assistance. Given his appearance, they could tell he'd been surviving on his own for some time. Sullivan looked back at them and motioned for Eliza to come out and help him.

Eliza stepped out of the SUV and took Sullivan's rifle and held it in front of her with ease. It surprised Nash that she was to able carry the gun with such comfort, given the size of it and her tiny stature.

"Stand up and spread your legs," said Sullivan.

The man clamored to his feet and opened his legs as Sullivan patted him down from top to bottom. Sullivan slid off the man's backpack and knelt down to search through it, just as he had the day he accepted Nash into the Treefort. The man smiled nervously at Eliza as Sullivan rooted through his bag. He went through the contents before he took out a small pocketknife and slid it into his own pocket.

"What's your name?" asked Sullivan.

"Barry," said the man as relief crept into his voice "Yours?"

"What exactly do you want from us, Barry?"

"You must have room in your car. Please, let me travel with you for a spell. I'm exhausted and I can't be out here alone any longer." Tears formed in his shallow eyes as he pleaded to be taken in by them. "Please, I've lost everything."

"What exactly have you lost?"

"Why wife and daughter. We were traveling…"

"What were their names?" interrupted Sullivan.

"Heather and Molly,' said Barry, not skipping a beat.

"What was Molly's birthday?"

"October 1st, 2012. She was born at 3:34 am in Leesburg, Virginia. Two of her toes on both feet were webbed, which Heather and I decided to have fixed when she was three. She went to Waterford Elementary School and her first grade teacher was Ms. Randall."

"That's enough," said Sullivan, keeping his eyes trained on Barry.

"Please, I just need a safe place to rest before I move on."

Sullivan looked back at Eliza, the gun still readied to fire with her slender finger resting beside the trigger. She nodded slightly at him before she handed the gun back and rejoined Nash in the SUV.

"Come on, get in then," said Sullivan, opening the back passenger side door as the man slid in behind Eliza. The man's smell, while nothing nearly as offensive as Mark's back at the Treefort, was enough for Eliza to leave her window rolled down.

"Thank you all so much," said Barry, getting situated and clicking his seat belt. "I'm so exhausted." He placed his head against the seat rest and closed his eyes.

"There's no second chances here, Barry," said Sullivan, taking one of his larger knives and handing it to Eliza. "She's quite skilled with a knife."

"I understand." Barry looked at Eliza with a nervous smile before glancing at the large knife.

"Were you with a group?" asked Nash.

"A while ago, yes. The dead ransacked our camp and we all got separated. We made it away safe but it didn't take long for us to come across another group of the dead ones. That's when I lost them for good."

"I'm so sorry," whispered Eliza, who listened intently as he told his story.

He didn't respond, but looked longingly out the window in solemn silence. She watched as a single tear slid down his cheek onto his collar.

"Do you have a group you belong to?" asked Barry, but received nothing but silence. Everyone knew better than to divulge any information of their group to a stranger, even one as sincere as him. There was still a sniper at large.

"We'll take you some place safe," said Sullivan, undecided on whether Barry would be allowed to enter into the Treefort.

"Honestly, anything would be greatly appreciated. One more day alone and I don't think I would have made it."

He reached down to his backpack, situated on the floor between his legs, and pulled out a weathered canteen. The water sloshed inside as he placed the nozzle to his lips, taking a long drink and watching Eliza stare at him from the corner of his eye. He kindly smiled at her as a splash of water escaped on to his chin. He released a small chuckle as he wiped it away with his palm.

"Here," he said and handed it to Eliza with a smile. "It's the least I can do."

"No thank you," said Eliza, tapping her own canteen with the tip of her knife.

Barry smiled and placed his canteen back into his bag. He let out a little giggle before pulling out a second canteen.

"This is where I keep the strong stuff," he said with a smile.

Eliza looked to the front of the SUV for a small moment as Barry poured contents of the canteen into his hand. He reached up and smacked her across the face, leaving a dark, bloody handprint across her mouth. She gasped in shock, looking down at his hand covered in thick blood and tasting it in her mouth.

"No..." she said softly with fear in her eyes.

"He's coming to get you! *He's coming to get you! HE'S COMING TO GET YOU!*" he squealed in a horrific singsong before he opened his door and launched himself into the rapidly moving landscape. Eliza lunged sideways and sliced his arm with her knife but wasn't able to stop him before he tumbled out of the backseat.

"*What the hell?*" yelled Sullivan, adjusting the rearview mirror to try and see find Barry.

Nash saw him hit the ground in his side view mirror, tumbling a few times before getting to his feet and hobbling into the distance.

"No, No, No! Oh my God I can already *feel* it!" screamed Eliza as she sobbed thick tears over her freckled cheeks. Nash turned quickly as she cried into her palms, seeing the pungent, sticky blood pooling on the floor from the open canteen.

"Sullivan you need to pull over!" said Nash as he watched her with a mixture of fear and confusion. Her tears stopped as she removed her hands from her face and revealed red bloodshot eyes that reflected a newfound rage.

"She's infected! Pull over *now!*" barked Nash as he looked into the face of a newborn howler in the backseat.

Before Sullivan could take his foot off the gas, Eliza lunged into the front of the SUV, screaming wildly as she crashed against the dashboard. She landed in a heap on Sullivan's lap as she thrashed her feet frantically back and forth. One of her powerful feet kicked hard against Nash's throat, which sent him into a fit of wheezes as Sullivan struggled for control of the dead girl.

Eliza flipped violently on top of Sullivan as he tried to maintain control of the SUV. Her legs snaked their way down below to where his feet were working the pedals, and as she continued to fight against his strength, her feet took control of the gas pedal and pressed it to the floor. Sullivan tried his best to remain in control of the vehicle but most of his attention was focused on her teeth as they clattered inches away from his as she eagerly tried to sink them into his face.

Eliza's unbridled strength was much more than Sullivan had ever expected as he held her throat in one hand his other hand on the steering wheel. The sounds of her teeth breaking as she smashed them together became less audible as the SUV continued at full speed, moving dangerously down the desolate road. Nash continued to try and regain his breath as a wave of nausea settled over him and sent a mouthful of vomit onto his chest and lap.

"Brace yourself kid! Keep your eyes and mouth shut!" yelled Sullivan hoarsely. "Eliza, honey, I'm so sorry."

He let go of the wheel and grabbed a handgun from his side, pulled it from its holster and fired a single shot into her temple. The windshield turned red as a spray of blood splashed across the glass. Her body fell limp with her arm caught in the steering wheel, pulling it as she slumped over and sending the SUV into a tumble. It flipped three times before it came to a stop upside down in the middle of the road. Nash and Sullivan remained buckled into their seats, hanging upside down in the mangled pile of metal and glass.

"Are you okay?" asked Sullivan as he placed his hand on Nash's chest.

"Yeah, I'm fine," he said, doing a quick survey of his body to make sure there were no injuries. His head was pounding hard and felt as if it had just gone through a washing machine.

"I'm gonna get myself out, then come around and get you. Keep your mouth shut, don't let any of her blood get in your mouth or eyes."

Sullivan unlatched his belt and fell to the ground, landing on one of the canteens belonging to Barry. He used his feet to open the door in one kick and sent it flying off the already damaged hinges in the process. He crawled out, cutting his hands on shards of broken glass and metal as he tumbled out onto the hot pavement. Sullivan moved his way quickly around the SUV, ripping his blood soaked shirt off in one loud tear as he moved.

Nash sat perfectly still and hung upside down as he waited for what seemed like an eternity for Sullivan to make his way to him. A drop of blood fell from above and landed on his chin, running down his face methodically. In the time it took Sullivan to get out and over to his side of the SUV, Eliza's blood covered almost half of it as he tightly clenched his eyes and mouth shut, using one of his hands to pinch his nose closed.

Sullivan opened the door gruffly and unlatched Nash's belt, letting him fall gently into his arms before he pulled him from the crumpled SUV. Nash quickly wiped the blood off his face and removed his shirt, tossing it aside in a bloody heap. Sullivan appeared from the back of the SUV with a bottle of water, opened it, and threw the top to the ground. He used the water to wash Nash's face and hair clean, making sure all the blood had been washed away.

"What the hell happened?" asked Sullivan as he knelt down to where Nash was sitting and feverishly making sure there was no blood on his face or hands.

"I think he had a canteen full of blood. He smacked her in the face with it on his hands."

Sullivan stood and looked off into the distance, trying to see if Barry was within view. "Dammit," he whispered, shaking his head as he looked down at the back of the SUV. Her body sat wedged against the back door, her bloodied face plastered against the only window left intact. "I didn't check his canteens."

"Why would you? Never in a million years would I have thought anyone would do that."

Sullivan helped Nash to his feet as they both stood and surveyed the wreck. Aside from some deep scratches and soon to be bruised arms and legs, the two of them had left the SUV with no major injuries. Sullivan walked to the back of the wreck and tried to avoid contact with Eliza's dead, bloodshot eyes.

"Son of a bitch!" he bellowed as he planted his foot against the crumpled metal and moved the vehicle a couple inches. He stood with his hands on his hips and looked up and down the road while hoping to catch a glimpse of Barry.

"We should follow him," said Nash, looking down the road where Barry had escaped.

"Trust me, I want to, but we don't even know which direction he went." He pried open the back door of the SUV as Eliza's body spilled out and landed on the pavement with her arm outstretched on the road. "We'd be best utilized getting back to the Fort. I'd rather be there, should he somehow find it, as opposed to wandering through these fields looking for him."

Reaching into the back of the SUV, he pulled out a large blanket, and unfolded it on the pavement. As gently as he could, he pulled Eliza's body from the wreck and placed it on the blanket. Sullivan carefully folded her arms across her chest and closed her eyes with his fingers.

"I don't even know what to say right now. She was alive ten minutes ago." Sullivan stood over Eliza's dead body as he helplessly stared down at her. Nash searched his mind for anything to say and came up empty, realizing he hadn't known her at all. Looking at her now, he wished he had.

Sullivan inhaled deeply before leaving her to rummage through the back of the SUV. The two of them picked through the bloody mess to salvage the most important items, most of which were coated in Eliza's infected blood. Nash used his bloodied shirt and wiped off the blood before passing it to Sullivan to do the same to his rifle. Sullivan stood stoically with his back to Nash, Eliza's body laying in front of him on an old blanket.

"Let's go," he said and walked down the road, pulling Eliza gently behind him. "Eyes alert."

It took them close to two hours of complete silence to get back to the Treefort. The words "*HE'S COMING TO GET YOU*" ringing in their heads like a nightmarish lullaby. Nash wanted nothing more than to discuss it with Sullivan, but he knew right now wasn't the time as they walked along the lonely road with the body of one of Sullivan's closest friends.

Sullivan stopped at the edge of the trees leading to the Treefort and looked both ways down the road in a last check that

Barry hadn't followed them. "I might be wrong in this, but I don't want people knowing exactly what happened to her. Not yet anyway." Nash nodded in silent agreement; he didn't quite know what was right either. "I want to talk to Dianna and Stu before letting people know the truth. For now, we'll say she was attacked by a howler leaving the exile site."

Sullivan marched into the trees in silence as Nash followed close behind. The woods seemed to have doubled in size as the two of them walked together, sharing the burden of awful news.

"Cole is going to be devastated," whispered Sullivan as they approached the Fort and alerted Dianna to their presence. Sullivan gingerly picked up Eliza's body, making sure that her bloody head was hanging away from his body. Dianna opened the front gate for them and the two of them walked in, Eliza's blanketed silhouette lying softly in Sullivan's arms. Dianna's hand raised to her mouth as she realized what was underneath the blanket.

"No…" she said as her eyes welled with tears. "What the hell happened?"

"I'll tell you in private. For everyone else, she was bit by a howler."

"Oh God! What happened?" Cole yelled, his eyes already welling with thick tears. Scott and Meghan shared a long look before they disappeared back into camp, eyes glistening.

Sullivan tried in vain to comfort Cole as Nash made his way to Melissa. She hung her head out of the sliding window as he approached to see what the commotion was.

"What's wrong?" she asked as she disappeared into the truck and came out the door to join him.

"Eliza's dead," he said softly with her hands in his.

"What? Why? Was it Duncan?"

"No, it wasn't Duncan. I'll tell you, but you need to keep it between us. You can't tell a soul." The realization that they were no longer alone settled upon her as he explained what happened.

Cole refused to move away from Eliza's body. Seeing his anguish, the group kept their distance, letting him come to terms with what had happened. It wasn't long before Scott and Meghan reappeared with shovels in their hands. They were quietly making their leave to ready a grave for burial when Cole saw them.

Cole shot to his feet quickly and knocked the shovels out of their grips. "I do this, not you! It's too fucking soon, anyway! She's not even cold yet!" Scott and Meghan stood for a moment as Meghan whimpered softly. Scott took her by the hand and led her away, leaving Cole alone with the shovels on the ground.

"*You!*" yelled Cole as he picked up a shovel and pointed it at Nash. "I wanna hear it from you! Tell me what happened to her!"

Cole marched toward Nash with the shovel at his side, huffing wildly with anger as Sullivan quickly stepped in front of Nash.

"Back off, Sullivan!"

"I already told you what happened, Cole. I know you're upset but this isn't Nash's fault."

"Isn't it though? It's his asshole father that had you all out there in the first place!"

"Hey!" Melissa countered, standing beside Sullivan. Sullivan placed his arm in front of her and created a barrier between her and Cole.

"This isn't his fault, Cole," said Sullivan as he tried his best to keep calm. "We're all upset right now, but you need to calm down and back away."

Nash remained sitting, hidden fully from Cole's view by Sullivan's massive stature. Cole stood in front of them all, bubbling with anger before he turned and disappeared out of the Fort with one of the shovels.

"I know he doesn't mean it," said Nash. "Doesn't mean he's wrong, though."

"Don't say that," said Melissa.

"No, he's right. If we'd never come here, she'd still be alive."

"It could have happened to any of us, Nash," said Sullivan. "Nothing that happened today is your fault. Take a few minutes and meet me in the war room please."

Sullivan walked away and joined Dianna and Stu at the front of the war room before they disappeared inside.

"He's right, Nash. This isn't your fault," said Melissa as she sat beside him and placed her arms around him. "I hate what happened, but at least we know now."

"Know what?"

"That something's coming for us," she said softly.

"We don't know that," he said. "That Barry guy was deranged."

"Go sort this out," she said as she placed her hand on his cheek. Find me when you're done."

Melissa gave him a peck on the forehead and headed back to the food truck with tears in her eyes. Nash walked with a heavy heart to the war room as Cole's words followed him like a venomous shadow. Scott and Meghan reached the war room at the same time, and Scott held the flaps open for Nash and Meghan to walk through.

"Keep your head up, kid," Scott said as Nash walked into the tent.

The inside of the war room had its typical hot, muggy air, but none of them seemed to notice. Nash sat down in the same spot he had the last time they met and looked over to the empty seat across from him. Scott zipped the front of the war room shut as they each flicked on their lanterns.

"Eliza didn't die because of a howler bite," said Sullivan. The already quiet room silenced completely. No one breathed. "We met a man named Barry driving back from exiling Duncan. Eliza spotted him running in a field so we stopped to see if we could help him. He seemed genuine and peaceful, honestly just looking for sanctuary. I searched his bag, confirmed he was unarmed, and allowed him in the SUV with us. Shortly, after we started driving, he took a canteen out of his bag."

Sullivan stopped, rested his hands on the table below him, and hung his head. Tears dripped onto the table below as he stood in silence, unable to tell the rest. Dianna got up and softly rubbed his muscular back.

"He had his own canteen he was drinking from but he had a second canteen full of infected blood. He poured it all over his hand and smacked her in the mouth." It felt as if the air had been vacuumed out of the room. They stared at Nash, dumbfounded over the thought of someone doing such a thing. "Sullivan is right. He was as genuine as they come. He was frail, unassuming, and the look in his eye was genuine loneliness. He played us hard."

"After she took a drink, he opened the door and jumped out. He disappeared after that and we weren't able to find him. Eliza turned within seconds and was in the front seat with us in a flash." Sullivan stopped, visibly shaken by the memories of the afternoon. "This is why we try and avoid the howlers at all cost. The strength she exhibited while I fought her to maintain control of the SUV was staggering. I had no choice; she was eventually going to bite me so I put a bullet in her head."

Dianna began to sob, leaning onto Sullivan's back. Stu and Scott sat with their gazes fixed on Sullivan, while Meghan leaned on Scott as she also began to cry.

"At that point, she slumped over and we lost control of the SUV. It flipped a few times and landed upside down."

"You two are lucky to be alive," said Scott as he put his arm around Meghan and nodded at Nash.

"We need to find this man," said Stu, his bruised and bandaged face rippled with anger. "We need to find him and *make him pay for this*."

"I'm afraid we may have something bigger to worry about," said Sullivan as he helped Dianna to her seat. "Right after she spit out the blood from the canteen, Barry started chanting something."

"He's coming to get you," said Nash, the sound of the singsong way Barry had sung it rang in his ears. It sent shivers through his core each time he thought of it.

"This is why I didn't tell you the truth when we first got here," said Sullivan, head down toward the table in exasperation. "I didn't want to cause a panic. I wanted to talk to you all first before saying anything."

"We need to tell everyone," said Meghan, sitting up from Scott's chest as she wiped her eyes. "People need to know what we're dealing with. This guy broke your trust and murdered Eliza. If he's part of a bigger group, we need to be prepared."

"I agree," said Dianna. "We all need to be ready for whatever could be out there."

"We don't know if anything is out there," said Scott who looked sadly at each of them as he spoke.

"No, Scott, she's right. Something is coming and we need to be ready," said Sullivan. "This place was built to hide us from the dead, not protect us from other groups. If we aren't vigilant with our security, we're just sitting ducks. I don't want to overreact and I'm not talking about arming everyone. I just think that we need to be prepared if someone does end up at our doorstep."

"What are you proposing?" asked Stu as the light from the lanterns illuminated his tattered face.

"Scott and Nash, I think I'd like the two of you patrolling the woods each day in two hour shifts. Stu and I will talk to the rest of the group and form other pairs we think would be good for the job."

They each sat for a moment in the harsh lantern light and contemplated the changing scenario around them.

"I can't believe she's gone," said Meghan when she began to cry again. Scott leaned sideways and took her into his arms, his eyes slightly tearing as well.

"Things have changed," said Sullivan softly. "It's a new world we're living in now and I have a feeling it's about to get a whole lot bigger."

"We'll gather everyone together," said Scott as he stood from the table with Meghan. "You can go over everything with them and then..." He stopped speaking, not wanting to vocalize that they'd have to bury her before the sun went down. "We'll check in with Cole and let him know what happened to Eliza."

Everyone stood together and exited the war room in silence, feeling numb as the story of Eliza's death slowly settled on each of them. Scott escorted Meghan out of the Fort as she wept, both of them off to break the news to Cole. Stu and Dianna ushered everyone to the meeting place as Sullivan stepped up on the platform.

"Everyone, please gather around," said Sullivan. "As you all know, Eliza was killed today. What you don't know is that it wasn't because of a howler..."

The look of shock in people's eyes was the same from person to person, a mixture of sadness and fear radiated from them all. Fresh tears flowed as the crowd processed exactly what her death meant to the safety of the group. Sullivan himself had to hold back more tears as he stood strong in front of the group and watched them all breakdown collectively.

"Something is clearly happening in the area around us," he said as he reached his hand into his pocket. "I think it's time that everyone knows what's been going on." He held a handful of red cloth strips in the air. "For a while now we've been finding some of the dead with these tied around their wrists. It's quite clear that they're all coming from the same place, but for what reason, I don't know."

"Why didn't you tell us sooner?" said a woman who stood at the front of the group.

"Why would I?" said Sullivan sharply. "I wasn't going to cause a panic among the group by feeding little pieces of information bit by bit. Information that may mean nothing. These," Sullivan held the little red ties higher in the air. "Could just be people who were in the same group at one time—or it could mean something else entirely. What we know now is that there is a very real threat nearby and we all have to be on high alert. Anyone interested in volunteering for security duty, please see me."

Sullivan headed back toward the war tent, his shoulders tense. Slowly, volunteers filed over to him.

By the end of the meeting, Sullivan had recruited ten other people to join Nash and Scott in securing the woods each day. Stu dismissed the group, but kept the new members of the security team back to go over their responsibilities and pair them off. Stu and Sullivan gave them an overview of what was required of them. They listened, nodding along. "We'll take notes on what we see and when. This way, if there is any correlation in movements we'll see it."

Almost everyone from the Fort joined them as they walked through the woods to the burial site. They moved in silence as the birds continued their late afternoon melody. Cole led the way with Eliza in his arms, followed by anyone who had known her well inside the fence. The burial was quick, with few words exchanged as everyone stood in disbelief. It didn't take long for Cole to place her in the ground and efficiently refill her grave with loose dirt as silent tears rolled down his face.

She was laid to rest among a collection of twelve other wooden crosses, each with a name scribed across the front. Sullivan stood in the back of the group as he leaned on a tree and surveyed the number of grave markers, Dianna beside him. They'd created a safe place to settle in the Treefort, but it was a dangerous world they lived and the gravesite was a reminder of that. Cole knelt beside the grave and fixed a cross with her name carved neatly across the front, making sure it was deep enough to stay upright. He stayed on his knees, slumped over as the group watched him in the dying light.

"Take everyone back to camp and give Cole some time," said Sullivan, watching as tears fell to the ground from Cole's eyes.

"Of course," said Dianna. She hugged him softly before she gathered the group. Before Nash and Scott could join them, Sullivan held out his arm.

"Let's go check in on the slowpokes you'd told me about by the creek."

They walked quickly together to the area along the creek where they had found the slowpokes before Duncan's exile. The three of them stood at the edge of the steep bank, looking down at the clueless monsters that still stood along the water below. Some of them had moved farther down the creek but most of them were located where they had been the day before. The dreadlocked slowpoke stood ankle deep in the water in front of them, gazing up at them with his wild, fiery eyes. There were a few more of them today.

"I could've gone without seeing him today," said Scott as he gazed at the slowpoke.

"This is concerning," said Sullivan, looking up and down the waterline as the dead continued their monotonous way of life.

"They must have migrated here together," said Scott as he looked at all of them with the red strips on their wrists. "Dammit I wish we knew what it meant."

"I get the feeling we're going to find out soon," said Sullivan. "Let's head back. I don't wanna get caught out here at night."

The sun had almost completely set by the time the three of them made their way back to the Treefort. Dianna opened the gate as usual. The Fort was blanketed with an eerie silence.

"Everything okay?" she asked, locking the gate as they filed in. Sullivan exhaled and pulled her in for a hug as Nash and Scott walked off to join everyone around the fires. Melissa and Nash locked eyes and smiled as a loud ruckus suddenly erupted from the armory trailer, followed by Mark releasing a wild string of profanity. Everyone looked over to see him on the ground, yelling as the door of the trailer hung open. Cole stepped outside with a large rifle strapped to his back, as well as a smaller handgun and a large knife strapped to his ankle. Sullivan sprinted to the trailer and helped Mark to his feet as Cole marched past him.

"What the hell do you think you're doing?" boomed Sullivan, following behind him as Mark continued to curse at Cole and shake his fist in the air. Cole paid no mind and continued his walk toward the front gate. "Hey! I'm talking to you!"

"Do I really have to say it, Sully?" spat Cole without turning around.

"You're not thinking clearly," said Sullivan as he caught up with him and placed his hand on Cole's shoulder. He spun around and knocked Sullivan's hand away.

"You think you can stop me?" He glared back at Sullivan through the firelight with red, bleary eyes. Sullivan stared back at him and saw the determination and stubbornness in his posture.

"Don't do anything stupid. Bring him back here, if you find him."

"The fact that you even think you have to say that is insulting," said Cole as he made his way to the gate. "When you're done getting what you need from him though, I'm going to kill him."

Sullivan unlocked the gate for him as he stepped outside into the darkness. He stopped and turned around as his face softened slightly in the pale light.

"Tell the kid I'm sorry for coming at him like that." With that, Cole disappeared into the darkness.

Most of the Fort went to bed early, mourning Eliza's death and fearing what was to come. The rest sat in silence around the fire. Sullivan sat across from them with his arm around Dianna.

"Do you think he'll find that man?" asked Melissa, her head resting on Nash's shoulder. Her eyes fluttered as she tried to stay awake.

"I sincerely doubt it," he said as Dianna tilted her head to look up at him. "Cole doesn't have any tracking skills and he's running off raw emotion right now. It'll be dumb luck if he finds anything at all."

"You're convinced there's another group nearby, aren't you?" asked Dianna as she leaned her head back into his shoulder.

"Seems pretty obvious at this point. What worries me is that recent events have all but confirmed that this other group, wherever they are, don't have good intentions."

About an hour later, Melissa whispered, "Take me to bed," without opening her eyes.

Tim Gabrielle

Nash helped her up and the two of them walked toward the RVs. Nash guided her slowly toward hers, only to be stopped by her smile.

"No. Take me to *our* RV."

Nash blushed and gave her a short nod. The door opened smoothly as he escorted her inside, but closing was a bit more difficult. The broken doorjamb would always remind him of his last night with Duncan, but nothing could ruin the way he felt at that moment.

They crawled into bed together and Melissa snuggled against him. "I feel so bad for Cole. I hope he'll be okay."

"Cole's angry, but he seems like a smart guy. He'll be okay."

"I hate losing people," she sobbed softly. Her tears dampened his shirt.

"Me too," he whispered. Nash hadn't realized it before, but she and Eliza had been close. Eventually, her sobs quieted and she fell asleep.

Nash listened to her breathing beside him as he replayed the events of the day. The image of Barry tumbling on the ground as he fell from the SUV, followed by Eliza's crazed attack replayed endlessly in his mind. The faces of the people in the Fort flashed before him as they realized that Eliza had been killed, each one knowing that it easily could have been any one of them. Nervous energy radiated through every part of his body.

He didn't sleep at all.

Chapter 14

Nash jolted out of a daze to the sound of heavy banging on the door of his RV. Melissa was gone, just like the morning before, only this morning there was no care package at the edge of his bed to greet him. He quickly put on clothes and opened the door to find Sullivan standing outside looking dreary-eyed and equally as exhausted as he felt.

"They let us sleep in," he said, stepping into the RV.

"I'm not sure *sleep* is what I'd call it," said Nash. "I don't think I slept a single minute."

"Me either," said Sullivan. He sat on a wooden chair at the end of the RV opposite the bed. "I can still feel her weight on top of me, Nash. All night, all I could think about was her gnashing her teeth at me."

"I kept thinking about it all night, too. I just don't understand why anybody would do what he did."

"He was sending a message," said Sullivan as he rubbed his eyes with his palms. "I think something really dangerous is coming and between you and me, I don't think we're ready. We haven't had a single person come through here with any kind of ill will, until Duncan anyway. I think we all just got comfortable thinking that everyone left alive was decent. I'm guilty of it and I got Eliza killed because of it."

"It wasn't your fault," said Nash; the emotions of the day before were still raw. "He could have fooled anyone. He fooled me. He fooled all of us."

"I know that. This whole thing has just made me realize how ill prepared we really are. Nobody would know what to do if someone were to come for us. I'm not sure I even know what to do."

Sullivan looked down toward the floor in frustration as Nash stared out across the open door at the line of people at the food truck. Nash wanted nothing more than to go and see Melissa, but he liked being accepted into Sullivan's inner circle so quickly.

Sullivan looked up at Nash, his eyes red with sadness. "Do you think she was present? You know what I mean? Did she know what she was doing?"

"I guess anything is possible, but I don't think so. I like to think if there were any part of her remaining, she would have been able to stop herself. Look at Melissa's parents; her dad ripped her mom apart without a thought. I think that once you're infected, that's the end of who you were."

Sullivan returned his gaze to the floor and silently wept. Nash walked over to where he was sitting and placed a hand on his broad shoulder, patting a couple times before he let his hand rest.

"She loved you, Sully." The short form of his name came out smoother than he thought it would. Only people close to him shortened it, and as he said it, it felt right. "They all love you. No matter how much you do to safeguard this place, bad things are going to happen. They all know that. Nobody out there is blaming you."

"I know," he said through his tears, his voice not wavering in the least. He inhaled deeply, letting the air sit in his lungs for a moment before he exhaled a long, powerful breath. "Let's get out there. Go see Melissa, I know you're itching to."

Nash smiled as Sullivan stood. He placed his dark sunglasses on his face to hide his red eyes, and patted Nash on the back before he ducked his head and left the RV. Nash watched Sullivan walk toward the middle of the camp as Melissa leaned out of the sliding glass window of the food truck. Any uneasiness he felt from the restless night washed away as he stepped out of the RV to join her.

He'd woken up thinking about her every morning since he got to the Fort, and time without her was starting to become a blur. She smiled wider as he approached, her eyes remaining sad from the day before. She placed a package of food onto the window ledge, similar to the one from the day before.

"I woke up a little later than I should have and people were getting hungry," she said as he reached the truck. "Sorry I didn't have time to bring it to you like yesterday."

"No worries. I can stand in line just like everyone else," he said with a smile. "How are you feeling after yesterday?"

"Better, I guess." Her eyes were visibly red from crying through the night. "I didn't sleep well, as I'm sure you can tell."

"I didn't sleep at all," he said as he opened the package of Pop Tarts and bit down without separating them. "Sullivan was up all night too. We were talking this morning, and he's not doing well. He thinks that everyone is going to blame him for Eliza's death."

"Poor Sully," she said, looking past Nash as Sullivan sat alone by a small fire. "None of us are in denial about the world outside the fence. It's dangerous, and not all of us are going to make it. Most of us probably wouldn't even be alive if he hadn't found us in the first place." She closed the glass window and joined him outside the truck, putting her arms around him as she rested her head against his chest. "How do you feel today?"

"Sore, but not too bad." Sullivan was gathering the group together who would work the security detail outside the fence, talking to them all from the platform he usually spoke from. "I should probably be over there."

He placed his hand on hers and squeezed it softly before he joined them. Sullivan stepped down from the platform and instructed the group to follow Stu to see the schedule and get further training.

"Not today, chief," he said as Nash tried to follow the group. "You and Scott are gonna patrol as a team, but not today. After yesterday, I'd be negligent to not give you a bit of a break."

Sullivan trotted off to help Stu with training the volunteers as the lack of sleep from the night before finally caught up with Nash. He looked back at the food truck, which now sported a considerable line of people waiting to get food. Melissa was busily dispensing breakfast and marking it in her ledger.

Knowing that she'd be a while at the food truck, Nash wandered back to his RV to try and get some rest. The inside of the RV was considerably warmer than it had been that morning as the sun continued to rise high above the trees. He unlatched some of the windows and cranked them open, letting the fresh air fill the space around him. He undressed all the way to his boxers, finished a half empty water bottle, and crawled back into bed.

****

He woke in the darkness of the RV, a fire roaring outside as an overwhelming sense of urgency flowed through him. Against his will, he stepped out of bed and went out into the darkness as he stepped barefoot onto the cold ground. The fire roared wildly in the center of the Fort, and other than his RV, the entire space inside the fence was empty. He kept quiet, looking from corner to corner and realized he was completely alone.

The front gate rattled softly, "He's coming to get you," a voice called. He walked toward the gate slowly, the rattling getting more vicious with each step..

"He's coming to get you," the voices chanted. Nash stopped at the gate and silence descended.

"Buddy Boy, Buddy Boy, let me in," Duncan's voice hissed. Terror grabbed Nash and he stood still listening as the voices hissed at him from the other side like hungry serpents.

"She's out here with us, Buddy Boy," Duncan cackled. "We've all taken a turn. She was worth the wait." A girlish giggle echoed through the air, a dark and twisted version of the laugh he had come to love.

The camouflage attached to the fence dissolved into mist revealing hundreds of angry, glowing eyes staring back at him. Black fingers curled their way through the chain link fence, shaking it until it shattered. Duncan stepped forward first, giggling with glee as Nash tripped.

The ghoulish giggling continued and Duncan descended upon him.

****

Nash burst into wakefulness. Even after they exiled Duncan, he still tormented Nash. Maybe there was no ridding himself of the monster. His head pounded with exhaustion as he reached for his watch to see that two hours had passed. Nash grabbed a bottle of water and drank half of it quickly. He opened the RV door as an engine roared to life nearby. He stepped outside and watched as Sullivan maneuvered one of the RVs along the fence, right behind three others now parked in a line.

"Redecorating?" asked Nash as he walked over while Sullivan stepped down from the RV cab.

"Security," he said and closed the door behind him. "Gonna move all the RVs along the walls so that we can patrol from up top. A lot of the RVs are empty so it only makes sense to have them here. The ones that are used for sleeping will be moved inwards a bit."

"That's actually a good idea," said Nash, looking down the row of RVs. Sullivan moved toward the line of RVs and stepped inside the one that Nash and Melissa shared, moving it across the Fort and parking it directly behind the other RVs.

"I can tell you're restless," said Sullivan, looking along the fence to make sure he left enough space. "If you're feeling up to it, why don't you go check out the creek and see if anything has changed. I know I said nothing today, but if you're like me, downtime doesn't help anything."

"Yeah, it's driving me crazy," said Nash as he turned and ran toward the armory to get his weapons. "Thank you!"

"Take Stu with you!" yelled Sullivan from behind as he walked toward another RV.

Mark stood up and opened the door as Nash approached before he sat back down in his chair with a grumpy look on his face. There was a yellowish bruise on his cheek from when Cole had knocked him to the ground. Nash waved with a smile and made sure to hold his breath as he walked past him and into the hot trailer. He quickly found his favorite knife and clipped it to his belt. He begrudgingly took a gun from the shelf and clipped the holster to his other hip, already hating the weight he felt hanging there.

"Grab me a knife, would ya?" yelled Stu from outside the armory door, keeping his distance from the trailer to avoid Mark's stench. Nash stepped out of the trailer and handed Stu a knife. He felt guilty when he saw the bandages and bruising on his face.

"How you feeling today?" asked Nash as Mark closed the door, muttering something to himself as they walked away.

"I'm doing okay. Dianna has me on some pain meds, which help, but it still smarts quite a bit. I'm really curious to see this slowpoke extravaganza."

"It's a sight to be seen," said Nash as he sent a wave to Melissa. Dark clouds began to roll in overhead as the two of them made their way through the gate and into the trees.

They hurried through the woods and hoped to beat whatever rain was coming. As usual, Nash could see the dreadlocked slowpoke on their approach. He stood with his head just crested over the bank of the creek and watched with a twisted grin stretched across his cheeks.

"He's been there in that spot since I found them all," said Nash as they came to a stop at the edge of the steep bank.

"He's a happy guy, isn't he?" said Stu, analyzing the dreadlocked slowpoke. Most of the slowpokes still congregated along the edge of the water, each doing their own mindless task, as Stu looked up and down the creek at each of them. The clouds opened with a low roll of thunder and thick drops of water began to fall from the sky. The canopy of trees above shielded them from the onslaught of raindrops but enough fell through to cool them as they stood and watched the slowpokes.

"I hope it doesn't rain too long," said Stu. "We collect a good amount of water when it rains like this but it makes camp messy."

"I never pegged you as a neat freak, Stu," said Nash with a smile. Stu responded with a look of horror, his eyes fixed on the area down the creek. Nash turned is head sharply to see what had shaken him so badly.

Far down the creek, a man stood his with back toward them, shirtless with an arrow sticking out of the top of his inflamed shoulder muscle. He swayed softly with his face to the sky as the rain fell into his open mouth. The water flowed down his back and ran overtop the dried streams of blood and tattoos that stretched from his back onto his muscular arms.

It was Cole.

"Oh my God," muttered Nash as the two of them took off, slipping in the mud in their haste.

"*No, No, No, No, No!*" yelled Stu as they ran, coming to a stop in front of the man who had just buried Eliza the day before. Nash placed his hand on Cole's arm and turned him around, which revealed a chest full of deep cuts and dried blood.

Cole looked back and forth between the two of them, with a sad, forgone look in his eyes. The pupils contracted back and forth. The falling rain cascaded down his chest, and slowly washed away some of the blood and revealed something they hadn't originally noticed.

"Those aren't just cuts on his chest," said Nash as he watched the rain flow off Cole in a pink waterfall. The harder it rained, the more blood and dirt washed away.

HE'S COMING

"Barry," said Nash as he looked up and down the creek. "This is bad."

"He was hardly gone a day," said Stu, tears welling in his eyes as he gazed at Cole. "What do we do?"

"I'm going to go get Sullivan," said Nash. "Stay here with him and check and see where he was bit." Nash took off running into the woods toward the Fort as Stu examined Cole for the bite mark. The rush back to the Fort was a blur as he darted in and out of trees on his way back.

"Dianna!" he yelled at the front gate, his jeans covered in mud from his quickened pace.

"What is it? Where's Stu?" she asked him in a panic, opening the gate as she spoke.

"Keep it down," said Nash as he tried to hide his own panic, gasping for air. His hands were shaking, so balled them into fists at his side. "I need Sullivan. We found Cole out by the creek. He's dead."

"What?" she hissed, visibly shaken by the news.

"Yes; kind of. He's a slowpoke." The words sounded false as they came out of his mouth.

"Not again," she said and rubbed her eyes with her fingers. "Sullivan is still moving the RVs. I'll go get him."

"Hurry," Nash pleaded.

Melissa jogged through the rain to join him, having noticed his exchange with Dianna.

"It's Cole," he said, before she could speak. "I took Stu down to the creek to show him all the slowpokes, and Cole was one of them."

"We're not safe here anymore," she said flatly. The reaction to Cole's death wasn't what Nash had expected, but he knew she was right.

"I know. I'm gonna take Sullivan down there now, and we'll talk. I don't have to tell you to keep it quiet."

"Of course not," she said as Sullivan walked up to them.

He said nothing, just left the Fort and broke into a full sprint. Nash on his heels as the gate closed behind them. He was quickly far ahead of Nash and moved swiftly through the sopping forest as Nash struggled to keep stride behind him. For how large he was, Nash was shocked at Sullivan's speed and agility. Nash reached the creek and joined Sullivan as he stood with Stu in front of Cole's empty shell.

"There's no bite mark," said Stu. "I looked him all over. There's nothing."

"They're using the blood as a weapon," said Sullivan as he examined the arrow that stuck out of Cole's shoulder. "Barry used the blood to turn Eliza. He took a chance and got lucky when she turned into a howler. This arrow was infused with infected blood, I guarantee it."

"First Eliza, now this?" asked Stu. "What the hell are we going to tell the group?"

"We have to tell them everything," said Sullivan. "They all need to know what we're dealing with."

"Crazies," said Stu while he looked at the carving in Cole's chest. "We are in over our heads here."

A soft, muffled giggle filled the air as the three of them quickly darted for cover.

"Who the hell is that?" whispered Stu, looking around as he tried and find the source.

Sullivan placed a stern finger in front of his lips and signaled them both to stay quiet.

"I know you're here, Barry!" boomed Sullivan before he ducked behind a large tree. "Come on out and talk with us." He placed his hand on the handle of his knife and adjusted his fingers around it tightly.

Another snicker in the distance echoed through the trees as rain continued to fall through the canopy. Sullivan noticed a tree, about ten feet away, that was large enough to hide behind. He pointed toward it and silently sent Stu to flank the left side while he walked around the right. He motioned Nash to hide behind one of the trees near them.

The snickering continued, getting louder and increasingly manic as they approached him. Sullivan silently made his way around the tree and found Barry with an arrow loaded and ready to fire at Stu.

"Stu, get down!" yelled Sullivan as he leaped forward like a jungle cat. The arrow released and hissed through the air, missing Stu by an inch as he hurled himself onto the wet ground. Barry hit the ground hard, laughing wildly as a canteen of blood spilled onto the mud.

"Hello *again*!" yelled Barry, his face pushed into the mud by one of Sullivan's massive palms. "I killed your other friend! Did you *see*?"

Sullivan yanked him up with one hand and punched him square in his teeth. His head snapped back, blood spraying from his mouth. He hung loosely in Sullivan's grip, laughing wildly as they stared at him in disbelief.

Sullivan placed his hand on Barry's throat and squeezed, watching his face turn dark red as blood continued to pour from his open mouth. Nash and Stu watched as Barry hardly broke character, still trying to giggle as Sullivan's face twisted with hate.

"Sullivan, *stop*!" yelled Stu while he tried to pull him away from Barry.

Sullivan released his grip and let Barry fall to the ground. He landed like a sack of old bones as he writhed on the ground and giggled through his gasps for air. Nash listened to the gasping, hacking cackle and knew he'd hear it again in one of his nightmares.

"Look," said Nash as he pointed down at the red cloth strip tied around his left wrist.

The three men stood around the crazed lunatic on the ground as he continued to chuckle and repeatedly dug his fingers in and out of the mud. Sullivan quickly frisked him and pulled him to his feet with one hand.

"Come on," he said, leading the charge along the edge of the creek. Stu and Nash followed behind, as Barry hooted and waved wildly at the dreadlocked slowpoke. Sullivan tightened his hold on the wriggling psychopath.

"Hey! Hey, buddy! *Hey, hey, hey, hey, hey hey, buddy*!" Barry shouted with his crazed smile. He continued to wave his hands as the slowpoke stared back, his grin widening as he watched Sullivan lead Barry into the trees.

"Shut the hell up," said Sullivan as he took a bandana from his back pocket and tied it around Barry's eyes.

"You really think I don't know where your camp is?" asked Barry as he looked up at Sullivan through the blackness of the bandana. "You should have seen how far away I was when I nailed your friend back there! Best shot of my life!" Sullivan landed a hard punch to his ribs, a snapping sound ricocheting around them. Barry lost his footing slightly after the punch but didn't show a shred of pain.

The rain relented momentarily as they reached the gate. Dianna let them in with a look of shock on her face as they led Barry inside. He knew he was inside their camp and immediately turned on the theatrics.

"Hi everyone!" he yelled loudly. "Thanks for having me!"

"Shut up, or I'll break another rib," whispered Sullivan sternly.

Barry pretended to whimper in fear for a moment before he let out a loud, hysterical cackle. "*I killed your friend! All those tattoos on his arms! Easy, peasy —killed him dead*!" The Fort let out a collective gasp and watched as Sullivan led him toward the holding trailer. He planted another blow to the same side of Barry's body, which broke another rib as Barry fell to the ground.

"Sullivan!" yelled Dianna from behind.

"Sullivan! Sullivan! *Sully, Sully, Sully*!" squealed Barry from the ground, lying sprawled in a pool of rainwater. "That's *two* of you I've killed! Ain't that a pip? How many more I wonder, I wonder, wonder! I hope some more."

Sullivan landed one final blow to his face, knocking him out and into a puddle. He stood above Barry's limp body, breathing heavy, as others began to crowd around.

"This is the man that killed Eliza. This is also the man that killed Cole." The group stood in silent shock and listened to him as the rain started again. "Cole is standing out by the creek with an arrow sticking out of his shoulder. There was a warning carved in his chest. It said 'HE'S COMING'."

"What the hell is going on, Sullivan?" yelled a man from the middle of the crowd.

"I know a lot of you were upset with me for not sharing certain things in the past, but I assure you, you know everything. Every one of you needs to be aware of what's happening in order to continue to live safely. We've had a fairly easy ride here at the

Treefort but that's all changing now. There's a threat at our doorstep and we need to prepare ourselves for the worst. I'm not going to sugarcoat things for any of you. We are in danger."

He paused and listened to the rain falling hard throughout the woods. Stu moved forward and scooped up Barry's frail, unconscious body from the puddle. Someone from the crowd joined him and they disappeared from the crowd, off to lock Barry in the holding trailer.

"Wherever Barry came from, they are using infected blood as a weapon," said Sullivan. "We found Cole with an arrow sticking out of his shoulder and not a single bite anywhere on him. Whoever these people are, they are dangerous, and they mean us harm."

"What's next?" asked Dianna from the front of the crowd.

"Once he wakes up, we'll use the information we get from him to formulate a plan. Until further notice, I don't want anyone leaving the Fort without talking to me first."

"What about Cole?" asked Melissa. "We can't just leave him out there."

"Myself and the security team will decide what to do with Cole but for the next little while, we need to keep our heads down and prepare for what's to come. I don't want any attention drawn to the Fort."

The rain began to fall harder than before, which sent everyone scattering to the RVs for shelter. Nash ran with Melissa to the food truck to close it down before the two of them locked themselves inside their RV. As soon as the door was closed, her arms were around him. They stood silently in each other's embrace. The air was surprisingly cool inside as the rain pattered the top of the RV He leaned his head down to her ear and brushed her wet hair away from it.

"I love you."

She removed her head form his chest and they stared into each other's eyes. He'd never seen them sparkle so brilliantly as he looked down at her, drops of rain still clinging to her face. Her fingers tangled in his damp hair as she pulled his head down to hers and placed her lips softly against his.

"I love you, too," she whispered softly.

The two of them crawled into their bed, kissing each other as they moved. Melissa pulled the blanket back and they slid under, removing their shirts in unison before starting to kiss again. Nash's heart pounded fast as her fingers pulled his shorts down before pulling off her own.

He touched her bare skin lightly; his nerves making his hands shake.

"Wait," Melissa said, sitting up and grabbing her bag from the floor in front of the bed. Nash held his breath, wondering what he did wrong. She rummaged through her duffle and pulled out a silver-packaged condom. "Here," she said and placed it in his hands.

"How long have you had this on you?" asked Nash, turning the package in his hands.

"I put it in my bag the day after you got here. They're in short supply, and I wanted to be prepared. Just in case." Her cheeks flushed with color. "I didn't plan for it —I just, well, thought I should have one."

"We'll I'm glad you do," said Nash with a smile as he awkwardly struggled with the condom.

The two made love for the first time as the rain thundered down around them. Their movements were awkward at first, each unsure where there hands should be on the other. But they moved slowly, listening to their bodies. It was over quickly, so they laid next to each other, listening to the storm outside. They curled into each other, both of them replaying their first experience in their heads. Barry's voice cut through the thunder, bringing them out of their trance and back into their reality. His voice was loud and jubilant, fighting with the rolling thunder.

"He's coming, he's coming, he's coming to get you!"

Chapter 15

Nash let the sadistic nursery rhyme run freely through his head as he dragged his fingertips along Melissa's bareback. The song continued as the rain came to a halt and amplified as the pattering of the raindrops on the RV relented. Nash slid away from the bed, making sure to cover her naked body with their blanket.

"I'll be right back," he said as she smiled up at him.

Nash stepped outside as others began to file out of their RVs as well. Barry was thrashing wildly in the trailer, hooting loudly until he noticed Nash standing nearby.

"Hey! Hey kid! I *know* what you were doing in there!" Barry stood with his face pressed up against the window of the holding trailer, his crazed eyes and twisted smile radiated from behind the dirty glass. Sullivan was already walking over to the trailer before Nash could even look for him to help.

"Dead, dead, dead. You'll all be dead!" squealed Barry as Sullivan opened the door and stepped inside, leaving it open as he quickly bound Barry with duct tape before he placed a strip across his mouth. Barry giggled behind the tape as Sullivan closed and locked the door.

"Thank you," said Nash as Sullivan walked away.

Melissa opened the door of their RV and stepped out into the muggy afternoon air, her hair moist in the unrelenting wet heat. She pulled it back into a damp ponytail and smiled at Nash as he watched.

"I'll be at the truck," she said as she kissed him on the cheek and ran off to the food truck. He loved how gracefully she moved, even in the muddy ground that he knew he'd easily slip and fall in if he'd try to run at her speed.

An engine roared to life behind him as Sullivan maneuvered the last of the RVs into position along the fence. Most of the RVs were now parked directly behind the other, leaving as little space between them as possible. Sullivan stepped out and closed the door.

"Can you gather the security team for me and meet in the war room? We have some things to talk about."

"No problem," said Nash.

The inside of the war room was hotter than normal, the humidity descending upon the Fort with a vengeance. They each took their seat, but left the door zipped open in hopes that it would cool the temperature inside. Nash walked in with Melissa and looked to Sullivan for his approval for her to be there, which he nodded in silent agreement.

"We have a couple serious things to discuss. First, we need to decide what to do with Cole." The group sat silent. "The way I see it, we have two options. We leave him be and let him roam, or we put him to rest."

"Can't we bring him in here? Let him stay with us?" asked Melissa as she tried her hardest to provide an alternative to the two harsh options.

"I thought about that too, and I don't think it's a good idea. He's not in good shape."

"He's right," said Nash, taking her hand into his under the table. "His body is all torn up and we all know that slowpokes don't eat so they deteriorate quickly. He'd wither away before our eyes."

"Exactly," said Sullivan solemnly. "I personally feel he should get a proper funeral, just like Eliza did. Does anyone object to that?" Nobody spoke so the matter was silently decided.

"After the meeting is over, I will tend to him and get his grave ready. We'll have the funeral before nightfall."

"What do we do about the prisoner?" Scott asked in an effort to change the subject.

"I'll be taking him off site to interrogate him later tonight. I don't want him thinking he has an audience so I'll be taking him to an old shack about a half-mile down the creek. I'll need a security detail with me to guard the area while I'm out there. Scott, I was hoping you could spearhead that for me."

"Of course," he said. "But why at night? Wouldn't it be safer in the daylight?"

"Barry's people are using infected arrows as weapons, so doing this at night takes that advantage away from them if they come looking for him. Nash, Scott and Stu, I need you to set up walkways across each RV by sundown. Between the three of you, I'm sure it's doable. Use whatever materials we have around and make them as sturdy as possible."

"Will do, chief," said Stu as he tapped his fingers nervously on the table.

"Dianna," Sullivan said, "Meghan, are you comfortable letting the group know about our plan for Cole?"

"Of course," said Dianna, wiping tears off her cheeks.

The group left the war room, each off on their way to the task ahead. Nash watched as Sullivan disappeared into Cole's RV and reappeared with a small bundle before he left the Fort with a shovel. Sullivan's shoulders were slumped, the weight of the current situation rested firmly on him as he made his way to bury another one of his friends.

Nash, Stu, and Scott all collected wood and tools from the camp. The first walkway was constructed within a half hour and the rest of them quickly came together as the three of them worked silently. Before they finished Nash ran along the top of each RV and made sure all of the walkways were secure before he climbed down.

"This was a really smart idea," said Scott as they stood together admiring their handiwork.

"I'm going to check in with Sullivan," said Nash. "See what else he needs."

"I'll join you," said Stu using his bandana to wipe sweat from his forehead.

Scott made his exit silently, and disappeared to prepare with Meghan for the interrogation later. The situation at hand was weighing heavy on everyone in camp and Nash could see the stress and fear in each resident's posture.

Thunder rolled in the distance as Nash and Stu exited the Fort and made their way to the gravesite. The ground was wet and slippery, which forced them to move slowly to avoid falling down or twisting their ankles. They reached the clearing where the group had met to bury Eliza the day before, an empty grave now dug beside hers, Sullivan no where to be seen.

"I can't believe they're gone," said Stu. "I feel like things are falling apart."

"He'll think of something," said Nash. "You've trusted him this far, he'll get us through this too."

"I do trust him, and that'll never change. We've just never dealt with anything like this before." Silently, Stu surveyed all the graves before them with his arms crossed over his chest. "This burial site is far too crowded for my liking."

The two of them made their way as quickly as they could to the creek, the sound of thunder nipped at their heels. The dreadlocked slowpoke smiled as they approached the creek banks, their welcome party. Sullivan was crouched down beside Cole's body. The arrow was gone and Sullivan had dressed him a new shirt. There were strips of bloody cloths collected neatly in a pile while Sullivan silently prepared Cole for burial. Stu placed his hand on Sullivan's shoulder as the three of them gazed down at their friend.

"Nash," said Sullivan, pausing for a moment before he continued. "Can you have Dianna get everyone moving to the burial site now? Stu and I will bring Cole."

Without saying a word, Nash walked back to the Fort. Everyone was gathered quickly and met at the front of the gate, ready to say goodbye to Cole. Just like Eliza's, not everyone joined in the march, but a great majority of the group attended. Most of those who stayed behind were fearful of leaving the Treefort's walls.

The sounds of mourning filled the woods as Sullivan and Stu each took an end of the sheet and lowered Cole's body into the ground.

Sullivan's jaw was clenched tightly as he attempted to keep his emotions in check. His hands shook slightly so Nash offered to take the shovel but was waved away. Stu placed the last shovelful on top as Sullivan planted the standard cross into the ground at the head of the grave, Cole's name painted across the front. They all stood in silence, mourning their collective loss.

"Scott, can you be ready to move at sundown?" asked Sullivan, breaking the silence.

"Yes. Meghan and I will both go with you."

Sullivan nodded once and made his way back to the Fort, Dianna's hand in his.

The sun set quickly as Nash aimlessly wandered throughout the camp, not quite knowing what to do as the evening descended on them. It was one of the first times since he had gotten there that he truly had nothing to do. The sound of the holding trailer's door swinging open drew his attention as he watched Sullivan step inside and come back out with Barry in tow. He could hear Barry's muffled giggling. Barry toppled to the ground, refusing to cooperate as Sullivan led him forward.

Without breaking stride, Sullivan scooped him up and slung him over his shoulder. Barry kicked wildly, giggling and coughing as best he could as the people in the Fort watched him be carried away into the night.

"Sully," Dianna whispered, moving towards him, wringing her hands.

"We'll be careful," Sullivan whispered before he kissed her softly on the lips.

Barry locked eyes with Dianna, a sinister smile on his mouth behind the duct tape. There was an eerie promise there that Dianna couldn't ignore. Fear blossomed anew in her chest as she watched the love of her life leave the Fort, death carried on his shoulders.

Chapter 16

The moon cast an eerie glow through the trees as they moved silently through the dark woods. Sullivan led the way, holding Barry by the arm with a knife trained on him with the other hand. Scott and Meghan followed closed behind, keeping their ears trained against the silent woods. Barry continued to giggle wildly as the dark silhouette of the shack slowly came into view.

"Stay alert," whispered Sullivan as they came to a stop outside the shack. "If you so much as have a feeling something is not right, let me know."

"Will do," said Scott as Sullivan opened the door and disappeared inside with Barry.

Sullivan quickly secured Barry to an old wooden chair before turning and shutting the door. He switched on a lantern and hanging from a hook on the ceiling, illuminating the windowless shack in an eerie glow. Sullivan stood in front of Barry, looking down at the giggling lunatic.

"I need your assurance that if I take off this tape, you're not going to cause a fuss," said Sullivan as he sternly looked into Barry's crazed eyes. "I'm going to take off the tape to talk. If you're loud, I will put it back on and cause you pain. If I think you're getting out of control, I'll kill you."

He pulled out a long Bowie knife, the cold metal reflecting the lantern's light. He was surprised when Barry stopped giggling at the sight of the blade and his eyes met Sullivan's with a touch of fear. He ripped the tape off Barry's mouth, peeling skin and hair with it as Barry grunted in pain.

"What makes you think I'm going to tell you anything?" Barry hissed. "Do you know what he would do to me if I told you his secrets?"

"I've already told you what will happen if you don't. The choice is yours."

"I'd rather die by your knife than at *His* hand as a traitor."

"Tell me about him," said Sullivan. Barry's eyes met his as a grin stretched across his face.

"He's going to kill you, I can tell you that. As for the rest of your group, as long as they fall in line, they'll be fine. He has plenty of room for you all at his mansion. You though; no, no, no…you're a goner!"

"So he lives in a mansion?" asked Sullivan as he tried to extract as much information as he could while he fought the urge to plunge his knife into Barry's chest.

"You'll find out soon enough. Well, you won't. Someone who'll for *sure* see the Mansion is that pretty little blonde you've got stored back at your campsite. She'll fit in quite nice." His eyes twinkled with madness as he spoke. "Pretty girls like her get the *royal* treatment under his watch!"

"What are these?" asked Sullivan, taking control of the conversation as he pointed to the red strip around his wrist. "Why are we finding so many of the dead wearing them?"

"She's a pretty little thing, isn't she? What do you think she tastes like?" he asked. "She looks delightfully tasty to me, but you never know. Might not be quite, *ripe*."

"Tell me about the strip on your wrist," said Sullivan, his fingers turning white as they gripped his knife tightly.

"You've thought about it, don't pretend you haven't. A man your size, you'd probably kill her!" He let out a loud chuckle at the thought. "You're better suited for that huge bitch you smooched when we left. She definitely won't see the Mansion. I'll kill her myself when he comes for you."

Sullivan lurched forward and buried the blade of his knife into Barry's left lung. Blood poured from the wound as Barry let out a yelp, but not once did he divert his gaze from Sullivan's. Sullivan watched the look of madness in his eyes as he smiled through the pain, giggling and coughing harshly as his lung quickly filled with blood. His breath turned into a gargling wheeze as blood dribbled from his mouth. He laughed one time, and uttered one last threat.

"He's coming to get you…"

Scott opened the door and peered in, already knowing what had happened by the sounds. Sullivan stood over Barry's lifeless, hunched body, his fingers still wrapped around the handle of the knife.

"He's gone," said Sullivan, eyes trained on the now blood soaked torso. "He's gone, Scott."

"I know, Sully," he said as he pulled Sullivan's hand away from the knife and guided him out of the shack. "It's okay, we heard it all. You weren't gonna get anything from him."

"What do we do with him?" asked Meghan as she looked at Barry's bloodied body from the door of the shack. Sullivan nudged her away as he reentered, grabbed Barry by his still bound wrists, and dragged him into the dark. Scott and Meghan stood motionless, listening to the sound of Barry being dragged through the leaves followed by a thud as Sullivan released him.

"Fuck him," he said as he rejoined Scott and Meghan. "He doesn't get a funeral. He can rot."

They walked back to the Treefort in silence. Barry's interrogation hadn't given them a lot to go by, hardly anything really. Only that there was a Mansion, and whoever *he* was, was coming. Sullivan wasn't sure if *he* knew where they were or not.

"*Where is he?*" Dianna asked in a panic.

"Dead," said Sullivan and marched away toward his RV to barricade himself for the night.

Barry's death was well received; Barry was the murderer of two of their friends and most everyone felt more at ease with him gone for good.

The group retired to their RVs earlier than most nights and after hours of trying, Nash finally fell asleep, Melissa tossing and turning beside him, trapped in a faraway nightmare. His sleep was dreamless, but not restful, as if the Duncan-howler was just on the outskirts of his slumber. He woke to the morning light to find Melissa already gone. Through the windows he could see Sullivan was talking with a small group of people who wore black riot gear he hadn't seen before. He dressed quickly and jumped from the RV to join them.

Four men, whom he'd not had the chance to meet yet, stood dressed in the gear, each with a rifle strapped to their back and a clear riot shield with the word POLICE printed across the front. They wore a matching helmet with a clear faceguard.

"Those are new," said Nash, looking at the riot gear as the men walked away.

"We've had the gear for a while but never really felt we had use for it. Until now anyway," he said as he watched the men climb the ladders to get on top of the RVs. There were two men on each line of RVs and they walked back and forth as they surveyed the area outside the Fort.

"I wouldn't mind helping out with this," said Nash as he watched the guards on top of the RVs.

"Actually, I had something else in mind for you. I want you outside the walls again."

"I thought we were putting a stop to that."

"I've seen the way you are outside the fence. I can tell that you and Duncan spent a lot of time on the road and you know what you're doing. You and Scott are going to be our only away team, until I've vetted some of the others. Just once a day, I want the two of you to do a quick patrol of the area, only after the sentinels have given you the okay to go."

"You like giving things names around here, don't you?" asked Nash with a smile. Sullivan looked up at the four sentinels.

"I guess I do," he said. "Don't go at the same time every day, either. If someone is out there watching, I don't want them catching wind of a routine."

"I assume you're in the loop now," said Scott as he walked up to the two of them. "Seems quiet, I was up there earlier. Wanna do a sweep?"

"For sure," said Nash, ready to get back outside to help in the security effort.

The two of them walked together to the armory to check out their weapons. Mark let them in with a toothless grin as the typical smell of body odor invaded their senses. Nash grabbed his favorite knife, as well as a handgun and began to clip it to his waist.

"Here," said Scott, handing Nash a large rifle. "Sullivan wants us to be armed to the teeth out there. Position of power should we run into any trouble."

Nash reluctantly took the rifle in his hands and hung it around his back like he'd always seen Sullivan do; he slumped slightly, surprised by its weight.

"You'll get used to it," said Scott with a smile.

"Do you think Sullivan would let me hang on to this knife?" asked Nash as he held it in front of him.

"I've noticed you like that one. Just keep it. I'll let Mark know that it's yours now."

He sheathed the knife and stepped out of the hot trailer and back into Mark's foul smell. Mark crossed the knife off of his list and smiled at Nash with a thumbs up. Scott opened up a large

154

compartment attached to the back of the armory trailer and pulled out more riot gear.

"He wants us wearing these when we're outside," he said as he handed Nash a collection of protective gear. It was a full set for both of them, designed to protect their chest, arms, back, and legs. They both brushed off dust from the face guards before they situated the equipment on their heads. Nash gave Melissa a salute as he walked, which made her smile nervously as she watched them walk toward the front gate. He knew she wasn't a fan of him leaving the Fort, no matter how much protective gear he wore, but part of keeping his promise to her was keeping the Fort safe.

"Be careful, you two," said Dianna as she shut the gate behind them.

As usual, the woods around the Fort were relatively calm. The sounds of birds singing in the sunlight echoed through the trees as they moved together silently, holding their rifles in front of them as they scanned the trees. Considering most of their previous trips had led them to the creek, they decided to branch off in another direction to explore other areas. After having walked for twenty minutes, they were glad they did.

They came across a small camouflaged tent with the front flaps left open, softly blowing in the breeze. It was situated behind a large tree, which blocked its view from the direction of the Treefort.

"How in the hell did we miss this," said Scott as he leaned forward to look inside. The tent was filled with empty cans of food and water bottles, scattered messily overtop a dirty sleeping bag. A quiver full of clean arrows sat on the ground next to an old bow and a canteen. Scott grabbed the canteen and spilled the contents out onto the ground, creating a thick pool of crimson blood.

"This is deranged," said Scott as he threw the canteen into the woods.

"I guess we have an answer to who the sniper was when I first got here," said Nash when he opened up the flaps of the tent and revealed a rifle laying on the ground.

"Sullivan will be glad to hear that, at least," said Scott as he picked up the gun and inspected it.

"Scott, look," said Nash, his eyes fixed on the back corner of the tent.

The two of them looked in silence at an old walkie-talkie that laid near the head of the sleeping bag. Nash looked around the inside of the tent to make sure there wasn't a trap set he couldn't see before he reached in and grabbed the radio. The two stood with it between them as they looked at the multiple knobs on its face.

"Whoever was leading Barry's group, he knows where we are." Scott turned the walkie-talkie over in his hands.

"Should we turn it on?" asked Nash.

"No," said Scott. "We need to take it back to Sullivan and let him decide. This is big, Nash. They've been watching us."

Before they headed back, the two of them did a large sweep of the area around the Fort and ended at the creek for a final check. The number of slowpokes had thinned out dramatically, and only three of them now stood along the water. The dreadlocked slowpoke stood idle as usual.

"Every damn time I see him, I inevitably have a nightmare that night," said Scott as the two of them made their way back to the Fort.

The sentinels who were perched atop the RVs came into view as Nash and Scott approached the fence. One of them gave a nod to the guys, and he signaled to Dianna that they had returned. She opened the gate for them and knew immediately from their demeanor that they'd found something in the woods.

"What is it?" she said as she secured the locks behind them.

"Something big," said Scott. "Where's Sully."

Dianna pointed toward the middle of the Fort, where they could see Sullivan as he played a game of checkers with a teenage boy. They walked toward Sullivan with the radio hidden discreetly inside Scott's side-bag. Sullivan put his hand up to Scott and Nash as they approached and let them know that he had no intention of leaving the game until it was finished. He made a move and the kid excitedly jumped two of his pieces, which ended the game in a fit of excitement.

"You got me again!" yelled Sullivan, clearly having let the kid win to move on to more serious matters. "Good game, kid. We'll play again tomorrow."

The teenager took off into the center of the Fort with a smile on his face and the checkerboard in hand ready to find a new opponent.

"We found something big," said Scott as he pulled the radio out of his bag and handed it to Sullivan.

"Where did you find this?" he asked as he looked down at the radio in Scott's hand.

"It was in a tent about twenty minutes' walk from here," said Nash. "Judging from the garbage inside, Barry must have been there awhile."

"We found another bow with arrows and a canteen of blood," said Scott and pointed to the bow and arrows slung around Nash's shoulders with the rifle.

Sullivan took the radio and turned it over in his hands. "Something, indeed. This is military-grade. It reaches for miles." He placed his fingers on the knob to switch it on, then thought better of it. "Let's head to the war room."

The three of them walked together to the war room, waving the other members in before they disappeared inside. Sullivan switched on a lantern and hung it from the top of the tent as it bathed the inside of the war room with artificial light. He took his seat at the head of the table and placed the radio in front of him.

"Nash and Scott found this in a tent nearby. It looks like it was Barry's."

"Have you turned it on yet?" asked Dianna, her eye contact was unwavering from the scuffed up army radio.

"No," said Sullivan. "That's why I brought you all in here. I'm assuming Barry's group knows where we are but if by chance they don't, my fear is that whoever is at the other end of this thing will be able to find our location by us using it."

"Is that possible?" asked Meghan.

"Very much so."

They all stared in silence as each of them were unsure of what to do.

"We turn this on and our world gets a lot bigger," said Stu. "Given what's been going on lately, I don't know that's necessarily a good thing."

"We could turn it on and just listen," said Meghan. "We don't even need to say anything."

"I don't feel comfortable with it being on," said Scott. "Sullivan is right. While they probably already know where we are, it's not a sure thing. It's a big chance we'd be taking."

"We found this in Barry's tent," interjected Nash. "I'm not trying to advocate either way, but it's pretty clear whoever's out there more than likely already knows where we are. Seems to me that we don't lose anything by turning it on."

They sat again in silence and evaluated the possible repercussions of flipping the switch. The air weighed heavy on them in the dimly lit war room with beads of sweat on their foreheads. The silence was deafening as they viewed the item of their possible demise. It felt as if the air was sucked from the room as Sullivan reached forward and turned the knob to ON.

A soft, static hum radiated from the beat up radio.

Chapter 17

A month after Sullivan switched on the radio, Nash woke up beside Melissa as he had every morning since. They had been up late the night before, sitting at the campfire with Scott and Meghan as they told stories and laughed late into the night. The mood around camp had become increasingly tense as time went by, each of them trying to live their lives while trying to stay vigilant.

He slid out of bed quietly so as to not disturb Melissa and looked at the small watch beside their bed. He was alarmed to find that it was just past noon, later than he'd slept since his first days of living at the Treefort. He yawned quietly and stretched his arms toward the ceiling, watching as Melissa slept under the light sheet they used every night. He thought about waking her but decided against it, knowing she needed the sleep just as much as he did. Most days she was awake before him and nuzzled him awake; some days they would make love, other days they would lay in bed and talk. They typically ended each day the same way, a routine that Nash was increasingly happy to have settled into.

He stepped out into the warm afternoon air as people moved about the camp like every morning before. He strolled over to the food truck and saw a small line of people waiting outside for their lunch. An older woman named Sarah stood inside, handing increasingly smaller packages of food and water to the people as their supplies began to dwindle. Sarah had volunteered to help Melissa with her duties and now the two of them alternated days, giving Melissa a much-needed break from the demand of the camp's food needs.

He grabbed their food packs and smiled at Sarah as he noticed the two chocolate bars she'd snuck inside. As he passed by, Nash noticed Sullivan alone in the war room. He had his feet up on the table as he leaned back in his seat. The radio sat in front of him and hummed its soft, almost silent, static. He shook his head as he met Nash's gaze, his arms folded across his chest.

This had become a daily routine for Sullivan, everyday around noon since the day he'd first switched on the radio, and again just before dusk, hoping to find some sort of life on the other end but each session ended in silent frustration. There were multiple channels he could have searched but he'd decided to stay on the same channel it was set to when he twisted the knob one month ago.

"You were up late last night. I could hear the four of you talking and laughing before I went to sleep."

"Sorry," said Nash as he stood at the opening of the war room. "I hope we didn't keep you up."

"No, not at all," he said before he stood and stretched his arms above his head. "It's a good message to everyone around here. We don't know when, or if, anyone will be coming for us. Everyone just needs to go on their way and act normal. We are as prepared as we can be."

Sullivan was right. In the month that had passed, he had expressed to everyone the danger that they were in and educated them as best he could in how to protect themselves. He'd weapon trained most of them and went over emergency procedures in the event that someone did show up at their doorstep.

As prepared and safe of an environment he had tried to create, there were still those who felt unsafe and left the Fort. Three families in total, equaling nine people, left the Fort to fend for themselves outside the woods. Sullivan and Stu had met with them on several occasions and pleaded with them to stay, but in the end they believed they were no longer safe inside the Treefort.

Their departure weighed heavy on Sullivan's mind and robbed him of multiple nights' sleep as he dwelled on their departures.

"Have you ever thought about leaving?" asked Nash as Sullivan sat back in his chair. "I mean, all of us could leave and find a new place to live."

Sullivan looked passed Nash into the distance and ran his fingers through his thick beard as Nash stood in front of him, fearing he'd asked the wrong question.

"The thought's crossed my mind," he said finally. "I think we're safer here though. I feel like we can protect everyone here more than we could out on the open road." He paused a moment more, and stroked his beard again. "I'm not giving up on this place."

Nash walked back to the RV, the door was open so he stepped inside to see Melissa dressed and pulling her hair back into a ponytail. He placed her food package on the bed beside her and leaned up against the wall of the RV, staring at her with a wide smile.

"Can I help you?" she asked with a smile.

"Nope," he said as he ripped open his chocolate bar. "You just look nice this morning."

"Blah! I look like a wreck," she said but still smiled from the compliment. "I see Sarah was good to you this morning."

Nash held up the chocolate bar and smiled with brown covered teeth, which made her giggle. "There's one for you too."

Melissa sat beside him, opening up her own chocolate bar. "Anything on the radio?" she asked. Nash shook his head.

"If I were them, once Barry was out of contact, I would have switched channels."

"Maybe try changing the channel then? I hate not hearing anything. The waiting is scarier than knowing something is coming."

"Maybe—" Nash said, opening a water bottle. "That's not my call though."

There was a knock on the door, ending their conversation.

"We went out a little later yesterday," Scott said, when Nash opened the door. "How do you feel about heading out soon to do our sweep?"

"Whenever you're ready," said Nash as he finished his bottle of water.

"Suit up! I'll meet you at the gate in ten."

Nash nodded and stepped back into the RV to put on his riot gear.

"You should have woken me up this morning," Melisa said from the bed.

"Trust me, I wanted to. You were obviously tired so I let you sleep in." He attached his vest around his chest and hugged her tightly.

"Tonight then," she said as she nuzzled her head into his neck.

He could see Scott waiting outside with his riot gear already on and his rifle slung around his back. Nash quickly placed the helmet on his head and grabbed the quiver of arrows and his bow. Melissa leaned up and kissed the faceguard of his helmet, which left a lip smudge on the front of the protective cover.

"Be safe," she said, as she did everyday he went outside the gate.

****

Scott and Nash moved through the woods methodically. Nash held his bow at his side, ready to fire at any kind of animal that crossed their path. It didn't take long for him to find a rabbit and he sent an arrow quickly through its small body. He'd become skilled with the bow over the last month and everyone was always thankful for the fresh meat he brought back. Before their sweep was done, Nash had killed three more rabbits, enough for a hearty stew residents could enjoy.

Just like every day since they discovered Barry's tent, they found nothing of concern in the woods. The birds in the trees were extra loud as they moved through the forest, something that happened every so often and always made Nash smile. One of the reasons he loved being outside the Fort was the simple, consistent sound of nature. Being in the Fort didn't completely drown out the sounds, but having other people around, it was easy to ignore the noises of the woods around them.

As usual, the dreadlocked slowpoke stood guard at the creek and watched with a smile as Nash and Scott waved at him. Scott had taken to calling him Sammy. Nash loved going on sweeps of the woods but enjoyed their trips to the creek the most. The sound of the rippling water filled their ears as the sun broke through the trees and warmed their faces. In a safer time, he would have taken Melissa there, but with the threat of poisonous arrows, he knew it wasn't an option.

They made their way back to the Fort with Nash's dead rabbits in tow. Stu was skilled at cooking game animals. He happily took the rabbits at the gate and disappeared to prepare them. He'd gotten used to Nash returning with meat and met them at the gate after most runs, a bag of spices and seasonings in his hand and a smile on his face.

"Good sweep today, bud," said Scott and extended his hand in the air for a high five. "Looks like she's waitin' for you."

The two of them could see that Melissa sat at the fire while she read a book with her feet up on an empty chair. On the days that Sarah worked the food truck, she and Nash would often be found around the fire as they sat close together and read independently.

"Looks that way," said Nash with a smile as he opened his RV door and jumped inside.

He quickly took off his riot gear and made his way to the fire with his book in tow. She was completely engrossed in the story that she was reading as he leaned in and surprised her with a kiss. He sat next to her and propped his feet up on the same chair with her. Without a word, the two of them sat comfortably beside each other and read for the remainder of the afternoon. Three quarters of the way through his book, Nash fell asleep and let the afternoon pass by as Melissa continued reading beside him.

"Finished mine!" yelled Melissa, jolting Nash awake and throwing her book at him. "You don't have much sun left, chump," she said, taunting him because she finished her book first.

It was a game between the two of them to see who finished a book first; a game, which Melissa regularly won. She stared at him with a smile and repeatedly pushed his feet off the chair in an effort to annoy him as he hurriedly tried to complete his book before the sun set. He finished quickly and flung it at her with a smile as other people began to crowd around the fire like they did every night.

Stu joined them at the fire with the prepared rabbits. Nash always enjoyed being around Stu while he cooked. Seeing the spices crackle on the meat while it heated and filled the air with the delicious smell that he loved so much. Nash and Duncan rarely had meat while on the road together and survived mostly on prepackaged foods they'd collected along their way. Neither of them had really known how to hunt, which left them at a disadvantage in a world full of flourishing wildlife. He was proud of himself for learning how to use the bow. Sullivan placed one of his large hands on Nash's shoulder from behind and startled him as he talked with Melissa.

"Is it okay if I separate the two of you for a moment?" he said with a smile, Melissa chuckling at Nash's surprise.

"Of course," she said. "He may need to change his pants though."

"Oh very funny," said Nash, who stood and followed Sullivan.

"I wanted to go over some ideas for tomorrow's sweep of the woods."

"Of course," said Nash as they entered the war room. Nash greatly valued his role in the Fort and loved being included in the security meetings. Scott was already inside and was at the table with a couple lanterns. Sullivan sat at the head of the table as usual and flicked the radio on for his nightly surveillance of the channel.

"How are things out there? I know you tell me things right away but I haven't heard much from the two of you lately."

"Things have been quiet," said Scott as Nash nodded in agreement. "We haven't seen a thing. Even the slowpokes down at the creek have pretty much vacated, except, of course, for Sammy and a few of his friends."

"Sammy? Is that what we're calling him now?" asked Sullivan and raised his eyebrows in the darkened tent.

"It's easier," said Scott. "I don't know what's crazier, the fact that I say hi to him every day, or the fact that I felt I had to give him a name." It was an odd feeling, this camaraderie they had with the slowpoke.

"Well, I was wondering if the two of you could use a break. I'm thinking about adding another team to outside detail. You two would alternate with them so you'd only have to be out there every other day."

Nash and Scott didn't necessarily need a break and hadn't spent much time considering the option. They'd grown to enjoy their time together outside.

"Obviously, we could have your day off coincide with Melissa's day off at the truck," said Sullivan.

The lighthearted tone of their conversation was stripped away as the radio squawked for the first time in a month. The three of them stared at it with wide eyes and nerves on end as they waited for another break in the soft humming.

"What do we do?" asked Nash as the hairs on his arms stuck straight up. Without hesitation, Sullivan grabbed the radio and squeeze the transmit button.

"We know you're there," he said and released the button to another squawk.

They sat and listened to the humming sound of the radio, awaiting a response from whoever was on the other end. They held up another minute before Sullivan hit the transmit button again.

"Who's there? Answer me." More silence as they sat in the artificial light of the war room. It released another squawk, followed by silence as the person on the other end held down the transmit switch.

"Rather demanding, seeing how I've got the high ground. With whom am I speaking to?" said the voice on the other end, followed by another squawk and the familiar hum of static.

"Seeing how I hailed you, I think it's common courtesy you identify yourself first," said Sullivan.

Stu poked his head in and saw that Sullivan was talking on the radio and left quickly and returned with Dianna and Meghan. They came in and sat around the table, waiting to be clued in on what was happening. Nash watched Melissa from where he was sitting. She looked happy as she watched the fire and laughed with some of the others that sat with her, right before Dianna zipped the tent flaps shut and lowered herself next to him.

"Whatever this is, they don't need to hear it," she whispered to Nash. "Let them be happy, while they still can."

The radio squawked.

"My name is Fletcher Crawford. Whom am I speaking with?"

"Don't tell him," said Dianna, softly.

"If this is who we think it is, he already knows everything about us," Sullivan said. "I think it's best we stay as honest as possible." He squeezed the transmitter. "You're speaking with Sullivan Grant."

"He's close," said Sullivan to the group. "His voice is crystal clear." Each of them seemed to feel themselves shrink as they basked in the nervous energy bottled inside the war room. Sullivan squeezed the transmitter again. "What do you want from us, Mr. Crawford?"

"Please, call me Fletcher. I get the sense that you're a smart man, Sullivan. I assume you've already determined that I'm closer to your location than you're probably comfortable with. Am I correct?" Sullivan sat silent with his finger on the transmit trigger but not squeezing it. "I want your allegiance. If I can't have that, I want your lives. It's that simple," said the voice. He paused, silent as he held the transmitter. "Here's how this is going to work. Tomorrow, at noon, all your people have the opportunity to join my family. All they have to do is walk out of your gates and make their way through the woods to the dirt road behind your camp. As long as they have something of value in tow, they'll be welcomed into my family with open arms. For those of you not interested in that, we'll be by later in the day to have a meet and greet."

The voice stopped and the radio returned to the static hum they'd listened to over the last month. Meghan got up from her seat and left the war room. She barely got the doors unzipped before she vomited onto the ground outside. Scott didn't follow after her, but sat shell-shocked in his seat.

"We'll leave. You can have everything inside the fence," said Sullivan as he tried not to sound like he was pleading. The voice didn't respond for a few moments and each of them eagerly awaited the reply.

"Any of your people try and venture off on their own will be killed on sight. Your people can live with me or die with you. Those are your options."

"Let's meet and talk about this," said Sullivan his knuckles ghost-white around the radio. "What's your location?"

They listened to the hum of the radio and waited for a response that would never come. They sat in silence for a half hour before Sullivan stood and slammed the radio onto the ground with a ferocious growl, which sent pieces of plastic and metal into the air.

"We fight," said Stu. "We've built something here, and we should defend it."

"That's not our call to make, Stu. We have families here to worry about. We don't know what we're dealing with and I can't lead us all blind into a fight we don't know we can win."

"How can someone be so calculated?" asked Dianna. "It's like we're nothing but numbers to him."

"We have been incredibly lucky, hiding here in the woods and under the radar from everyone. I always knew it was a matter of time before we dealt with another group, but I never thought it would be like this. I never thought it would *end* like this."

"Who says it's the end?" yelled Stu as he stood and slammed his fists onto the table. "Why are you giving up so easily?"

"Look around, Stu," said Sullivan, his voice weighted with sadness. "We aren't ready for a battle. We're a group filled with families, kids, and the elderly. I tend to think his offer is real."

"*Why the hell would you believe him?*" yelled Stu, louder than his original outburst. "*He's a lunatic!*"

"If he wanted us dead, he could've marched in here at night and killed us all," said Nash. "He's been watching us for a while. He knows what he's dealing with and he's calculated his odds. I'm with Sullivan on this one." Stu sat down and fumed.

"We can't waste any time here. I'm going to go brief the group. Those that want to go will be encouraged to go. Those that want to stay and fight will be allowed to. It's not my place to force anyone here to do anything either way. The Treefort was always about safety and freedom and I can't provide either of those here any longer."

The group remained still as tears flowed from Dianna and Scott's eyes. Nobody objected to Sullivan's plan. They opened up the flaps of the war room and found Melissa hunched over Meghan, who sat on the ground with her arms wrapped around her knees. The others around camp watched in silence as the security team shuffled out of the war room.

"If any of you know of people who are asleep, please go wake them and bring them to the fire," said Sullivan loudly to the Fort. It was still early in the evening and most everyone was still awake, but still some people went to their RV and brought back a sleepy friend or family member. Melissa slid her hand into Nash's as the two walked to the fire where Sullivan and the rest of the inhabitants had joined together.

"I love all of you," said Sullivan, his soft voice echoing across the silent Fort. The spaces in between his words were filled with nothing but the sounds of crickets and the aggressive crackling of the fire. He wiped tears from his eyes as he continued to speak. "The radio we found in Barry's tent last month finally went live tonight and each of us has a very personal decision to make by morning."

Sullivan went on to explain the conversation he'd had with the stranger named Fletcher Crawford. He explained all the points that had been discussed in the war room and gave as much information as he possibly could before they made their decision. The group was immediately broken into two camps; those who were brought to tears and those who bubbled with anger.

"We stay and fight! All of us!" said a man who sat at the edge of the fire. Many others stood and cheered in agreement, only to be met by Sullivan's hands in the air to quiet them.

"I urge you, please think past your emotions and make the best call for you and yours. Do not let loyalty to me, or to this place, cloud your judgment in anyway. Those who would like to leave, and I urge you *all* to take Fletcher up on his offer, will be given a package of goods to bring to his group. Your choice to leave the Fort will not be looked upon as abandonment or cowardice. This is about survival, and that is what I want for all of you. If there are any of you who wish to stay behind and fight, I will be here. If there is any chance that we can keep this place alive, I will be here to exploit it, but I do not in any way mean for any of you to follow me into this madness."

The group disbanded for the most part and returned to their RVs in tears to map out their decisions. The security team stayed around the fire and mulled over their own best course of action. Melissa stayed at Nash's side and held his hand tightly while she leaned against him as she softly wept.

"You're leaving with the Fletcher group tomorrow," said Sullivan to Dianna as she rested her head on his broad shoulder.

"Like hell I am!" she said as she pushed away from him in shock.

"The group leaving tomorrow is going to need someone to guide them and keep things steady with the transition. More importantly, I love you too much to have you here when the shit hits the fan."

Tears welled in her eyes upon the realization that he was right. She knew he couldn't go to Fletcher; as the leader of the Treefort, he'd be killed on sight. They all knew that a man like Fletcher would never let another group's leader live among his community, which made Sullivan's decision to stay behind and fight for the Treefort an easy one. Without question, Stu opted to stay behind and fight with Sullivan, as did Meghan and Scott.

"I want the two of you to go," said Sullivan to Nash and Melissa who sat quietly across the fire from him.

"That's not your decision to make," said Melissa as Nash sat beside her in silence.

"Melissa, I'm serious. People who stay behind will more than likely be killed. I think we all know this," said Sullivan. The group nodded in solemn agreement. "It would be horribly irresponsible of me to allow the two of you to stay behind."

"I won't allow it," said Dianna. "I'll drag the two of you out of here by your ears if I have to."

Nash and Melissa stood together, not saying a word as they turned and walked back to their RV in tears. They crawled into bed together, faces wet as they held each other long into the night.

"They're right. You know they're right," said Nash into the darkness.

"I know," she said softly as a fresh stream of tears flowed over her cheeks.

Not a single member of the Fort slept that night. By dawn, everyone was outside their RVs as they cried and said their goodbyes. In total, about three quarters of the group inside the Fort decided to leave, Melissa and Nash included. Nash wanted nothing more than to have fought alongside Sullivan but he knew it would mean certain death. Fighting a battle against an unknown enemy wasn't part of the silent promise he'd made Melissa.

The food truck was left open for anyone who wanted to take from it, but it sat untouched all morning as people huddled together around the fire, scared of what was to come. The people who had chosen to stay and fight had taken to the armory and were fitted with weapons and riot gear. It was mostly single, younger men who volunteered to stay, hoping to stand against Fletcher's men to save the Treefort.

Sullivan and Dianna silently pieced together packages of goods for each person who left the Fort to bring with them, as per Fletcher's deal. Everything, with the exception of the riot gear and weapons being used, was sent away.

"There has to be another way," whispered Dianna as she packed food into duffle bags and wept softly.

"I wish there were. I spent the whole night thinking of what to do," said Sullivan. He placed his bag down and grabbed her by her shoulders. "I will make it back to you. I'll fight for as long as I can, but if things get rough, I will call for a retreat. This isn't goodbye."

Dianna zipped up the final duffle bag as Sullivan pulled her in for a tight hug. They both knew that his words, as comforting as he had intended them to be, were only that; words. Sullivan went into the afternoon knowing that what he had built would fall, as well as himself and his group of fighters. It was the end, and with as much gusto as he could manage, he looked directly into his destiny and felt no fear for himself. Sullivan stood at the front gate and held Dianna while the rest of the people leaving crowded around to say their goodbyes. Sullivan kissed her softly and embraced her in his broad arms as her tears wet his beard.

"I will always love you," he whispered to her as he stared into her red and glassy eyes. He could have stared at her forever, but they let go and she made her way through the gate and allowed the others to say their goodbyes to him. Nash and

Melissa were last to get to Sullivan, as the rest of the leaving party waited on the outside with Dianna. Melissa fell into his arms, and sobbed loudly onto his chest as he held her close. Nash looked on in sadness as tears welled in his own eyes as he watched. Stu, Scott, and Meghan stood with Nash, shell-shocked as they thought about the task at hand.

Melissa let go of Sullivan without saying a word and walked through the gate as she continued to sob. Nash hugged Sullivan and both of them patted each other's back hard as they embraced.

"Thank you for everything," said Nash as he tried not to be overly emotional.

"You've a survivor, kid," he said. "I know you'll be okay." They let go of each other and shook hands firmly. "Keep her safe," he whispered.

Nash nodded his head and allowed the tears to flow freely from his eyes as he left. Melissa fell into his arms and continued to cry as Sullivan stepped forward.

"It's been a pleasure knowing all of you. Stay safe and stay together. I know you're all scared; I'm scared too. You're all survivors though; make no mistake about that. I may have brought you here to the Fort, but you are all alive because of your own resilience."

With that, Sullivan shut the gate and disappeared into the Fort with the remainder of its inhabitants, readied to fight. The group made their way to the back end of the fence and disappeared into the woods, headed to the forest road to meet Fletcher Crawford. Dianna led the group from the front as Nash and Melissa walked in the rear, hand and hand as they marched in silence. Nash only looked back once to find the sentinels as they climbed onto the RVs, ready to begin their final post.

The group made their way toward the creek, far away from the area where Nash had always seen Sammy. He actually found himself feeling sad that he was unable to see him one last time before he moved on. He imagined that Sammy would be killed by one of Fletcher's men as they descended into the Fort, as well as the rest of their group that had been left behind. If Fletcher's group were anything like Duncan, and he had a feeling they were, there wasn't much that would make it out of the woods alive.

They could tell their exodus from the woods was almost complete as the sound of engines idling registered in their ears.

"Remember what Sullivan told us. We are survivors," said Dianna as she turned to talk to the group briefly. "Do what he says and try to stay together. We'll get through this."

They exited the trees and filed out onto the shoulder of the dirt road. The light from the afternoon sun was blinding as they laid eyes on two large, idling transport trucks. Three men stood on each of the trucks, holding rifles and grinning down at the group. Waiting in front of the two trucks was a black BMW, and two men in black suits and sunglasses were standing guard beside it. Spread out around the trucks were more men with guns, and a sharply dressed man leaned against the truck directly in front of them. He wasn't tall, well under six feet, with thick, receding brown hair, brushed backward in a wispy style that revealed his broad forehead. A pair of expensive looking sunglasses sat on his face and hid his eyes from them as he watched them all spill out of the woods. He was slightly chubby, but athletic, and looked to be in his mid-forties. He was surprisingly clean and wore a dark blue golf shirt with a designer suit jacket over top, and jeans that ended at a pair of brown leather shoes.

"Hello everyone," said the man as Nash and Melissa stepped forward from the woods. He walked confidently and stood in front of the group with a friendly smile on his face. "My name is Fletcher Crawford. You've made the right decision today."

He placed his thumbs into his pockets and stood looking up and down the line of people as he sized them up one by one. He nodded his head as he moved down the line and made mental notes about everyone who stood in front of him. His eyes stopped at Nash at the end of the line as a frown crawled across his face.

"I'm not going to stand here and try and convince you that I'm a nice guy. You've all made up your minds about me, and I guess that's fair. You'll see, in time, things aren't so bad out here." He walked forward to the middle of the group and used his hand in a chopping motion to divide the group in two. "I want this half of the group in that truck, and the other half in the other. I know it's not going to be a comfortable ride, but we expected most of you would be joining us and couldn't think of a better way to move you all at once."

The two groups made their way to their respective trucks, heads down in fear of what was to come. They all trusted they'd made the right decision, but as they were ushered into the back of dark transport trucks, they easily questioned themselves. Nash and Melissa stood still as the rest of their group moved toward the trucks. He watched as a man held his hand out to help Dianna get into the back of her truck, which she quickly slapped away and took his place helping people into the back of the transport. Fletcher moved forward and stood in front of Nash and Melissa, sweet smelling cologne clogging their senses. It was impossible to deny that Fletcher Crawford had more charisma than he had use for.

"I've been told what you do around here, kid," he said, talking directly to Nash. "You'll be an asset to our family, if you so choose. What's your name?" Nash stood still, unwavering in his decision not to answer.

"I'm guessing you already know," Nash said finally, not breaking his gaze from Fletcher's dark lenses.

Fletcher smiled and took off his glasses to reveal a set of piercing blue eyes. "You'll warm up. I suggest it happen sooner than later." He shifted his gaze to Melissa and looked her right in the eyes. "Go ahead and get on the truck. We'll be home shortly."

Nash walked with Melissa, his hand on the small of her back as they prepared to be the last two loaded. He could hear the sound of the other trucks' sliding door slam shut as he helped Melissa into their transport. One of Fletcher's men came around the truck as Nash was about to climb in, wearing a black ski mask over his face. The man tore off the mask in one fluid motion and Nash's heart sank.

"*Buddy Boy!*" yelled Duncan with a smile as he planted the butt of his gun against Nash's head. He heard Melissa scream as he fell and landed on the dirty road before he blacked out.

Chapter 18

Sullivan locked the gate as the group departed. He did a quick check of all the weapons he had on him and made sure he was ready for whatever Fletcher Crawford had in store. He knew it would end today; but he wanted to make sure it ended for some of Fletcher's men too. His rifle hung on his back, as usual, with knives secured to his boots and handguns on his belt. Strapped to his belt were four grenades that he'd kept since he had started the Fort. He caressed the metal, he knew the damage they caused, had seen it before. When he was originally stockpiling supplies he had hesitated about bringing these kinds of weapons into the Fort. He had never wanted to use them—had hoped he wouldn't have to— but now was glad for their presence.

"You ready for this?" Sullivan asked Scott and Meghan. They stood beside him wearing their riot gear, their faces obscured by the face shields.

"As ready as we're going to be," said Scott.

"I wish you would have left with Dianna," said Sullivan.

"No way in hell," said Meghan. "You've been good to us and kept us safe all this time. If we die, we die together."

"Why don't we send a scout or two out into the woods, see what they can see?" Stu suggested.

"No," said Sullivan. "He's been casing out these woods for a while, at least a month. He's handed us a death sentence."

"It's been an honor," said Stu. He held his hand out to Sullivan, and Sullivan ignored the outstretched hand. Instead, he pulled Stu in for a tight hug. The two stood embracing for a moment before Stu released himself.

Sullivan joined the sentinels on top the RVs and scanned the area with a pair of binoculars. It was hard to see very far due to the dense forest, but the trees were one of their best lines of defense against whatever was coming. He handed the binoculars to one of the sentinels and climbed down the ladder to the ground and exhaled deeply as he placed his feet back into the dirt. Everyone stood silently at their posts not knowing exactly what to do or what to expect. Including Meghan and Scott, fifteen people stayed behind to help defend the Treefort. Sullivan addressed them quickly, went over last minute strategy plans, and let them know that if things got rough, they were expected to try and escape into the woods. They each shook his hand and felt the frustration and anger that flowed from him as his giant hand covered theirs.

Far in the distance, they could hear the sound of transport trucks barreling off down the dirt road as Sullivan stood in the center of the Fort, second-guessed his decision. He tried to think of other possible options to have dealt with the threat but came up with nothing.

A crow cawed in the distance, followed by the great calamity that would bring the Fort to its death. With slicing precision, four arrows flew through the air and landed in a soft spot of each of the sentinel's riot gear. All four of them fell backward into the Fort and landed hard on the ground below. They writhed wildly on the ground and gasped for breath as blood pooled and sprayed from the arrows that stuck out of their throats.

Each of the remaining members of the Fort took cover and watched in horror as the four sentinels turned. One by one, three of the deceased sentinels stood and released a monstrous howl while tearing at the riot gear. The forth got up slowly and stumbled like a fawn standing for the first time. He stood still, looked at his riot gear, and softly tapped it with his hands.

"*Everyone, be alert!*" yelled Sullivan as he took a shot at one of the newly formed howlers. A howler towards the east side of the Fort screamed once before he latched onto one of the younger Fort defenders. The young man, Edgar, Sullivan thought, grabbed at his open throat before he sank to his knees—mouth opening and closing in surprise.

Sullivan could barely spare a second to watch Edgar's body twitch once more before it stilled. Sullivan knew it wouldn't be long before Edgar got back to his feet, either as a howler or a slowpoke. He sighted in Edgar's form but couldn't get a solid shot off to keep him from rising so he turned away to focus on more pressing matters.

Another sentinel stood, eyes wild with arms outstretched. Stu and another man charged towards it. They tackled it to the ground, and Stu plunged his knife into the back of the howler's skull.

"*Son of a bitch!*" Stu's partner screamed. He pulled his hand away from the howler, skin hanging off his wrist.

Stu closed his eyes momentarily before he took the man by the shoulder, "Try and take some of them down before you turn." And then Stu was up and running towards the main fire at another howler. He sliced into the raging creature just as a large metallic mass careened over the fence and landed in the fire.

Sullivan held his breath, not daring to look away as the projectile erupted into flame engulfing Stu, the howler, and a number of other Fort residents. Their screams echoed around the empty Fort as the fires licked at their flailing bodies.

The smell of his burning friends sent a wave of nausea through him as he moved towards their charred bodies. Flames licked the ground around him as one of the burning men stood up behind him, its skin blackened from the fire as it tore flaming pieces of flesh from its body. It let out a violent scream before it lunged at Sullivan with its flaming lips gnashing wildly. Sullivan reached out and grabbed it by the throat to stop its advance. Flames bit at Sullivan's arm as he planted his knife through the howler's temple before he tossed it to the ground. His arm was alive with burning pain as he surveyed the dying fort.

He grabbed one of the grenades from his belt and pulled the pin before he tossed it over the fence in the direction the firebomb had come. It exploded with more ferocity than he had expected and blew open a part of the fence. Screams of pain came from outside the Fort. The fire from the grenade caught quickly and spread from tree to tree across the dry, crackling ground.

Sullivan sent a stream of bullets through the remaining portions of the fence as the forest fire continued to expand. The members of the Treefort were falling quickly, as he watched them run wildly through the dying Fort. One of the newborn howlers sprinted into the woods through the broken fence and sank its teeth into one of Fletcher's men as he fell to the ground. A loud, ear-piercing screech came from behind him, a scream he thought he recognized. He swung around with his rifle held in front of him as his heart sank into his stomach.

Meghan knelt over Scott, her face nuzzled against his neck as she tore at his flesh. Sullivan cried out again, hardly able to comprehend what was happening around him as Meghan swung to face him. Her beautiful, sparkling eyes were now red and full of madness, blood and gore hanging loosely from her lips. She screamed violently at him and the flesh fell to the ground as Sullivan squeezed the trigger of his rifle and placed a bullet between her eyes with trembling hands.

He hoped he'd somehow be able to save Scott but knew it was too late. Meghan's body had fallen backward on top of him, their blood pooling around them. Scott looked up at Sullivan with an open-mouthed grin. The gaping wound in his neck pulsed, gurgling as air passed through his windpipe. The life drained from his eyes and he died with a smile on his face as he looked up at Sullivan with empty eyes.

Gunfire obliterated the fence around him and he dove to the ground as bullets whizzed above his head. He grabbed a grenade and threw it to the back edge of the fence where the bullets were coming from. It exploded wildly and sent debris high into the sky as the air filled with screams again. He rolled sideways and narrowly avoided a falling piece of flaming fence as he unleashed another barrage of bullets into the woods. He used his free hand to pull the pin from another grenade as he continued to fire his rifle. He rolled a grenade through the exposed fence into the burning woods The sounds of agony continued to crash all around him like sonic-waves, amplified by the explosion.

The woods behind the Fort was empty, filled with downed trees and growing flames. He heard voices near the front of the Fort as he sprinted past the mangled fence and into the flames, feeling them lick his skin as he passed through. Before anyone could see him, he ducked behind a large tree and pressed his back against it.

He peaked around the tree and saw a group of seven men flood into the Fort from a section of the fence they'd torn down. He gave them time to search the area and confirm that nobody was left alive inside before he pulled the pin on his last grenade and tossed it into the area where they stood. He took off deeper into the woods and listened to the blast echo through the woods.

The creek was deserted, void of any of the slowpokes that had previously dotted the banks. Even Sammy was gone, which left Sullivan alone as the Fort burned behind him. He heard a thud nearby, followed by an earth-shattering explosion. His life at the Treefort flashed before his eyes, the loss clawing at his insides as the flames from the blast cascaded across his face. He fell to the ground, looking straight up into the blue afternoon sky wracked with sobs. He could see a cloud as it floated softly in the sky above the waves of smoke that billowed upwards. He gazed at it, and in his stupor he could see Dianna's face as his mind faded to black.

Chapter 19

Nash awoke in a frenzy with Melissa's arms around him.

"You're ok. We're in the back of one of the transports," said Melissa.

It took his eyes a moment to acclimate to the darkness of the transport truck.

"Duncan," he whispered.

"Yeah," said Melissa as she placed one of her hands into his. "How are you feeling?"

"My head is pounding."

"You fell pretty hard after he hit you."

"How long have we been moving?"

"An hour, maybe?"

Her features were barely distinguishable in the darkness of the trucks. He could feel the presence of all the others trapped with him as they sat quietly in their own despair.

****

The truck came to a stop and shut off its engine, which gave way to the sound of motorcycles in the distance. Sounds of the dead swarmed nearby mixed in with the loud, high-pitched roar of racing bikes. After a few moments, the sounds of bikes and the dead tapered off into silence, followed by the truck engine roaring back to life.

The trucks rumbled down the unseen road as Nash propped himself up on his knees beside Melissa. They struggled to keep their balance while the truck plotted along the bumpy road. They could hear muffled voices outside as it came to a final stop, the people in the front cab letting out a chuckle as they shut off the engine and stepped out of the cab. Footsteps tapped on pavement alongside the truck, followed by the sliding of the door being opened which sent bright afternoon light into the back of the truck.

"Welcome home, fuckers!" yelled Duncan as he stood in front of them all with a smile on his face. The Treefort residents blinked into the sunlight, their eyes tearing.

Nash and Melissa stared back at him in silence.

"Dial it back a bit, Duncan," Fletcher ordered as he joined him at the opening. "I want these people to feel welcome here! Please, everyone, join me in the light."

Duncan reached his hand out with a grin to help Nash out of the truck. Nash batted it away and hopped onto the hot pavement before he helped the rest of them down while Duncan stood directly behind him. Fletcher reached out and gently maneuvered Duncan backward, sensing his anger toward Nash.

"Please, follow me, everyone," said Fletcher as he and Duncan walked to the front of the truck. The group waited for Nash to move first before they followed Fletcher. Everyone from the back of the first truck had already been unloaded and waited for Nash's group to join them.

"Everyone okay?" asked Dianna with red eyes.

Nash nodded to her as his group settled in beside hers. Fletcher stood in front of all of them, Duncan leisurely sitting behind on a park bench.

"Take a look around," said Fletcher, hands in his pockets as he talked. "It's not nearly as bad as you'd imagined, right? Again, I'm sorry for the crude transportation. Everyone okay from the ride?"

Most of the group stood motionless with the exception of a few who acknowledged him with a nervous nod. Nash kept his eyes firmly trained on Duncan, who stared back at him with a grin.

"Is this going to become a problem?" asked Fletcher as he looked over the top of his glasses. Nash and Duncan silently challenged each other as Fletcher frowned.

"Not one bit," said Duncan with a wink at Melissa. She ignored him and took Nash's hand, gently pulling him closer to her side.

"I think it'll be for the best if you move on your way for now, Duncan," said Fletcher without turning toward Duncan. Duncan's smile faded as he sat with his arms resting along the back edge of the bench. "Whatever differences you two have had in the past can be sorted out at another time. I won't have either of you spoiling everyone's first day here."

Duncan begrudgingly stood and tried in vain to mask his frustration over being ordered away.

"You're the boss," he said.

Fletcher readjusted his sunglasses and stepped forward to where Nash was standing. "I know enough from what he's said that there's history between the two of you. I also know that there's two sides to every story. If you can mind your manners here, I'll make sure he minds his. Fair enough?"

Nash stared back at him until Fletcher stepped back to where he'd originally been standing.

"I'm sure you're all wondering what these are," said Fletcher as he held up his left wrist and pulled down his sleeve to reveal a red strip that hung loosely from his wrist. Nash looked around at Fletcher's men and realized they all wore the same strip. "This is the sign that you belong to my family. I realize a lot of my former family members ended up wandering around your camp in the last few months. Why they made their way so far from here, I'll never know. Apparently they were a little more adventurous in their death than they were in life."

"Do a lot of your family members end up wandering dead outside your walls?" asked Dianna with a stern look on her face.

Fletcher looked back at her with a clever smile as one of the truck doors opened and slammed shut.

"That'll have to wait for another time, my dear," he said, looking toward the truck as footsteps approached. "Dietrich, my boy! Welcome home."

Nash's body tensed as the person came into view from the other side of the transport truck. He was covered in moldy, tattered clothes and his dreadlocks still hung loosely behind him.

It was Sammy.

"Dietrich's an invaluable member of my family here," said Fletcher, soaking in the shock he could see flowing from Nash. "There's only a few of you who would know who this man is, but he's the one who initially found your little group and volunteered to keep watch until today."

Nash stared at him and felt betrayed by the man he'd once referred to as Sammy. For a moment, as he stared at his mud-soaked figure, he thought he caught of a flash of remorse in Dietrich's eyes.

"So," said Fletcher with a clap of his hands. "Let's get a move on, shall we? My men will escort you to your new homes. As you can see, this little township you're standing in was a little on the ritzy side and I've made sure to keep it that way. Just because the outside world has gone to shit, doesn't mean we can't live like royalty!"

Fletcher was right; the houses situated inside the walls were large and luxurious, easily able to give all of them much more room and privacy than the Fort had been able to offer. The homes were the beautiful, well maintained structures you'd find in *Home & Garden*. Surrounding the entirety of the community was a large brick wall with guard towers located at each corner. At the front and back of the wall were two entrances, both sealed with thick, reinforced iron gates. It seemed far less maniacal than any of them had imagined, but Nash could tell the Mansion had been built to keep people in just as much as it had been built to keep people out.

"As much room as we have here, the houses will have to be shared by multiple families. Couples and families will be kept together, so please, do not worry over such things. I'd like to personally meet with all of you later in the evening, so settle in and feel free to explore the town. Each of your homes has a working clock, so please make sure to be at the church at 5:00, sharp. Until then, make yourself comfortable."

Fletcher disappeared into the back of the BMW as the armed men took the front seats and drove off down the road before they parked in front of a church near the middle of the compound. It was the kind of church that could easily be found on a country postcard, with a tall steeple that gave way to a large meeting place behind. Fletcher and his men walked together to the front steps to join an angry Duncan. A sharply dressed man opened the large double doors for Fletcher and his men as they approached and let them disappear inside before he closed the doors and continued his watch.

"I know this is a lot to take in and you're all probably quite nervous," said Dietrich, with a voice much more calm and pleasing than Nash had expected. "Nash, please come with me. The rest of you, know that you're safe, and allow these men to escort you to your new homes."

"Are the guns really necessary?" Dianna asked.

"Everyone stand down," said Dietrich. "These people are unarmed."

Fletcher's men put their guns away and ushered the group towards a large group of houses. Dianna glanced at Nash with a grimace before allowed herself to be ushered along. Nash looked at Dietrich with as much hate as he could muster. Melissa clenched on onto Nash's hand tightly as he glared at Dietrich.

"You have no reason to trust me right now, I understand fully. Please though, come with me. The home you've been assigned to is more removed than the rest and I'll take you there."

With noticeable hesitation, Nash moved toward him while he still held tightly onto Melissa's hand. A man in a tattered flannel shirt and jeans opened the back door of an idling black BMW and motioned them to climb in. Nash stopped in his tracks as the man smiled at them while rapping his fingers on the handle of a large knife that was sheathed on his belt.

"Oh for goodness sake, I said to stand down," said Dietrich to the man that held the door open. The sound of motorcycles once again began to register, followed soon after by a riotous song of the dead. "Get ready to let the runners in. I'm sure Fletcher doesn't want any mistakes like last time."

The man scowled at him and made his way toward the front gate and fiddled with a large set of keys as he moved. Dietrich gave another one of his kind smiles and opened the back door for them as he motioned politely again for them to get in. Nash and Melissa slid into the back of the BMW as Dietrich shut the door behind them. The leather seats were surprisingly cool, the air conditioning circulated throughout the cab. They allowed themselves to enjoy the cool air until the moment Dietrich opened the driver's door and sat down. He put the car in gear and drove toward the church where Duncan and Fletcher had disappeared.

"My name's Dietrich," he said as he passed the church and made his way to the far end of the compound. "I wanted to apologize for the trickery."

"Trickery?" Melissa asked, looking at Nash.

"Ever since I started doing sweeps of the woods with Scott, Dietrich's been standing down at the creek, pretending to be a slowpoke so he could spy on us." Nash's words were cold and full of factual malice as he stared out the tinted window.

"Nash, it wasn't easy being out there and seeing you everyday, knowing what was going to happen."

"Then why'd you do it?" asked Melissa. They drove for a moment in silence as Dietrich weaved his way through the compound.

"I think in the short time you've been here, you've realized how persuasive of a man Fletcher Crawford can be. I honestly expected that all of your group would join with us, but I was wrong. Coming forward and talking to you or alerting you to the fact that I wasn't one of the dead would only have endangered your entire community."

Dietrich took them past the back gate of the compound. The iron gates stood firm as the dead pressed their faces and arms as far as they could through the slats.

"There's something you're not going to hear from a lot of people around here, but it needs to be said; I'm sorry for what's happened to you and your group. I truly am."

"Where were these feelings before they stormed our camp?" said Nash.

"Again, Fletcher is a very persuasive leader," said Dietrich, pausing for moment as he continued through the compound. "We all have our motivations."

Dietrich turned the car down a street lined with new looking houses. Men with rifles were leading members from the Treefort into their new homes as they passed by in the BMW. He took them up a longer driveway and parked at a beautifully tended to colonial home. It was one of the only homes that sat atop a hill with a large manicured lawn spreading out in front. They sat in the air conditioning and stared at the house as they absorbed the cool air.

"I'm not going to lie to the two of you, this is going to be a very hard transition for your group. You need to be prepared that some of them may *not make it through*."

"What do you mean, not make it through?" asked Nash coldly as Melissa continued to tighten her fingers in his hand.

"I've seen entire groups come in here and be all dead within a week. The ones you were finding around your camp, they all belonged to a group we raided two months ago. I don't think there's anyone left living here from that group. If you're not with him, you're against him. My suggestion to you and your folks is to just fall in line…for now."

"For now?" asked Nash.

"Come with me," said Dietrich as he turned off the car and stepped outside.

They followed Dietrich up the walking path to the home while they admired its outside and tried to not show any sign of appreciation. Nash had never even been near a home so large, let alone given one to live in. Dietrich pulled out a pair of keys and unlocked the door, then handed them to Nash.

"Welcome home," he said and stood aside to let them into the house. The inside was just as perfectly put together as the outside. The entire main floor, including the stairs that led to the upper levels, was made of dark cherry hardwood. The walls were painted a soft taupe, with beautifully framed wildlife scenes throughout.

"This place is huge," said Melissa as she admired the molding and the carved intricacies of the staircase railing.

"Yes, it is. Biggest house in Mansion Heights, actually, and it's all yours," said Dietrich.

"Mansion Heights?" asked Melissa.

"Yeah, that was the name of the community here before the world ended. He's just shortened it to the Mansion."

"How do you have electricity here?" Melissa asked, feeling the cool air.

"Fletcher has had a few engineers join our group over time. They were able to get the power grid up and running awhile back. It's not perfect; we have some outages every so often, but it's better than nothing."

"Why does everyone else have to share while we get this place all to ourselves?" asked Nash.

Dietrich exhaled and sat on the steps as he looked up at them through his mangy dreadlocked hair. "I guess you have me to thank for that. I vouched for you; I told him that after deceiving you for a month, it might lessen the blow. As much as he likes Duncan, I think he's grown to have a bit of a soft spot for you. Not sure how long that will last, so enjoy it while you can."

"No thank you," said Nash sternly. "We don't want special treatment. We want to be with our people."

"See, Nash, it's that kind of talk that's going to get you killed. We're your people now, whether you like it or not. I have my reasons for wanting you apart from everyone."

"Yeah? What's that?" asked Melissa.

"In time," he said before he got up and walked to the open door. "I hope you've taken my advice to heart. Just know that you have friends here, and I don't mean the people you came in with."

With that, Dietrich shut the door and returned to his car. They placed their bags down in the foyer and watched him as he drove away, turned a corner, and disappeared out of their view. Nash pulled Melissa toward him and hugged her as they stood in the foyer soaking up the cool air.

"What now?" she asked, her arms still around him as her head rested on his shoulder. "I don't want to go out there."

"I don't either," he said and looked around at the ornate carpentry of the house. They walked around the space together, surveyed their new belongings as they moved from room to room. The kitchen was bigger than the entirety of their RV and was stocked with all sorts of canned goods and frozen meat. They climbed the staircase to the upper levels and looked around at the five bedrooms, each perfectly readied to accept a guest.

"This isn't right," said Melissa as the two of them stood at the doorway of the main bedroom. A king size bed stood before them, ready to accept them whenever they were ready to give in to the Mansion's way of life. "Everyone who stayed behind at the Fort is more than likely dead and we're…here."

"Come on," said Nash as he took her hand and led her into their new room.

The two of them crawled into the huge bed, cuddling together in the middle as they both sobbed into each other's arms. As wrong as it felt to be lying in the comfortable, air-conditioned room, Nash felt that Dietrich was right. This wasn't their home, and eventually he'd find them a way out. For now though, he knew they had to fall in line.

With that thought, he drifted off to sleep with Melissa still in his arms.

Chapter 20

Nash and Melissa were torn from their sleep to the sound of banging that came from the main floor of the house. Morning light illuminated their room as Melissa brushed stray hairs from her face and strained her eyes against the harsh morning light. Nash rubbed his eyes in a stupor as the banging continued downstairs.

"This bed is dangerous," he said as he stood up and stretched quickly as Melissa joined him.

"We were supposed to meet Fletcher last night with the rest of the group!" she said as she adjusted her hair in the mirror the best she could.

The two of them hurried downstairs and looked through the window beside the door to see Fletcher standing with his hands in his pockets. He was wearing the same designer jeans and shoes, but now wore a green t-shirt instead of the golf shirt and jacket from yesterday. Melissa and Nash gave each other an uneasy glance as Nash opened the door.

"Good morning!" said Fletcher cheerfully.

"Wakey, wakey!" cooed Duncan from behind him.

"May we come in?" asked Fletcher.

Nash hesitated for a moment as he watched Duncan glare at him with the demented grin that he hated so much.

"Of course," he said and stepped backward, allowing Fletcher and Duncan to join them in the foyer.

"We missed you last night at our little meet and greet," said Fletcher who stood with his hands in his pockets as Duncan closed the door behind him. "I assumed you'd fallen asleep, which is understandable. Our friend here gave you a bit of a jolt from what I heard last night, and for that, I apologize."

"*Bop!*" yelled Duncan as he mimicked hitting Nash with the butt of the rifle. Fletcher gave Duncan a disapproving look before he continued on.

"You've got the best house on the block here. You can thank Dietrich for that. I guess he owes you that, seeing how you're really the only one he spent the last month deceiving. I trust you slept well?"

"Yes, thank you," Melissa said quietly, her head down. "The house is beautiful." She was playing the game already, leaving Nash impressed and ready to participate.

"I'm glad you like it. I want you to know that I understand the reservations your people have about this place. Like I said yesterday, I truly feel if you embrace the Mansion for what it is, you'll grow to love it."

"Give it time," said Nash. "It's a big adjustment for everyone. They'll come around."

"I certainly hope so," said Fletcher. They stood in silence as Nash and Melissa tried to hide their nervousness over his presence. "Anyway, I come bearing gifts!" He reached into his pocket and produced two long, red strips of fabric. "Everyone else was fitted last night at our meet and greet."

"He usually doesn't do house calls," said Duncan with a grin. "You should feel honored."

"I'd feel more comfortable if he were outside," said Nash as he watched the smile slither from Duncan's face.

"Of course. Duncan, please wait outside," said Fletcher without taking his eyes from Nash.

Duncan stood steady in the foyer as his anger toward Nash bubbled inside him. After another moment of silence, Duncan left, slamming the door behind him.

"He's a wonderful number two, but he's all about the theatrics," said Fletcher, confirming just how close Duncan was with the man in charge.

"That's an accurate assessment," said Nash.

"I understand that the two of you have a bit of a history."

"What has he told you exactly?"

"Bits and pieces. He's not overly fond of you."

"The feeling is mutual," said Nash while he looked outside to see Duncan with his zipper undone, urinating on the hedges. "How exactly did he end up here?"

"That's a story for another day. Miss, if I could please have your left hand." Fletcher's undeniable charm was quickly chipping away at the murderous façade they'd conjured in their heads. He gently turned Melissa's hand over so her wrist was facing up as he tied the strip around it. The loop was loose around her wrist, but the knot was tight and strong. He did the same for Nash afterward, clapping his hands together once he was finished.

"Welcome to the family!" he said loudly with his hands in the air to celebrate. "And how rude am I, I've never asked your name."

"Melissa," she said with a shy smile.

"Well hello, Melissa, and welcome to the family. I think you two are going to fit in just fine around here. I'd like for you both to stop by the church sometime today."

"Of course," said Nash. His stoic facial expressions hadn't cracked once during the encounter with Fletcher. The underlying tension between the three of them dissolves as Fletcher nodded and left their house with a smile.

"He's a charmer, isn't he?" asked Melissa while she looked at the red strip now tied firmly around her wrist.

"That's an understatement. He looked pretty chummy with Duncan too, which tells me everything I need to know about him."

The two of them made their way up the stairs to investigate their new surroundings. Melissa walked into the ensuite bathroom and found it fully stocked with toiletries and fresh towels. She turned on the faucet and let water flow as she tried to hide the smile that crept to the surface. She opened the door of the shower and turned it on, watching the hot water fall freely from the nozzle as it slowly filled the room with steam. Before she knew it, her clothes were off and she was closing the shower door behind her.

"Hot water!" said Melissa. "I feel awful for caring after what happened yesterday but I have to say it's an upgrade from the rain water we used to collect."

"Nobody would blame you for enjoying a hot shower, Mel." Nash pulled back the curtains of the large window that overlooked the community. He squinted against the bright sun. The Mansion's sprawling properties were bathed in a fairytale glow, a deceptive illusion given what he knew about Fletcher and his group. Far in the distance he could see the front gate, secured tightly as the dead pressed their bodies against it. It would be impossible to hear them from where he stood, but his memories were flood with them.

The steam from the shower had completely overtaken the bathroom as he stood and leaned in the doorway. He used his palm to wipe the mirror, creating a circle in the middle of it. Dirt from his hand left smudge marks on the mirror and taunted him to take a shower as he looked through them at his reflection. He hadn't really had the chance to look at himself in months and marveled at the newfound ruggedness of his face.

"Have I always been this dirty looking?" he asked as he unwrapped a new toothbrush from the counter and applied a line of toothpaste onto it.

"You should see the dirt flowing off me right now," she laughed. "I think we were all a little dirty."

Melissa turned the water off and grabbed the towel she had draped over one of the walls of the shower. "I could have spent the whole day in there," she said, reaching for a second towel to dry her hair. She opened the door and stepped out, the oversized towel wrapped around her as Nash spit his toothpaste into the sink. He looked at her as she stood clean and smiling in front of him, and was surprised by the new butterflies in his stomach.

"I want this with you," he said, admiring her as she stood in front of him. "I want a life like this and I want you with me, but not here. This isn't right."

"I know," she said. "It's like Dietrich said though; we need to blend in and play the game. If I show up without showering today, Fletcher will know something's up. I know this can't last, but I'm going to enjoy it while I can."

"I guess you're right," said Nash as he took off his clothes and stepped into the shower himself.

He let the hot water rush over him in waves as he absorbed the therapeutic heat. He hadn't had a real shower in over a year and it was a feeling he missed terribly. He looked around to find the shower had been stocked with all sorts of soaps and lotions, a few of which Melissa had already gotten into. He used a bar of soap to lather himself and grabbed a bottle of shampoo and squirted an unnecessary amount into his palm before he massaged it into his scalp. The smells of the soaps brought a smile to his face as he stood there inhaling the scents.

He quickly patted himself dry and wrapped the towel around his waist, stepped out of the shower, and noticed a heart drawn into the fog on the mirror. He smiled and moved into the bedroom to find that Melissa was standing in front of a spacious walk-in closet.

"Wow," she said as she stood back from the closet.

Nash joined her and looked inside to see it completely stocked with brand new clothes, ready for them to slide into. There was a large dresser inside, filled with all sorts of clean underwear and socks for both of them, ranging in sizes like they weren't sure who would be occupying the space next.

"I don't even remember what it feels like to wear fresh underwear," said Nash as he slid into a brand new pair. He picked out a pair of jeans and a blue t-shirt that seemed like it would fit and laid them on the bed. He grabbed a pair of socks and left Melissa to pick out her outfit. He sat on the edge of the bed and slid on his socks, feeling the fresh fabric on his feet as Melissa stood in a matching set of bra and panties as she fingered through the numerous dresses.

"There's nothing but sundresses in here," Melissa said as she rifled through the clothes. "Would it be too much to ask for a pair of jeans and a t-shirt?" Nash threw her old, dirty clothes at her and they landed at her feet. "I see your point. A dress it is."

Nash had completely dressed himself and was trying his best to style his hair in a mirror outside the closet. She walked out of the closet with the dress she'd picked, settling just above her knees. It was a thin, pale-blue sundress with white polka dots that clung softly to her clean skin. She nudged Nash away from the mirror with a smile and admired the dress as she tied her damp hair into a bun.

"Not practical at all but it sure is cute."

"You're adorable," said Nash with a smile. She closed the closet door before she kissed him on the lips. She didn't say a word, just lovingly smiled at him before she walked to the window and looked out over the community.

"The Mansion," she said. "What a funny name."

"I think we have to be ambassadors around here, Mel," said Nash when he joined her by the window. "I get the sense that

Dietrich might be someone we can trust. If we can all play nice and be patient, I think we could have a future here."

"I thought you didn't want to stay," she asked as she took his hand and looked out the window.

"I said *we*," he repeated as he stared at the church in the distance. "That doesn't include Fletcher Crawford."

Chapter 21

"This is more unbelievable than the closet," said Melissa, standing in the kitchen as she marveled at the assortment of food.

"It almost feels like nothing happened to this place," said Nash as he pulled out a can of peaches and used an electric can opener to pry the lid off.

Melissa opened the freezer to find it stocked completely full of meat and vegetables and the fridge filled with an assortment of fruit and fresh milk.

"Nothing here feels quite right," she said as she took out the milk and sniffed it before placing it back. "What's our plan for today?"

Nash handed her a fork as the two of them ate the fruit out of the opened can. "I think we should check in on everyone else from the Fort and see how they're settling in. After that, I guess we should go meet with Fletcher."

"Ugh," she said as she finished the peaches and tossed the can into a wastebasket in the corner of the kitchen. "I hate having Duncan around again."

"I know," said Nash as he placed the two forks in the sink behind him. "He's close to Fletcher, which makes him more dangerous than he ever was before. It's not going to be comfortable but I think we need to just roll with the punches around here until we decide our plan of action."

Nash closed and locked the front door and jiggled the doorknob before they made their way down the driveway and onto the road. A pickup truck pulled up and two men in overalls stepped out, not taking notice of Nash and Melissa as they closed the doors. They were both rough looking men in their thirties, with long straggly hair and sullen faces. Nash and Melissa watched as they pulled gardening equipment from the back of the truck and made their way up the walkway toward the house, not saying a thing as they began their work.

"Gardeners?" whispered Melissa as they turned and watched them. One of the men started a lawn mower and pushed it along the edge of the house.

"Apparently," he said. "This just gets weirder by the minute."

The two of them walked down the street together and listened to the hum of the lawn mower as the cries of the dead continued to cascade over the brick wall. Nash stopped in the middle of the road and walked to the line of trees that ran along the wall.

"What are you doing?" asked Melissa as she watched Nash climb up one of the trees with lower branches.

"I want to get a look at the other side," he said. He didn't have to climb very high into the tree to get a good vantage point of the carnage outside. Hundreds of howlers and slowpokes stood before him, screaming at him as he stood on a thick branch. They weren't smart enough to try and scale the wall, or even apply enough pressure to weaken it; they simply screamed in anger as they met his gaze from above.

"Nash?" said Melissa from the ground. He turned to see that she was looking backward as Dietrich approached from down the street. Nash took a final look at the howlers and climbed down quickly, joining her in the middle of the street.

"Quite the view, isn't it?" said Dietrich as he approached them with his hands in his pockets. The month of dirt and grime had been washed away; his facial hair had been trimmed and his mane of dreadlocks were pulled back and tied behind his head. He wore a pair of khaki shorts and a plain green t-shirt, with gray boat shoes on his feet.

"It sure is," Nash said as he listened to the cries of the dead. "Mel, there's hundreds out there."

"*Hundreds?*" she asked, shocked by the number. Neither of them had seen anywhere close to that amount.

"They span the length of the wall, for the most part," said Dietrich. "Fletcher's learned how to control them easily enough. They really are manageable."

"People don't leave here often, do they?" asked Nash as they continued to walk down the street.

"No; no, they don't. He's all about power and allegiance. Keeping us all safe in here is his way of guaranteeing those two things."

"Do you feel safe?" asked Melissa. Dietrich smiled and looked at the ground for a moment while they walked. She hadn't noticed it before, under all the grime and mud, but he was quite handsome.

"Like I told you both yesterday, if you can play his game, you'll be fine. It's those that don't fall in line that have trouble here. I get the feeling the two of you aren't ones to just fall in line."

"I get that same feeling about you," said Nash as they turned a corner and walked past more homes.

"I have my reasons for sticking around," he said.

"Care to elaborate?" asked Melissa.

"We all have our reasons for staying here. You'll find yours in time. Has he asked you to come to the church yet?" asked Dietrich.

"He came by this morning to give us our bracelets and told us to come by whenever," said Nash. Dianna stepped out on to her porch at that moment, and Nash felt a surge of relief when he saw her. Melissa ran ahead toward her. "Anything we should know going in?"

"Dietrich!" yelled Duncan at the end of the street. He looked irritated as he watched Dietrich and Nash talking to each other.

"Just fall in line," he said to Nash. "You've got friends here." Dietrich bounded off toward Duncan and the two of them disappeared around the corner. Nash caught up with Dianna and Melissa who were standing on Dianna's lawn. Nash walked up with a smile, but it faded when he saw their faces.

"Everything okay?" he asked as he joined them on the grass. Melissa had tears in her eyes.

"You look nice and clean today, Nash." Dianna's voice was deadpan, her face unreadable but still covered in dirt and grime of the Treefort. Nash and Melissa both picked up the smell of alcohol on her breath. "Settling in quick I see. Even making new *friends*."

"Hold on Dianna," said Nash, holding up his hands in surrender.

"Don't you tell me to hold on!" she screamed, tears cascading down her cheeks. "Our group was torn apart yesterday and you know as well as I do that Sullivan was murdered!" Her tears paved clean tracks down her face, and she smudged them away with angry swipes.

"We don't know that," Melissa started, her hand hovering near Dianna as if afraid to touch her.

"Oh, yes we do, *my dear*," she said with a sneer. "While you two were having a nap yesterday in your fancy house, his team came back and confirmed it. Everyone who stayed behind was killed. Imagine my surprise when I see you two strolling down the street today, all done up nicely with that *vile* man." Dianna's chest was heaving, her anger barely checked — hate and hurt bubbling up from her soul.

"Let's go inside and talk about this," said Nash as he motioned toward the door.

"You can both go to hell for all I care," Dianna shouted. She spun on her heel and left the two of them on the lawn, slamming the door behind her. Nash and Melissa stood staring at the house, dumbstruck.

"I knew it was the case but it's hard hearing it," she said as she sobbed softly.

"I know," he whispered to her. "She'll come around. She's just in mourning. I'll try and talk with her later."

"She was supposed to lead us," said Melissa. "She was supposed to keep us safe here without Sullivan."

"She will," said Nash as he took her by the hand and stepped back onto the road. "She's grieving, give her time. She'll come around, but for now, we'll have to depend on ourselves."

The two of them walked together to the center of the Mansion where the church was located. In front of the church was a large green space, dotted with benches and a jogging path that wound its way throughout. A stern, athletic looking couple jogged past them on the track as gardeners worked diligently on the grounds around them. A few children from the Treefort played carelessly on a playground as their nervous parents watched nearby, still wary of their new surroundings.

"Don't worry about Dianna," Nash said. She'll understand eventually."

"I know."

The church felt out of place inside the walls of the Mansion; it was a smaller building with a large double-door archway and a tall bell-tower in the front. Judging by the newer construction on most of the homes, it almost seemed to Nash like the community had been built around it. Standing in front of the large double doors were two sharply dressed men who held rifles in their hands.

"We're here to see Fletcher," said Nash, Melissa at his side.

"*Mr. Crawford* is inside," one of the men sneered. He opened the door and allowed them to enter.

The inside of the church was warm and inviting, the smell of apples and cinnamon floating through the air. The walls were decorated with stained glass windows, which made the inside seem like a colorful mirage. Each side of the aisle was lined with hardwood pews, upholstered with a soft cushion on the seat and back. If there had ever been a podium or lectern at the front of the church it had been removed and replaced with the large ornate chair in which Fletcher sat.

"Nash! Melissa!" he cooed as the door was closed behind them. "Thank you for coming. Please, come up here and let's talk!"

The first three pews were filled with dead women, sitting shoulder to shoulder with their hair done as if they were ready to be escorted to prom. Fletcher smiled as Nash and Melissa nervously made their way to him and tried their hardest to hide their confusion and fear.

"Don't mind them," he said as he acknowledged the women between them.

Nash slowed his approach. The women sat motionless with makeup painted perfectly on their faces. Each wore the same red sundress and looked forward with a smile on their face.

"Dead women tell no tales," said Fletcher with a slight grin as he gauged Nash and Melissa's reaction.

"You asked us to come by," said Nash as he sharply changed the subject, forcing himself to look at the man and not the empty eyes of the women behind.

"Yes, yes I did," he said. His demeanor began to change as they moved forward in their conversation. "I've met with a few of your people today. Lovely people, really, every one of them. They've been relatively responsive to the way I run things around here, which I was pleased to find out."

"Glad to hear it," said Nash.

"I'm sure you're wondering how exactly I do run things around here," he said while he tapped his fingers on the arm of his chair.

"A little bit, yes," said Nash, as one of the women sitting in the pews let out a soft moan from behind them.

"Communion," he said, unwavering from his postured stance in his chair.

"I don't see any wafers or wine," said Nash.

"Well no, you wouldn't. What I have to offer isn't nearly as archaic," he said, not breaking eye contact with Nash. "It's much more gratifying for everyone involved."

Melissa stared intently at the women who sat on each side of them. They continued to smile, sitting still with their hands folded on their laps. As she watched, one of them slowly turned her head and made eye contact with her, which sent a vibrant chill down her spine.

"Please, don't be scared," said Fletcher. "It's quite simple, actually. Everyone living here is loyal to me, to a fault. They have their jobs and they do them well, and in return, they're allowed to partake in my communion."

"I'm not understanding," said Nash.

"We live in a world of tension, Nash, and people long for the comforts of old. Alcohol, narcotics, authority, sex. People's vices come back full force when given the opportunity. Even yourselves, there has to be something you miss from the past."

"So you're just creating a community of addicts to follow you?" said Melissa.

"Our people will have none of it," said Nash.

"Is that so? The first three pews were filled this morning," he said as he motioned to the women in front of him. There were five spots that were empty.

"These women are being used for sex," said Melissa, almost to herself but coming out for them all to hear.

"Yes, my dear, they are. By *your* people, no less. I told you yesterday that you're part of my family, so it's time to stop thinking of yourselves as different groups before you find yourself filling one of these spots."

The threat echoed in Nash's mind as the color drained from Melissa's face. She stood dumbstruck in front of Fletcher as Nash silently took her hand.

"I'm sorry, that came out very aggressive. Please accept my apology."

Nash nodded at Fletcher, Melissa's hand crushing his with fear.

"Take your time and think it over," said Fletcher as he smiled at the women in front of him. "You do need to know that communion is not an option here in the Mansion. You will work for me and you will take part in how we do things. You've seen outside the walls and I'm sure you're not interested in braving the beasts. Let me assure you though, it can be just as dangerous inside these walls for those who do not comply, rules are there to keep *everyone* safe."

Fletcher reached to the side of his chair and grabbed onto an elaborately decorated scepter. He pounded it three times on the floor as the front door of the church opened. Taking that as their dismissal Nash and Melissa turned and retreated down the aisle, leaving Fletcher to sit alone at his throne with the dead women around him. The guard who had opened the door closed it as they walked through and quickly made their way down the front steps, trying not to show their haste. More joggers had joined the track since they had went into the church, but for the most part the Mansion seemed deserted.

"I see why Dianna acted the way she did this morning," said Melissa as the two of them sat together on a bench near the playground. "Nobody really knows this but before the dead started biting, she was an alcoholic. She would've died a drunk if Sullivan hadn't found her when he did."

"I knew I smelled alcohol on Dianna this morning. He must have already gotten to her last night when they all met. Damn it."

"We're in over our heads," said Melissa. "If Dianna is already doing this communion thing, we're screwed."

"It's not just her either, if he's to be believed."

The two of them sat on the bench in silence, watching while the gardeners worked together in beautifying the grounds around them. The joggers continued their rounds, passing by the playground that was now completely empty.

"Where are all the other people?" asked Melissa as they sat on a bench that overlooked the well-manicured park space.

"He made it pretty clear he's surrounded himself with addicts. This place is pretty quiet so my guess is everyone's in their homes, strung out on whatever drug he is giving them."

"I don't think we have to worry about our group," said Melissa as she watched a familiar face from the Fort walk rounds on the jogging track.

"Are you sure about that?" asked Nash while he looked at her tanned face as she stared over the park. "Did you really know any of them before coming to the Fort? Addiction is a driving force for a lot of people and it seems like he already got a few people to take him up on his offer."

Nash thought back to the women who sat in the pews as the two of them watched the gardeners continue their work. Fletcher had seemingly handpicked the women he used for his communion brothel and chose only beautiful women to sit in his shrine. He thought about the empty seats and cringed at the thought of Fletcher's threat.

"Who from our group gave in already?" she asked as she thought about the empty seats.

"I'd rather not think about it. I'm only concerned with you and me, Mel. Everyone else can do as they please."

"What about Dianna?"

"She's a grown woman, Mel. I know it sounds harsh but there's not much we can do for her right now. You saw her."

"I think you should at least limit the time you spend with Dietrich," she said abruptly. "We don't know if we can trust him and it just looks bad to everyone."

"I know," he said softly. "I do feel like he's someone who could help us though."

"He could have helped us at the Fort," she said with an angry twinge in her voice as she wiped a tear from her cheek. "He could have warned us all. We could have prepared for Fletcher's group. Instead, he let him kidnap us and kill Sullivan and the others."

"I know," he said as he placed his hand in hers and intertwined their fingers. "That fact doesn't fall from me, don't worry, but the way he carries himself and how he talks about Fletcher, I get the sense he's an ally. Or at the very least, an enemy of Fletcher. And isn't the saying, 'the enemy of my enemy is my friend'?"

A figure stood across the park, bathed in shade as it leaned against a tall tree. Nash squinted slightly and confirmed what he already suspected; it was Duncan. He couldn't see from where they were sitting, but he knew that Duncan was watching them with that sinister grin on his face. A spray of ashes illuminated for a moment as he flicked a half-smoked cigar away from him.

"Let's go," said Nash as he got up without letting go of her hand and walked briskly away. She'd learned enough about him to know when he was moving with purpose so she followed easily and without hesitation. "This place isn't safe, especially for the two of us. Please keep by my side."

"I know," she said and clenched his hand as she looked back to see that Duncan still leaned against the tree.

As they walked, they observed a group of people from the Treefort outside the church, being let in one by one to speak with Fletcher about their communion. Others from the Fort were outside, roaming the streets while they explored the area. Dianna's door was still shut with the curtains drawn, hiding her inside from the world.

"Should we go talk to her?" asked Melissa as they slowly walked past the road that led to her house.

"I don't want to talk to her until I've talked to Dietrich. I can't approach her without a solid explanation of what is going on under the surface around here."

Nash looked up into a window of a home as they passed and made eye contact with a familiar face from the Treefort. The curtains had all been drawn in the rest of the home and he was about to close the last set when he saw Nash. Standing behind him was a woman, with a blank look on her face as she stared at him from behind. The disappointment flowed from Nash's eyes as the man pulled the curtains closed hard.

"That's Phil," Melissa whispered. "He used to help build stuff for the kids back at Treefort."

"I wonder what he's doing for Fletcher in return?" Nash asked as they passed by. The sounds of the dead filled their ears as they walked along the wall and listened to them clamor. They could see Dietrich sitting on their front porch, eating a bag of chips as they approached.

"Are you sure you can trust him?" Melissa asked as they cut across the upward slope of their front yard.

"Nope," he said while he made eye contact with Dietrich.

"So...did you take communion?" he asked as he closed his chip bag and placed it beside him on the porch.

"I think you know we didn't," said Nash, a stern look on his face. "Can we talk inside?"

Dietrich smiled and nodded, then stood up and let Nash and Melissa pass. The new lock took the key smoothly as Nash turned it and opened the door.

"You saw the women I assume," said Dietrich.

"Yes, we did," said Melissa.

"And I'm assuming he pointed out the missing spots in the pews to you."

Nash replayed the image of the man from the Fort closing the curtains as he passed.

"Have you ever been with one of them?" asked Melissa coldly.

The question hung angrily between the three of them. Dietrich's usual easygoing demeanor broke, visibly stunned by the question.

"In a way, yes," he said plainly. "It's not something I'm fond of talking about though."

Nash took Melissa's hand in an attempt to calm her. "Let's cut to the chase. You've said we have friends here and I assume you mean yourself. Either let me know what's really going on around here or we're done here."

Dietrich exhaled deeply and scratched his forehead. He showed himself into the living room next to the foyer and opened up the curtains, revealing the view of the path that led up to the home. He sat in a comfortable looking leather chair as Nash and Melissa followed him and sat across in a loveseat.

"I play the game well but I don't fit in here." Dietrich kept his voice down and calmly looked out the window as he spoke. "These aren't my type of people."

"You seem to fit in just fine," said Nash. "You didn't have to spy on us all that time by the creek. You could have warned us what was coming."

"I didn't have a choice, Nash. You've seen what he's built here and I'm sure you can tell the caliber of people who are loyal to him. If I had given up my post and warned you all, he would have stormed in and murdered every last one of you. I think you know he would have destroyed your group if that had been the case. He has the firepower and the manpower. I knew he'd make the offer to have you all join him if you didn't fight, so yes; I let it happen."

"Tell me about your communion," said Nash as he circled back to the original subject. "You say you don't fit in but you've been with one of his girls from the church."

Dietrich sat silent for a moment and tried to hide the fact that his own eyes were starting to well with tears.

"About a year ago, my wife and I were living in an abandoned school a few miles from here. It was a community similar to your own, but we were severely under prepared when he came calling. He gave us the same offer he gave your group, only the coward in charge of our group disappeared without alerting us to his offer. I'm sure you saw with Barry that Fletcher likes to use the dead as weapons, and that's precisely what he did. He flooded the halls of the school with those monsters in the night and by morning, most of us were dead, including my wife."

Everything about Dietrich's secretive behavior came into focus as he sat in front of them.

"He could see pretty clearly that we had no idea that he'd offered us the chance to join him and took pity on the ones of us that had survived. I don't know why but he took a liking to me, up until Duncan anyway. He knew I was out of sorts after my wife's death and kept his distance, but his empathy only lasted so long before he was ready to start manipulating me with his communion."

He stopped talking for a moment to check his watch, something he'd done a few times while he sat in the chair.

"I'm sorry," said Melissa.

"It's okay," he said. "I would have done the same if I'd been in your position. He beckoned me to the church one afternoon, just like he did to you today. I walked up the aisle, just as you did, and there he was sitting in that ridiculous throne of his. I saw all the women sitting there, staring forward like a bunch of living mannequins. You can imagine the strength required to not react to seeing my wife sitting in the second pew, wedged in with the rest of those poor girls."

"I'm so sorry, Dietrich," said Melissa.

"He explained to me about his communion and what he required of me in return. I somehow kept my composure as I explained to him that my wife was sitting in the pews. That alone was easily the hardest thing I've ever had to do. He initially offered her to me once a week, like any other communion offering he gives to his subjects, which I was unwilling to agree to. In the end, I basically committed to being his official servant. He calls me his handyman. Anything he needs, anything he wants, I get it done. In exchange, I get my own home to live with Sherry. He set me up with everything I need to keep her healthy and I've been living with her ever since."

Dietrich constantly looked around, as if he was waiting for someone to catch him talking about things he shouldn't. There was resolve in his posture, but fear in mannerisms, which made Nash equally as paranoid.

"You want him dead..." said Nash abruptly. He wanted to grab the words back the moment they left his lips.

For a moment, Dietrich just stared back at him and Nash thought he had made a big mistake. But he took a long inhale, held it and then with unblinking eyes said yes.

"I want to take this place from him and turn it into something proper. In better hands, this place could be a safe haven. Taking this place from him is going to be a delicate, complicated affair so please keep all of this between us."

"Of course," said Nash.

"As awful as it sounds, I got lucky with having Sherry here. It was an easy out, not having to partake in his communion like the other junkies here. The two of you will have to figure something out soon though. He won't be okay with you making him wait."

"I know," said Nash.

"I've already prepped him that you're good outside the walls. We've been here for a while but there are still plenty of areas around to explore. He sends groups outside daily to monitor the surrounding areas and to bring back supplies. He already knows I want you on my team, so if you ask him, he'll let you."

"And what about Melissa?" Nash asked.

"We can either get her an easy job in here or we might be able to get her on my team as well. You'll have to play your cards really well, Nash. You'll have to play the game."

"I know what to do," said Nash and stood with Dietrich as he shook his hand. They could see that Duncan was walking down the street with one of the gardeners who had finished his daily duties and noticeably strung out on his communion.

"I'll keep you in the loop as much as I can, but for now, the less you know the better," said Dietrich as he patted Melissa on the shoulder and made his way to the foyer.

With that, Dietrich left the house and joined Duncan and the junkie as they walked down the street. Nash could see through the edge of the curtain that Duncan was straining his neck to see into their windows.

"I never would have guessed he'd gone through all that," said Melissa as she rubbed her face in exhaustion.

"I had a feeling he wanted Fletcher gone but I never knew his motivation."

"You said you had an idea on what to do for communion," she asked.

"I do; it's going to make our house a little weird for the next while."

Church bells began to sound loudly, like an alarm.

"What's going on?" Melissa asked, eyes wide. She pointed towards the windows as a dark silhouette ran past.

Nash leapt to his feet at the sound of the front door opening, expecting to see Duncan but instead, a somewhat panicked Dietrich appeared in their foyer.

"You need to come with me, right now," he said, as people ran wildly through the street behind him.

Chapter 22

"What's going on?" Melissa asked nervously as they joined Dietrich outside.

"Just follow me, and please, keep calm with what you're about to see," he said as they hurried down the road. "Any erratic behavior is going to show your hand and he'll have you killed on the spot."

The streets were dotted with people as they made their way toward the center of town. Some of them moved quickly with big smiles on their faces, while others walked at a normal pace, expressionless as they went down the road. Melissa nudged Nash and pointed to the steps of a house as they passed. A woman sat on her porch, barely able to hold herself upright as she sat immersed in the trip of some drug she had taken.

The church bells continued to ring loudly as Dietrich led them to join a growing group of people heading for the back of the church. Other members of the Treefort had gathered too and were intermingled with the members of Fletcher's group. It was the first time they'd seen everyone gathered at once, and each of them had the same shallow, empty stare that Nash easily recognized from when he'd first met Barry.

Fletcher stood centered on a large platform situated directly against the back of the church as the group crowded around him. He raised a walkie-talkie to his mouth and a moment later the bells atop the church stopped chiming.

"Thank you all for coming," said Fletcher. A scepter was resting on his shoulder while he spoke. "Most of you know what this meeting is all about, but for those who don't, this is an atonement ceremony."

The group stood in silence and watched him speak, as they hung on his every word. Nash and the rest of the Fort members listened to him with a nervous curiosity.

"Bring her up," said Fletcher as he tapped his scepter on the wooden platform.

Duncan walked up a set of stairs at the edge of the platform, pushing a woman in front of him. The woman had her hands bound in front of her as she struggled to keep her balance, Duncan nudging her from behind. Her eyes were sunken in and empty, and once again, Nash was reminded of the day he'd met Barry on the roadside.

"*Please*," said the woman, the word barely audible as tears rolled down her face.

"*Quiet!*" yelled Duncan and smacked her across the face with an open palm. She sobbed loudly as members of the group laughed and mocked her.

Nash looked at Dietrich in horror, shaken by seeing Duncan so aggressively violent toward the woman on the stage. Dietrich looked forward, his face unwavering, which sent a message to Nash to keep his cool.

"Most of you know Rose," said Fletcher as he placed his arm around the lady's shoulder. "Rose has been with us for about four months and she's done wonderful things while working at our beauty salon. But, what she did last night was anything but wonderful."

The woman continued sobbing loudly. Nash could see the imprint of Duncan's hand across her left cheek.

"Communion is a very, *very* simple idea," continued Fletcher. "You tell me what you want and I give it to you. In return, you work for me. You help me in keeping this oasis of ours afloat. The key to that statement is *I give it to you!*"

Fletcher's anger drew some light applause and a few whistles from the overly faithful.

"You get your communion from me, *weekly*. You don't go around my back to try and get more and you *especially* don't break into the storehouses and steal from me. Like I said, it's a very simple idea, which means there's no room for second chances."

"Please, Mr. Crawford! It won't happen again, please!" Rose's words were slurred, the drug she'd stolen clearly altering her senses.

"I know…" said Fletcher.

With that, he removed a large Bowie knife from behind his back and ran it quickly across the woman's throat. Blood sprayed from her neck as she fell to her knees, gasping and gargling as she tried in vain to take in air. Duncan put his arms underneath her armpits, which forced her arms out to her side as she bled out helplessly in front of a now cheering crowd.

"For you new folks, this is a perfect example of how things go around here, and for everyone else, let this be a reminder. *My* rules are not to be trifled with."

Fletcher placed his index finger into the flow of blood that came from Rose's throat. Behind him, on the outside of the church, were dozens of reddish-brown tally marks. He walked up and ran his bloody finger on the wall, leaving a new, crimson-red tally beside all the others. Fletcher left the platform, which left Duncan behind to hold the dead woman up in front of the now silenced crowd. He began to wiggle her arms about wildly and made her corpse dance in front of him like a marionette.

"That's enough, Duncan!" yelled Dietrich from the crowd.

"Too soon?" asked Duncan as he looked over to the edge of the stage to find that Fletcher stood and motioned for him to join. "You're no fun, *Dietrich*."

Duncan let the woman's body fall in front of him into a growing pool of her own blood as the group slowly dispersed.

"Let's go," said Dietrich, snapping Nash and Melissa out of their shock.

Chapter 23

The atonement ceremony had closed and the group had mostly departed, save for a few junkies who stayed behind to poke and giggle at Rose's body. Dietrich led Nash and Melissa to the park across from the church and sat in the shade of a large oak tree.

"You could have warned us!" Melissa hissed.

"No, I couldn't have," said Dietrich as he sat on the bench in front of them. "There is nothing you could have done to help her and I didn't want the two of you going in with chips on your shoulders. I am sorry though. It's not an easy thing to watch."

"How often does that happen?" asked Nash.

"Often enough. Usually more often after a new group has joined us; someone trying to escape or taking more than they were allotted in their communion."

"Can you take Melissa back to our house?" asked Nash.

"*Pardon me?*" Melissa reeled. "I'm not going *anywhere* with anyone but you."

"I'm going to Fletcher to take our communion and I don't want you around while I do it. I'm dreading what I have to do, and I don't want you to see it."

Melissa sat for a moment, staring at him with apprehension in her eyes before she stood to join Dietrich.

"Good luck," said Dietrich.

"I'll need it," he said to himself.

He inhaled deeply as he sat alone on the bench, looking at the church that loomed nearby. A church was not a place to sell your soul. It was supposed to be a place where you could save it;

or at least redeem it. That's how Nash chose to look at this moment. That's how he would live with his communion. Take communion, save Melissa. He repeated this mantra in his head as he made his way to the doors of the church.

The guards opened the large double doors as he approached and smiled at him as he walked up the steps and into the church hall. Fletcher sat on his throne at the end of the isle, his legs crossed with a book in his lap.

"Nash!" he cooed as he adjusted his glasses and closed his book. "Come on up here, my boy!"

Nash walked briskly up the aisle, glancing briefly at the women sitting in their pews as he walked. He noticed a few more open spots as he approached and his stomach clenched.

"I'm sure you and Melissa were shocked by the atonement ceremony. I'm sorry about that."

"I'm not going to lie Mr. Crawford, it's not what I expected to see once the bells started ringing."

"Oh please, my name is Fletcher. I don't think we'll ever be seeing the two of you on that stage so don't worry yourself too much. What can I do for you?"

"Well, I have a few things actually," said Nash, his hands in his pockets as he talked. "I was talking with Dietrich today and he was telling me there are groups that do sweeps of the area outside the walls."

"That is correct," said Fletcher. "Dietrich told me you handle yourself well out in the wild."

"I did daily trips outside the fence back at the Treefort," he said. "I'd like to do the same for you here."

"I see," said Fletcher as he sat forward slightly in his seat. "That could be arranged, I suppose."

The two of them stood in silence as they listened to the soft breathing of the women around them.

"I think you know what's expected of you next," said Fletcher with a stern face.

"Melissa and I talked a long time about what we could possibly take for communion. It wasn't an easy talk, and I learned a few things about her I hadn't known before. She would have come with me but she's too embarrassed. I hope that's okay."

"Of course. I will eventually like to speak with her about her communion, in the future when she's more comfortable."

"I do have one condition, though," said Nash, timidly.

"Go on," said Fletcher as he grabbed his scepter and leaned back into his chair.

"Melissa comes with me, outside the walls, whenever I'm out there."

"You're worried about leaving her alone in here with Duncan."

"Yes. He's threatened her in the past," said Nash. "Do we have a deal?"

"We do. Tell me, what is this communion that your girlfriend is so embarrassed over?"

"This is confidential, I assume?"

"Of course," said Fletcher. "Don't worry, he'll never know."

Nash came forward and stood beside Fletcher, scanning the women who sat in the pews.

"I never would have guessed," said Fletcher with a smirk. "Take your pick."

"They're all gorgeous," said Nash as he scanned the women in front of him. "How do you keep them so fresh looking?"

"Well," said Fletcher as he got out of his throne and stood next to Nash. "I have a few beauticians living here and they take good care of them daily. Rose was one of them, so I guess I should say I *had* a few beauticians. They dress them, wash them, do their makeup and hair. These women live the good life here, as you can see."

Nash locked eyes with a woman in her early twenties, sitting in the front pew right in front of him. She had shoulder length red hair, with slight freckles on her cheeks and big green eyes. Her makeup was done to perfection, with bright red lipstick and thick black eye lashes.

"She's splendid," Nash said as he stepped forward and ran his hands through her hair.

"Oh yes," said Fletcher. "She's in the front row for a reason. Easy to look at, isn't she?"

"That's putting it lightly."

"Go ahead," said Fletcher, goading him. "Take a closer look."

Nash ran his hands up and down her soft, exposed arms, surprised at how warm she was for a slowpoke. Knowing Fletcher was watching him, he cocked his head to the side and ran his hand under her dress, cupping one of her breasts and squeezing softly. Fletcher watched him with a smile, rapping his fingers on his scepter.

"Take a look under the hood," he said.

"I think she'll do just fine," said Nash, looking into the deep green eyes of the redhead.

"Is she for you, or the girlfriend?"

"Oh, she's definitely for both of us."

"Alright then," said Fletcher, laughing slightly as he watched Nash with a smile.

"We want her full time."

"That's a tall order," said Fletcher. "She's quite popular around here. You'd be breaking a lot of hearts by taking her out of rotation." Nash stood determined, looking intently at Fletcher as he waited for his response. "Then again, the thought of that cute

Tim Gabrielle

little girlfriend of yours in the sack with Samantha here makes me smile. I'll allow it."

"Just curious…how do you keep them sitting still like this?"

"The dumb ones are actually quite trainable. Newer girls will try and get up and walk around but if you just keep sitting them back down, they eventually stay put."

"Never would have guessed," said Nash, inspecting Samantha with his eyes.

"Anything else I can help you with, Nash?"

"No, I think I'm all set. Thank you, Fletcher." Nash smiled as he took Samantha's hand.

"I think you'll both be very happy with her. Her physical upkeep is up to you at this point, but our beauticians are available whenever you'd like. To keep them nourished, we have a formula we've created that she can drink, three times a day. Easy as that."

"Thank you," said Nash as he smiled beside Samantha.

"Why the change of heart, Nash?" asked Fletcher, showing his skeptical side. "You seemed pretty stuck in your ways last time we spoke."

"Dietrich," said Nash. "He was at our house earlier today and told us about the woman he lives with and made it sound so nice. I was shocked when he left and Melissa said we should do the same."

"He's a good man to have around," said Fletcher. "And she sounds like a wildcat! You're a lucky man, my friend."

"Thank you," said Nash and shook Fletcher's hand.

"Go, enjoy her. Have fun. I'll talk with Dietrich and get you set up with a field partner and you can start tomorrow."

Nash forced a smile and walked away, leading Samantha by placing his arm around her waist and guiding her in the same direction. Fletcher chuckled as they walked together, side by side.

When the doors closed behind them Nash felt the need to apologize to the dead woman, "I'm so sorry," he whispered. He was mortified by the way he had to touch her in front of Fletcher. He was disgusted by the way this seemed natural to Fletcher and his men.

Dietrich stood across the street from where they walked, talking to one of the gardeners as they worked. He gave Nash a slight nod as they continued down the road. The sun was getting low and the sounds of the dead amplified, always louder as the sounds of the day receded and gave way to the quiet of night.

He opened the door and led Samantha inside. Shocked didn't begin to describe the look on Melissa's face. Fear, hurt, disdain, all fluttered across her features.

"What the hell Nash?" she demanded. Nash released the slowpoke and locked the door behind him.

"Say hello to Samantha," said Nash.

"I see, Samantha, why is she here Nash?" Melissa's voice was just a decibel lower than a screech.

"She is our communion, or at least she's our fake communion." Realization dawned on Melissa's features and she looked Samantha over again.

"She looks so...*alive*."

"I know. They all do."

"How'd it go?" she asked, as she inspected Samantha.

"Horrible," he said and hugged her tightly. "What they think is normal is scary. But I had to convince them." Melissa nodded, hugging him back – her gaze not leaving Samantha.

"And did you?"

"I think I did," he said. "Fletcher thinks you're a wildcat."

Melissa snorted, surveying their guest. "She's gorgeous."

"He has people taking care of their looks. The woman that was killed today was one of them."

Nash and Melissa jumped as a knock came from the front door. Samantha stood without reaction, looking at the door with a blank smile. Nash looked through the side window to see the familiar silhouette of Dietrich, standing alone on their porch in the dark. He opened the door as the cries of the dead flowed into their foyer.

"I see you chose Samantha," he said as Nash closed the door behind him. "She gets a lot of use around here. I'm glad you got her out of the rotation. When do you have to have her back?"

"We don't," said Nash as he looked out the window again to make sure nobody was around.

"How the hell did you swing that? You didn't promise him too much did you?" asked Dietrich as they all moved into the living room beside the foyer.

"Not at all. I did exactly what we talked about. He said he's going to be talking to you and placing me with a partner tomorrow. I made it all seem like it was Melissa's idea to have her here. The thought of her and Samantha together was enough to get what we wanted."

"He hides it well, but Fletcher's downfall will be his perversion with women. Not many people know this, but the part of the church he lives in is filled with women like Samantha."

"Melissa is coming with me, outside the walls," said Nash. Both Dietrich and Melissa looked at him, surprised by the idea. "I'm not leaving her inside alone with Duncan. He's been watching us since we got here and I'm not taking any chances."

"Good call," said Dietrich. "I'm going to go talk with Fletcher now, get you all set up. I'm going to have you out there with a girl named Emma. She's a friend."

"How many *friends* do we have in here?" asked Melissa as she guided Samantha onto the couch and sat next to her.

"Not many," he said. "We have to wait for the right opportunity. I need to caution you both not to cross his guards.

Any of the men wearing the black suits are his personal security detail and they are the most depraved individuals inside the walls. Their communion is horrific and they take it whenever they want. They'd die for him without question."

"What do you mean by horrific?" Melissa asked.

"Nobody really knows these things," he said as he looked out the window through the side of the curtain. "I'm not sure which one, but one of them has a taste for children and Fletcher has a few younger dead ones stored somewhere in the church. I don't know where."

"That's…that's just…," she stuttered.

"Horrifying?" Dietrich offered. Melissa nodded, her face white.

"Why not tell everyone these things?" asked Nash. "I'm sure if everyone knew that sort of thing, they'd be ready to throw him out themselves."

"Everyone here is so wrapped up in their own communion that nothing else matters. I can tell you that a good amount of your people have already given in. I've seen drugs, alcohol, and women already given out to them. You two are young and probably didn't have the kind of vices that older members of your group had before the rise of the dead. Addiction is a strong motivator, and Fletcher knows it."

Neither of them had any clue that so many in their group would fall so easily to the communion offered by Fletcher Crawford. There was a small glimmer of hope that maybe the residents of the Treefort were doing just as Nash was —faking it.

"We have a friend from our group. Her name's Dianna," said Nash. "She was partners with Sullivan, the leader of the Treefort. She could be an asset to our cause."

"I think I know who you're talking about," said Dietrich. "She's a taller, larger framed woman, correct? Long, brown matted hair?"

"Yes, that's her," said Melissa.

"She's knee deep in a pool of alcohol right now," said Dietrich. "I saw her leave the church earlier with a duffle bag. All I had to do was walk past her to hear the clanging of the bottles inside. I saw the look on her face as we passed. She's mourning and old vices die hard. I think the best thing is to just keep her safe until we are ready to act."

"I never would have guessed she'd have been an alcoholic," said Nash as Melissa leaned onto his shoulder.

"There's a lot about your group you probably don't know, or want to know for that matter."

With that, Dietrich walked past them back into the foyer. He left the soft scent of cologne, a strange smell that neither of them were used to smelling but were learning to appreciate.

"I'll have Emma come by in the morning to get you. We don't have the kind of protective gear I saw you wearing back in the woods, so you'll have to be on guard. You're sure you're comfortable with this, Melissa?"

"I'm sure. I'm safer with Nash out there than I am in here."

"I would agree," he said as he opened the door and stepped into the dark. "See you tomorrow."

Nash shut the door and watched him disappear into the night. They stood together in the foyer, looking into the living room as Samantha sat alone.

"She makes me so sad," said Melissa while she watched Samantha smile back at them.

"Let's get her upstairs and into a bedroom," said Nash as he walked into the living room and helped her up.

The three of them made their way upstairs; Nash in the lead, holding Samantha's hand as Melissa followed behind. Melissa came around and opened the door to the bedroom that was directly next to theirs, which was just as lavishly decorated as their own.

"Stay with me for a minute," he said as he flicked on the light to illuminate the room. He wasn't used to having electricity again but he was quickly becoming accustomed to it. "I want to see if she was bitten."

"I never even thought about that," said Melissa. "You don't think he would…"

"Yeah, I do," said Nash as he slipped the straps of Samantha's dress off her shoulders.

The sundress fell to the floor in a crumple as she stood naked in front of them just as she had with so many men before. She continued to smile, her breasts protruding in front of her as Nash and Melissa awkwardly began their inspection.

They each took one of her arms, turning it over in their hands as they looked for any sign of a bite mark. After inspecting her legs, Nash stepped back to let Melissa inspect her breasts and buttocks. They sat her on the bed and inspected the bottoms of her feet and in between her toes, not leaving a single inch of her uninspected. Nash looked up to see her smiling back at him, which made him blush with awkward nervousness.

"It's okay, Nash," said Melissa, smiling as she continued to look at Samantha's right foot.

"This is just so weird," he said as he pulled Samantha back onto her feet and placed the sundress on over her head. He and Melissa looked together behind her ears and all throughout her perfectly done hair.

"I didn't see a thing. Not a single bite mark or scar," said Melissa.

"That's because she wasn't ever bit," said Nash as he met Samantha's smiling gaze. "He's handpicking girls for his brothel."

"Right from the people he brings back…" Melissa's thoughts trailed off in the same direction as Nash's.

"We can't step out of line, Mel. Not a single toe, not for a while." Melissa swallowed hard.

A shared fear swam through both of their minds as Melissa leaned into Nash's shoulder, feeling Samantha's gaze on them the whole time. Finding not a single bite mark on her had confirmed a fear that Nash had already been holding onto since they met him at the church.

Fletcher Crawford wanted Melissa for his collection.

Chapter 24

Emma showed up the next day, just as Dietrich said she would. She was a short woman in her early thirties, with short cropped, brown pixie hair. She wore a tank top, which revealed arms covered in tattoos from wrist to shoulder. Nash and Melissa stood shell-shocked at the open door, looking at the woman who almost in every way reminded them of Eliza.

"Everything okay?" asked Emma. Her deeper voice contrasted with their memory of Eliza's higher pitch.

"Yes, sorry," said Nash as he introduced himself and Melissa. "You remind us a lot of someone we used to know."

"Good thing or bad thing?" she asked.

"Good thing," said Melissa, smiling.

"Dietrich caught me up to speed," said Emma as she handed them both a loaded handgun and Bowie knife. "Try not to use these unless needed. When we're outside the walls, stay with me and you'll be fine. I'm sure I don't have to explain to you what it's like out there."

"We know all too well," said Nash. He knew how to handle himself outside the walls, but for Melissa, this was a first. "We'll follow your lead."

Emma reached down and handed them each a duffle bag, which they both slung over their backs as they walked toward the center of town. Nash looked up Dianna's street as they passed, only to see the curtains still drawn—no signs of life.

"I checked on her this morning," said Emma as they continued passed the street. "Dietrich told me about her and that you were worried. She's liquored up something fierce, but she's okay."

"What is she doing for Fletcher that she has so much time to sit around drinking?" asked Nash.

"Fletcher knows that she and your group's leader were an item, and she was supposed to be the one in charge coming in here," said Emma. "I think he's just letting her self-medicate herself into oblivion to keep her out of the game."

"Guess that makes sense," said Nash. "He's very calculated, that one."

"Other than the gardeners and the people from our group, we've hardly seen anyone out and about," said Melissa.

"That's about right. Most everyone around here barricade themselves inside throughout the week, either strung out on drugs or screwing their days away. Makes me sick to my stomach."

"Where's he getting all these drugs?" asked Nash.

"It's only one drug, actually. He has a team here that makes it for him, his own recipe. It's ingestible and he's had them craft it to look like a communion wafer."

"He has a bit of a God complex, doesn't he?" Nash asked. He watched the guards let in another familiar face from the Fort into the church. Emma simply smiled as they continued walking.

A man with thick flannel shirt sat on a bench with a rifle resting on his lap. He had his legs crossed, with tattered jeans and thick work boots.

"Good morning, sexy," he said as they approached.

"Just open the cover, Brad," she said sternly. Nash could tell this was something she dealt with often.

"Okay sweetie, don't get your panties in a bunch…if you're even wearing any. Are you?"

The three of them stood silently as Emma and Brad stared each other down. Nash fought the urge to stand up and say something in her defense, but knew from their short interaction that she was more than capable to stand on her own.

"Oh well, a man can dream," said Brad and grabbed a crowbar from beside him to pry open the manhole cover.

The three of them climbed down the ladder leading to the sewer below as Brad placed the cover back. The musty air choked them slightly as they inhaled and Emma flicked on a powerful flashlight, which illuminated the long underground tunnel.

"This is the best way to get out of the Mansion without drawing attention from the dead," she said as they moved through the tunnel. They walked in silence for a few minutes before coming to a stop near another ladder that led up to the street. Emma led the way, stopped at the top, and knocked five times on the cover with a pair of brass knuckles. A few moments later, the end of another crowbar appeared in one of the holes of the cover and it was lifted from its base.

"Thank you, Allan," she said as she climbed out of the hole and into the sunlight. Nash could tell she had said it with a smile. They came out of the sewer one by one and were greeted by a tall, tanned man with a ponytail. He had a thick beard, which hid the tattoos on his neck that seemed to join tattoos on his chest underneath a sleeveless t-shirt. He leaned down and kissed Emma on her smiling lips.

"Nash and Melissa, this is Allan," she said. They shook hands quickly and exchanged small talk before they headed off down the road toward a row of burned down homes.

"How long have you been together?" asked Melissa as they walked.

"About a year, actually," she whispered. "His camp and my camp were brought here within days of each other."

They stopped for a moment as Emma surveyed the area with a pair of binoculars. Most of the dead from the area were drawn to the Mansion, which made the area around them relatively safe. Looking back, Nash could see the Mansion, complete with hundreds of howlers squawking as they attempted to breach the walls. They covered the entirety of the wall and made it almost impossible to pass without sending out the motorcycles to draw them away.

All around them were burned or torn down homes, many of them having X's painted on the doors. Nash knew without asking that those were the houses that had already been searched, which gave Fletcher's group no reason to return. They walked through the streets, littered with bodies and broken down cars. The occasional slowpoke scowled or smiled at them as they passed, a few of them even slowly followed them through the street. They wove their way through the broken down subdivision, finally making a stop in front of a two level home surrounded by a white picket fence.

"It's pretty basic," said Emma as she pulled out her knife and opened the gate of the fence. "We go in, we take anything of value, and then we leave. Keep your knives out and your guns ready."

"Do you find a lot of howlers inside the houses?" asked Melissa as she looked at the row of untouched homes.

"Howlers...I like that," said Emma as she continued up the walkway. "Most of them are drawn to the Mansion but you'll find one every so often."

Overgrown grass nipped at their legs like the fingers of the dead as they made their way up the walkway. They each surveyed the windows of the home, remarkably untouched by time, and tried to find any hint of movement inside. The front porch was sturdy and didn't creak at all as they walked up the hardwood steps and made their way to the door, which hung open halfway. Emma placed her hand on the door, ready to push it open, but stopped and turned toward them.

"I've always called the slow ones smileys. What do you call them?"

"Slowpokes," said Melissa with a smile. "I like smileys too."

Emma smiled again and nodded her head before she pushed the door open and stepped inside. It creaked angrily as it swung open and revealed a house completely torn apart by a long gone howler. They walked silently from room to room, checking for the dead, before they looked for anything to salvage. The three of them entered the dining room and saw two slowpokes sitting at the kitchen table as if expecting a meal to be served to them. Their skin was pulled back harshly against their bones as the two of them sat together, hand in hand slowly fading away. Pictures on the walls around them showed the couple in their days before the fall, smiling down at the empty shells of their former selves.

"It's almost romantic," said Emma as she regarded the couple together at the table.

"It's heartbreaking," said Melissa, her arms crossed in front of her chest.

Nash and Emma both walked forward and drew their knives as they positioned themselves behind the couple. They both silently slid their knives into the back of each slowpoke's skull as the couple lurched forward and fell dead onto the table.

The rest of the homes were completely void of any howlers or slowpokes. Nash understood why the Mansion had done so well for so long, seeing how they each walked away with their duffle bags completely full. They worked meticulously, moving from one house to next, marking the ones they'd looted so no one repeated the same job twice.

The last home of the day had looked as typical as the other ones on the street. The picket fence opened easily, just like every other house, as did the front door. There were no signs of the dead, but unlike the rest of the homes, it had been completely looted and emptied.

"Why just this house?" whispered Nash as they stood quietly in the empty kitchen.

"Spread out, eyes open — first sign of danger make a bee line for the front door," Emma ordered. It was like following Sullivan on one of their rounds, and Nash felt a pang of loss clench his heart.

They covered the main floor quickly, finding it just as empty as the kitchen. Other than the sound of their footsteps the house seemed eerily quiet. Emma nodded toward the stairs and they slowly made their way to the upper level.

As they crested the stairs, they were hit with the putrid stench of death. "Someone died," Melissa whispered. Emma held a finger to her lips and she and Nash took each side of the hallway.

Two doors hung open on either side of the hallway. Facing them from the end of the hallway was a closed door with a pool of dried blood seeping out from underneath.

Nash stepped in front of Melissa and Emma took the lead, un-holstering her gun. The smell got worse the closer they got to the closed door. Melissa hid her nose in her shirt, eyes watering.

Emma reached her hand toward the doorknob but stopped as the sound of soft sobbing registered from behind the door.

The three of them stood frozen and watched the door as they listened to the sobbing continue. Emma stepped back and drew her gun and gestured for Nash to open the door as she readied herself. Nash turned the knob and opened the door slowly to reveal a dead body hunched over on the tiled bathroom floor. The floor was covered in garbage, piled all around the body. Beyond the corpse, hiding in a clear but mildew-stained shower curtain, was the silhouette of two huddled figures. The sobbing continued as Emma moved toward the shower, her gun now holstered as she held her knife at the ready.

"Please…" said one of the voices, weak and tired from behind the curtain.

Emma froze with wide eyes and stared at the murky curtain as the silhouettes nervously continued sobbing. Nash moved past her and flung open the curtain and revealed two girls in their early twenties, dirty and frightened, who flinched at the site of their knives.

"It's okay," said Nash as he put his knife away, motioning Emma to do the same. "You're safe."

The two girls wiped their tired eyes and quieted as best they could as Melissa rushed in to join them, her face shocked by their condition. Their faces were sunken with hunger as their dirty clothes hung from their frail bodies, making it obvious they'd been on their own for a while.

Nash and Melissa helped the girls out of the bathtub, the smell of body odor and filth stirring through the air as they stepped out of the tub. One of the girls began to sob louder at the site of the dead body.

"Just close your eyes," said Melissa as she helped her around the corpse.

Nash and Melissa guided them to the biggest bedroom and sat them on the bed as Emma did a final sweep of the other rooms. Behind the dirt and fear, they could tell the two girls were twins. Their hair was long and stringy, having stopped caring for it long ago.

"My name is Nash, and this is Melissa and Emma."

The girl sitting on the right was much more visibly shaken by the experience. Her gaze remained on the floor the entire time.

"I'm Jessica," said the girl on the left, wiping the tears from her eyes as she spoke. "This is my sister, Courtney."

"How long have you been here?" Emma asked.

"I have no idea," Jessica said. "A month, maybe? We were traveling with our mom through the area and ended up in a chase with some of the fast ones. We ended up here and haven't left since." Courtney sobbed again and the thick tears fell onto her lap. "My mom injured herself pretty bad during the chase. That's her in the bathroom."

"I'm so sorry," said Emma as she reached out and took Jessica's hand.

"Are you from that group inside the wall?" asked Jessica, with hope in her voice as she spoke. Emma looked at Nash, not knowing quite what to say. "We've wanted to make it there for a while, but it's too dangerous around the wall."

"It's not much safer inside the walls," said Melissa, who stood behind them in the doorway.

"Anything has to be safer than what we're doing now," said Jessica, looking past Emma and Nash at Melissa.

"No, she's right," said Emma. "It's not safe inside the walls."

"If you're not going to take us there, you can just leave," said Courtney, her sobs having been replaced with sharp anger. Jessica placed her arm around her sister in an effort to comfort her.

"It's going to be safe soon," said Emma as she took her bag off her back and dumping the contents onto the ground against the wall. "The place inside the wall is being run by a very bad man. Bringing the two of you in there would be certain death for you both."

"We have plans to change things," said Nash as he dumped half his bag into Emma's so she didn't return empty handed. "We just need time. We're telling you this to protect you."

"What do you suppose we do then?" Jessica snapped, looking at the food and water bottles now sitting in a pile.

"Just be patient a while longer," said Emma. "Eat, drink, and stay safe. Once things are different inside the wall, we'll come back for you."

"You cannot leave this house though," said Nash. "We're not the only patrol that's out here so you have to stay hidden. We're going to mark the outside of the house so that everyone knows it's been checked, but you can't be seen, under any circumstances."

"And how do we know we can trust you," Courtney asked when she finally looked up to meet Nash's gaze.

"They gave us all their supplies, Court," said Jessica. "Plus, we don't have much of a choice."

"I'm outside the wall twice a week," said Emma. "I'll check in on you as much as I can. I'll knock five times on the wall at the bottom of the stairs so you'll know it's me."

"Just stay hidden and you'll be fine," said Nash. He lifted up his pant leg to reveal the knife from the Treefort. Jessica inhaled sharply, and leaned away, shielding Courtney with her body. "It's okay," Nash said, holding a finger to his lips. "This is my favorite knife; it's light and sharp. Here," he held it out to Jessica. "Keep it for now, just in case. When we bring you back to camp you can give it back to me."

"Thank you," said Jessica, a glimmer of hope starting to return to her eyes. She cradled the knife in her hands and sat up a bit straighter.

"Most of the dead are going to be attracted to the wall, so you shouldn't have to worry too much about them. Just stay hidden and we'll see you soon," said Emma.

The two girls smiled slightly as the three of them left the room. Emma pulled Nash aside to the bathroom and waved for Melissa to join them.

"We can't leave her here," she said, grabbing an oversized towel from the towel rack.

Emma laid the towel on the ground beside the dead woman and rolled her onto it. Her skin was stuck to the bathroom tile in a pool of dried blood, which created a wet, tearing sound as her body fell limp on the outstretched towel. Melissa turned away, disgusted by the decomposing woman as Jessica and Courtney came into the hallway.

"Don't look girls, we're just taking her outside," said Melissa. "We can't bury her because a grave would arouse suspicion, but we'll find somewhere peaceful for her. I promise."

Courtney tucked her tearstained face into her sister's shoulder. Jessica wrapped her bony arms around her and the two cried softly as Nash and Emma passed them with their mother.

Melissa walked ahead of Nash, opening the front door. Beside the house, they found an old garden, overgrown with weeds and yellow flowers. Nash and Emma gently placed the dead woman on top of the tall grasses and the flowers and greenery enveloped her.

"We'll bury her one day, if we can," said Emma as she left the woman behind as she returned to the front door. She shook a can of orange spray paint wildly before spraying a large X on the front of the closed door. "That should do it."

"Should we expect this kind of thing every day?" asked Nash with a smile.

"Don't count on it," Emma laughed.

The street was void of howlers, but a few slowpokes dotted the scene as they made their way back to the wall. Allan stood atop an old van and waved at them once they came into view.

"Hello again," he said with a smile and climbed down the ladder on the back of the old camper van as he noticed the concerned look on Emma's face. "Is everything okay?"

"Yeah," she sighed. "At least I hope so. Found two girls out there—pretty shaken up." Allan climbed back onto the roof and looked back toward where they had come, using his binoculars to search the area for the house Emma described.

"I think they'll be okay," he said. "I can't see the house you were talking about. As long as it's tagged, they'll be fine."

"Hopefully they can join us, sooner than later," said Emma as Allan climbed down from the van again and kissed her once more.

He opened the manhole for them, Emma dropping down first to catch the duffels Nash tossed down to her. When they got down in the manhole, they secured the bags to their backs before heading back toward camp.

Emma again took the lead, and climbed the ladder leading to the Mansion first. She rapped five times on the metal before the cover was lifted. She handed her bag up through the hole to a waiting hand, and then pulled herself up and out of the ground. Nash and Melissa followed suit.

"Have a good time out there, *Buddy Boy*?" asked Duncan as Nash climbed into the street.

"Where's Brad?" asked Emma as Duncan replaced the manhole cover.

"Why?' he asked as he took his seat again on the bench. "Feeling a tad horny, are we?"

"You're a pig," Melissa snapped as they walked away. Emma chuckled her agreement.

"You have no idea, sweetie," said Duncan.

"Please don't engage him," said Nash as they moved toward the road back to their house. "It'll never end well."

"I know. I couldn't help it, it just came out," she said as she looked up to see Fletcher standing on the steps of the church. He motioned for them to join him before he disappeared inside.

"I don't want you checking on the twins," said Emma. "You're too new and I don't want anyone watching you and catch you going there. I go on a run by myself once a week and I can check on them then. You both did great today."

"Thank you," said Nash as she took their duffle bags to deposit in the storage area.

They walked hand in hand to the church, moving up the steps to the open doors that awaited their entry. Fletcher was just sitting down on his throne and nursed a bottle of soda as they walked up the aisle.

"I love this stuff," he said as he held up the bottle of purple liquid. "It's one of life's greatest little gifts."

"I'd have to agree with you on that," Nash said with a smile when they came to a stop in front of him. Sitting in a pew midway up the aisle was a couple they both recognized from the Fort. They sat, still and silent, their facial expressions changing sporadically.

"Don't worry about them, my dear," he said as Melissa cocked her head to look at them. "They're both very much alive. They've simply taken communion today. Once they come back down, they'll be part of the church's cleaning crew. I like to keep a clean home."

"I can see that," said Nash as he looked around at the immaculate church. He scanned the rows of dead women and saw many more empty spots compared to the last time he was there.

"So tell me, how was the first night with Samantha?" he asked as he leaned forward while still holding on to his bottle of soda. Melissa smiled and blushed while she looked down at the floor.

"She's something else," said Nash, smiling as well.

"Well I'm glad you're enjoying yourself so far. How'd today go?"

"It went well. I find going through the homes exciting. Makes the time fly by," said Nash. Melissa stood next to him, still bashfully not making eye contact with Fletcher.

"Dietrich told me you'd be perfect for that detail and I have a feeling he was correct. Emma typically goes out every other day, plus once by herself throughout the week. She and that Sam have a romp in the streets on her solo days, but that's not my business."

Nash and Melissa looked back at the couple sitting in the pews as a soft moan came out of the girl's mouth. They were starting to come back to reality, blinking their eyes as they fidgeted in their seats.

"It's about time!" Fletcher said and clapped his hands together once, jolting the couple slightly. "Nash, Melissa...go enjoy your day! I saw the bags you came in with and I'm very impressed with your first haul."

"Thank you," Nash said as he turned to leave with Melissa. She smiled at Fletcher hoping her sweet and dumb routine was working. It must have been, because Fletcher's eyes never left her body as she and Nash walked together down the aisle.

Chapter 25

Nash and Melissa made their way from the church as Melissa grappled with the show she'd just put on for Fletcher.

"That's not easy," she said. She still felt Fletcher's searing gaze on her.

"I know. Trust me, I know too well," said Nash as he thought back to the night before when he brought home Samantha.

Melissa stopped him in the middle of the street and looked down the line of houses to where Dianna had barricaded herself. Dietrich was sitting on a park bench outside her house, with his legs crossed while he read a book.

"We should check on her," said Melissa as she walked down the street and pulled Nash behind her.

As usual, the streets were bare, save for a man and a woman from the Treefort who sat together on a porch swing, each holding a bottle of whiskey.

"Is there anyone from our group that didn't take his communion?" asked Nash as they joined Dietrich at the bench.

"Doesn't appear that way," he said as he closed his book. "I'm assuming you're here to check on Dianna."

"We were thinking about it," said Melissa as she sat on the bench next to him.

"She's been blacked out for a while. I've been checking on her periodically, just to make sure she's okay. Duncan's been skulking around the street all afternoon."

"For what purpose exactly?" asked Nash as he looked down the street and saw Duncan walking away.

"Your guess is as good as mine, but I imagine it isn't good. For whatever reason, he minds his manners more when I'm around, so me just sitting here has kept him away."

"Have you actually talked with her at all since she came here?" asked Melissa.

"No. She was personally escorted to Fletcher the day you got here, before anyone else had a chance to talk to her. He knew she was important to your group and wanted her in control quickly. I'd say he's done a pretty damn good job because she's been drunk ever since."

"We needed her," said Nash as he rubbed his eyes. "You have no idea how beneficial she could have been to us. I think she expected Sullivan to survive."

"The best we can do is continue to keep an eye on her. How was your first day outside the walls?" he asked.

"I think you should go and talk with Emma," said Nash as Melissa stood and joined him. "Everything's okay, but you should speak with her."

"Alright," said Dietrich, standing with a puzzled look on his face. "I'll come by your place later."

The two of them stood together on the sidewalk as Dietrich disappeared down the street. The blinds were all pulled shut in Dianna's house, with no signs of life at all as she lay blacked out in the upstairs bedroom.

"I feel so bad for her," said Melissa as she put her arm through Nash's and leaned into him. "I have no idea what to do."

"I don't think there's much we can do. She's a mess because of what happened to Sullivan and if Fletcher keeps feeding her booze, nothing will change. Dietrich is right, though; we just have to keep her safe."

The screams of the dead filled their ears as they made their way along the wall on the road to their house. The church bells began to ring again, indicating another atonement ceremony.

Doors along the street burst open as people flooded into the streets, running toward the middle of town to join in the excitement.

"We'll skip this one," said Nash, taking Melissa's hand as he continued toward their home.

"I think I'd be happy never going to another one of those ever again."

People continued to make their way toward the church as the two of them disappeared into their house. Nash closed the door and Melissa made her way into the kitchen. He turned to join her, but stopped at the sight of a dirty smudge right above the doorknob. He leaned forward and took a closer look, since he hadn't noticed it that morning when they'd left for the day. He racked his brain, trying to remember if either of them had dirty enough hands to have left a mark and he knew that neither of them had. A loud banging jolted him from his gaze and made him jump backward away from the door.

"Knock, knock, fucker," said Duncan from the other side of the door.

Nash double-checked that the door was locked before he headed to the kitchen, leaving Duncan alone on the front porch.

"Was that Dietrich?" asked Melissa with her head inside the fridge as she pulled things out to make lunch.

"Far from it," he said as Duncan appeared in the window above the sink.

"You two can't ignore me forever," he said, his face almost pressed against the window. "Why aren't you at the atonement ceremony?"

"Goodbye, Duncan," said Nash as he pulled the curtains shut and Melissa stood nervously behind him. They stood motionless and watched his silhouette from behind the safety of the curtains.

"I put my dick on your doorknob earlier. Enjoy that."

With that, his shadow moved away from the window and disappeared. Nash glanced from behind the curtains to see him walking across their yard, not leaving before he unzipped his pants and urinated on their grass again. Melissa had a can of disinfectant spray in her hand before Nash could even turn around.

"He's disgusting," she said as she disappeared into the foyer to clean the doorknob.

Nash unwrapped a granola bar and followed behind her as the church bells stopped ringing. The smudge from the door had been wiped away, smeared on the cloth that Melissa was now using to disinfect their front doorknob.

"I wonder how often they do these ceremonies?" asked Melissa as she feverishly scrubbed the doorknob.

"I imagine the people here aren't the most stable or predictable. It's a miracle he's been able to keep any order at all."

"I feel so bad for Courtney and Jessica," said Melissa, putting the can of disinfectant on the porch as she sat on the top step. "They were both so scared when we found them."

"They're lucky we found them before any of his other people did. We shouldn't be talking about this out here."

Nash opened the door and let her inside when a round of cheers scattered into the wind as Fletcher delivered another deathblow for the crowd. They sat together in the kitchen and ate cans of fruit as they talked about the twins they'd met that morning. The streets became loud again as the people of the Mansion made their way through the streets, hooting and laughing from the show they'd just witnessed.

"I hate this place," said Melissa as she looked past Nash and outside the window in disgust.

"I know. Try not to focus on it too much. Eventually, it'll be different."

A gentle knocking sound came from the foyer as they exchanged a nervous glance. Melissa walked to the kitchen window and craned her neck, trying to see who was there with no luck.

"I swear it better not be Duncan," said Nash as he walked slowly to the foyer. He was relieved to see Emma and Dietrich standing outside, waiting patiently to be let in.

"Let's have a drink," said Dietrich as he held up a bottle of whiskey as he and Emma entered the foyer.

Melissa went into the kitchen to retrieve glasses while Nash led Dietrich and Emma into the living room. The furniture was brand new and still smelled of new leather. Melissa placed four glasses on the coffee table before sitting next to Nash.

"Those two girls don't have any clue how lucky they are that you found them," said Dietrich, leaning forward as he poured the whiskey into the glasses. "A set of twin girls would for sure go right to his personal collection."

"He'd have no way of telling if they'd turn into a howler or a slowpoke," said Nash as he grabbed his and Melissa's glass and sat back on the couch.

"He'd accept the risk," said Emma, drinking the whiskey in one shot and then poured herself more.

Melissa and Nash held their glasses in front of them, smelling the liquid nervously. Dietrich smiled at them as he watched them silently debate the alcohol.

"I'm not too worried about the drinking age these days," said Dietrich with a smirk. "You don't have to partake if you don't want to."

Nash and Melissa looked at each and shrugged before clinking their glasses together and downing the liquid. Melissa immediately spit it back into the glass and coughed while Nash placed the glass on the table with a grimace on his face. Dietrich poured himself more while he and Emma laughed at their reactions.

"Wow!" said Nash with a smile and a cough.

"That'll be it for me," said Melissa while putting her glass back onto the table.

"How about some cards?" asked Dietrich as he unwrapped a deck of cards and shuffled them quickly.

The four of them played cards and talked throughout the entirety of the afternoon. The laughter and lightheartedness was finally broken by the church bells ringing once again as sunset approached. The street outside once again erupted into fits of wild laughter as the group made their way to yet another execution.

"People don't learn around here, do they?" asked Melissa.

"It's rare that it happens twice in one day like this but when Fletcher finds someone skirting his system, he doesn't hesitate to drop the hammer," said Emma, as she gathered up the cards and placed them back in the package. "We should go. We missed the last one and he usually expects us to be part of them."

"Lucky you," said Melissa as they all stood together.

"This was a lot of fun. Took my mind off everything going on around here," said Nash as they moved into the foyer together.

"Well, we'll make sure to do it more often," said Dietrich as he opened the door and let Emma outside. "Have a good night, you two."

Nash and Melissa followed them outside and stood on their porch as Dietrich and Emma joined a group of three people walking toward the ringing bells. The sun was creeping toward the horizon and cast an eerie glow over the Mansion.

"I am unbelievably tired," said Melissa, yawning as she leaned against him.

Nash led her to their bedroom. Melissa kissed him on the cheek before she disappeared into the shower, leaving him in the hallway outside their room. The sound of the shower filled the upstairs as he went into Samantha's room. She was sitting at the edge of her bed, smiling at him as he came in to visit her.

"Hey Sam," he said as he pulled back the covers of her bed and helped Samantha to her feet. She met his gaze with the same goofy smile she always wore. "It's time for bed."

Nash situated her under the blankets and stood beside her, looking down at her clueless face. Having her in the house with them still felt strange to him but her absent-minded smile almost conveyed a sense of appreciation.

"Goodnight, friend," he said as he left her alone in the room.

The shower was still running as Nash walked into the bedroom, kicked off his shoes, and took off his shirt. He contemplated joining Melissa, but the exhaustion of the day compelled him to lie on the bed and wait his turn. The rhythmic beating of the water against the shower floor echoed in his head as he closed his eyes and immediately fell asleep.

Chapter 26

Nash woke up to the smell of blueberry pancakes. The early morning sun illuminated the room as he tossed the heavy comforter to the foot of the bed. There was a bluebird on the tree outside his window, singing its morning song as Nash got to his feet and stretched his arms high above his head.

"Nash! Breakfast is ready!"

His mother's voice echoed through the house as he opened his door with a yawn. The light outside his room was blinding, stopping him in his tracks to rub the sleep from his eyes. The sound and smell of crackling bacon bombarded his senses as he made his way down the stairs to the kitchen where his mother was waiting for him.

"I hope you're hungry, I made extra today!"

Her voice sounded strange to him, almost as if someone was trying to impersonate her. The light from outside continued to blind him as he walked passed the windows. He used his hand to shield the fierce glow. He squinted through the light and saw their front yard glimmering outside. The light gave everything a shimmering, hazy shine, as if it were a mirage at the end of a highway.

"Honey, come eat," said the voice in the kitchen, still sounding strangely foreign to him.

The kitchen was bathed with the same wild glow as every other room in the house. His mother stood in front of the stove with her back toward him as she continued to cook. Nash sat down at the table and watched her with a smile, ready to devour his favorite Sunday breakfast.

She began to hum a song he didn't recognize as she moved a pancake from the skillet to a plate already piled high. He watched her as she rhythmically moved back and forth from between the bacon and pancakes while she hummed a song and bobbed her head to the tune. The crackling of the bacon was interrupted by a sound in the distance, a familiar sound that seemed to vibrate the harsh light in the kitchen. He listened intently as it approached, getting louder and closer. He wracked his brain and tried to pinpoint the source of the sound.

He felt a sudden wave of terror as he realized the source of the sound. It was a low, deep chuckle that radiated through his mind like a hot iron. It was something he thought he'd never have to hear again and something he'd never wanted to hear again. Coming closer, second by second, was the unmistakable giggle of Barry.

His mother stepped back from the stove and dropped her spatula. The laughter got louder, almost seeming to be right outside the window as the metal spatula came to rest on the tiled floor. The laughter stopped and sent the room into a deafening silence that seemed to numb his mind. His mother's terrycloth robe had loosened slightly, and the fabric belt fell to her side. The light blue strap hung loosely beside her, the tip drenched in blood and dripping onto the floor.

"Mom?" he asked, frozen in fear and unable to move from behind the table.

She stood for a moment, motionless, hardly even breathing while Nash continued to watch her from his seat. The fabric belt of her robe continued to drip endlessly, creating a pool of blood on the tile below. Her head turned slightly toward him; the room was so quiet he could hear the tendons in her neck stretch.

****

Nash opened his eyes in the darkness as Melissa breathed softly beside him. Moonlight had replaced the harsh, shimmering glow of the sunlight in his dream. He laid still in the darkness and thought about his mother making breakfast for him as Barry's laugh echoed in his mind. As time went on, he found he didn't think about his mother as much as he had when he was alone on the road with Duncan. Even if it had just been a dream, he found himself wishing he'd been able to see her face again.

He gently removed the comforter and sat on the edge of the bed. The stench of the days sweat reminded him that he'd fallen asleep while waiting for the shower. He undressed slowly, his head still swimming from his dream as he turned on the water. The water took a moment to warm up but steam quickly filled the room. The hot water rolled over him in waves releasing the tension in his shoulders and clearing his mind.

Silence returned to the room as he turned off the water and stepped through the shower door. He dried off quickly and brushed his teeth, something else he'd forgotten to do before he accidently fell asleep. He slipped on a clean pair of boxer shorts and stood at the bedroom window, looking out across the dark Mansion. Most of the houses had electricity but the streetlights were left off during the night, coating the streets in darkness. He could see patches of orange glowing here and there where people sat around fires.

A small shriek came from Samantha's room, just loud enough that Melissa stirred slightly. Slowpokes would sometimes shriek during their sleep, something he'd always known but still took some getting used to. He pulled the comforter over Melissa and left the room to check in on Samantha. The moonlight illuminated the room enough for him to see her still tucked into her bed where he'd left her. Her eyes fluttered endlessly behind her eyelids as her lips moved from a smile to a grimace over and over again.

"What do you dream about?" he whispered to himself out loud.

He imagined Samantha getting glimpses of her old life, which brought smiles to her face before flashes of her life now chased them away. He left her alone and made his way down the staircase, heading to the kitchen to get a drink. Walking down the moonlit staircase as if he was walking through a ghostly storybook, he reached the kitchen and took a can of soda out of the fridge. Soda was something he missed terribly from before he hit the road with Duncan, and having a fridge full of it was one of the perks of living in Fletcher's compound.

The sound of the can opening echoed through the silent house as he lifted it to his lips and drank half of it in two gulps. He put the can back in the fridge and stood in front of the kitchen window, looking out across their dark yard. He'd already learned to ignore it, but the sound of the dead behind the wall echoed loud throughout the night; a constant reminder of what was hidden just out of reach.

Just as he turned to leave the kitchen, a small orange light appeared at the edge of their grass before it faded into nothing. He watched for a moment until it appeared again, only to disappear once again.

"Damn you," he whispered into the darkness. "What are you doing here?"

The cigar faded in and out a few more times before it shot across their yard like a falling star. Nash strained his eyes through the darkness just enough to see Duncan's silhouette fade into the night.

"Unbelievable," he said and left the kitchen to make sure the doors were locked and secured.

Chapter 27

On the two-month anniversary of settling at the Mansion, Nash and Melissa collected supplies outside the walls with Emma like they did every other day. The routine never changed; they collected supplies, looked for survivors, and marked the houses with their spray paint. In the time since they found the twins, they'd discovered no other survivors in the suburb surrounding the Mansion.

"I'm not feeling this today," said Emma, the bags under her eyes dark as she spray painted an orange X on the door of a house they just searched. She used a cloth to blow her nose before throwing it onto the grass. "What do you say we pack it in early?"

"Probably for the best," said Nash as he comically stepped away from Emma as to not catch her cold.

"Oh stop, if you're gonna get it, you'd have it already!" she said and tossed the spray can at him playfully.

"Ok, stop flirting, you two," Melissa laughed.

Allan greeted them with a smile, as usual, and kissed Emma on the lips before they made their way down the manhole. The three of them climbed out of the sewer and into the streets of the Mansion just as the church bells began to ring.

"We'll skip this one," said Nash, walking with Melissa toward their house as Emma disappeared into town.

"I need to ask you something," said Melissa as they made their way down the road.

"Oh boy," said Nash, knowing a serious discussion of some sort was on it's way.

"This might sound strange, but have you ever felt like someone else has been in our house?"

Nash thought back over the last months and tried to recall anything he could to support her question. "I remember finding a really distinct dark smudge on the inside of our door in our first few days here. I don't think either of us had left it. We got distracted and I think you cleaned it after that so I forgot to mention it to you. Why do you ask?"

"I dunno. Maybe it's just a feeling, but I've noticed little things here and there. Nothing big, which is why I never mentioned it to you."

"The night of our first day outside the wall, I caught Duncan watching our house from the road in the middle of the night."

"You're just telling me this *now*?" asked Melissa.

"Well I didn't want you to worry. I don't know if he saw me watching him from the kitchen but he hasn't been back since. Not that I've seen, anyway."

"Nash..." Melissa said, staring at the group of people staring at Fletcher on the stage.

"Oh God..." Nash said as Fletcher stood with Sarah in his grasp.

"What the hell could she have done wrong? She's the sweetest woman I've ever known." Melissa remembered how kind she had been, volunteering to help her with the food truck rations.

"I have a feeling he could find an issue with any of us from the Treefort."

Fletcher shook Sarah, trying to get her to cry or respond to the accusations he was leveling at her, but Sarah stood firm. She found Nash and Melissa in the crowd and stared at them with sad, tired eyes. Fletcher followed her gaze to the two of them, watching from the stage as they stared back with sorrowful eyes. Fletcher straightened his posture and instead of the usual slice on her throat, he stabbed her in the stomach repeatedly until she finally cried out in pain and slumped to her knees.

Nash and Fletcher continued to stare at each other as Melissa turned and walked away. Fletcher placed his boot on the back of Sarah's head and pushed hard, sending her flying forward onto the wooden stage. Her blood reached the edge of the stage and started to pour like a waterfall as Nash turned and hurried to catch Melissa.

"Mel…"

"I don't want to talk, Nash. Let's just get back to our house."

They walked back to their house with Sarah's scared face carved into their minds. Atonement ceremonies had begun to happen almost every other day, sometimes even daily. On Dietrich's advice, Nash and Melissa had started attending most of them, simply to be seen by Fletcher in the crowd. They'd walk together to the town center and watch Fletcher murder a new person, but usually stood far in the back as to not be too close to the action. Each time someone from the Treefort was dragged on stage was hard for them but something about Sarah's murder sent their minds ablaze.

"I need to get out of here," Melissa said as they approached their front door."

"I know…"

Nash stepped onto their front porch and stopped in his tracks, listening to the sounds of someone rustling around inside. The sound was faint but as he locked eyes with Melissa, he could tell she heard it as well.

"Stay here," said Nash as he slowly opened the door.

Nash stepped inside and grabbed a baseball bat from the coat closet at the base of the steps before he slowly worked his way up the stairs. As he climbed upwards, it was clear to him that he was listening to the sound of Samantha being raped in her bedroom. As his eyes crested the top step, what he already knew was confirmed as he watched a half-naked Duncan in Samantha's room, on top of Samantha as he violently moved against her.

"*You son of a bitch!*" yelled Nash as he ran into the room and swung the bat at Duncan's head.

"Hey, Buddy Boy!" yelled Duncan while he used his forearm to block the bat and falling off Samantha in pain. "*You little prick, that fuckin' hurt!*"

"*Get out of here!*" screamed Nash and positioned the bat for another blow.

"Take it easy, *you cock*," yelled Duncan, pulling his pants up while he winced in pain. "I think you broke my fucking arm. You're in so much shit, you don't even know."

"If I ever see you here again, I'll kill you!" said Nash as he let Duncan out of the room and followed him down the stairs.

"Sure you will, big guy," said Duncan as he cradled his forearm and fumbled hurriedly down the steps. "*You're* not fucking her! Somebody's gotta!"

"*What the hell's that supposed to mean?*" asked Nash as he chased Duncan outside.

"You're a lucky girl!" yelled Duncan to Melissa as he passed her outside. "That Samantha's a good lay!"

"*Oh go to hell you damn pervert!*" yelled Melissa as Nash guided her back inside.

"Don't," Nash said as they made their way up the steps.

"*Don't tell me what to do!*" she yelled as he closed the door behind them.

"*I'm trying to protect you!*" Nash yelled. It was the first time he'd raised his voice to her and he immediately felt bad. He reached forward to pull her in for a hug only to have her push him away with both hands.

"I can't do this, Nash. This is all too much! We need to leave!"

"*Keep your voice down!*" Nash whispered, forcibly. "Do you think I *want* to be here? I hate this place and these people just as much as you! Dietrich has something in the works and we just have to trust him. All I can do right now is trust him and keep you safe in the meanwhile."

"I know. I'm sorry," said Melissa, putting her arms around Nash. "I appreciate you watching out for me. My blood just boils when he's around. Was he doing what I think he was doing?"

"He sure was. He's probably been doing this whenever we are outside the walls, which might explain you feeling like someone has been in the house."

Melissa visibly shivered at the thought as the two of them walked up the stairs to check on Samantha. She was laying on the bed with a smile on her face as they entered the room. She fixed her gaze on Melissa as Nash picked up her sundress to cover her up.

"Not yet," said Melissa, taking the dress from him and placing it on the messy bed. "She needs a shower. A very hot, thorough shower."

The two of them helped her from the bed and into the bathroom. Nash left Melissa alone to clean Samantha and went back into her room to clean up the mess Duncan had left. The entire room smelled of sweat and aggression. Nash ripped the blankets and sheets off the bed and tossed them aside in favor of clean sheets. He was tucking the last corner of the mattress into the sheet when the church bells began to ring again in the distance.

"Are you kidding me?" yelled Melissa from the bathroom. "*Again?*" She turned the shower off and patted Samantha's skin dry.

He could hear the crowd cheering in the distance as Fletcher took the life of another of his residents. Melissa led

Samantha into the room, covered in a robe with her wet hair hanging against her neck.

"I'm not in the mood to do her hair right now so she gets to have frizzy hair this afternoon," said Melissa, dropping Samantha's robe as she quickly slid a clean sundress over her figure. "Should we say anything to Fletcher about what Duncan did?"

"I think we may have a bigger problem," said Nash, his arms crossed in front of him and moving to look out the window. "I think Duncan knows we aren't using Samantha for sex."

"I heard that," she said, sitting Samantha on the bed. "He's been watching us, hasn't he?"

"I think so. This is bad, Mel. I feel like I need to let Dietrich know."

"Well he can't do anything, can he?" said Melissa. She sat beside Samantha and rubbed her shoulder soothingly.

"No, I suppose he can't."

"I can't take this place anymore, Nash. Do you think Dietrich is almost ready to move forward with his plan?"

"I don't even know what the plan is but I hope so. Dietrich is smart and calculated; he's not gonna make his move until the perfect moment presents itself."

"Sooner than later, I hope," she said, wiping away another tear out of her eye.

Banging from the front door rattled the entire house as they turned away from the window.

"What now?" Melissa said. She followed Nash out of the room, leaving Samantha perched at the edge of the bed. Nash motioned for her to stay behind him as the crept down the stairs toward the foyer.

Through the front door window they could see Fletcher standing on the front lawn about ten feet from the door, Duncan and another of Fletcher's henchmen stood on the porch.

"Don't open it," said Melissa and stepped back nervously.

"I have to, Mel. Fletcher's with him."

Nash steeled himself and unlocked the door. His hand hovered over the doorknob while he prepared to put on his smiling face when the door burst open and knocked him to the ground. Duncan stormed in first while the second man, a hulking beer-bellied mass, came into the foyer and shoved a shotgun in Nash's face, forcing him to the ground.

Duncan grinned at him from the foot of the stairs before he charged up. Melissa's face shifted from surprise to horror as Duncan headed for Samantha's room.

"Duncan! What is this?" Nash yelled.

"Just let it happen, my boy," Fletcher yelled from the front yard, his demeanor calm as usual. "That's two ceremonies you've missed today, for the record."

"Oh, God," Melissa whispered when Duncan reappeared at the top of the stairs. He dragged Samantha down the stairs, tossing her at Melissa's feet.

"Come on, *darlin'*!" Duncan crowed. He grabbed Melissa by the hair and shoved her face toward Samantha.

"Let go of her!" yelled Nash as Melissa winced in pain.

"Shut up!" the man growled, shoving the gun against Nash's head.

Duncan roughly let Melissa go and delicately brushed a strand of hair behind Melissa's ear. He leaned in close, and cupped the back of her neck in his hand, directing her to look at the slowpoke on the ground. "Fuck her," Duncan whispered.

"What are you doing, Duncan?" Nash demanded.

"Another word from you and I'll put a hole in your head," said the gunman.

"I said, *fuck her*," Duncan whispered, his lips grazing the side of Melissa's temple.

"Why are you doing this?" asked Melissa as tears ran down her cheeks from her red eyes.

"Oh come on, honey! If you're anywhere near the pervert that Fletcher's told me you are, you'll probably enjoy it more with us watching!"

"I know I'd enjoy it," said the gunman, grinning.

Samantha stared up at Melissa with the same trusting smile she had every day, her happy face sending chills down Nash's spine as he watched helplessly from the ground. Duncan grabbed Melissa's hand firmly and shoved it hard between Samantha's legs.

"Work your magic for us, honey," he said, taking his hand away as he watched the tears continue to rush down her face.

"Why are you doing this?" she asked as she struggled to get the words out.

"I knew it, you little *bitch*," said Duncan as he pushed Melissa to the ground. He snagged Samantha by the hair and dragged her out to the front lawn.

"*Stop!*" yelled Nash as the man shoved the barrel of the gun firmly against his chest.

Samantha continued to smile as Duncan roughly flung her around. The gunman dropped his weapon from Nash's head and followed Duncan outside, whistling. Nash rushed to Melissa's side and took her in his arms.

"Come on outside, *Buddy Boy*!" yelled Duncan.

"I'm sorry, Nash," Melissa croaked. "I couldn't do it."

"It's okay," Nash soothed, brushing her hair.

"What's going to happen if we go out there?" Melissa whispered.

"Nash." Fletcher's voice cut across the lawn. "I need to see both of you down here. Now, please."

"We have to do this, Mel," he whispered to her.

Melissa wiped her eyes the best she could before she nodded to him and rose to her feet. Nash walked at her side, his arm around her waist. Each step felt like it was a mile long. They stepped out onto the front porch and found the three men standing on the lawn, Samantha on her knees in front of them. Her dress was lying beside her on the ground and she smiled wider at them as they exited the house.

"The day we met, Nash, I *knew* you were going to be trouble," said Fletcher. "Duncan has always told me you were a pain in the ass, but I had high hopes for you. To be perfectly honest, I still do. You seem like a reasonable kid, so I think you can still be reasoned with. It's not a hard concept to grasp; you do something that benefits me that you were already doing at your old camp, and in return I give you *anything* you could ask for."

Nash watched as Dietrich came walking up the road but stopped far away to observe.

"Everyone from your camp, and I mean *everyone*, fell in line, except you two. I give you the nicest house this place has to offer. I give you the freedom to work outside the walls, *with* Melissa, as per your request, and this is the thanks I get. I even gave up my most beautiful girl, for the two of you to do as you please, and I find out today it was all just a lie."

"*You son of a bitch*," yelled Melissa as she lunged toward Duncan as Nash grabbed her.

"She's a feisty one, Fletch!" said Duncan as he and the gunman laughed together.

"What did you expect from us, Fletcher?" asked Nash. "There's nothing we wanted from you. We just want to live in peace."

Silence filled the space between them as Fletcher regarded them. "You've done me well, kid," Fletcher said, finally. "I don't have any reason not to believe that's going to stop. With that being said, this kind of behavior is unacceptable. This isn't how I saw today going, but I think this situation warrants it."

Without breaking eye contact with Nash, Fletcher held out his hand for the shotgun.

"Please, Mr. Crawford, don't," said Melissa. She started forward, but Nash grabbed her arm and held her back.

"Honey, a little tough love goes a long way," said Fletcher. He grabbed Samantha by the hair and pulled her into the middle of the yard. He took a couple steps backward before firing the shotgun at the back of her head.

Samantha's head erupted into a splatter of blood and flesh as she crumpled forward to the ground. The two men on each side of Fletcher cheered, clapping their hands with smiling faces. Fletcher handed the gun to Duncan and stepped in front of Nash and Melissa.

"I hope you understand the seriousness of this situation," he said calmly. "This is your final warning."

"Fuck you!" Melissa yelled. Fletcher stared at her as she gazed back at him intently.

"She don't get it, boss," said the man standing with Duncan.

"No, Paul, I don't believe she does," Fletcher said. He continued to stare at her, silently weighing his options. "Grab her."

"No!" screamed Nash as Paul stepped forward and put his muscular arms around Melissa. Melissa began to scream but stopped when Paul smacked her hard across her face. Duncan stepped forward and secured Nash as Paul carried Melissa away with Fletcher walking beside him. "Fletcher, you gotta let me fuck her before she's turned! I can't leave it to chance that she'll be a slowpoke!"

Nash wiggled his arm free and landed a punch against where he'd hit Duncan with the baseball bat. Duncan wheezed in pain as he let go but was able to grab Nash's left wrist as Nash turned to run. Nash turned and swung his right fist as hard as he could and connected with Duncan's mouth, sending him backward to the ground in shock as Nash took off.

"Stop," said Fletcher, calmly pulling a handgun from behind his back and pointing it at Nash. "Give me one reason why I shouldn't put a bullet in your brain and sit Melissa in one of my pews?"

"I'll mind them, Fletcher," said Dietrich, joining them. "Leave them in my charge. They're both excellent outside the wall. They're two of the only ones here that are easily trusted not to be drunk or high when on a run. Please, leave them with me. I'll keep them in line."

Fletcher held the gun in one hand while pointing it at Nash. He looked at Dietrich, considering his offer in silence. "Anything goes wrong and you'll be the one putting them down. Understood?"

"Yes, I understand."

Fletcher lowered the gun and smiled at Nash. "See, I can be reasonable. Paul, put the girl down. Duncan, let's go."

Paul dropped Melissa to the ground with a chuckle as the three of them left the property. Nash quickly helped Melissa to her feet with tears in her eyes. A large, red handprint had already formed across her cheek. Duncan looked back at them from the road with a scowl and a trickle of blood on his lip.

"It's time," Dietrich said, glaring back at Duncan until he disappeared out of their view.

Chapter 28

Nash guided Melissa up the stairs and into their bedroom. She sat on the edge of the bed, her face throbbing with pain from Paul's slap. Her eyes were a deep red, filled with shock and sadness as the bathroom filled with steam from the shower.

"I love you," he said when he pulled her to her feet and wrapped his arms around her. "It's going to be okay."

"I want to leave," she said as she pulled back and looked into his eyes. "The next time we go out on a run, I want to leave."

"You know we can't do that," he said as he brushed a wet strand of hair off her cheek. "He'd find us, and kill us. If he can't find us, he'd kill anyone associated with us here."

"Is it almost over?" she asked.

"Yes. You heard Dietrich, he's ready to move."

Without saying a word, she walked slowly into the bathroom and shut the door behind her. Nash ran both his hands through his hair and exhaled deeply, trying to release the tension of the morning. He still felt the sensation of the gun pointing directly at him, turning his stomach as he relived the fear in his head. The shower continued to run as he left the room to stand in the doorway of what had been Samantha's room. Duncan's dirty footsteps left marks on the carpet from the door to her bed and back.

"You son of a bitch," he said out loud as he closed the door and made his way down the steps. He found a shovel and an old plastic tarp in the basement and brought them outside to find Dietrich already digging a grave at the edge of their property.

"Thank you for being there," Nash said, grabbing his shovel and starting to help dig. "I don't think there was anything I could have said to stop him."

"You're right about that. Melissa would have been turned by now if it wasn't for me being there. He's going to have the two of you under a microscope now."

"So what's the next step?"

"Give me some time. He's really expedited our timetable here. It's happening soon, just know that."

With the two of the digging in unison, the grave was finished quickly. They rolled Samantha onto the plastic tarp; her body covered with wet grass and blood. They stood looking down at her draped in the blue plastic.

"Should we get Melissa for this?" asked Dietrich as he looked back at the house. He caught a glimpse as she watched from the second floor window before the blinds shut in a flash.

"No, I don't think so. I don't think she could handle it right now."

The two of them shoveled dirt into the hole, covering the tarp until it was no longer visible. Nash wiped the sweat from his forehead and once again caught a glimpse of Duncan, who stood down the street in the shade of a tree.

"Duncan's been spying on us," said Nash. "That's how he found out that we weren't doing anything with Samantha."

"He's been standing there since you took Melissa inside," said Dietrich as he looked back to see Duncan walking away from them. "I know that you already went out today with Emma but I want to take you out on another run."

"Sounds good; any reason in particular?" asked Nash.

"There's something I've been wanting to show the two of you and today seems like the day. Meet us in an hour at the exit point."

Dietrich walked around the grave and patted Nash on the shoulder before he disappeared down the road. Nash grabbed his shovel and walked back toward the house. He felt a flash of anxiety as he made his way around the blood-streaked grass and up the stairs to the front door. He hadn't noticed it before, but there were splashes of blood on the steps and porch, which he slyly dodged as he disappeared into the house. Melissa was dressed and leaning on Samantha's doorframe.

"You okay?" he asked as he put his arms around her and placed his chin on her shoulder.

"He's just so *cruel*. She was living fine with us, away from all those horny bastards."

"I know," he said. "I'm going to go shower. Dietrich wants to take us out on another run today. Are you feeling up to it?"

"There's no way in hell I'm staying in here alone. Why does he want us to go out again?"

"No clue. The fact that he wants to show us personally means it could be big."

He kissed her on the forehead before he disappeared into the bedroom to shower and get ready to meet Dietrich. As he stood underneath the hot water, letting the events of the morning wash away, the shower door opened and Melissa stepped in with him, fully clothed as fresh tears ran down her cheeks. She closed the door behind her and hugged him tighter than she ever had.

"I can't live like this any longer," she wept as the water ran down her clothing and stuck to her skin. "It's too much; *he's* too much!"

They stood together in the hot water as she continued to cry and the underlying stress of living in the Mansion finally bubbled to the surface. He held her until she stopped crying, the steam rising above them like a dense fog.

"I'm sorry," she sighed, opening the shower door.

"It's not your fault," he said.

Nash quickly scrubbed all of Samantha's blood off his skin before he stepped out to dry off. He could hear Melissa still crying in the bedroom as she changed out of her wet clothes. Fletcher's threat of having to find a replacement for Samantha in his brothel terrified him. He shivered at the thought of Melissa sitting in the front row of his church, smiling as she waited to be given to someone as their communion. Listening to her sob in the next room, he felt more committed to that promise than ever.

He dressed quickly and found Melissa sitting listlessly on the bed as she stared blankly out the window. Seeing her lost in her sadness brought him to the edge of tears, her posture reminded him of all the girls in the pews.

"Mel?"

"Practicing," she spat. "If we stay here much longer he'll make me take her place."

Nash grabbed his backpack from the corner of the room and pulled out the empty Pop Tart package she'd given him in the first few days at the Treefort. The little red heart she'd drawn on the silver packaging stared up at her as she looked down at it with a smile.

"It might not feel like it right now but it's going to be okay," said Nash with his arm around her as he sat next to her on the bed.

"I know. When do we need to meet Emma and Dietrich?"

"Half hour or so. I'm going to go make us some food before we have to go. Are you okay?"

"I'll be fine," she said.

Nash kissed her on the forehead and left their room, closing Samantha's door before he headed to the kitchen. Melissa joined him shortly after and ate quickly before they left on their second run. Dietrich met them halfway, greeted them with a smile, and gave Melissa a hug.

"I'm sorry about what happened this morning. I promise it'll all be over soon."

"Either way it will be," she replied, her voice hollow.

"Emma will be joining us again. She'll be meeting us in a half hour. I told you to come early because I wanted to introduce you to someone."

The armed guards stood at the ready as the three of them walked in front of the church. Dietrich nodded to them as they walked and each of the guards nodded back as the trio passed by the church. The green space across the church was filled with people Nash had never seen before.

"I've never seen so many of Fletcher's people outside before," said Nash while he watched the crowd of people congregating outside.

"They're all between communions," said Dietrich. "When the streets aren't as busy, you can assume people are inside and strung out. We have a lot of drug users here."

They stopped in front of a large house, smaller than Nash and Melissa's but larger than many of the others around it. They walked up the sidewalk and Dietrich opened the door, letting them in first before he joined them inside.

"Welcome to my home," he said and closed the door behind them.

"It's beautiful in here, Dietrich," said Melissa as she looked around at the immaculately decorated home.

"Sherry always liked a neatly decorated house. I do it for her. Please, have a seat."

Nash and Melissa sat on a couch in the living room as Dietrich disappeared down a hallway. Nash could see Duncan on the road outside.

"Go to hell," said Melissa as they watched him pass.

Dietrich walked slowly into the room with a slowpoke at his side that had an emotionless face.

"This is Sherry," said Dietrich, as Nash and Melissa stood to meet her. "She's not a smiler, as you can see."

Sherry stood in front of them, dressed in a knee length dress and bare feet. Her chocolate brown hair was pulled back into a bun on the top of her head, with streaks of gray starting to appear at the base of her scalp.

"She's beautiful," said Melissa as she looked at the well-kept woman who stood in front of them.

"Thank you," said Dietrich with his arm around his wife. "It's not easy seeing her like this, but it's better than not having her at all. I'm sorry it took me so long to introduce you to her. I keep her private for the most part for fear of what happened this morning."

"You don't need to explain," said Nash. "We understand."

"I don't know why I brought you here," he said with a chuckle as they stood together in his living room. "I just wanted you to meet her."

"We're glad you did," said Melissa.

"I miss her terribly," he said while he looked at her longingly with a sad smile. "I'm sorry. Let me take her back to her room and then we can head out."

"I feel awful for him," whispered Nash as he watched Dietrich move slowly with his wife.

"It's actually kind of beautiful," said Melissa. "In a creepy way."

Nash nodded, "I can understand his refusal to let her go." Melissa squeezed his fingers once as they waited.

"We should go," said Dietrich as he closed Sherry's door and joined them in the living room. "I have something to show you outside the walls."

"I thought meeting Sherry was what you meant when you said you had something to show us," said Nash.

"Oh, no, not at all. Come with me and I'll show you something special."

They joined Emma at the sewer exit, her patience obviously stretched thin by one of Brad's advances as she stood with an angry scowl on her face.

"This cold is going to be the death of me," she said as she handed them each their guns before she disappeared into the manhole.

Dietrich tossed the empty duffle bags down the hole before climbing in himself as the cover slammed back into place. They were at the second ladder quickly and moved up fast after Emma knocked on the cover five times, as she always did.

"Hello again," said Allan with a smile as they each filed out of the sewer. He tried to kiss her on the lips but diverted him to her cheek before she sneezed into the wind.

"Steer clear, Al. She's a mess," said Dietrich with a smile as they shook hands. "Keep an eye out for us. If someone comes through, we'll need you to keep them busy."

"Will do," said Allan and smiled at Emma again before he climbed back onto the van and continued to survey the area.

"How have the twins been," asked Nash as they walked through the decimated streets.

"They have been amazing, actually," said Emma. "We've been making sure they're fed and healthy. I think you're going to be surprised by how much better they look."

"Oh, we're going to see them today?" asked Melissa with a smile.

"We're going there right now," said Emma.

Since the first time Nash and Melissa had come outside the walls with Emma, they'd looted hundreds of houses, each having an orange X on both sides of the door. They'd killed dozens of howlers and the area was vastly more secure than it had been back then, even though the area around the Mansion was thicker with howlers that it had ever been. They approached the home the girls had been hiding but Emma and Dietrich kept moving.

"Weren't they staying there?" asked Nash as they passed.

"We moved them shortly after you found them," said Dietrich. "We wanted them to be hidden farther away from the Mansion, just in case. We moved them about three weeks ago."

They walked down a street filled with mostly burned houses; a few dotted here and there were untouched by the flames. They walked up to a home with burn marks covering the entire right side of the home but otherwise in good shape. There were orange X's on each side of the door, which indicated it had long been looted and left behind to crumble.

Dietrich opened the door and stepped in, letting the rest of them walk in too before he closed it behind them. The stairway that led to the upstairs was a disaster, with broken furniture and glass sprayed up and down the steps. Dietrich knocked seven times on the wall before he scaled the disaster of a staircase.

"Watch how I climb, but stay here until I call you," he said as he moved up the stairs with ease.

It looked as if a howler had, at one point, peeled through the house and tore things from wall to wall, but as Dietrich moved up the steps and found precise footing among the debris, it was easy to see it all had been placed there intentionally. Dietrich disappeared down a hallway up the stairs as the sound of a door opening and closing echoed through the house. He was gone for a short moment before the door opened and shut again, followed by Dietrich reappearing at the top of the stairs to wave them up.

They climbed up easily enough, taking care not to disrupt the carefully crafted disaster scene. The top of the stairs was less obstructed than the steps, but still enough to ward off anyone who came looking.

"Here we go," said Dietrich as he came to a stop in front of a closed door at the end of the hall.

He turned the doorknob and pushed it open.

"Nash! Melissa!" said Courtney, who was sitting on the bed next to Jessica.

The twins shot to their feet and greeted them at the door with a hug. They each glowed with health, having spent the last two months being able to eat and drink freely and living a relatively tension free life as they awaited Fletcher's demise. There was something else in the room that quickly drew their attention away from the twins and reduced everything else to a blur. Both Nash and Melissa looked with tunnel-like focus.

Sitting in an armchair beside the bed with his legs propped up was Sullivan Grant.

Chapter 29

"Hey," said Sullivan with a smile, taking his feet down from the bed as Melissa and Nash looked at him from the doorway.

His trademark thick, straggly beard had been replaced with stubble, which revealed a bare patch on his left cheek where he'd been burned by the grenade blast at the Treefort. Melissa walked toward him quickly with watery eyes, collapsing into his arms as he caught her.

"How?" asked Nash as he looked at Dietrich. "He was confirmed dead."

"He *was* confirmed dead," said Dietrich. "By one of our friends, who I placed on the team that attacked the Treefort."

"How'd you find us here?" asked Nash as he struggled to believe Sullivan was in front of him.

"The last thing I remember was a grenade going off near me."

"Our guy found him shortly after that, passed out on the ground, but alive," said Dietrich as he ushered them into the room and shut the door behind them. "There wasn't much our guy could do to help during the attack, seeing how he was outnumbered by Fletcher's men, but he did his best to hide Sullivan and confirmed the kill."

"I woke up that night, the woods on fire around me. I'm lucky I woke up when I did because I would have easily burned to death. There's not much left in the woods; it's basically all gone."

"Fletcher's group left but circled back and torched the trees. He's luckier than he knows," said Dietrich, patting Sullivan on the shoulder as he looked out the curtained window.

"After that, I made my way the best I could. I was slow moving at first, seeing how this was healing and intensely painful." He pointed at his face, wrinkled and scarred from the grenade blast. "It's healing nicely and I look a lot more badass."

"That you do," said Nash as he shook his hand with a smile. "It's good to have you back around."

"Out there on your own, it's a nightmare, but here I am."

Nash looked around the room and realized it was covered in maps and written plans, as well as the names of key Mansion personnel.

"You've built another war room, haven't you?" asked Nash.

"I suppose I have."

"You're not going to like the state of our group," said Nash. "It's disappointing."

"You haven't told them yet?" asked Sullivan while he stared at Emma and Dietrich as they stood in the doorway.

"Told us what?" asked Melissa as she sat on the bed with the twins.

"It was in your best interest that you didn't know yet," said Dietrich. "I felt horrible keeping this from you, but I had to keep you safe."

"I feel like today is just full of surprises," said Nash while he prepared for the news.

"Fletcher's been bluffing you. I just realized it myself last week."

"Bluffing how?" asked Nash as Melissa grabbed his hand.

"He's been killing off most of the Treefort group," said Sullivan. "It's been happening from day one. Anyone who wouldn't partake in his communion, he's been having them killed or thrown outside the wall."

Nash and Melissa stood silent, trying to make sense of the news that had just been told to them.

"Think about it, Nash," said Emma. "The only people from your group you've seen are the ones whoring around with those slowpokes or strung out on his drugs."

"Oh my God," said Melissa, letting the truth of the situation settle in as she connected the pieces in her head. "How many are left?"

"Less than half," said Sullivan. "The only reason Dianna is alive right now is because of the damn alcohol she's drowning in. Pretty much all of the remaining civilians from the Treefort are taking his communion regularly, just to stay alive."

"He knows we haven't taken his communion," said Melissa.

"I know. Dietrich briefed me before bringing you up," said Sullivan. "That is why things are moving quickly now. We don't know how much time we have."

"Why don't we just stay outside the walls?" asked Melissa. "Tell him we ran, tell him we died, I don't care! We're safer hiding out here than we are in there."

"If we don't come back, he'll know something's up," said Nash. "We have no choice, we have to go back and play his game."

"He's right," said Emma. "You're on his radar in a big way after this morning. The pieces of the revolt are all in front of him; he just can't see it yet. If you run now, it won't take much for him to put the pieces together. You'd be putting the entire operation in jeopardy."

"*Quiet!*" hissed Sullivan. They became silent and gazed at him with nervous anticipation. From behind the door, there came a soft crunching, followed by the sound of banging down the stairway. Dietrich crashed through the door quickly, looking down the stairs to see the front door thrown open into the foyer.

"Look outside!" yelled Dietrich as he flew down the stairs quickly with Emma right behind him.

Nash flung open the curtains just in time to see Duncan disappear behind a row of houses as Dietrich and Emma spilled out onto the street. He opened the window and leaned out, pointing in the direction Duncan had run off.

"It's Duncan! He went that way!" he yelled and his voice cracking from frustration and fear.

Dietrich and Emma took off running in the direction Nash had pointed them in. Dietrich moved like an Olympic runner, jumping fences as he moved through the backyards of the homes to catch up to Duncan. Emma kept pace behind him with her gun drawn and held at her side as she ran.

"This is bad," said Nash as he stood with everyone else at the windows and watched as Dietrich and Emma disappeared from view.

"Who's Duncan?" asked Jessica as she rose with her sister and looked out the window.

"He's one of the higher ups at the Mansion," said Nash. *"How the hell didn't we see him following us?"*

"We need to move," said Sullivan as he started to take all his notes and maps off the wall.

"They have to stop him," said Nash as he helped Sullivan with the papers.

"It doesn't matter at this point. Whether he gets back or not, Fletcher will know. We need to prepare for the worst."

Melissa and the twins quickly filled an empty duffle bag with the food stored in the room and Nash and Sullivan did the same with the plans scattered across the walls. As they worked, a gunshot rang across the dead subdivision, followed by the sound of Emma's screams. They all froze in unison before running to the window to see if they could view anything.

"This is the last thing we needed today," said Sullivan as he listened to Emma's cries from the window. "Grab the bags, we're going down there."

Sullivan grabbed the heavy bags full of food and barreled out of the room, made his way down the stairs in a flash, creating a path from the others to follow behind. They filed out of the house together as Dietrich and Emma returned in a frenzy, holding up Allan between them as his legs listlessly tried to match their pace. He was shirtless and covered in blood as he held his balled up shirt against his chest.

"*Oh God, no!*" yelled Melissa as she placed a hand over her mouth.

"Duncan shot him," said Dietrich as he and Emma supported Allan the best they could between them.

Allan made no attempt to talk, but simply looked at them all with eyes that seemed to stare right through them.

"This is serious," said Sullivan as he replaced Emma in helping to carry Allan. "We need to move."

"He's going to have people tearing these houses apart to find us," said Dietrich. "We need to hurry."

Sullivan and Dietrich led the way while they supported Allan between them his balled shirt soaking wet.

"We lost our window, didn't we?" said Dietrich quietly as they walked.

"Let's just focus on getting to safety," said Sullivan as the group disappeared deeper into the subdivision; each of them knowing their world had just changed drastically.

Chapter 30

The sun set softly over the houses nestled inside the walls of the Mansion and cast long shadows across the well-maintained lawns. The inhabitants gathered outside, laughing and cheering as the sound of the dead fought to be heard. Fletcher Crawford stood in the middle of the street that led to the front gate and smoked a cigar as his parishioners continued their riotous symphony.

Loud, heavy metal music vibrated through speakers as the men and women inside cheered with delight and chanted lyrics of a song they'd heard hundreds of times. Most of them were inebriated in some way, reveling in their extra rations of communion. Fletcher watched the howlers outside that were pressing against the reinforced iron gates. Their long, gnarled limbs reached viciously toward him as their faces smashed angrily against the hard metal. He smirked slightly as he puffed cigar smoke into the air, not taking his eyes off them. It was a perfect image of what he'd created; a community where nobody comes in, or leaves, without his permission.

Except of course the traitors. But they wouldn't be traitors for long. His fingers itched to wrap around Melissa's throat – to force her to drink his special undead cocktail. She would be the perfect addition to his harem.

Duncan approached the wall with a ladder and placed it against the stone wall near where it connected to the gate. He climbed to the top, taking particular care to make sure he was completely out of reach of the dead, before he unzipped the duffle bag that hung from his shoulder. He reached in and took out two round objects and placed them on the ledge of the wall, making sure they were not in danger of rolling forward into the crowd of ghouls below. He turned and raised his hands triumphantly in the air to the cheers of the drunkards behind him.

Fletcher puffed more cigar smoke into the air as he and Duncan locked eyes. He nodded in approval as Duncan climbed down the ladder and flung it against the side of the wall. With a stoic look on his face, Fletcher admired the sixteen objects Duncan had deposited; eight lining the wall on each side of the gate. The heavy metal music continued to pump into the air as he finished the cigar and flung it to the ground crushing it with his designer shoe.

He walked back to the church as his congregation continued to cheer—the tables were turning.

Chapter 31

Allan died in the night as the sound of distant, muffled music flowed into the home they'd taken refuge in. Emma held him long after he'd passed, weeping softly as the rest of the group sat in shock. Sullivan stood guard through the night, watching from the upstairs windows for any sign of movement in the dark street. The music finally died after midnight as half the group struggled through a restless sleep.

"I feel like I need to prepare you for something," said Dietrich as he scanned the street with Sullivan.

"I know she's dead, Dietrich," said Sullivan as he crossed his arms in front of him. "Probably the rest of them too. I know the kind of man he is."

"Why bother returning then?" asked Nash. "We have nothing to go back to, so why risk it?"

"Your group isn't the first he's done this to," said Dietrich. "The amount of people he's killed is staggering. We can't leave him alone to just do it again to someone else."

Nash sat beside Melissa on the king sized bed as the twins slept beside her. He held her hand, rubbing it softly while he thought about the days to come. Emma stood and made her way to the second window, wiping tears from her eyes as she scanned the darkness.

"He knows I'm involved now," said Dietrich. "Sherry's gone, I know it. When we get inside the Mansion, I'm the one to kill Fletcher."

The room stood silent, the soft breathing of the girls in bed was the only thing that broke the quiet.

"Understood," said Sullivan. "Everyone should get some rest. We don't know what tomorrow will bring."

Dietrich and Sullivan took Allan's body into the garage of the home and laid him on the concrete floor with a sheet tucked around his body. Emma leaned in the doorway, watching them as she wiped fresh tears from her face.

"He needs to suffer," she said as she joined them beside Allan's body.

"I know, dear," said Dietrich, as he pulled her into a hug. Sullivan placed a hand on her back before he left the two of them alone in the garage.

"I'm going to stay in here tonight, if that's okay," she said.

"Of course," said Dietrich, letting her go as he disappeared into the house. He returned with some couch cushions and blankets.

"Thank you," she said as she laid the cushions on the floor and walked to the garage door, looking out the window into the deserted street.

"Get some sleep," said Dietrich as he closed the door behind him and left her alone with Allan in the garage.

Sullivan stayed awake the entire night and watched the streets for any sign of life as the rest of the group struggled through a restless sleep. Just as the sun began to warm the house, Courtney erupted from a nightmare with a scream. The entire house burst from their beds on high alert.

"What is it?" Nash demanded, scanning the room.

"I'm so sorry," Courtney sniffed as she rubbed her eyes. "I...I...I had a nightmare."

Nash's body visibly relaxed and Melissa dropped her knife to sit next to Courtney.

"It's okay, we all have nightmares." Courtney nodded, her sister holding tightly to her hand.

Emma joined them in the panic, a look of fear across her tired face.

"It's okay," said Dietrich as he started to open cans of food for everyone's breakfast. "Courtney had a nightmare."

"I'm sorry," Courtney said again. Emma gave her a sad smile and sat at the dirty table with Dietrich.

"What's our plan?" asked Nash as he joined Sullivan at the window and handed him a can of baked beans.

"As of yesterday, I was leaning more toward a tactical approach," he said while he was still staring out the window. "But now, I've changed my mind."

Sullivan turned around and held a grenade in the palm of his hand.

"Where the hell did you get that?" Emma asked, staring at the grenade.

"I swiped it from Fletcher's armory awhile ago," said Dietrich. "Given our current situation, I guess that's a good thing."

"What do you suppose we can do with one grenade?" asked Emma, taken back by Sullivan's change of plan.

"With one grenade? Very little, but think about what a hoard of howlers would do to that place. I think we blow the gates and let the howlers do the work for us."

"What about our people?" Melissa asked with alarm.

"Mel, honey, I can guarantee you they are all dead by now," said Dietrich. "He knows Sullivan's alive now. There's no way he'd allow them to stay alive, communion or not."

"Don't you think he'd keep them alive to try and lure us in?" asked Nash.

Dietrich shook his head no. "I know him. It's not his style. Now that he knows, he's going to purge the Treefort group, then come after us. I've seen him do it before."

"Then we come to him first," Sullivan said. "I can't leave him alive to do this to some other group."

"Before we do anything, we'll need to find weapons," said Emma. "Not everyone is going to die from the howler attack, especially Fletcher. I think it's safe to assume that whoever survives the initial attack will be heavily armed."

"Where do you suppose we're going to find the kind of weapons we'll need to finish the job?" asked Melissa.

"I can get us guns," said Sullivan. "Back at the Fort, I always kept a cache of weapons buried in the ground. When I woke up that day, there wasn't a chance in hell I was going to be able to get them with the fire, so I left. Nash, Melissa, and I will go and get the cache and regroup here later this afternoon."

"Take the twins with you," said Dietrich. "In the event that we run into trouble, they'd be safer with you, away from here. Emma and I can hold our own until you get back."

Sullivan led the way, moving quickly through the streets until they reached the interstate. It was clogged with cars and trucks, just like any other major roadway, and it didn't take them long to find an SUV with the keys still in the ignition.

Sullivan drove it across a grass field until he reached a back road and turned onto it, leaving a cloud of dust in their wake.

"This brings back bad memories," said Nash, sitting in the passenger seat as Sullivan drove.

"Yes. Yes, it does," he said as he squinted through the sun as they drove.

They'd been driving in silence for about an hour before Sullivan pulled the SUV into a familiar town, which Nash quickly recognized as the town they'd used to exile Duncan. A lot of the buildings were now burned to the ground; some of them crumbled completely into ashen piles.

"Fletcher likes to see things burn, doesn't he?" said Nash as they watched the blackened buildings fly by quickly as they exited the town. They drove past the remains of the SUV from the day Eliza died, which was still sitting upside down. Sullivan didn't slow in the least.

"That's where she died, isn't it?" asked Melissa. Neither Nash nor Sullivan responded.

Sullivan pulled the SUV over to the side of the road in the same area where Nash and Melissa had originally been loaded into Fletcher's trucks. They got out and stood at the edge of the blackened landscape, while they scanned the field of burned and fallen trees in front of them.

"I never thought it would look so awful," whispered Melissa, almost to herself.

"Come on," said Sullivan, squeezing Melissa's shoulder softly as he guided them into the remains of the forest.

The ground was covered in thick soot that crackled under their feet as they moved and sent black and gray ghosts into to the air as they walked. They crossed the murky creek, complete with a few burned slowpokes that had congregated there the morning of Fletcher's attack.

"Here we go," said Melissa as they approached the burned shell of the Treefort.

Parts of the fence still stood upright among the fallen trees and debris like blackened tombstones. The burned remains of both the people who once lived there and the people who came to destroy it lay strewn about the silent grounds. The RVs were nothing but charred skeletons, sitting eerily in the shadow of the once dense woods like phantoms in wait. Sullivan walked to the middle of the Fort and stopped at a pair of charred, flaking masses.

"Scott and Meghan," he said as he stood reverently above them while Nash, Melissa, and the twins joined him.

"Once this is all over, we're coming back to give them all a proper burial," said Nash as he stared down at their remains.

Sullivan walked away toward one of the burned down trailers along the fence. He disappeared inside, only to reappear a moment later with an old, rusty shovel. He walked to the corner of the Treefort and speared the shovel into the ash, which created a plume of soot around him. It only took him a few powerful strokes before he pulled out a large, black duffel bag.

"This is how we win this fight," he said as he unzipped the military-grade canvas bag and the group circled around it. The inside of the bag was full of rifles, handguns, and ammunition. There were a few knives, which Sullivan reached in and passed out to everyone. Courtney and Jessica looked at the sheathed knives, their lack of comfort visible on their faces.

"There will come a time when you'll need it, trust me," said Nash as he clipped his sheathed blade to his belt. Melissa nodded her head, clipping her own knife to her beltline.

"Let's head back," said Sullivan. "It's still early enough that we could do this tonight."

They walked together through the blackened woods and left a roadmap of footprints behind.

Chapter 32

Sullivan parked the SUV and the group rushed back to the house. The afternoon sun rested harshly on their shoulders as they moved through the dilapidated subdivisions. Dodging a few howlers as they maneuvered toward the house, Sullivan guided them into the backyard of a house near the home they'd slept in the night before.

"Stay here," he said. "I want to make sure Dietrich and Emma are safe before we go marching in. Wait for my whistle."

He disappeared around the house and left them in the overgrown backyard, the rusty playground equipment squeaking as it moved slightly in the wind.

"We're not going to have to fight, are we?" asked Courtney.

"No," said Nash. "You, your sister, and Melissa are going to stay back during the attack."

"*Excuse me?*" asked Melissa. "That isn't your decision to make!"

"I'm not taking you back there, Mel. If anything happens and he gets his hands on you, I'd never be able to forgive myself."

Melissa gave him an irritated look but didn't press the issue. A sharp whistle rang in their ears as Sullivan reached the house. They ran together, Nash in front, and filed quickly into the house and up the stairs. They entered the room they'd slept in as Dietrich fitted a rifle around his back and clipped handguns to his waist as well.

"Wait; we're doing this now?" asked Nash, surprised at seeing Sullivan and Dietrich arming themselves.

"Not yet, but soon," said Dietrich. "We're going to survey the area. We need to get a lay of the land before we mount our attack. We won't be long, Emma will break down the plan for you."

"We're going to attack as soon as they get back," said Emma. "We figure that Fletcher won't suspect us coming so soon after our cover was blown."

"This is of course assuming that our friends are dead, right?" Melissa asked solemnly.

"If Sullivan and Dietrich see anyone from your group left alive, they're going to stand down."

"What's the plan?" Nash asked as he took Melissa's hand.

"It's incredibly simple, actually. I'll use Sullivan's grenade to blast the front gates open. There's a good chance that we kill a lot of howlers; but not all of them. With the gate gone, they'll flood inside and make quick work of the people inside. Most of them won't even know what hit them. Sullivan and Dietrich will come around the rear and scale the back fence. Anyone trying to escape that way, we'll get."

"So we're just going to kill all these people?" asked Melissa, incredulous.

"We don't have a choice, Mel," said Nash. "The people living with him aren't good people. If they had the chance, they'd kill us themselves."

"Trust me when I say that running away isn't an option for us," said Emma. "We bested him; we planned to kill him. He won't stop looking until we're dead."

"What am I doing?" asked Nash.

"You'll stay outside the walls in the rear, should any of his men try and escape. I'll be doing the same at the front."

"You really think that two men, alone for the most part, can take down the entire community?" asked Courtney, who was sitting with Jessica on the bed.

"I think we can count on a great number of Fletcher's men being killed by the howlers," said Emma. "The ones that remain shouldn't be an issue for Sullivan and Dietrich. Jessica, Courtney, and Melissa, you'll stay back here. I have a flare gun. If things don't go our way, I'll fire it. If you see the flare, that means you need to run. Run for as long as you can and hide."

"We have Sullivan on our side. We won't have to use the flare," said Nash as he took Melissa's hand and gave a reassuring look to the twins.

Emma smiled before she turned and looked out the window, waiting nervously for Sullivan and Dietrich to reappear.

Chapter 33

Dietrich and Sullivan made their way through the deserted streets, weaving in and out of the broken down cars as they moved toward the Mansion.

"Why the hell is it so quiet?" whispered Dietrich as he crouched between cars.

"It's strange." The silence was deafening all around them, but it didn't prepare them for the strong, pungent smell that enveloped them as they got closer to the mansion.

They climbed into an abandoned school bus and stepped over decaying bodies to find a set of open seats. Dietrich crouched down below the line of windows as Sullivan sat up slightly and peered through a pair of binoculars.

The ground smoked violently as all the howlers lay in a carpet of dead, charred bodies. A man walked on the outside of the wall, spraying the pile of dead with a flame-thrower.

"Shit," he whispered and handed the set to Dietrich to view. "That son of a bitch moves fast." Heads lined the wall of the Mansion, each one a member of the fort.

"That he does," said Dietrich as he scanned the wall outside the Mansion.

"Sherry..." whispered Dietrich, his eyes glued to his wife's severed head. He handed the binoculars back to Sullivan before he slumped into one of the bus seats, his eyes closed, his breath erratic.

"My wife."

"What?" Sullivan asked, pressing the binoculars to his face. He scanned each of the staring faces of the people he'd once shared the Treefort with. His gaze stopped at Dianna's face, which looked directly his way with open, milky eyes. A violent mixture of rage and sadness bubbled in his core. He clenched his teeth, his eyes burning with furious tears.

"What now?" Dietrich asked, his voice soft. Sullivan placed the binoculars back in his bag.

"We leave. We start fresh, someplace new," he said, voice flat. "It doesn't matter how many weapons we have. Without the howlers to start the attack, we're massively outgunned. He's won."

"I won't accept that," said Dietrich, following Sullivan off the bus. "He needs to die. He needs to pay for what he's done."

Sullivan stopped him in his tracks and placed his hand on Dietrich's shoulder.

"Another day," he said. "Think of the others."

"He killed my wife."

"He took everything from me and my people — I understand your rage. I feel it too. But the kids need us more than we need our revenge."

Chapter 34

They made their way down a long country road, the quiet afternoon interrupted only by the sound of their footsteps on the pavement. It'd been two weeks since they left the Mansion, and although they'd met their fair share of howlers, they had not come across a single living person. The countryside was dotted with abandoned farmland and rolling hills that stretched out in each direction.

Dietrich and Sullivan led the group. Each of them walked with purpose, a rifle at their shoulder. The rest of the group followed close behind, Nash fitted with a rifle, the girls with knives and handguns. Melissa had originally put up a fuss about the men being the only ones with rifles, but once the rifle was place in her hands, she quickly returned it in favor of her smaller firearm. They heavy weapon weighed her down much more than her pistol.

Sleeping at night in the open was a chore. They laid there restlessly under the night sky, fearing an ambush by Fletcher's men. They knew he would be hunting them and expected the worst at any every moment.

So they walked, covered by the shadow of a thick canopy of trees and aimlessly looked for a safe place to exist. They'd stayed away from interstates, choosing to keep to back roads and country paths.

They hadn't seen any traces of Fletcher's group since they had fled but on the fifteenth day, Sullivan stopped suddenly to the side of a dirt road. His hand shot into the air to signal for them all to stop. Dietrich stepped up next to Sullivan, weapons at the ready.

"I'm coming out," said a woman's voice. "Please, don't shoot."

An elderly woman, with long gray hair pulled into a messy ponytail, stepped out from the bushes with a basket full of berries. She made her way to the middle of the road, her hands out in surrender with a basket of berries in the crook of her elbow.

"I'm alone," said the woman. Sullivan continued to train the barrel of his gun on her, responding only with silence. "Please, just leave me alone. I'm only picking berries for a pie. I just want to be left in peace."

Sullivan stood a moment and glared at her from beneath his dark sunglasses before he lowered his weapon and gestured for the rest to do the same.

"We'll be on our way," he said as he moved past her. They walked past her in single file. The twins pulled up the rear, smiling in unison at the warm-faced woman.

"Those look tasty. Good luck with your pie," whispered Courtney as she passed.

"Wait," said the woman from behind. The group stopped as she approached them, her basket of berries now held at her side. Sullivan's gun aimed once more at her. She stared at the weapon for a moment before she turned her gaze back to the twins. "Where are you all heading?"

They stood silent, unsure how to answer until Dietrich stepped forward. "We're not sure, to be perfectly honest. Somewhere safe, hopefully."

A conflicted look fell over the woman's face as she looked at the group of armed strangers in front of her.

"My group lives not far from here," she said, slowly. "It's not a big place, and not very secure, but we don't get much traffic in these parts, either living or dead."

"Where?" asked Sullivan coldly.

"About a mile down this road. You're heading that way anyway so I may as well walk with you and let you talk to Paxton."

"Who's Paxton?" Sullivan demanded from the back of the group.

"He's my husband. I suppose you could say he's our leader."

"Dietrich will walk with you to meet with your husband," said Sullivan. "We will come later, once he's assured us that it's safe."

"That won't be necessary, my dear," the woman said with a smile.

There was another rustling as an older man came walking from a path in the woods with a concerned look on his face as he surveyed the group. He held a basket of berries as well, but in his other hand he supported himself with a twisted, homemade walking cane. His white beard extended past his shoulders and ended halfway down his chest while his white hair reached his jawline.

"You old coot," said the woman as she walked over to the man. "Stalking me again, I see."

"I thought I'd surprise ya," he said and handed her the basket, which she combined with hers. "Seeing your new friends, I reckon I'm glad I did."

"Hello, sir," said Dietrich, stepping forward with his hand outstretched. "My name is Dietrich Campbell. My group and I were just passing through."

"Oh, nonsense," said the woman as the old man feebly shook Dietrich's hand. "I was just going to bring them to meet you. My name is Sally and this is my husband Paxton."

The group smiled and waved slightly. Sullivan stood stoic as ever.

"We haven't agreed on anything yet, ma'am," said Sullivan "My group isn't stepping foot into your camp until we know it's safe."

"Well regardless of what my sweet wife may've told y'all, I ain't gonna welcome you into our camp until I know *you* ain't no threat."

"Don't mind him," said Dietrich, picking up on Paxton's distrust of Sullivan's militant stance. "We've been through a lot. We're sort of refugees."

"Refugees of what?" asked Paxton as he leaned on his walking stick.

They stood in the shade of the road, and Dietrich struggled to find the words. "We were part of a group," he began. "We were not willing to conform to their ways—we didn't want to participate in their debauchery. We're the only ones that escaped, but they may be after us."

Paxton sized up the group, looking at each of them quietly before exchanging a long, debating look with Sally. "We ain't goin' anywhere until you shoulder them rifles," said Paxton, looking uneasily at the rifles the men were holding. After a moment of hesitation, Sullivan nodded to Nash and Dietrich and they all shouldered their weapons. "Come on, then."

The group walked together, Sally offering her basket of berries, which the twins and Melissa accepted with smiles. It took a half hour before they came into the town Paxton and Sally called home. The pavement gave way to dirt road as the approached a sign at the town limits, which read *Hillcrest*. Old school buses and vans sat idle, lining the street outside the town.

"Getaway vehicles, I presume?" Sullivan asked.

"You got it, friend. Ain't never had to use any of 'em," Paxton said. "Not yet, anyhow. Got a whole other line of 'em down yonder."

The tree canopy became thicker as they made their way down the dirt road. The homes in the town were old, brick farmhouses dating as far back as the Civil War. People nodded from their front porches as they walked, welcoming the new people being led by Paxton through the town.

"How many people live here?" asked Nash as he locked eyes with an elderly couple that sat on their front porch, their gazes filled with concern.

"With Paxton and myself, twenty," said Sally. "Some old folks, like us, but we have quite a few young bucks who do their best to keep us safe and secure."

"I don't see any line of defense," said Sullivan as he towered over Dietrich and Paxton while he walked behind them. "How do you keep the dead out?"

"I'm sure you noticed how long a walk it is to get back here," said Paxton. "We hardly see any kind of movement in these here parts. You're the only people we seen, livin' or dead, in months."

"And we've always been here," said Sally.

"I was born here and I reckon I'll die here," said Paxton. "When everythin' went south, people here pulled up stakes and headed for the safe zones the government was talking about, didn't turn out to be so safe, I reckon. Been quiet as a mouse 'round here ever since."

Sally and Paxton led them up a walkway to an old, stone home that was beautifully landscaped all around. Paxton opened the front door, allowing his wife in first, followed by the rest of the group. The inside of the home was well kept and smelled of fresh baked goods. From the spot they stood, they could see right into Sally's kitchen and immediately knew she had been preparing to bake before she went out in search of the berries.

"Ladies, would you be so kind as to assist me with this pie?" asked Sally with a smile. Melissa and the twins showed no resistance and moved into the kitchen with her. Emma stood with an indifferent look on her face as Dietrich softly nudged her with his elbow.

"Fine," she said begrudgingly and left the men behind and she moved into the kitchen.

"Please, this way," said Paxton as he opened a door and ushered them inside. The walls inside the room were covered in framed black and white photos of the town before the turn of the century, complete with tattered photos of Civil War soldiers who stood and posed for a photo in one of the towns sprawling fields.

"These are fantastic," whispered Nash, looking at the photos. The rest of the group sat down at a long, wooden table.

"All originals, my boy," said Paxton from the head of the table. "I consider myself a bit of a collector. I have more upstairs that I can show you some other time."

Nash sat down at the table and admired the obvious craftsmanship that had gone into its construction.

"I need to make one thing clear," said Paxton, his arms folded on the table in front of him. "We here are a peaceful group. We ain't gone lookin' for trouble and trouble hardly finds us. We'd like to keep it that way."

"We understand," said Dietrich while he mentally prepared to pick up and leave Hillcrest.

"With that being said, I can't, in good conscience, send y'all back out to the eaters. Just 'cause we don't go lookin' for trouble don't mean we ain't prepared for it. From the looks of it, y'all come pretty prepared yourselves. You're welcome to stay here as long as you like, assuming you can mind you manners and all."

"Will the rest of your community be as accepting of us as you have been?" asked Dietrich.

"Especially given the trouble we may possibly bring to you your doorstep," said Sullivan.

"It's a funny thing, but a lot of the people living here have a military background," he said. "We ain't scared of no fight. Plus, it seems like you've put some distance between yourselves and this *Mansion*."

"Did you serve?" asked Sullivan.

"The people here refer to me as the Colonel, but no," he said. "I've always been fascinated by the Civil War, as I'm sure you seen. I had ancestors fight for the North, though."

"A group full of ex-military being led by a civilian," said Sullivan. "That's something to be proud of."

"I supposed it is," said Paxton with a smile. "But like I done said, we ain't seen much trouble here. I'm just a figurehead. A peacetime leader, if you will."

"A leader, nonetheless," said Dietrich as he reached across the table and shook his hand. "We thank you for your hospitality. I'm sure my group would be happy helping with anything they can while staying with you."

"I'm sure, in time, we'll find suitable tasks for y'all, but for now, let's get you settled in," said Paxton as he stood and headed for the door they'd entered through. "Let me show you to your home."

Paxton walked down the street, his back slightly bent when he walked, his walking stick bracing each footstep as the group followed behind him. People along the street smiled and nodded as they passed with polite apprehension. Laughter filled the air from somewhere down the street, followed by the sharp screech of a bird overhead. The summer breeze brushed passed them as they followed Paxton, and for those that had been there, the memories of the Treefort wound their way into their minds.

"Here we are," said Paxton, stopping at a white picket fence with a large colonial home behind it. The exterior was an old, red brick, with black shutters and white curtains.

"I've grown to distaste colonial houses," whispered Melissa to Nash.

"Go on and get settled in. I'll come by later," said Paxton as he slowly walked back to his home. "We're having a town meeting tonight and now that you've shown up, I have a feeling it's gonna go later than expected."

The group filed into the house and quickly chose their rooms. Nash and Melissa selected a room on the second floor that overlooked the dirt road they'd entered the town on. There was a knock at the open door as Dietrich leaned into their room.

"We're meeting downstairs to talk," he said before making his way toward the stairs. Nash and Melissa made their way down, settling themselves on the bottom step.

"We were fortunate to find this place," said Dietrich, while he leaned his back against the front door. "But we need to decide if we should stay. I personally feel Fletcher will not stop until he finds us. Staying means we're bringing the fight to Paxton's doorstep."

"He sounds like he's ready for a fight," said Nash. "If we were going to be taken in by anyone to help us with Fletcher, this is the group."

"It's not their fight," said Sullivan as he watched a couple of men walk past on the street outside, glancing at the house as they did. "They may have the know how, but they're out-gunned. They have no visible defenses either—we're sitting ducks here."

"We have to stay," said Melissa. "If Fletcher makes it this far out to find us, he's gonna find Hillcrest anyway. We need to help them defend themselves. You think he'll just let them stay here?"

"She's right," said Nash. "They'll need us as much as we'll need them."

"It's settled then," said Dietrich and pushed himself away from the door. "I think we've found something special here."

The group spent the rest of the afternoon in their new house, relaxing and waiting for the town meeting. Until they'd been formally introduced, they wanted to keep a low profile. Sullivan stood watch at his window, ever vigilant, as he searched the streets for any danger. He listened to the sounds of the birds outside, warm air flowing in through the open window. For the first time since he left the Mansion, Dianna's face appeared like a ghost in the back of his mind. Not the morbid, milky-eyed version he'd seen on the Mansion wall, but the smiling woman he'd known and loved back at the Treefort. Fletcher would come, he knew that, they just had to be ready.

About an hour before sundown, Sally knocked on their door. The group had already been gathered downstairs, with the exception of Sullivan who continued to stand guard from his upstairs bedroom.

"Hello, dear," said Sally as Dietrich opened the door with a smile. "Paxton is already on his way to the meeting house. Would you all be so kind as to help me carry my pies down to the hall?"

"Oh I think that with pie involved, you shouldn't have any trouble getting our assistance," said Dietrich with a smile as he opened the door wide and they all filed out into the warm evening air.

The large double doors of the schoolhouse stood open and revealed Paxton leaning against a large podium at the front of the room. People stood all around inside talking as they waited to meet the new residents of Hillcrest.

"Are you ready?" asked Sally.

"Ready as ever," said Dietrich as he returned her smile and motioned to her to lead the way.

Chapter 35

The rubble and ash from the burning buildings choked him as the flames crept closer. He groaned with pain, clutching his left arm tightly as he hobbled away from the wreckage. The fire roared behind him, but the screaming and gunfire grew louder with each step away from the flames. He kept low, hoping to avoid any stray bullets—the screaming wasn't just from the living and so he tried to keep his watering eyes on his surroundings.

A ragged bullet hole in his left bicep sent excruciating pain up and down his arm, but he sighed in relief that it wasn't a bite. The dead were swarming the fire, so he let his injured arm hang at his side and pulled his pistol out of his waistline. He squeezed the trigger, dropping a biter as it turned its attention on him.

The screaming continued as he made it to a line of abandoned cars covered with dirt and dust from years of neglect. He opened the first one, only to find the ignition empty; the next few cars in front of him fared the same. As he frantically searched for a workable car, a group of the dead noticed him and sprinted forward, falling over each other as they gnashed their teeth wildly. They were steadily gaining on him.

He moved to the next vehicle, a battered blue pick-up. Through the murky window, he could see keys hanging from the ignition. He wrenched on the door, but it was locked. Not wanting to waste any bullets he flicked his safety on and used the butt of the gun to break the window. He launched himself into the front seat of the truck as the dead reached the line of cars. He slammed the door and turned to the key. To his relief, the engine roared to life and drowned out the voices of the dead outside.

One of the dead reached in through the broken window and grabbed his arm as he peeled away. He clipped the car in front of him as he did, jolting himself. The dead one hung on for a moment as it screamed and snapped its teeth together before it finally let go, bouncing off the pavement as the man drove away from the burning disaster behind him.

Chapter 36

Three months after entering Hillcrest, Dietrich entered into Paxton's study like he did every afternoon. He took a seat in the same chair he always did and sipped the same cup of tea he had every day. This had become a custom for the two of them. Once the day's responsibilities were complete, the two of them always retreated to Paxton's study to talk and theorize together. In the short time they'd been there, Paxton and Dietrich had become close.

"Would you looky here!" said Paxton as he put down his teacup and looked out the window behind Dietrich.

Sullivan and a couple of men from the newly formed security team pulled a large deer behind them on blue tarp. Sullivan stopped in front of Paxton's house and knocked loudly on the door.

"You, sir, are my damn hero," said Paxton as he opened the door with a grin. "I can't remember the last time we had venison for supper 'round here!"

"I can get it prepared to roast. Just tell me where?"

"There's an old shack near the schoolhouse used for that exact purpose. It ain't been used in a good while but you should have everything you need there!"

"All right, then," said Sullivan. "I'll bring the meat over as soon as I'm finished."

Sullivan joined the two members of the security team and continued to drag the deer down the street. "That man is something else," Paxton said.

"That he is," said Dietrich. "I think I'll cut our chat short today. I'm sure he could use some help."

"Well I'm not gonna argue that," said Paxton. "The two of you should stop on by when you're done for a spot of whiskey. My treat!"

"Will do," said Dietrich with a smile and placed his hand on Paxton's shoulder before he left.

Dietrich made his way down the street to join Sullivan. He glanced between two houses to the farmland behind and saw Nash and Melissa as they finished their day's work in the fields. Hillcrest was surrounded by abandoned farmland, portions of which had been taken over by Paxton and his group and brought back to life. Nash and Melissa had spent every morning in the fields and learned from the group how to tend to them properly.

Jessica and Courtney normally worked with Sally in the kitchen, learning how to cook. Dietrich noticed the three of them wandering back from the fields. They each held a basket filled with vegetables and fruit for the night's meal.

"Did you see what Sully brought in today?" asked Sally with a smile.

"I sure did," said Dietrich as he passed. "I'm on my way there now to help him."

"Whenever you're ready, just bring the meat on over and we'll get it cooking!"

"Will do!" said Dietrich, reaching the deer shack and disappearing inside.

Dietrich and Sullivan worked late into the afternoon as they butchered the deer. They spent their time together sharing stories back and forth, reminiscing about the time before the world changed. It wasn't something either of them dwelled on often, but it felt right as the two of them worked in unison to prepare the meat.

"She used to wear this pear perfume," Dietrich laughed. "It was horrible, I held my breath anytime she came near me.

Smelled like rotting fruit and meatloaf. She was a good lady though, always brought me sweets, my Nan."

"I didn't have much family," Sullivan said. "Just an aunt and a brother by the time the world lost its head."

"Hurry up in there chatty Kathys!" Courtney squealed from the door. "The town is starvin'!"

Chapter 37

The savory smell of cooked venison filled the air as Nash and Melissa made their way to the one-room-schoolhouse where the town met each night to eat together. The sounds of laughter and conversation boomed out of the open doors and windows of the building.

"This place reminds me of a restaurant," said Melissa as she looped her arm into the crook of Nash's elbow. "You know, before everything changed."

"I know what you mean," said Nash with a smile. "Come on; let's see if we can get Sullivan to wait on us."

Melissa giggled as they walked inside, greeted by Dietrich waving them to their spot with two plates already prepared for them. They sat down across from him and Emma, with Sullivan and the twins on each side of them, already eating their food. Dietrich had a deck of cards beside his plate, ready to be shuffled and dealt after they'd finished eating. Dinner and cards had become a nightly routine for a lot of the residents at Hillcrest, something that Dietrich had started.

Meals were finished quickly and the plates were taken away by the younger kids. They were responsible for setting the tables and cleaning the dishes afterwards. Most everyone stayed behind to play cards, while some of the more senior group members retired for the evening to their homes.

Out of the Mansion group, Sullivan stood first, reaching his arms above his head as his joints popped loudly.

"Well, I'm tired. I'll see all of you in the morning."

"Would you be a dear and escort us old timers back to our house?" asked Sally with a smile.

"Us too!" said Jessica, as she and Courtney stood and joined him.

"I'd be delighted," said Sullivan, allowing Sally to link her arm through his as they left the church.

The deer meat Sullivan had brought to the town that day had made for one of the best meals the town had enjoyed in months. The mood at the town's nightly dinners was always happy but there was something about tonight that felt different to them all.

"I'm done for the night," said Emma, forcing her words out through a deep yawn as she threw her cards onto the table.

"Until tomorrow," said Dietrich with a smile as he gathered the cards together and placed them back into the pack.

The group walked through the warm night air as crickets sang their evening song in the darkness. Nash and Melissa walked in the front with a lantern as Dietrich and Emma followed behind talking quietly, an occasional laugh echoing into the night. Melissa glanced back to see Emma quickly pull her hand out of Dietrich's.

The four of them slinked into the house and held back laughter as the stairs creaked slightly as they walked.

"Goodnight, you two," Dietrich said to Melissa and Nash as he closed his door.

"Night!" whispered Melissa as she exchanged another silent grin with Emma.

"Emma and Dietrich are together!" she excitedly whispered to Nash as they got into bed.

"Shut up," said Nash with a smile as he pulled the blanket over the two of them.

"When we were walking tonight, I looked back and they were holding hands. She pulled it away real quick but I saw it!"

"Hmm. Yeah, I guess I could see that."

"Keep your mouth shut for now, you blabbermouth!" she said as she scooted next to him and kissed him on the lips. Nash put his arms around her and pulled her close against him.

The two laid in silence while the crickets' chirped outside their window. Nash was just at the verge of sleep when her soft voice started him back awake.

"Do you ever wonder what's happened with the Mansion after we left?"

"Every day," he said. "I've had nightmares of them finding us and dragging us back there."

"Do you think he will ever find us?"

"I'm not sure. Us being out here really doesn't have any impact on him. I feel like if he were to have gone after us, he would have found us by now."

"You're probably right," she said after a long, silent pause.

"It doesn't matter if he were to find us, Mel. I'd never let anything happen to us."

Chapter 38

The truck sputtered to a stop as the man made his way down the abandoned country road. Smoke billowed from the hood as he stepped out into the warm morning air. The sun baked hot from beyond the canopy of trees, which created a dry humidity that made his wounds ache all the more.

He gingerly pulled a long jacket over himself, letting the hood hang loosely onto his forehead. He'd created a makeshift sling for his arm and cradled it inside the jacket as it burned wildly underneath. He'd done what he could with his foot and covered it tightly with a cloth to try and stop the bleeding. Even with all he'd done, it continued to ooze and sent waves of pain up his leg. He knew the distance he had to travel, and at his current speed, he knew it could easily take a couple days. He slung a backpack over his shoulders and hobbled toward Hillcrest.

Chapter 39

The group was woken by loud rustling outside in the early morning. Nash rolled out of bed and rubbed his eyes, and Melissa sat up groggily. People were gathering outside Paxton and Sally's house, each looking concerned as they stood in the street talking.

"Get dressed," he said without looking away. "Something's going on."

"What is it?" she asked as she slid on her shirt.

"I'm not sure but it doesn't look good."

The two of them left their room just as Emma and Dietrich came walking out of his bedroom. Dietrich's eyes widened as he looked back and forth between Nash and Melissa.

"Um…this isn't what it looks like," he said while he scratched his forehead.

"Never mind that," said Nash as Sullivan came into the hall.

"Something's up," said Sullivan as he closed his door and moved passed them and down the stairs, fully dressed and armed.

"What's wrong?" asked Emma as she watched Sullivan sprint down the stairs.

"I don't know but something is going on down the street," said Nash.

The group shot toward the stairs as Melissa knocked once and poked her head into the twin's room to see them still fast asleep.

"Let them sleep," said Nash as he grabbed her hand and ran down the stairs to join the others.

****

They joined the congregation outside Sally and Paxton's house. Sally sat on the porch and sobbed softly as one of the women from town sat with her arm resting gently around her shoulders. The front door to their house was open and they could see people moving about inside.

"What's happened?" Sullivan asked to the group.

"Paxton died in his sleep," said an older man, not taking his sad eyes off the house.

"Oh no..." said Dietrich under his breath as he left the group and made his way up the walk to where Sally was sitting.

"This can't be good," said Emma, watching as Dietrich knelt beside Sally as she leaned against him.

"He was fine last night," Melissa said.

Jessica and Courtney wandered out of the house to join them. "What happened?" Jessica asked. Courtney rubbed the sleep from her eyes as Dietrich consoled Sally on the porch.

A man came outside and whispered in Dietrich's ear before he disappeared back inside. Dietrich talked with Sally for a moment as she nodded softly, standing to his side as he helped her down the walkway toward the street.

"Paxton's time on this earth has come to an end. Bless you all for your concern," she said through her tears to the people standing before her.

Without saying a word, Sullivan walked up the path toward Sally's house and disappeared inside. Melissa and the twins stood together, crying softly like much of the rest of the people who watched the house. Emma joined Dietrich when he disappeared into the schoolhouse with Sally as Sullivan and a couple men dressed in military fatigues walked out side with Paxton's body on a makeshift stretcher, a white sheet covering his frail body. Sullivan let the two men take the lead as they guided him and Paxton's body to an empty house where they would keep his body until burial.

"I can't believe it," said Nash as he put his arms around Melissa and the twins as they continued to cry.

The street slowly emptied after Sullivan and the men disappeared inside the house with Paxton's body. It wasn't long before he reappeared with a couple other men each holding shovels as they disappeared to dig Paxton's grave.

"I'm going to go check in on Sally," said Nash as he left the girls alone to console each other.

"Nothing to check in on, sweetie," said Sally, approaching them in the street as Dietrich and Emma followed behind. "I'm fine. I've lost my husband today and our town has lost its leader, but the last thing Paxton would want is for us all to be sulking around all day."

"I tried to stop her," said Dietrich, shrugging as he met Nash's gaze.

"Oh nonsense!" said Sally as she turned and swatted at Dietrich. "We need to carry on. We need someone to lead this place and my choice is Dietrich."

"Now hold on a second," said Dietrich, a surprised look on his face. "Shouldn't this be a town decision?"

"Oh to hell with 'em! You'd be his first choice and everyone knows it. I just didn't want you to be taken aback when I bring up your name tonight at dinner."

"I'd be honored to serve this town, but only if everyone is in agreement."

"I don't want anyone moping around here!" said Sally as she waved her index finger at them all. "You go on and spread the word. Today and tonight, we celebrate him. I'll have no doom and gloom on my watch!"

"Yes ma'am," they all said in unison.

"Courtney, Jessica, come with me. We've got a lot to do today and I could use all the help I can get."

The girls each took one of Sally's hands, "Melissa and Emma are welcome to join us," she called over her shoulder.

Melissa gave Nash a quick kiss on the cheek before she joined Sally. Emma grunted loud enough for Dietrich to hear. He smiled as he nudged her forward to join the girls.

"I'd rather not—" she started, but Dietrich waved her off.

"She just lost her husband, she could use the distraction."

****

The streets were deserted, save for Dietrich and Nash, who stood together in the street. Storm clouds were slowly starting to roll in over the town and brought with them low rumbles of thunder in the distance.

"What a day for a storm," said Dietrich, his hands crossed over his chest as he looked into the sky.

"I'm glad she wants you in charge," said Nash as he reached out and shook his hand. "So what do I call you? Colonel Dietrich? Captain? Mayor?"

"Let's not get ahead of ourselves, funny guy," said Dietrich with a grin. "I'm honored she'd want me in charge."

"I think her word will go a long way with the others. They won't have any qualms with you taking charge."

"We'll see," said Dietrich as another roll of thunder echoed through the town.

Sullivan reappeared in the street, looking up at the sky as he joined them.

"The grave is almost done. If it's okay with Sally, I think we should do the burial soon."

The clouds continued to darken overhead and the thunder was getting louder with each roll. Dietrich went into Sally's house and briefed her on the coming weather, and with her blessing, the group gathered the town's people to bury Paxton before the storm overtook them. Dietrich and Sally led the group to the small cemetery that had served the community for decades as Sullivan followed behind with Paxton's frail body in his arms.

Sally stood at the edge of the grave, her arms crossed in front of her as she silently allowed tears to fall down her cheeks. Paxton's body lay in the open hole, wrapped in a white sheet as the group stood above. Sullivan and a few others stood quietly aside, as their shovels sat at their feet, awaiting her word.

"He was loved, and he loved us all," said Sally and nodded to Sullivan to start the burial before the rain broke. "I know the weather looks dicey, but dinner tonight is mandatory. Everyone must attend."

With that, Sally and her group of helpers returned to her home as the rest of the town scurried back to their homes. The rain let loose with a fury, coming down in sheets as it cascaded on the town for the majority of the afternoon. Nash considered volunteering with Melissa at Sally's house but thought better of it, knowing she had more than enough people in the small house to be helpful. Unsure of what to do with his time, Nash picked a book from a large bookcase in the living room. He pulled a book called *Final Flight* by Kurt Saunders from the second room of the shelf and carried upstairs to his bedroom. He'd never heard of the book or the author but he was engrossed in the book almost immediately.

Halfway through the book, he was startled by the sound of a ringing bell outside. He panicked for a moment before realizing it was the dinner bell.

"Good book?" asked Dietrich.

"Yeah, actually. Are we ready to go?"

"After you," said Sullivan as he opened the door to the wet world outside.

The three of them entered the already busy schoolhouse to find the lavish buffet of food that the girls had spent the day preparing. Spanning the front of the schoolhouse was a wide range of dishes, finished with different kinds of pies and cookies to end the meal. Melissa placed a plate of hot pasta on the table and joined Nash.

"Thanks, it looks great!"

"The amount of non-perishable food they have is staggering," Melissa said. "Honestly they have enough boxes of dry pasta that we could build a fort."

"He read all afternoon," whispered Sullivan with a grin.

"Oh? How nice for him," she whispered and nudged Nash firmly with her elbow before she let him put his arm around her.

People continued to file into the schoolhouse, filling it quickly as they all sat with each other and ate. The meal was loud, as usual, but much less than it had been on other nights. Paxton's death hung heavy over all of them. Sally finished first and made her way to the front of the schoolhouse. She stood behind a lectern and pounded her fist on the top to get the group's attention.

"Thank you all for coming tonight. I know I said it was mandatory but it means the world to see all of you here. What I'm about to discuss might seem too early but it's important enough that we can't worry about the standard rules of mourning. We need to appoint someone to run this place and I propose it be Dietrich."

The group sat silently and listened to Sally as she gave her recommendation. Dietrich stood and joined Sally at the front, feeling everyone's eyes on him as he moved.

"As many of you know, I became quite close with Paxton over the past few months. We talked daily about this place and the nature of what it means to lead in a world like this. If it's your will, I would be honored to serve in that capacity."

"This does feel a bit rushed, Sally," said a man who sat at the front of the schoolhouse.

"Do you really think Paxton would want this drawn out? We're safe, and we've been safe for a long time, but the last thing he'd want is for us to be so comfortable in that safety that we wait too long to get the town back up and running," Sally said.

"I don't know how many of you have spent time out on the road, but it's dangerous," Dietrich chimed in. "Before coming here, my group used to live in a walled-in town, surrounded by the dead. We didn't go a day without seeing one of them and since we've been here, we haven't even seen one of the slow ones. This place is an anomaly. We've been safe for so long but we can't get too comfortable in that. It just takes one group of those monsters to come wandering down the road and they could dismantle everything we have here."

"I think that Dietrich's experience makes him the perfect person to take charge," said Sally. "If there are objections, please make them known."

There was a small moment of silence, followed by a round of applause. Dietrich stood awkwardly in front of them all, giving a nervous wave as the group continued to applaud.

"Ok, everyone," said Sally with a smile. "Settle down and have some pie!"

The rest of the night was dedicated mostly to people stepping up front to share memories of their time with Paxton. The schoolhouse was filled with tears and laughter as people took their turn up front. Most everyone left the schoolhouse just before midnight and each of them took the time to shake Dietrich's hand before they headed off into the dark.

"You'll do great," said Sally as she held Dietrich's hand and kissed him on the cheek. One of the town's younger men escorted her back to her house, which left only the Mansion group alone in the schoolhouse.

"I'm glad it's you," said Nash as he patted Dietrich on the back.

"Thank you. I supposed we should get some sleep."

"That sounds wonderful," said Jessica, Courtney curled up beside her, barely awake.

"She worked us to the bone today," said Melissa who could barely stand from exhaustion.

"Party-poopers," said Sullivan. He got up to turn off all the lanterns around the schoolhouse

Sullivan hardly slept anymore and spent most nights sitting in front of the window as he watched the darkened street below. He'd doze off periodically, have a dream or nightmare that involved Dianna, and wake up to his dark reflection in the window. Knowing what he had sentenced Dianna and the others to threatened to tear him apart as the guilt ate at him daily. Each night before bed he pictured Dianna's face; the way her eyes crinkled at the corners when she smiled, her deep rumbling laugh, the way her face would flush when he caught her staring at him. Tonight though, he felt tired, and stretched out on his bed for a long, dreamless sleep. Dianna's face barely fluttered in his mind before he drifted off.

Dark clouds blotted out any chance of morning light as the wind tossed leaves and stray branches through the street.

"We haven't seen a storm like this in months," Melissa said, staring past him out the window.

"I know. It's pretty bad out there. Way worse than yesterday."

****

The group stayed in their rooms for most of the morning as they watched and listened to the storm as it pounded the small village. Sometime after eleven, Sullivan got up and went downstairs into the kitchen to get food ready for the group.

"Some storm, huh?" said Sullivan.

"That's putting it lightly," said Melissa as a flash of lightning illuminated the kitchen.

Nash watched Sullivan, standing in front of the window and felt sad for him. Sullivan had been different since they left the Mansion. He was still the strong, steady protector he'd always been, but Nash and Melissa could tell something had been left behind that day at the Treefort.

A flash of lightning touched down in a field across the street from them, which made everyone jump. After the initial shock of the crash of lightning, Nash realized Sullivan hadn't moved an inch, but simply stood idly in front of the window and held the now empty pie plate.

"Something is coming," whispered Sullivan.

"What do you mean?" asked Dietrich as he stepped up beside him and looked outside. "Do you see something?"

"Just a feeling I get," said Sullivan as he lifted a bottle of water to his mouth and took a sip. "I can't explain it."

Dietrich stood next to him, arms crossed over his chest, as they looked through his reflection out to the rain.

Chapter 40

By midafternoon the rain had completely subsided as the residents of Hillcrest came out into the muggy afternoon air and surveyed the damage from the storm. Trees had fallen down throughout town, covering the road, which made parts of it impossible to pass. Dietrich, Nash, and Sullivan worked together on one of the trees, sawing at it before they cast the branches in a pile by the roadside. A man wearing army fatigues ran up to them from down the street, his long shaggy hair wet from working in the rain.

"Dietrich," said the man as he brushed the hair away from his face.

"Hi, Derek," he said as he turned and shook his hand. "What can I do for you?"

"Well, seeing how you're in charge now, I should probably show you something. Do you have a moment?"

"Of course," he said with a smile and brushed his hands on his jeans as they walked down the street.

Derek led him to the schoolhouse, which was narrowly missed by a large tree that now lay alongside the building. Dietrich smiled at the group of people working to remove the tree as he followed Derek inside.

"I think you'll like this," said Derek as he reached the lectern at the front and moved it aside to reveal a closed hatch underneath.

"How did I never notice that?" asked Dietrich with a grin.

"Guess that means it's in a good spot," said Derek and pulled open the hatch to reveal an area underneath.

The space underneath the lectern was filled with handguns, loaded and ready to fire, as well as a collection of large knives. The two men stood overtop the open hatch, looking down at the hidden collection of weaponry.

"We don't advertise that we have an armory, but here it is," said Derek. "It's not very big, but it'll do in a pinch."

"That it will," said Dietrich as he stared at the weapons beneath them. "Let's just hope we don't ever have to open this hatch again."

"We've never had to fire a single shot here," said Derek as he closed the hatch and replaced the lectern. "We'd prefer to keep it that way."

"As would I," said Dietrich, patting Derek on the back as they walked out of the schoolhouse together.

Sullivan joined him outside the schoolhouse as Derek returned to the tree he'd been helping remove. The entire town was outside working diligently to restore the town.

"This place doesn't need a leader," said Dietrich as he watched everyone work together to clear the streets. "Paxton was a figurehead; someone to point to. I think it's the same for me."

"You're wrong," said Sullivan. "There's going to come a day when they're all going to need us, and we'll need them as well. I see you found their armory."

"I did. Derek showed me. When did he show you?"

"He didn't," Sullivan said with a smile. "I eagle-eyed that hatch day one. I snuck in there one night and saw for myself."

"You're a good man to have around, Sully," said Dietrich, smiling as he watched everyone move about the village.

It took the better part of the afternoon and early evening for them to get Hillcrest to look and operate the way it had prior to when the storm came through. Nash and Melissa went with a group of others to inspect the farming fields and made sure their crops hadn't been destroyed during the storm. Save for a few areas that had been uprooted by the wind, most of the farmland remained intact.

After having spent the previous day creating the elaborate meal for Paxton's memorial, Sally advised the town that there would be no dinner at the schoolhouse that night. The townspeople prepared their own food at home, which left the town quiet as the sun began to sink below the horizon. Dietrich sat with Emma in the schoolhouse, going over a census Paxton had commissioned that had been made available to Dietrich after his death.

"That man was all about procedure," said Dietrich as he looked through the pages of information he'd collected on the residents. "I feel like a vice president being ushered in after an assassination."

"It's kind of like that, I guess," she said with a smile as she sat in a chair and watched the sun go down through one of the windows. She took his hand from the census papers and interlocked their fingers.

"Did you hear what Sullivan said earlier this morning?" asked Dietrich, putting the papers down as he took her other hand.

"About something coming? Yeah, I heard that. He has nothing to go by to say that, but I trust him."

"Me too," he said, thankful for what was underneath the lectern. "We'll all just have to stay vigilant. Keep our eyes open. Maybe we should have some patrols around here. What do you think?"

"Probably a good idea," she said, watching as the sun descended outside. "I'm really surprised nobody here thought to do that before we showed up. Seems pretty basic."

"Paxton was comfortable. He was comfortable, and very lucky. It could have been anyone who had strolled in here. That's not going to happen on my watch."

"You're a good man, Dietrich Campbell," she said as she leaned in and kissed him on the lips.

A loud, coughing sound echoed forth from the street as they both shot away from each other. They were still trying to hide their relationship from the rest of the group. They watched as a lantern bobbed slowly down the damp road toward the schoolhouse, moving slowly and methodically.

"We don't have anyone here that moves that slowly," said Emma as she watched intently. "Not anymore."

The cloaked figure reached the schoolhouse and stopped for a moment. It turned and walked toward the open doors, the lantern revealing a man wearing a long jacket who hobbled toward them.

"Hello there," said Dietrich, trying to decipher who it was that was joining them in the darkened schoolhouse. The man stepped through the open door and placed the lantern on the floor before he flipped the hood off of his face.

"Hello, old friend," said Fletcher Crawford, as Emma and Dietrich looked at him in horror.

Chapter 41

Dietrich pulled a handgun from the back of his waistband and trained the barrel on Fletcher.

"Come on, my boy. Do I look like I care if you kill me right now?" he said, standing in the soft lantern light as he coughed wildly.

Fletcher let the jacket fall to the ground, which revealed that his left arm was coated in dried, angry crimson. His foot was also covered in thick blood as he stood looking at them with sunken eyes and shook softly as a fever ravaged his system. His skin looked pale behind ragged burn marks that cast shadows across his tired face.

"Emma, would you please go get Nash and Sullivan?" asked Dietrich, not breaking eye contact with Fletcher. Emma disappeared out the back of the schoolhouse.

"I always thought the two of you would make a wonderful couple," said Fletcher before he broke into another coughing fit.

"What the hell are you doing here?" scathed Dietrich, still pointing the handgun at him.

"You've already sent Emma to get your friends," he said. "Why don't we wait until they get here?"

"I'm not so sure you'll have much time to say anything at all once they get here."

Emma returned quickly with Nash, Melissa, and Sullivan who filed in through the back of the schoolhouse where she'd left. Sullivan walked forward without question and Fletcher's eyes met his fierce gaze as he walked.

"Sullivan, I presume?" said Fletcher who kept his eyes locked on Sullivan's as he moved toward him.

Sullivan frisked him quickly and checked to make sure he was unarmed as he winced. Nash and Melissa flicked on more lanterns, which gave the schoolhouse an eerie glow. They all stood together and stared at the shadow of what had once been one of their biggest adversaries.

"Hello, everyone," he said, the usual bravado in his voice having melted away as his temperature continued to rise from the infection inside him.

"Tell us what we want to know," said Sullivan as he rejoined his group and crossed his massive arms in front of him. "The way I kill you will depend on how helpful you are."

"Fair enough," said Fletcher. "I expected that much when I came here."

"Where are your men?" asked Dietrich.

"I'm alone," he said. "I drove here with a truck, which broke down a few miles away from here. You can check for yourself."

"Why are you here? How the hell did you find us?" asked Dietrich.

"For about a month after you left, we searched for you. We checked every area around the Mansion, day in and day out. Obviously, we didn't find you. I grew tired of the chase and called off the search, which in retrospect is why I'm here now in the shape I'm in."

"That still doesn't explain why you're here," said Nash.

"I'm here because of your manipulative bastard of a stepfather."

"What does he have to do with anything?" asked Nash.

"He's a pain in the ass, which I guess you could have told me from the start. I should have picked up on his bullshit along the way. Didn't think he was smart enough to pull his shit."

"Get to it," said Sullivan.

"About a month ago, Duncan went on a supply run and didn't come back for days. Turns out, he was searching for you, and he found you. He came back and reported where you were and to be honest, I couldn't be bothered. I was on to new things, but he was like a dog with a bone. He *begged* me to go after you, and I just kept saying no. It wasn't long after that he took the Mansion from me."

"Fuck," whispered Emma.

"*Fuck*, is the right word, yes," said Fletcher. "He rounded up a posse in the middle of the night and killed off my guards, knowing it was the only way to get my attention. Before I knew it, Duncan was living in the church and I was stuck in the house where Nash and Melissa used to live. I know you thought it was horrible when I was in charge but you have no idea what it was like under him. People were taking communion left and right. The entire place became a hedonistic playground. I couldn't stand seeing it any longer."

"You firebombed the Mansion, didn't you?" asked Melissa when she saw the burns on his face.

"Indeed I did," he said. "He basked in his own glory for a while, running the Mansion as he saw fit. Once he finally started making plans to come after you, I decided to act. I've had a bit of a change of heart in regards to how I see the world. Having your kingdom yanked out from under you by a psychopath will do that."

"I know the feeling," said Sullivan as he stared at him with an emotionless scowl.

"Yes, I suppose you do," he said. "I thought I'd be able to topple the Mansion when I set those charges, but I'm afraid I've only quickened their approach."

"They're on their way?" yelled Emma.

"Honey, they were always on their way," said Dietrich. "I've thinned their numbers, and without me, you'd have had no warning."

"Why are you doing this? Why come all this way and warn us?" asked Dietrich as he stood behind the lectern.

"My hatred for Duncan exceeds anything I ever felt toward any of you. You're my best chance at seeing him dead. Who knows; maybe I'm feeling a little sentimental due to this damn infection." He erupted into another string of coughs.

"How close are they?" asked Sullivan.

"I have no way of knowing," he said. "I didn't just leave the Mansion, I escaped. The fire was out of control and Duncan and his people were aggressively trying to stop me. He's quite mad at me, as well as all of you. I don't see any scenario where he isn't far behind me."

"Why should we believe anything you say?" asked Dietrich. "All those people you killed when we left. Dianna, Sherry…"

"All Duncan," he said as he unraveled the bandage on his foot to readjust it.

"That's bullshit," said Nash. "There's no way he pulled this off himself."

"You're right. He didn't. When Duncan caught you that day, it was the beginning of his takeover of the Mansion. He didn't even come to me first after finding you. He grabbed a machete and went for Dianna and Dietrich's house. He threw their heads at my feet when he came to tell me. Made a terrible mess of the floor, if I may say so."

"*You shut your damn mouth!*" yelled Sullivan as he remembered Dianna's dead eyes staring at him as he looked through the binoculars.

"And the rest of the residents from the Treefort that you had beheaded?" asked Emma.

"Duncan had apparently been planning this for some time. All the while you were planning your little revolution, he was planning his. Duncan had a lot of men working with him and your people were dead before he came to me that day in the church."

More storm clouds began to sprawl across the sky above them as a roll of thunder rattled the town.

"You can kill me now," said Fletcher who looked exhaustedly into Sullivan's vengeful eyes.

Chapter 42

"If he tries anything, shoot him," said Dietrich, as he handed his gun to Nash before he exited the schoolhouse with Sullivan.

"Do we believe him?" asked Dietrich in the darkness, rain lightly falling around them.

"Yes," said Sullivan, looking back inside through the double doors as Nash continued to train the gun on Fletcher. "His information helps us. I think Duncan wronged him and he's simply looking for revenge before he dies, which from the looks of things, won't be too long from now."

"Are you okay going out on a night patrol? If he's right, Duncan could be right on his heels."

"I'm already on it," said Sullivan. "I'll bring Derek with me."

"We'll work up some plans for the morning to amp up security…"

"Shhh," hissed Sullivan as he strained his ears through the darkness. The two of them listened intently, as a soft humming sound got louder and louder.

"What the hell is that?" asked Dietrich as the sound continued to amplify.

"Go get the guns," said Sullivan and took off into the darkness. "Tell everyone to keep inside and try not to panic!"

"Good luck with that," Fletcher said.

"Something's coming!" said Dietrich as he closed the double doors behind him.

"Everyone wake up! Stay inside and arm yourselves! Be alert!" yelled Sullivan in the distance as he banged on the doors throughout the town.

"Dietrich, what is it?" asked Emma as she looked out the window into the darkness.

Dietrich pushed the lectern over, letting it crash loudly onto the ground as he tore open the hatch.

"Everyone, take a gun and a knife. I'm not sure what's coming, but I think we're in for a fight."

"Listen!" yelled Nash as he strained his ears to listen to the hum as it radiated loudly through the town. "It sounds like a motorcycle. Something else too but I can't figure out what it is."

Everyone jumped when Sullivan banged loudly on the door. Nash opened it and let him in before he closed it tightly again.

"Here we go," said Fletcher as he held his arm with a delirious look on his face.

"Did you see what it is?" asked Melissa with a panicked look on her face.

"It's a four-wheeler," he said as he took a couple handguns from the hatch. "It's dragging people—they're using the bodies and the noise to lead a pack of howlers here."

"Oh, *that's* smart," said Fletcher while he laughed through a heavy coughing fit.

"How many?" Nash asked. He stared out of the window as the headlights of the ATV illuminated the street.

"A lot," said Sullivan.

The moonlight cascaded the town with a fiendish glow as the howlers descended on the town. The ATV rider flew quickly past the schoolhouse, leaving the town as a bolt of lightening illuminated the crowd of monsters in the street. They all watched from the windows of the school house as the howlers banged and screamed at the doors of the houses while they broke windows and poured inside to the screaming of the townspeople.

"*We have to do something!*" yelled Nash as a dozen howlers slammed against the sides of the schoolhouse.

"Gun?" asked Fletcher as he held his hand out to Sullivan.

"*Go to hell,*" he said and slapped his hand away harshly. "Melissa, guard the hatch. If he tries anything, kill him!"

"This should be interesting," said Fletcher as the howlers shattered the windows.

Melissa watched from where she was standing as the howlers broke down the front door and came screaming inside. She raised her pistol and fired. Each of them squeezed off shot after shot as the tide of dead clamored toward the living.

Townspeople were being forced from their homes as the monsters crashed through doorways and forced their way through windows. Once they were in the street they were overpowered by the masses of the dead.

"What's the plan?" Emma screamed over the angry screeching of the howlers.

A flash of light erupted into the sky as the first home burst into flame. The first blast was followed by a dozen more as Duncan's men firebombed Hillcrest.

The schoolhouse was filled with dead bodies as the group stood untouched, formed in a line against the back wall. Sullivan opened the hatch again and handed out the remainder of the guns to everyone as the shrieking continued in the streets.

"You stay here! If I see you outside I'm putting a bullet in your gut," yelled Sullivan into Fletcher's face."

"Like it matters at this point, Sullivan," Fletcher said, listening to the carnage all around them.

The group poured out into the chaos as the dead, now courting new members from their community, ran wildly throughout the muddy street. Fires had spread from house to house and gave the town a hellish glow. They watched as a silhouette in the distance threw a flaming bottle through a window and the bottom floor erupted into flames.

"If you see someone you don't know, kill 'em!" called out Sullivan as he shot a man with a flaming bottle in the distance and watched him fall, screaming in agony as the bottle erupted around him.

"Nash," Melissa said, horrified.

"What is it?" His gaze followed her pointed finger. Sally stood in the middle of the street, her cheek torn open to reveal her teeth behind it as she stood looking lazily into the sky.

"Damn it," he whispered.

By the time they'd killed most of the howlers, all of the buildings were ablaze and the town was illuminated by the bright firelight. Duncan's men had used the chaos of the howlers to distract them long enough to set fire to their town, and forced the Hillcrest residents out into the open to either be bitten or shot.

Sullivan's group took cover the best they could, hiding as they listened to the fires burn in the empty streets. They could hear sporadic screams from the monsters in the distance, followed by gunshots as Duncan's men finished them off. Sullivan fought the waves of guilt he felt, reliving the fall of the Treefort and wishing they'd kept moving the day they'd met Sally. He found Nash and Melissa's gaze and saw the same guilt in their eyes.

"I know you're out there, *Buddy Boy*," called Duncan as he stood in the middle of the street with his men. "Why don't you come on out, and nobody else has to get hurt."

Nash looked across the street at Dietrich and Sullivan who were hiding behind a building as it burned. They both shook their head no at Nash.

"*Alrighty then!* You always were a chicken shit! What about you, Dietrich? Sullivan? Emma? I know for a fact

Fletcher's here somewhere! *Daddy's home!* Come on out and give me a big hug!"

"Where are the twins?" whispered Melissa into Nash's ear.

"To be honest, I'm not here for any of you. I'm just here to fuck that tight little blond my boy has been porking since we lived in that forest shithole!"

Melissa squeezed Nash's hand even harder, the sound of Duncan's voice sending chills down her spine. The group stayed quiet as the fires continued to burn.

"Come on out, sweetheart. *We both know you want it.*"

His men chuckled as they stood in the middle of the street and waited for them to come out. Duncan squeezed the trigger of his rifle and sent a barrage of bullets into the night sky. Each of them tensed in fear as the gunshots echoed through the air.

"Have it your way, fuckers!"

They listened as Duncan's men dragged two figures into the middle of the street. The twins were huddled together on the ground, Jessica's lip bleeding as Courtney cried loudly beside her.

"Oh my God…" said Melissa as she placed her hands over her mouth.

"I'm not fucking around!" screamed Duncan, as he put the barrel of his rifle to the back of Jessica's head and pulled the trigger. The shot rang through the town as she fell face first into the mud as her arms flailed to her side like a ragdoll. Courtney screamed, clawing at her sister's body.

"No!" Courtney sobbed, tugging on her sister's arm. "No, no, no!"

"Stop!" Sullivan yelled. He stepped out from behind the brick wall, his hands in the air. "Leave her alone."

"The rest of you, come out now, or I'll shoot this one too!"

Nash gave Melissa's hand a quick squeeze before he stepped out from his hiding spot as well, Melissa tucked tight against his back. Dietrich and Emma each stepped out from their own hiding spots; hands in the air.

The street was littered with the bodies of the townspeople, mixed with the howlers that had been ushered into the town. Derek stood on the sidewalk in his army fatigues, a bloody gouge out of his arm as he absently smiled at them. Duncan fired another shot into Derek's head, which sent his limp body backward into a burning building.

"That's better," he clapped. "Hiya, Nashy!" Duncan moved forward, his men close behind; only one didn't move, instead keeping his gun trained on Courtney.

Nash looked at Duncan through the rain and hardly recognized the crazed man in front of him. He stood tall, hulking with a rifle in hand, with six other armed men behind him. For as long as he'd known him, Duncan had always been clean-shaven, but he settled himself in front of Nash with a scraggly, dirty beard.

"Cat got your tongue?" asked Duncan and smiled as he leaned in close to Nash. "That's fine. I expected so much. So…let's drop our weapons and get down on our knees."

The group hesitated for a moment before they tossed their weapons in front of them and knelt in the muddy street. Nash watched the smile on Duncan's face continue to widen at the carnage all around him. As usual, Duncan carried himself with a theatrical bravado and spent more time entertaining himself with his prey than actually taking action.

"Tell me…where's Fletcher Crawford? I'm sure he filled you in on our little spat."

"He was in the schoolhouse when you came into town," said Dietrich.

Duncan walked slowly and crouched down in front of Dietrich. He stared into his face, revealing his teeth as he smiled fiercely.

"I very much enjoyed killing that slutty wife of yours. Took her for a spin before I cut her head off, too. Dry as a bone, as I'm sure you remember, but nothing a little lube couldn't fix."

He moved down the line but stopped in front of Sullivan and gazed into his stern eyes.

"Even more, I enjoyed cutting off the head of that husky bitch you were after," he said as he smacked Sullivan's chest two times with the back of his hand. "Big, strapping guy like yourself! You could've done much better!"

"What exactly is it that you want, Duncan?" asked Nash.

"You, you, you, you, and you…all dead, at my feet!" he said as he pointed to each person in line while he spoke. "Oh, and Fletcher…Fletcher's gotta die too, but before that, I made Nash a promise a long time ago, and I intend to keep it."

"No…" whispered Nash, looking up at the horrible shell of the man Duncan had evolved into.

"Oh, *yes*!" Duncan cheered, standing in front of Nash as he looked down with a smile.

Duncan snapped his fingers and two of his men stepped forward, pointing their guns at Dietrich and Sullivan as another of his men tore Melissa away from Nash.

"*No*!" Nash lunged forward to grab her but she was out of range. Duncan stepped forward and fired four rapid shots into the ground in front of Nash. Mud and water shot into the air as he fell backward in shock.

"You keep your distance, *Buddy Boy*, and keep your eyes open," he said as he unzipped his pants and waved his erection around in the rain. "*Let papa show you how it's done!*"

Like a horn blast indicating the start of a great battle, a gunshot rang out in the darkness. Nash looked into the darkness to see Fletcher holding a gun in front of him. The man who guarded Courtney fell to the ground clutching at his throat. Blood sprayed from beneath his hands. Fletcher moved further into the street and fired another shot, connecting with the shoulder of the man who held Melissa.

"*Oh for fuck's sake!*" screamed Duncan as the man holding Melissa fell to the ground and brought her with him as Duncan fumbled for his rifle.

Nash lunged forward, grabbed his gun, and planted a bullet in the temple of the man still holding on to Melissa. Blood sprayed across her face as she fell backward with a scream, landing on the wet ground. Sullivan sprang toward Duncan and punched him hard across his face. Duncan squeezed the trigger of his gun as he fell and sent bullets wildly into the air. Melissa screamed in pain as one of the bullets connected with her leg, just below the knee.

"Get her out of here!" screamed Sullivan as he held Duncan to the ground. The rest of the group scrambled for their weapons and opened fire on the remainder of Duncan's men. A bullet zipped close to Sullivan's head and tore his ear into jagged shards, as Nash picked up Melissa. She groaned in pain as Nash hurried her to the schoolhouse. He kicked the door open and set Melissa down on the floor inside.

Sullivan wound up for another solid punch, but Duncan's knee came up hard between his legs. Sullivan hesitated just a moment, before his fist connected with Duncan's nose with a sickening crunch. Blood spilled from Duncan's face, and he flailed about, kneeing Sullivan twice more in rapid succession before he wiggled out from beneath him.

Duncan went for the rifle as Sullivan slowly recovered from the previous blow, but Dietrich was gaining on them. A loud pop echoed nearby and Duncan released a screech of pain; blood blossoming on his shoulder from the bullet wound.

"Oh fuck you, Dietrich!" yelled Duncan before he sprinted into the darkness between two houses. Dietrich disappeared after him as Emma ran to Sullivan's side.

"Come on!" she said and tried to help him up.

"No!" he coughed through the pain. He pointed to Courtney, who was hunched over her dead sister in the rain. "Take her to the schoolhouse. Help Nash."

Sullivan remained on his back in the mud and looked up into the dark sky, a flash of lightning illuminating the dying town. The fires slowly descended from the heavy rain, and returned them to the darkness that had started the skirmish. Dietrich joined him in the street and knelt beside him.

"He's gone."

"It's fine," said Sullivan as he let Dietrich help him stand. "We'll find him."

The two of them hobbled their way toward the schoolhouse, going quickly up the walkway, Melissa's cries of pain echoing inside.

Chapter 43

The group left the schoolhouse together as the sun crested over the horizon, shedding light on the true amount of carnage from the night before. Bodies were sprawled about in all directions and a few slowpokes were left standing confused in the mud. Dietrich and Sullivan walked through the town and collected the dead bodies of those who had lived with them, finding a few survivors who had waited out the night in hiding. They laid the dead in the schoolhouse, carefully placed next to each other on the floor.

Sullivan personally gathered the few slowpokes that were hanging around and laid them down as well, placing a covering over their face before he slid his knife into the side of their heads. The final slowpoke he put to rest was Sally. The bodies of Duncan's men were left to rot in the streets, a silent decision they had all agreed upon.

"Sullivan," said Dietrich as he called him over to the side of the road. The two of them looked down into a small ditch at the body of Fletcher Crawford.

The two men looked down at the man who caused this madness, and the man who helped save them in the end. Without saying a word, the two of them reached down and picked him up, water and blood cascaded from his body as they carried him from the ditch and placed him with the others inside the schoolhouse. The others watched them lay him down, some conflicted with the decision to lay him to rest with the other Hillcrest residents.

Dietrich grabbed a shovel leaning on the inside of the schoolhouse and walked out, followed by Sullivan who stopped and stood in the doorway, looking back at the blanket of dead bodies in front of him. He felt incredible guilt as he gazed at them, each with a cloth covering their faces, and knew he could have done more to protect them. He took a lighter and lit a Molotov cocktail and tossed it into the room. He shut the door and joined the rest of the survivors in the street.

They stood together as the old building caught fire, each of them making their own sort of peace with what had happened there. Sullivan walked up the street, stepping around the soggy bodies of the dead, and covered Jessica's body with a sheet, before he picked her up.

Courtney led the way—she would choose her sister's final resting place.

Nash helped Melissa along as she hobbled with a thick bandage wrapped around her leg, moving along the roadside as the morning sun chased away the night's clouds. The bullet had only grazed her calf and left a nasty wound, but she had stopped bleeding rather quickly.

"There," said Courtney, as she pointed to a hilltop shaded by a beautiful oak tree.

Sullivan placed Jessica's body in the grass and took the shovel from Dietrich. He dug the grave, the others comforting Courtney as she knelt beside her twin.

Courtney stood up and held on to Dietrich, her face against his chest as Sullivan gently lowered her sister in to her grave. She sobbed as Sullivan settled shovel after shovel of wet dirt on top of her until the grave was full again.

No one moved for sometime, and the silence was almost serene on the hilltop.

"We can go now," Courtney said, breaking the silence. Her voice was hoarse from crying, but her face was dry. She had no more tears left inside her.

The group walked together down the hill and made their way back toward the road, when Nash suddenly stopped in his tracks.

"Wait," he said as he strained his eyes in the bright morning light.

A silhouette of a man stood out against a line of trees, standing with his back toward them while he inspected the burning schoolhouse.

"I'll be right back," said Nash, letting Sullivan support Melissa as he walked toward the man with his gun in hand.

He approached the figure with caution, his gun held out in front of him as he walked slowly toward it, although he was fairly certain he wouldn't have to use it.

"Turn around," he said as he stood close to the man with his gun in front of him.

Nash lowered his gun as Duncan turned slowly. His clothes were wet and bloodied as he revealed a gaping bite mark on his neck. His face was covered with a deep sadness, unlike anything Nash had seen before. Nash's eyes filled with tears, a sensation he hadn't expected at all, as he raised the gun toward Duncan's head. He held it steady, pointed directly at Duncan's forehead, before he lowered it and placed it back in his waistband.

He looked at the monster that had once been his stepfather as a whirlpool of emotions tossed and turned inside him. Anger, hatred, pity, sadness, fear, but above all, hope. Fletcher was dead, and now standing in front of him was the man who had been a monster long before he'd been turned. He thought about his mother, and her smiling face flashed in his mind as he stood pondering Duncan's empty shell. Nash was finally free of Duncan's tyrannical hold, but as he stood watching him, he couldn't help but be overcome with a strange sort of sadness.

"Goodbye," he whispered as thick tears crawled down his face as he left Duncan to stand alone in the damp field.

"You okay?" asked Sullivan as he approached.

"Yeah."

Dietrich ran up ahead and looked at each of the vans and school buses, sitting in a line on the outskirts of the town. He climbed into the driver's seat of one of the yellow buses and turned the keys as the engine roared to life. They each silently filed onto the bus and took their seats as Dietrich pulled onto the road.

Chapter 44

The sun set warmly over the group of people who danced and celebrated together in the dying afternoon light. Fires had been started, and lanterns hung from the trees lining the old dirt driveway that led up to the aging plantation home as the night slowly descended upon them. Underneath the massive pillars in the front of the plantation were men and women playing folk music in the dying light.

A bride and groom held each other close, and smiled into each other's eyes as the music fluttered through the evening air. In that moment, as they danced with each other, as their friends and family watched and danced along, it was easy to forget the wall at the edge of the property that protected them from the dangers of the outside world. It had taken a month to find the abandoned plantation and the better part of a year to erect the sturdy wall around it. Those that found them were welcome with open arms.

Dietrich stood smiling, his arms around Emma as she tapped her hand against his to the beat of the music. Courtney stood with Sullivan, her head on his arm as she admired the dress she had created for the bride. Sullivan smiled while he watched the people he loved celebrate in the safety of what they had simply named, The Plantation.

The sun crested downward over the horizon as Nash twirled his bride softly, both of them smiling at each other in the twilight.

Melissa stared at the man she loved, the man who had promised to keep her safe, and who had kept his promise. In the dying light, they knew they were home. They'd found the place they were always meant to be: in each other's arms, surrounded by the ones they loved. They'd found their place in this land of monsters.

About the Author

Tim Gabrielle is a married father of three beautiful children living in Tecumseh, Ontario. He spent the first eighteen years of his life in Paeonian Springs, Virginia, hiking and thinking up adventures in his head. Bringing his southern roots with him, Tim moved to Ontario in 2003 where he's lived with his wife and kids ever since.

If Tim isn't writing, you can usually find him spending time with his family, playing rec league dodgeball, drinking Cherry Pepsi, or cheering at inappropriate volume levels for the New England Patriots.